The Kokuran II

In Full Blossom

The Kokuran II
In Full Blossom

Jordin Mack

Vaughn Publishing

The Kokuran II – In Full Blossom.

FIRST EDITION

Library of Congress Cataloging–in-Publication Data is available.

ISBN: 978-0-9971544-3-6

Also available in eBook formats

Cover and jacket design by Elm Street Design Studio.

Fanfare and Acclaims

When I released my debut novel, *The Kokuran,* it was well received in both US and International markets. The passion and realism of my style has been compared to African American legends such as Ms. Maya Angelou, Zora Neale Hurston, and Alice Walker while the contemporary flavor of my stories have been compared to the works of Terry McMillan mixed with the rawness of Zane. I receive these compliments with the highest level of respect and regard to these great literary artists.

What Fans Have Said About *The Kokuran:*

"A suspenseful emotional ride, filled with joy, sorrow, anger, intimacy and love before the exhale."

"Reads like a modern-day 'Color Purple' with sexy, hip hop swag."

"The characters and story-line are so real that you forget the story is fiction."

"A powerful female protagonist surrounded by an unforgettable cast of characters."

Dedication

This book is dedicated to the women in my life that have influenced me in some way.

To Max, my aunt, my first fan, and admirable critic. After reluctantly agreeing to read my debut novel, "The Kokuran", she said that it was outstanding and was anxiously awaiting the release of the sequel. Unfortunately, she passed away before it was published. However, she will always be remembered as a role model in humility, loyalty, and unconditional love for family.

To Cina, my big sister. The one who blazes trails and bears the scars of a true warrior. She is the embodiment of courage, and is persistent in her faith walk and truth talk. She is always there with a shoulder to lean on without hesitation.

To Bobbi, my aunt, for always being there for everyone in need; a pillar of strength for her family, friends and community.

To my baby sister, Angie with a heart as big as the universe, who loves and cares without limits.

To my namesake, my grandmother, my "Gigi" who inspired me beyond limits; believing that anything is possible and that mistakes can always be forgiven and overridden. Above all, she believed that nothing can hold you back but yourself.

To my mother, the one who brought me into this world. Without you, "The Kokuran" and dreams birthed would not be possible. You have motivated and inspired me in ways that I have only recently uncovered and have yet to discover.

And to all the other women in my life, those who have loved, educated, encouraged, and inspired me.

Table of Contents

One

The Restart

I woke up in the morning feeling refreshed and happy as I looked at my wedding ring and then glanced at our wedding picture in the Waterford crystal frame on the nightstand next to our bed. Then I heard the shower running, so I got up, went into the bathroom, and opened the shower door.

"Good morning, my beautiful wife," my husband said. "What took you so long?"

I smiled as I stepped into the shower and hugged him, and then we began French kissing. After we played around a bit, I closed my eyes and turned away from him to wash my hair. I asked him to pass me the shampoo, but he didn't respond. I turned around to look at him, but he wasn't there. I stood there, startled and confused, absorbed by the heavy steam and wondering where my husband was—my sweet, loving Joey.

That's when I'd usually wake up, feeling scared and discombobulated. I sat up in bed and looked around my room, only to realize I had been dreaming once again, and that Joey, my fiancé, died before we could marry.

I've had the same reoccurring dream at least once a week for the past year. Sometimes I could shake it off and go on with my day. But other times it would hurt me to my core, and I'd spend an hour sobbing in despair before I could pull myself together.

On a few rare occasions, I'd wake up feeling like the Kokuran, the black orchid—that rare, distinctive flower with an esoteric symbology characterized as mysterious, beautiful, strong, and powerful. It was Gigi, my mother, who introduced me to the flower and the significance of it. Gigi gave me her synthetic black orchid as a keepsake right after Joey died to remind me of its importance in my life. It was the same flower she brought with her from New Orleans when she eloped to Detroit with my father, Big John. Gigi believed the traits and energy of flowers could be infused into one's life. She told me on numerous occasions that I was like the Kokuran, and I tried to believe that as well.

On those special days when I'm feeling inspired by the Kokuran, I blast my hip-hop music as I'd get dressed, throwing on a tight-fitting dress that displayed my side-view and rear-view curves along with my other voluptuous assets. I'd let my hair down and walk with my shoulders back in my sexy, four-inch stilettos. I'd think to myself as I'm driving, *Yeah, that's right, I'm all that. So don't fuck with me today.* That's usually a good day for me. However, those days are far and few; in fact, I haven't had one of those 'good' days in a long time, and I'm not sure if I'll ever have one again.

While I had the black orchid placed strategically in my bedroom to ensure I saw it every day, most of the time I forgot it was there. It seemed to blend in with all the other silk plants and household furnishings with no significance at all.

As time went on, my connection to the flower slowly dissipated, taking away everything that it had given me, especially my sense of power. But I wasn't quite ready to give up. Perhaps the little strength I had left would be enough to help me find my way back and recapture my essence.

It had been almost two years since Joey passed, and despite my best efforts, my life had not yet resumed any form of normalcy. On the surface, everything looked fine, but nothing was as it appeared. My body was fierce, my skin was flawless, and my hair was flowing in the wind. Of course, thanks to Gigi's genes, I still had my youthful good looks; I could easily pass for thirty. However, with all my external beauty, I still felt disconnected from my interior. Naturally, I fell back into my old pattern of maintaining façades.

My career and spiritual life were seemingly intact, but my social life was practically nonexistent. Apart from going to work, I spent the first year after Joey's death being a recluse and a year later, not much had changed. I spent most weekends reading self-help books, studying other languages, and indulging in my new signature cocktail, tequila and lime, and my favorite treat, cannabis. I wasn't an addict, but I knew I was smoking far too much weed lately. It was the only thing that calmed me and quieted the thoughts that ran constantly through my head. Besides, it was better than taking all those pharmaceutical meds that Dr. Bina prescribed for me.

Dr. Bina, my former therapist, had reached out to me several times over the past year, trying to convince me to resume my therapy. I saw her a few times, but she wasn't very helpful. It seemed that Dr. Bina only wanted to pump me full of drugs and hear my torrid life story to publish in one of the many journals that featured her work. As far as I was concerned, she needed to find someone else to advance her career. Besides, I couldn't quite put my finger on it, but I thought she was a little on the cuckoo side—counseling me about relationships with the men in my life while she had never been married or had a current boyfriend. *Huh, she was the one who was crazy, not me.*

While my career appeared to be going well, it wasn't the same as before the incident with Joey. I still worked for the same company and had the same fabulous office and salary, but the context of my role had changed. My interaction with my colleagues was different. They were courteous to me, but I was clearly not the big shot that they once envied, admired, and sometimes hated. I felt they no longer respected me; instead, they pitied me, especially Scott, my boss. He treated me like I was a delicate flower that would break under pressure, which was probably why he drastically reduced my workload. During conversations, he often patted my shoulder and said, "It's going to be alright. Time heals everything. Things will be back to normal soon. Let's take things slowly." It was becoming obvious to me that my career at Wyatt, Jones & Steinberg was coming to an end. While my firm would never throw me out, they would find a way to make me want to leave. I knew it was time to move on, but I didn't know what I wanted to do next or where I wanted to go.

Regardless of my ambivalence, I would have to decide soon, before the firm decided for me.

As a result of my self-imposed exile, I lost touch with many of the friends and associates that Joey and I shared, mainly because of their choice, not mine. It seemed like Joey's family and our mutual friends hated me. None of them attempted to contact me after the incident, not even during my hospital stay. I wrote letters to Joey's family, but they came back unopened. I wasn't surprised though; my family would have felt the same if the circumstances were reversed. Nonetheless, I still felt a need to explain to Joey's family what really happened, that it was his best friend, Marcus, who pushed him over the edge. I also wanted them to know how much I loved and missed Joey. But that was wishful thinking. That conversation would never occur, because I would be forever known to Joey's family as the woman who caused him to kill himself.

Just after Joey's birthday, I went to visit his burial site, taking along a bouquet of orchids to plant near his headstone. I figured it would be safe, since his birthday was a few days earlier, and no one would be there. However, when I arrived at the cemetery, his mother and siblings were there, so I jumped back into my car and sped away. That was supposed to be my final step to put closure on my relationship with Joey. Mustering the courage to go to Joey's burial site was a tall feat for me. I had attempted to go there several times before but was unable to go through with it.

Later that day, I called Dr. Bina and told her about seeing Joey's family at the cemetery. "You should go back," she said, "perhaps in a few days. You must put closure on your relationship with Joey. Why don't you come by my office tomorrow, so we can talk in person? If you're feeling anxious, I can give you something to help with your stress."

There was Dr. Bina again, trying to drug me and get me back on her patient roster. I lied and told her I would go back to the cemetery next week and then come to her office. Truthfully, I wasn't sure if I could ever attempt to return to Joey's grave. And I definitely wasn't about to start seeing Dr. Bina's crazy ass again. Whatever was going on in my life, no matter how broken it was, I would manage it myself.

The next morning, as I was drinking my coffee, I took a moment to reflect on my life. I realized it had come full circle. In some ways, I felt like I did when my tumultuous eighteen-year marriage to Philip ended. He was my first everything—lover, batterer, and father to Junior, my one and only child. Among other things, my divorce left me feeling uncertain about what the future held for me. And years later, I was back at that same place; a life filled with more ambiguity. Just like before, the interior of my life was out of sync with my exterior. The only thing that was constant was my family and my three best friends: Zoe, Val, and Tara. Thank God I still had my girls for support; they would help me get through yet another life-changing transition.

Zoe and I remained close, but we had not spent much time together. Over the past year, she frequently invited me to galas and various political social events, but I usually declined. After a while, I think she became tired of me saying no, so she stopped extending invites altogether. We still had spa days occasionally, but that was the extent of our socializing. Zoe didn't believe in letting grass grow under her feet—not for me, not for Brad, not for anyone. She continued to be Zoe, dedicated to her career, playing hard, and still fishing, when time permitted.

Val and Tara had both visited me over the past year. They also accompanied me when I went to my condo on the Cape. Despite their love and support, I still put up a front with them, making them believe I was doing much better than I was. Yes, I remained highly skilled at putting on a false face to hide my true feelings, which I did often. But similar to what I had done with Zoe, I kept Val and Tara at bay. I wasn't ready to explain to anyone why I hadn't or couldn't move on with my life. It was easier to lie than allow people to see the real me: weak and powerless.

For a while, I stopped going to church too, since I no longer attended Joey's family's church. However, at Gigi's urging, I reluctantly joined Pastor Jay's church, the pastor who helped me through my grief following Joey's death. While Pastor Jay was a great spiritual teacher, I was concerned about the elitist status of his congregation. Most members were doctors, lawyers, entertainers, local politicians, and so on. I couldn't see that group as my church family at all. Gigi always said that people were people. It was a person's interior that defined them, not their exterior packaging. I had come to know that all too well, especially after my experience with Philip, a true Dr. Jekyll and Mr. Hyde. I'm still haunted by memories of him today.

Although I didn't attend church regularly, when I did go, I usually attended the sunrise service because fewer people were there. That made it easier for me to avoid the occasional whispers and stares that still plagued me. One Sunday after service, Pastor Jay stopped me as I was leaving and asked if I would be willing to help with one of the fundraising campaigns. I agreed and met with the church secretary to sign the required forms.

After that, I made a quick dash to my car, so I could get back to the comfort and quietness of my home. Of course, the quietness was only temporary because every Sunday, Gigi would call and lecture me about various aspects of my life, particularly my dating life, and then offer her usual unsolicited advice on what I should be doing to get over Joey. One thing that had not changed was my Sunday afternoon movie date with myself. I still looked forward to watching my Lifetime and Netflix movies.

A few days later, I received a call from the chair of the church's fundraising committee. To my surprise, it was Dr. Bolton (a.k.a. "Doc"), my former neurologist. "I was pleasantly surprised when I saw your name on the list of volunteers," he said, "so, I knew I had to call you right away. Why don't we have lunch or dinner and talk in person about your role on the committee?"

"Okay," I said hesitantly, "how about next weekend?"

"Why so long? Can we meet today? You know my schedule is hectic and subject to change on short notice. I'm free this evening. Let's have dinner later. Please?"

"Well, if you insist, then today it is. I'll do anything for a good cause." Who was I kidding? I was bored to death, and I could use a little stimulating adult conversation.

I left work at five and headed to a sushi restaurant downtown to meet Doc for dinner. When I arrived, about fifteen minutes early, he was already there. "I never like to keep a lady waiting," he said as I got seated, "so I'm always at least thirty minutes early for a date."

"Oh," I said, "I didn't realize this was a date; I thought it was a business meeting." We both laughed and then ordered cocktails.

"Wow, you look beautiful," he said. "How are you doing?"

"I have no complaints."

"Well, that's good to hear, because now that I've found you again, I don't want to lose you." He took my hand. "This time, I'm going to stay close by, if you'll allow me. I should have spoken up when I first met you, but I can be shy sometimes."

I was surprised by his comment. I had no idea that he was still interested in me, especially after all this time and the incident with Joey that landed me under his care. We continued to make small talk. We had a lot in common, both having one college-aged child and the unfortunate experience of losing a loved one. His wife of twenty years had passed away from cancer six years earlier, and he had not had a serious relationship with anyone since.

We lost track of time as we talked about everything for hours. We didn't leave the restaurant until our server said we were welcome to stay, but the cleaning staff was about to start.

Doc walked me to my car, firmly holding my hand. "Look, I'm not going to play games with you," he said once I was seated in my car. "I'm much too old for that. I want to see you again and have a real date. Can we do that?"

"Sure, I'd love to go out with you," I replied without hesitation. I'm not sure why I agreed to go out with him. Perhaps I was bored. I wasn't particularly interested in him at that time. I figured we would go out once or twice, but nothing lasting would come of it.

As I drove home, I turned on the radio and heard an advertisement about a fundraising event memorializing the second anniversary of Joey's passing. Needless to say, I quickly forgot about Doc.

With the second anniversary of Joey's death approaching, the media and the sensationalism surrounding it was in full throttle. It seemed that the city would not let Joey rest in peace. They memorialized his death as if he was a renowned political figure. Of course, the media always brought up the circumstances surrounding it, which meant the spotlight would be on me as well. I barely survived the first anniversary of his death. Even though I was at my condo in the Cape, TMZ and the other paparazzi still found me and harassed me. Burke, my public relations rep, said it would probably take at least five years for my name to disappear from the headlines. He also said that eventually Joey's foundation would only want positive images and stories associated with his name and would ward off any negative publicity.

Initially, my plan was to stay in Atlanta and deal with the chaos surrounding Joey's memorial, but that proved more difficult than I anticipated. With the media coverage, I found myself thinking excessively about Joey, which made me feel sad and lugubrious. I also realized I wasn't ready to start dating seriously. That's when I told Doc I wanted to keep our relationship platonic.

"I understand," he replied, "but I'm not giving up on us. I don't want you to disappear again."

"I'm not ready for anything serious," I replied. "I need more time; I'll be in touch soon."

To avoid the drama in Atlanta, I went back home to Detroit to visit Gigi. The timing was ideal since I hadn't seen her in almost six months. I knew that if I didn't pay her a visit soon, she would pay me one, but for a lot longer than I cared for her to stay. Now that Gigi was retired, she had become even more preoccupied with my life, even though she had ten other children and too many grandchildren to count. Apart from serving in her church, working in her garden, and the volunteer work she did at the hospital, her focus was always on me. Like a broken record, she always said, "You can't find a man if you stay in the house all the time. You know, if you stop using it, it might lock up on you." That was Gigi. Sex was always on her brain and part of her lectures.

"And you need to stop smoking that stuff; that's part of your problem. You don't have any ailments that require you to use medicinal marijuana. I'm old, but you're not fooling me, sneaking around smoking that stuff all the time. If you keep smoking it, you're going to turn into a zombie. It's a drug, you know. There are studies out there that show it's addictive too. Do you need me to send you some literature on it?"

I laughed. "Gigi, it's not that serious. I hear you though." I wasn't sure whether it was addictive, but it had certainly become a part of my life.

My plan was to spend a week with Gigi and then go to my condo on the Cape for an additional two weeks. I was in no hurry to get back to Atlanta. I needed a change in scenery.

When I arrived at Gigi's house that Saturday, I was surprised to find it untidy and her napping in bed. That was unusual for Gigi, who was usually a ball of energy and didn't know how to sit still. She said often that she would have plenty of time to rest when she went to heaven. If nothing else, she always found time to work in her garden and her greenhouse, which both looked neglected.

Later that evening, Gigi made dinner for us, and then we talked awhile, but I could tell she wasn't herself. The next day, I awoke to find her still sleeping. That's when I knew something was wrong because Gigi never missed church. When I tried to talk to her, she mumbled something, but the only thing I could make out was that she was tired. She seemed incoherent, and her breathing was shallow. I knew this was serious, so I called an ambulance. En route to the hospital, I called Deana, my oldest sister who also lived with Gigi and told her what happened.

Hours later, after all the commotion at the hospital settled, we learned that Gigi had suffered a stroke. Even worse, she had been suffering from congestive heart failure for years but had kept it to herself. I was scared. I couldn't bear the thought of Gigi dying. She was more than my mother; she was my everything. I wasn't ready to let her go.

Before that day, I never had any thoughts of Gigi not being in my life. I guess I assumed she would be around forever. For the first time in my life, my security blanket was gone. I found myself wondering how I would function without her.

By the following day, most of my siblings had arrived, including my sister, Nikki, who was a physician. While I had three other siblings who were also medical doctors, Nikki seemed to outrank them. Whenever there was a question or debate on any medical topic, Nikki's opinion usually prevailed. Perhaps it had to do with her genius-level IQ and the fact that she had graduated high school at age sixteen to begin her pre-med program. Not to mention the many accolades she had received and the numerous medical journals that featured her work.

Nikki and her husband worked at Johns Hopkins Hospital and did not spend much time with our family. Whenever they made it home for Christmas, they usually stayed at a hotel, while everyone else stayed at Gigi's house. Gigi always said that family was important, and the only holiday she required us to spend together was Christmas. That meant we all would be in Detroit for at least a week. To make matters worse, Nikki and her family usually left the day after Christmas, jetting off to Aspen or some other extravagant place for their winter vacation. Nikki knew her short visits and occasional absence during the holidays were upsetting to Gigi, but she didn't seem to care. It was as if her actions were deliberate.

Nikki and I were the closest girls in age—she was nearly seven years older than me—but our relationship was anything but close. She had always been contentious toward me, and I still don't know the source of it. I used to think it was sibling rivalry, but over the years, I realized it was something that ran much deeper. When we were younger, we argued constantly, and even when we grew into mature adults, not much had changed. We generally acknowledged each other and then stayed in our respective corners until we parted company. Unfortunately, not even Gigi's illness changed our feelings for each other.

While my siblings took turns visiting Gigi at the hospital, I never left, except to go home to shower and change clothes. Seeing her lying in the bed with oxygen and intravenous lines hooked up to her body terrified me. But I wanted to be with her when she awoke, or God forbid, the unthinkable happened. Nothing else mattered. I was prepared to stay in Detroit for whatever amount of time was necessary, until Gigi came home.

I decided to settle in my old bedroom and remove some of the junk that Gigi stored in it. I started cleaning the closet when I found a box that contained bullets and a small handgun. I also found several papers, including Gigi's gun permit. *That was odd.* I wondered why and for how long Gigi had owned a gun. I decided to leave it where I found it, on the high shelf in my closet. I would ask her about it later.

I visited Gigi faithfully each day, as if it were my job. Finally, after a month, Gigi's health stabilized, and she was released from the hospital. Although I was relieved that Gigi was well enough to come home, I was still worried. Her doctor said her condition would most likely get worse over time. I knew at some point I would need to prepare myself for the inevitable.

I decided to stay in Detroit with Gigi awhile longer. Although Gigi still had her delightful smile and spunky attitude, something was different about her. Her body was obviously fatigued, but her spirit was restless too. As much as I hated to acknowledge it, I knew this was probably the beginning of Gigi's downward spiral.

One day, while we were talking, Gigi said, "Baby girl, I have a lot to do, but I don't have much time. I need you and Deana to help me get things in order."

"Gigi, what are you talking about?" I replied anxiously.

"Never mind," she said. "I'm worried about you. I need you to be okay before I leave here."

I started to cry. "Gigi, please stop talking like that."

"Listen, I'm old and I'm sick. I have congestive heart failure. There's no cure for that. My body can stave off this disease for only so long. I'm not saying I'm going to die tomorrow, but my death is imminent. This world can be cold and cruel, full of hurt and disappointment, and nobody gets a pass. You have to be able to navigate through those difficult times and stay on the course God has designed for you. You can't fall down every time life throws you a curve." She paused, took a deep breath and then elevated her voice. "Girl, you need to stop acting like a victim. You know what you are. You're the Kokuran. When are you going to blossom?"

At first, I didn't respond. I just laid my head next to her and cried as she rubbed her hands through my hair. "You'll be okay," she said. "You're stronger than you know. Remember what I've always told you, you're just like the Kokuran, and don't forget it."

Yes, I was like the Kokuran—strong, bold, and all that other stuff—but why did I still feel so weak and broken?

As I was leaving, Gigi said, "Listen, you know Deana is my right-hand, so if you ever need anything, you can go to her just like you would me. Deana was also very close to Di, your birth mother; they were like twins. You know she's always loved you, just like you were her daughter. She's always been a caretaker, too busy taking care of everybody else. I guess that's why she never married or had any kids. She'll be there for you whenever you need her, just like I've been here for you."

"Okay, Gigi," I said, and then I left her room.

Afterwards, Deana went into Gigi's bedroom and closed the door. I knew they were having a conversation that was not meant for my ears, so I went for a drive.

For some reason, I found myself near Gigi's church, located in our old neighborhood near the Gardens. Although the Gardens were long gone, replaced by new low-income housing, the neighborhood looked the same: a strong scent of poverty, storefront churches and Muslim temples, and liquor stores on every other corner.

As I drove down Joy Road, the men from the area mosque were walking in the intersection passing out their Muslim newspaper and selling bean pies. While waiting at the stoplight, I felt a lump in my throat when I saw a ghost from my past. That face, albeit a little order was unforgettable. It was Ricky, walking across the street right in front of me. He was neatly groomed, wearing a white shirt and black bowtie, looking like a normal law-abiding citizen and nothing like the pedophile that he was. Perhaps he had changed now that he was a Muslim. I heard many times that Islam had transformed many criminals and wayward souls. But that didn't matter; he would always be a monster to me.

Suddenly, I heard a little voice in my head say, *Run him down. Just floor the accelerator. Do it now.*

I was absorbed in thought until I heard the cars behind me blowing their horns for me to drive through the green light. I ignored the voice and continued home.

I felt myself beginning to unravel. The anxiety was building fast, and I knew there was only one thing that could help: my weed. Since I didn't have a prescription with me, my only option was to find a "street pharmacist." I called Mr. Lee, the handyman that Gigi used for small projects around her house. I figured that since he attended Gigi's church and lived in the surrounding poverty-stricken neighborhood, he probably knew of people who dealt in such illicit activities. One thing about Detroit— one could always find a drug dealer in a slum neighborhood. Sure enough, Mr. Lee pointed me in the right direction.

As I pulled into a local city park where the virtual street pharmacy was located, I lowered my window slightly and waited for a seller to approach. Minutes later, a young man riding a bike with a backpack approached my car. "Whatcha want, lady? I got everything you need to make you fly high or lay low. Cause I'm your med doc." Then he rattled off some code words that were totally foreign to me. He sounded like he was singing Rap lyrics to a hip-hop song. He must have seen the confusion on my face, but he continued speaking his urban slang at rapid speed. "Hurry up, whatcha want? That white, brown, or green? I got them Percs, Zanax, and Oxy too. Hurry up, lady, you wasting my time. Whatcha want?"

"Just keep it simple, and give me a small pack of plain marijuana," I replied.

He laughed. "Oh, I know you ain't from around here talking like that." Then he swung open his jacket to let me see he was strapped. "You better not be Detroit's Finest."

I shook my head. "No, I'm not the police."

"Oh, you want that boom-boom, that nasty skunk, that jolly green from across the border."

I laughed. While I found him entertaining, I didn't understand a word he said.

Finally, he paused and spoke in a more serious voice. "Lady, you wanna a quarter, a fiddy, or a C-pack?"

Having never purchased street marijuana before, I had zero knowledge of the prices or packaging quantities. "Just give me the cheapest pack, please."

"Are you sure? It's not very much."

I nodded. "Yes."

"Alright, since you're a new customer, I'll throw in a few loosies for you too. You know where to find me when you want some more."

I quickly learned that "loosies" were cigarettes. We completed our transaction, and then I found my way to the freeway heading back to Gigi's house in the suburbs. The fact that I had spent the last ten minutes in an urban war zone didn't seem to faze me. A few years earlier, I wouldn't have been caught in a place like that. I'm not sure if it was courage, desperation, or stupidity that made me oblivious to my surroundings and the illegality of what I had done. It just didn't matter to me.

Once I made it Gigi's house, I poured a drink and went to the patio to sneak a few puffs of my homemade marijuana cigarette. While I was feeling calm and mellow, I still couldn't get the image of Ricky out of my head. Of course, with it came the pain from memories of him raping me as a child. I laid my head in my lap and sobbed.

Moments later, Deana appeared with a knowing look. She turned on the patio's ceiling fan and then sat next to me and grabbed my hand. "Astrid, it's going to be alright. You know how Gigi likes to exaggerate; she's not going anywhere."

"I hope you're right."

Deana had no clue about the real source of my pain. Even though we were close, I couldn't confide in her. I could never tell her about Ricky; that would remain Gigi's secret and mine.

"Goodnight," I said and then went to bed.

That night, my sleep was restless. I tossed and turned. I thought I was dreaming, when I heard the voice speak again. After all this time, the voice had returned. *I told you, there's only one way to get rid of him,* it said. *Stop being a coward. You know what you have to do.*

I tried to ignore the voice, but it kept talking. Finally, I got out of bed. However, for some reason, I went to the closet and looked at Gigi's gun again. Knowing it was there gave me a sense of comfort.

I still felt anxious, so I took an Ambien to help me sleep. With everything else I had taken earlier, it did the trick. I didn't wake up until noon the next day. I still felt uneasy, totally disconnected. My world was falling apart, and it was beyond my control. My life in Atlanta sucked. I had no man to love me, my career was practically nonexistent, Gigi was ill, Junior was studying abroad in Europe, and that monster, Ricky, had resurfaced. Could life get any worse? What happened to the strength and power I found within? Wherever it was, I needed to find it again, quick, fast, and in a hurry.

Feeling anxious, I continued to spiral downward. Although I had my weed, I needed a different distraction, something euphoric to shift my mind away from reality. After pondering my dilemma, Damien popped into my mind. If nothing else, I knew a good fuck would lift my spirits. Although we had not spoken for some time, I knew he would be ready and willing to indulge at the drop of a dime. I sent him a text message, letting him know I was in town and that I wanted to see him.

An hour later, Damien called. "You know I'm always happy to see your fine sexy ass. Just say when. I would invite you over to my place, but I have a situation."

"I'll get a room," I said. "Let's meet at the Marriot in the Renaissance Center."

"Oh, you want to skip the subtleties and go straight to home plate," he replied, as if he was surprised. "Mmm-hmm I got you. You know you can get this dick anytime you want it, baby. I'm glad you called. I could use a distraction too."

Damien had not changed one bit. His fierce, sexy looks were still breathtaking. Later that evening, we had a drink in the bar at the Marriot and then went up to my room. He wasted no time disrobing. We climbed into bed and went at it like two wild animals in heat. Even though I had been celibate for almost two years, my lava flowed generously, and my pussy easily ingested his horse-like penis. It was as if she remembered him from before. After sucking, licking, flipping, and dipping me all over, we laid in bed, breathless and sweaty. *This was just what I needed,* I thought, *a sexual release from Damien, my sexual defibrillator.* Of course, nothing was ever easy with Damien, as I was about to find out.

As we laid in bed making small talk, Damien told me about his recent setback. "My situation is dire. I had to let my band go, and my record label just dropped me. To make matters worse, I'm flat broke, my car has been repossessed, and my home was foreclosed."

"Oh, I'm sorry to hear that," I replied. "You're very talented. I'm sure you'll get another record deal soon."

He shook his head somberly. "I don't know. The music industry is changing, and the demand for smooth, sexy ballads is shrinking. I'm too old to start singing hip-hop, and I'm not ready to resign myself to simply doing studio work."

"Yeah, I know how you feel. It's one thing to make a career change when you want it, but it's very different when that change is forced upon you."

"Speaking of change," he said, "it's time for me to make a move. I should have left years ago. I'm ready to leave Detroit." Then he dropped the bomb. "Can I come to Atlanta and stay with you for a while? Just until I get on my feet and get my career back on track. It shouldn't take long. I have some good contacts in Atlanta. I could probably get a new record deal there within a year."

While I noodled over his request, I remembered what Tara had said about him years earlier, that he was a kept man and could be targeting me for that purpose. As much as I liked his dick, and as tempting as the notion of him living with me was, I couldn't do it. I was lonely, but I wasn't that lonely. I told him I could loan him some money instead. Before I left, I gave him a check for $5,000 and told him I would talk to my contacts in the industry to see if I could help him. He looked embarrassed and pitiful. "Thanks," he said. "I'll pay you back as soon as I can."

As I drove back to Gigi's house, I realized Damien was just like me. He had a beautiful exterior, but he was broken inside. It was then that I decided to block his number. I knew he would be calling me again to borrow more money or something else, and I might be vulnerable, given my state of mind. I certainly didn't need anyone like him in my life.

Upon entering the house, I was drawn to the library where Gigi kept the family pictures displayed. As I stared at my siblings and their family portraits, I found myself thinking about Di, my birth mother. I hadn't thought much about her since college. Like so many other painful things in my past, I tried to forget about her. Perhaps Gigi's near-death experience had triggered something in me. Even though Di disappeared a few days after I was born, leaving me to be adopted by Gigi, her mother, I longed to know her or at least know more about her. I knew that, after all these years, neither Gigi nor my siblings would ever discuss Di with me, so I decided I would investigate her whereabouts myself. Besides, I had a lot of idle time on my hands at work, so it would give me something substantive to do while I was pretending to be busy. That's exactly what I would do, search for my birth mother, even if it led me to her grave.

At Gigi's insistence, I went back to Atlanta to resume my nonexistent life. However, before I left, she made me promise I would open my heart to love again. "The spirits told me that you would find your true and greatest love in Atlanta," she said. "He will never forsake you. He will be everything that you're looking for and fulfill dreams you have not yet had."

That was Gigi, always full of optimism, praise, and encouragement.

Two

Sage – Another Spicy Woman

Once I returned to Atlanta, I decided to take Gigi's advice and at least open my mind to dating seriously. I decided the best person to help me re-enter the dating scene was Zoe. She had recently been elected to a new position in the state attorney general's office and had dialed down her undercover nightlife. She spent most of her time hobnobbing with Atlanta's political socialites and traveling back and forth to DC.

Lately, Zoe seemed like a very different person from the woman I had met years earlier, especially regarding her career. I knew she had ambitious political aspirations, but I didn't realize their extent. I couldn't reconcile her voracious sexual nature with being a subdued public figure; the two roles just did not mix. Perhaps that was my naiveté. Her conversations of late were always about politics: Gallup polls, super PACs, liberal vs. conservative policies, and so on. Zoe either knew, or was trying to get to know, everyone who was prominently seated in Washington and other high-powered political realms. She had even gone as far as to switch her political party affiliations.

While Zoe was still loving and kindhearted toward me, it felt like we were associates and no longer the close friends that we once were. Unlike before, she wasn't as readily available to me as she had been in the past. But I assumed she was still active in her "other" social life.

After calling Zoe a few times, she finally called me back. When I asked her about hanging out and attending a few "fishing" events, she said her schedule was hectic and left little time for such activities. I was surprised by how much Zoe had changed; I guess her party days were over.

One day, after a few months had gone by, Zoe and I met for lunch. She had done a complete makeover, trading her form-fitting cleavage-bearing dresses for a plain conservative style. She had even cut off her long locks and was sporting a classic shoulder-length hairstyle. She was still beautiful and definitely looked the part of her new role as attorney general.

While we were at lunch, Zoe shared some surprising news. "Brad and I secretly got married a few weeks ago." I was shocked, but before I could inquire about the details, she smiled and said she had another surprise. "I'm in my second trimester. Yes, I'm pregnant. At first, I thought I had food poisoning, and then I thought it was the flu, but it was neither. My swinging days are over, at least for now. My doctor says the baby and I are doing fine, but it's still a high-risk pregnancy, so she has me on a ton of restrictions. I don't mind though, knowing it's good for the baby.

I'm not sure about how this parenting thing is going to work for me, but the timing is perfect, because you know I'm planning to run for a Senate seat in two years. Nothing looks better than a nuclear family on the campaign trail. Seriously, I would have become Mrs. Brad Patterson sooner, but when my doctor told me a few years ago that I couldn't have kids, there was no rush to get married. Besides, I knew Brad loved me and would marry me at the drop of a dime. I'm ecstatic," she said, smiling and giddy, "but I'm scared too. You're going to have to help me with all this baby stuff. I've been reading books on parenting, but I know that's not enough."

"Aww, you know you can count on me to help you. Auntie Astrid will always be here for the little one and you too," I said as I pointed at her tiny bulging stomach, in awe as I digested the news of Zoe's pregnancy and the thought of her being a mother.

"I know you're shocked," she said. "I was too. With all the risks, we decided to keep the pregnancy a secret until I was further along. It wasn't as if I was trying to conceive; that was the last thing on my mind. But here I am, pregnant and married. Who would have thought this would be my life?"

"I think seeing you married and pregnant has shocked everyone," I replied. "But you look happy, and you wear the role of wife and expectant mother well."

As we were about to leave, Zoe grabbed my hand. "My life has changed, but not everything has changed." She pointed to her heart. "You're in here. I've never stopped loving you. I can still remember the taste of your sweetness."

I was caught totally off guard by Zoe's words of affection. I didn't know how to respond. We had not been intimate in years, not since before I met Joey. I recalled a few occasions when I caught Zoe staring at me, but I never thought much about it. Nor did she ever approach me in that way. I had no idea that she still had those kinds of feelings for me.

"Zoe, we shared a special moment at that particular time in our lives, but that's over now. That's not who I am. I can only give you my love as your friend, nothing more. But you have to know that if I wanted to love a woman that way, it would definitely be you."

Zoe smiled. Then we got up and walked to the door.

When the valet brought Zoe's car, we hugged and said goodbye. I felt sad as I watched her drive off. It was like I was missing a friend who was leaving to go back to her home in another state. In some ways, that was true. I was missing a friend, the old Zoe.

The conversation with Zoe reminded me of a time when I was, indeed, confused about my sexuality, well before I discovered that Philip was bisexual. Shortly after I married Philip, I learned he was into pornography, normal stuff like vintage *Playboy* and *Hustler* magazines. I didn't think much about it. I figured all men had girly magazines hidden somewhere in their home. However, it became a problem for me when Philip started renting porno movies and forcing me to watch them with him before we had sex. It seemed his preference was watching threesomes or lesbian couples. I was innocent back then and was disgusted by them, but I pretended to watch anyway, hoping to please Philip and maintain the façade of a happy marriage. Needless to say, Philip began pressuring me to have a threesome. After a while, I gave in to his request, thinking it might help our troubled marriage.

The night we were supposed to have our ménage a trois was the point at which I began to question my sexuality. Philip brought a woman home from a bar he frequented. She was a little older than me, shapely and pretty, and obviously quite experienced. The evening started off with her attention focused solely on me while Philip watched. I closed my eyes as I savored her soft caress, but when she attempted to French kiss me, it scared me, so I ran into the bathroom and locked the door. Philip tried to persuade me to come back and continue where we left off, but I refused. Minutes later, I heard the woman say, "Pay me now, so I can leave."

When I resurfaced, Philip was unsympathetic and noticeably upset. "Next time, you had better do everything I tell you to do."

There's not going to be a next time, I thought.

Over the next few months, Philip continued to pressure me for another threesome, but I always said no. It wasn't that I was turned off by being intimate with a woman; quite the contrary, which left me feeling confused and unsure. Back then, my sexual maturity was very low, even among my peers. It didn't help that neither Gigi nor my sisters ever talked about threesomes or lesbian and gay relationships. I'm not sure when or where it came from, but somewhere during my childhood, I had been raised to think that same-sex relationships were taboo.

Philip became unrelenting in his quest for a threesome and on a daily basis said, "I understand you were uncomfortable the first time, but this time you'll enjoy it. I saw you getting into it. There's nothing wrong with enjoying passion with a partner of the same sex. You'd be surprised at how many married couples engage in such activities."

"No, no, and no," I would reply. "I'm not doing that again. If it's that important to you, buy yourself two hookers and have at it."

The last time he asked me about the threesome, Philip reminded me of how nasty and cruel he could be. "I was trying to be nice, but you won't let me. Like I told you before, your body isn't sexy at all. Your face is alright, but your body looks like shit. No man is ever going to desire you. You're skinny and flat, from front to back. You're lucky I still want to have sex with you; the least you could do is try to fulfill some of my desires. This is why I do the things I do to you."

Then he paused and smiled. "What if I invite a man next time?"

I turned away from him without uttering a word.

"I was just kidding," he said. "I just wanted to see your reaction. You look mortified. Well, if you won't give me what I need sexually, then I'll get it from someone who will."

Looking back, I think Philip was trying to explore the limits of how he could integrate his closeted bi-sexuality into our relationship, given what followed years later when I caught him in our bed having sex with a man. That was the final straw and the catalyst that led to our divorce.

After that time, he never approached me about having a threesome again or discussed anything about same-sex couples. But I remained confused by the encounter with the woman until I gained my freedom from Philip. In fact, it was Zoe who helped me overcome the discord I felt with my sexuality. The intimacy I shared with Zoe helped me to realize I didn't have to use labels to define my intimate relationships or lifestyle. It opened my eyes, my mind, and my heart to the fluidity of love. When it came to my sexuality, I was confused no more.

I have to say, Zoe was actually glowing. Pregnancy seemed to agree with her, and I knew she'd make a good mother. Underneath her wild exterior was a tender, nurturing quality. So much for partying and turning it up in the ATL with Zoe; those days were over for now, maybe indefinitely.

Now that Zoe was on activity restrictions, I started going to the spa alone and taking yoga classes. One day after class, I met a young lady named Sage. She was in her early thirties and had recently moved to Atlanta from New York. She had a vivacious personality. As we sat on the floor drinking cucumber water, she told me more about her background and what brought her to Atlanta.

"I'm a former accountant, but I spent the last five years as a personal trainer, which has led me to my true calling."

"What's that?" I asked.

"I subscribe to the religious tenets of Buddhism and Hinduism, particularly around the wellness and purification of the mind, body and soul. That's why I want to open a yoga wellness center."

"Aren't they one in the same?"

"Not really. It's essentially a yoga studio integrated with meditation. I don't want to limit my customer base, so it won't have any religious tenets. I'm looking for a space to lease near the downtown area."

"Well, it sounds interesting."

I was curious about Sage. Besides looking more like a teenager than a thirty-something woman, she was rough and edgy, as if she was a former gangbanger.

At first, I thought she was a lesbian. She always wore her short, nearly bald hair under a baseball cap and wore sweats and hoodies instead of cute yoga outfits.

"Where can I find some dick around here?" she asked as we were leaving. "It's been a while for me. The last asshole I dated ended up being married."

Shocked by her directness, and the fact that she liked men, I laughed. "Well, you know, this is Atlanta, and there's a mixture of everything here. But if you look in the right places, you can find whatever you want."

"Can we get together sometime?" she asked. "Maybe you can show me around town. You seem cool, not like these other bitches around here. They're fickle as hell. They're either intimidated, jealous, or on some other shit."

"Well, I'm not known for being a girl on the town, but sure, that's cool. We can hang out sometime."

"And the answer is no, in case you were wondering," Sage said. "I never play in the lady pond. I'm not into tasting cat or hearing purrs or meows. However, I do enjoy looking at a beautiful woman occasionally, and I may get a feel in at a topless bar, but that's where I draw the line. I'm probably a nymphomaniac, and I prefer a dick that's long and thick—attached to a baller."

You're cute, I thought, *but you don't look like the arm candy that ballers hang out with.* Frankly, she looked more like a teenage boy with a foul mouth than a model or beauty queen.

She nodded and smiled. "Mmm-umm, you know what I mean?"

I smiled in agreement and laughed, and then we exchanged phone numbers.

A few days later, I resumed talking to Doc. I liked him, but I never felt fireworks when we talked. Nevertheless, I agreed to start seeing him again. I recalled Gigi's words of wisdom: "You can grow to love anyone if they treat you well. Hell, you can grow to love a monkey if you hang around it long enough." Gigi had an answer for everything and most of the time, she was right.

Over the next few months, Doc and I went on the usual "get to know you" dates: romantic dinners, theater, concerts, sporting events, and evening sails on his yacht. But we had yet to have any form of sex. Our intimacy was limited to holding hands and polite kisses. It was quite the opposite of my past dating experiences. I usually had to slow the sexual pace of the relationship, not wait for the man to jump-start it. However, back then, my motives for dating were altogether different. I was playing a dangerous game of love 'em and leave 'em, which was not my purpose for dating Doc. For the moment, I would just wait and see what happened.

One night, after one of our dates, Doc asked me to spend the night with him. I looked at him in shock. "What took you so long?"

He smiled. "I was waiting for the right time. You could have invited me to your place to spend the night as well."

Although I didn't have an overnight bag, I decided to stay over. I showered and then I climbed into bed with him. I was surprised to see him wearing a T-shirt and pajama bottoms. Although I was naked from head to toe, it didn't seem to matter to him. We cuddled in bed, but he didn't attempt to engage in sex or foreplay. At first, I was confused, but then I remembered Doc was active in the church and probably wanted to take things slow. That was fine with me. It wasn't like my pussy was really craving him anyway.

The next morning, we had coffee on his terrace, a bit of small talk, and then I left. As I drove home, I thought about how indifferent I felt about Doc and that I couldn't keep seeing him much longer if sparks didn't start flying soon.

After several invites, I finally decided to hang out with Sage. We planned to go to an adult entertainment bar, which was quite common among women in Atlanta: professional, straight, gay and otherwise.

I made it to the club as scheduled, but it appeared that Sage was a no-show. Then, about thirty minutes later, she finally made a grand entrance. The DJ even said, "Damn, baby! You over there wearing that cat suit, I wanna go home with you tonight."

When I turned and looked at Sage, I did a double-take as she walked toward our table. Her makeup was flawless, and her spiked hairstyle was a perfect complement to her attire. She was wearing a black patent leather cat suit that fit her hourglass figure like a leather glove. However, it wasn't until she sat down that I noticed why the men in the bar were gawking at her. The back of Sage's cat suit was made of sheer black fabric, similar to a pair of women's nylons. She was completely naked, her bare ass on full display. I could see everything from the top of her neckline, down her back, over her cute round booty, and down to her ankles.

"You look stunning," I said. "I guess we won't be buying any drinks tonight."

And we didn't. About every five minutes, our server came over to say one man or another had put our next drink on his tab. I only had two drinks, while Sage had several. I lost count after she threw back her fourth shot. I enjoyed hanging out with her; it was a lot of fun. After dancing and mingling with a few guys, I watched Sage get turned up and get her feel in, lightly slapping a few big booties. It was getting late, so I said goodnight, but she told me she was ready to leave too.

On the way out, I noticed she was extremely intoxicated, so I drove her home. When we got to her place, I discovered she had lost her keys, and her roommate was gone for the weekend. I had no choice but to invite her home with me. She could barely walk as we made our way through the lobby of my building. I helped her get settled in the guest room before she passed out.

The next morning when I awoke, Sage was already up, wearing one of my running outfits and shoes. She had also made me some kind of green smoothie. It tasted surprisingly refreshing. "If you drink this daily, you won't have to keep smoking weed," she said. "It will help you relax and quiet those voices in your head."

I was stunned by her remark. At first, I didn't respond, as I wondered how she knew about my weed, let alone the voices that plagued me occasionally. "How did you know I smoked weed?" I asked finally.

She smiled. "It takes one to know one. I used to be just like you. I saw the yellowing on your fingertips, and I knew you didn't smoke cigarettes. Your kind are usually pill poppers or weed heads. Based on my impression of you, I figured you to be the latter. And I was right. Like I said, I used to be just like you. Getting high to numb my pain and sorrow, so I know what you're going through."

"I'm not going through anything," I replied. "I enjoy smoking weed for recreational purposes. You know, there are benefits to smoking marijuana."

"Listen, I'm not trying to pry, nor am I judging you. I just want to be your friend and offer my assistance. Did you forget? I'm a yoga instructor, and I'm trained to recognize stress. Life can be pretty fucked up at times."

Still stunned by her words, I quickly shifted the conversation to another topic. "Has anyone ever told you that you're a walking contradiction? In one breath, you're meditating and talking about purity of mind, body, and soul, and then with your next breath, you're cursing like a sailor."

She laughed. "I'm a work in progress. I'm still trying to cut out the profanity."

I suggested we go for a quick jog before we started our day, and off we went.

A few hours later, I told her that I had plans and would take her to get her car on my way out. That's when she told me about her dilemma. She had been staying with a friend, and they had an argument over a guy. Her friend had essentially kicked her out. She asked if she could stay with me for a few days. She was expecting a huge wad of cash from one of her baller friends.

"I don't think that's a good idea," I said. "I like my space and my privacy."

"I'm really in a bind," she said, giving me a pitiful look. "I don't have anyone else to call."

"Okay," I said finally, feeling sorry for her. "You can stay, but we'll do this day by day."

"Thank you, and don't worry; you won't even know I'm here. I'll be quieter than a mouse. I promise I'll be gone in a week at most."

"Okay, one day at a time," I repeated.

OMG, I hope I don't regret this.

I packed my overnight bag and spent the balance of the weekend with Doc. We still had not yet increased our level of intimacy, but I didn't mind. I was gradually becoming comfortable with only cuddling and sleeping next to him. He made me feel safe and loved, even though he never said he loved me. For the moment, I would have to settle for intimacy on Doc's terms. Besides, just because Doc and I were not having sex didn't mean I couldn't have sex with another man. He was the one practicing celibacy, not me.

When I returned to my condo, I discovered that Sage had rearranged some of the furnishings. "The energy in this place is dark and negative," she said, "so I Feng Shui'd it for you. I hope you don't mind."

I didn't believe in Chinese or any other religious or philosophical "isms," but I didn't mind the changes. With the mood I was in lately, I was open to anything that might lift my spirits. We continued our conversation, which centered on my life. By the time I had my third glass of wine, I was in deep throes of whining and complaining about my job.

"Why don't you just quit?" Sage asked. "Start a business, teach, or do whatever puts a smile on your face. I was a certified public accountant for a major accounting firm and hated every minute of it. The upside is that my hatred for my job led me to find my true quest: my desire to get involved with health and fitness. I don't make a lot of money, but I love what I do, and that's worth a lot more to me."

"I understand, and I'm still exploring my options."

The next day at work, I sat in my decadent mahogany-furnished office, twiddling my thumbs, looking over some contracts that one of the law clerks could have easily handled. That's when I decided to leave. I would negotiate a hefty exit package and then perhaps seek an adjunct professorship while I figured out the next steps in my career. In the meantime, I would use my idle time to search for my birth mother. I wanted to know everything about her.

When I arrived home, Sage had made us a seaweed salad for dinner. I threw a few shrimps on mine and was good to go. I also told Sage about my decision to leave the law firm. She congratulated me, and we celebrated by toasting with one of her green health drinks.

Over the next few weeks, I hung out with Sage. Each morning before I left for work, we did yoga, and in the evenings, we worked out in my building's fitness center. However, I spent my weekends with Doc. It was while talking to Doc about Sage that I realized she'd been staying in my home for almost a month.

"Don't you find it strange that she's invited herself to stay in your house for so long without asking your permission?" Doc asked. "There's something fishy about it to me. You should at least do a background check on her or ask her to leave."

"You're right," I replied. "I don't know much about her. I'll take care of it when I get home."

By the time I got back to my condo, Sage was seated in the great room, as if she was expecting me. "I have some good news. I found a place. I can move in tomorrow."

Then she presented me with an envelope. I peeked inside and saw it was filled with cash. I looked up at her in surprise. "What's this?"

"I know it's not much, but I wanted to give you something to show my appreciation for letting me stay here. You've been a real blessing to me."

That's when I did the unthinkable. "I was planning to talk to you about your situation. I know your finances aren't very good right now, so why don't you stay here permanently, maybe for a year? This two-story penthouse is certainly large enough to accommodate both of us. I'll only charge you a nominal amount for rent. The only rule is that you can't bring anyone to my house for any reason, period. I don't like strangers in my home. Besides, staying here will allow you to save money for that building you've been eyeing in the Atlantic Station for your yoga studio.

"I would love to stay here with you," Sage replied. "This place is magnificent. Who wouldn't want to live here? Thanks Astrid, this means a lot to me. I promise you that I'll repay your kindness one day."

Just like that, I had a new roommate.

Three

Finding Love Again

Doc and I had been dating seriously for a few months but still had not had any form of sex, which concerned me. By then my feelings for him had deepened. I found him very attractive, especially for an older man. He was tall, about 6′2″ and had a full head of wavy salt 'n' pepper hair that adorned his caramel complexion. His body was fit and strong as he wrapped around me like a python when we slept, which stimulated my sexual craving for him.

Before long, my libido was fully awake and required immediate attention. I decided that if Doc wasn't going to take the lead and turn up the heat on our intimacy, then I would. I didn't care if Doc needed a little help in the bedroom; that's what Viagra and Cialis were for. After all, he was a doctor and certainly knew how to prepare a rocket for orbit. Little did he know, he would be doing a lot more than holding my hands on our next weekend excursion.

Doc and I were meeting some of his golf buddies at Hilton Head for the weekend. After he finished playing his eighteen holes, I would be waiting for his final stroke in the nineteenth hole. I didn't care if he used a long stroke or a short stroke or whether he hit a bogey or an ace, as long as the mission was accomplished.

As we were driving, I looked at Doc and smiled as I imagined how passionate our first time together would be. He would finally taste my juices and feel the flow of my lava, and I would feel the thunder and roar of his loins. Although Doc appeared to be reserved and shy, I had a feeling that he had been holding back. He was probably skilled in every way a woman wanted a man to be. He would taste my soufflé, part my Nile as wide as he could, and then plunge so deep, he would emerge breathless when he resurfaced. I would introduce him to all the things I shared with Joey but this time, no games. We would indulge and engage faithfully and truthfully.

After Doc and I spent the day playing golf, we went back to our room to shower and change for dinner. It was then that I decided to give Doc a sneak preview of the night's activities. Five minutes after Doc stepped into the shower, I joined him. He seemed surprised as he gave me a light smile. I grabbed the soap and began rubbing it all over his back as I kissed him gently on his shoulders and in the mid of his spine. I even washed his firm butt. Finally, I made my way to the front of his body. That's when I noticed how beautiful his body was. I had never seen a naked man in his late fifties. Doc's body was impeccable, no flab or sag anywhere. I knew he worked out intensely, and the results definitely showed.

After washing his bulging chest and ripped torso, I slowly kissed the nape of his neck, his earlobes, and then his lips. He pulled me close, and we began savagely French kissing. Then I pulled away and began kissing his stomach, working my way down to his pelvic area. Just when I dropped to my knees to give him a taste of my oral sensation, he stopped me.

"Stop. Get up. That's enough." Then he opened the shower door. "Let me finish showering by myself."

I was shocked by Doc's reaction. I couldn't believe what was happening. I didn't say anything; I just left the shower as he requested and went to the adjacent bedroom and finished my shower. I didn't know what to think about Doc's reaction. Half of me felt embarrassed, while the other half felt rejected and hurt. I closed my eyes as tears streamed down my face along with the water from the shower jets. When I opened my eyes, I saw a quick flickering image of Ricky and Philip with smirks on their faces. As I gasped for air, I closed my eyes again. When I opened them, the image was gone. *What the fuck? This can't be happening again*

As I was drying off, I planned to get a rental car and drive home, but when I stepped out of the bathroom, Doc was waiting for me with a solemn look on his face. "I'm sorry about how I reacted. Please, forgive me. I thought I was ready to take our relationship to a more intimate level, but I'm not." He paused briefly and looked away. Then he turned to me and grabbed my hand. "I'm crazy about you, but I'm not a hundred percent."

"What are you talking about?" I asked. "I'm not a hundred percent either."

"Do I have to spell it out for you? Listen, I'm sorry. I should have told you, but I really like you and wanted to make love to you. I thought I was alright, but I guess I need a little more time. Listen, sweetheart, I don't want to be selfish and ask you to make this kind of sacrifice, even if it's only temporary. I'll understand if you want to stop seeing me."

I was still confused about his "hundred percent" problem, but I figured we would discuss it in more detail later. After a moment of silence, I let out a long sigh. "I'm glad I didn't do anything to turn you off."

"Never, and not in a million years," he said. "Quite the opposite. You're beautiful and sexy. I want you in every way, and maybe for my wife someday. But you're still young, and I don't want to deprive you of a complete relationship, and I certainly don't want to share you with another man."

"Why don't we slow down and let things evolve naturally?" I asked. "We have a lot more between us than sex. Look at how close we are, and we haven't even had sex yet. Besides, you're not getting rid of me that easily."

We hugged, and then he pulled back and smiled. "Let's go to dinner now."

Doc and I spent the next few days having fun in the sun, but sex was not part of it. We kissed, hugged, and cuddled, but that was it. I thought we would eventually grind a little and indulge in oral sex, but that didn't happen either.

When I got home, I told Sage about Doc's medical condition, and she agreed that I should continue seeing him, especially since I had started developing feelings for him. "You need to stop worrying so much, Astrid. Let your relationship develop organically. Don't try to control so much. Time will tell if he's in your life for a season or a reason. Just be patient; you'll figure it out eventually. Look at all the guys you've fucked over the years. What has it gotten you?"

"Several very satisfying orgasms," I replied. "Need I say more? We need it just like they do."

We both laughed, and then I shook my head. "You're right. I need to be patient with Doc. I'm not always going to have the answers or a roadmap for my future."

Sage was very supportive of me and of anything that might bring me happiness. No matter how dark a situation looked, she always saw the bright side, which was one of many qualities that endeared her to me.

In some ways, she reminded me of Gigi with her calm spirit and wisdom but far more savvy, like a tough urban ghetto girl. She, no doubt, had a high street IQ and good survival instincts. Perhaps she was the person I might have become if I had remained in the Gardens and assimilated into its urban environment. But no thanks to Ricky, I fled the Gardens at age ten to attend boarding school and had a different life instead. And I never looked back.

As time went on, Sage became my self-appointed personal assistant. She was very well organized and started handling personal business matters for me. Every morning, during breakfast, Sage and I would review the to-do list that she had prepared for me. It consisted of various tasks with a corresponding timeline. She would often say, "You need to stop procrastinating and move on to your happy place." The problem was, I had no idea if such a place existed or how in the hell to get there.

As the days passed, my life fell into a triangular pattern with my job, Sage, and Doc. While this allowed for some stability in my life, I still felt disconnected from my essence. Something was still missing, and that cloud of depression was always lingering nearby. Even though I was in a relationship with Doc, I still missed Joey and continued to dream about him. Sometimes, I thought about going back to see Dr. Bina, but then I would change my mind. I also thought about finding a new therapist, but I couldn't go through with that either. It was going to take a lot more than therapy to get me out of this mind funk.

Gigi always said that prayer and a little time could heal anything, but neither seemed to be working. Perhaps because I had not done a lot of praying lately. I attended church regularly, but sometimes during the sermons, my mind would drift elsewhere. I would have to rely on my weed and tequila for healing, at least until enough time had elapsed and my prayers kicked in.

One thing that always perked me up was a call from Junior. He hadn't visited me much since the incident with Joey, but we talked or Skyped at least once a week. I was happy to see him maturing and growing into a young man in pursuit of his dreams. While Junior had let me back into his life, it was still different from the closeness we shared before my divorce from Philip.

One evening, Junior and I were having our usual Skype conversation, which consisted of him telling me about his studies in Europe and the multitude of girls he was dating. It was obvious that Junior was not interested in getting serious with anyone. I hoped his feelings were based on his youth and not tainted from his parents' divorce, but we both steered clear of that topic.

Then, out of nowhere, Junior said, "Now that Dad is moving to Atlanta, it will be easier for me to visit with you. I won't have to split holidays between you guys anymore. He's already purchased a home there, and they're moving in a few weeks."

It felt like someone had just stuck a knife in my stomach. Without realizing it, I stepped away from my iPad as I felt an anxiety attack coming on. Sweat ran down my face as my breathing became labored.

"Mom, are you still there? Are you alright? Is something wrong?"

"I'm here," I replied. "I needed to grab some water. I've had a sore throat the past few days. I think I'm coming down with the flu or something."

Moments later, I remained speechless, still in shock and reeling over the fact that Philip was moving to Atlanta. I had not spoken to or seen him since our divorce was finalized, nor did I have any desire to do so. Sometimes during my conversations with Junior, he would mention his father in passing. The context usually pertained to some event that he had attended with Philip but never anything in depth.

"I'm not feeling well," I said, still overcome with shock. "I'll call you back tomorrow."

"Okay, Mom. Take care of that cold. I hope you feel better. I love you. Goodbye."

I didn't even say goodbye as I ended our Skype session. Thank God Sage wasn't home. I poured a double shot of tequila and then went into my bathroom. I threw back the tequila and then lit a joint. I took two quick puffs and began to feel better. I decided to light a few candles to absorb the aroma from the weed, run a hot lilac bath, and soak awhile to decompress.

While bathing and listening to jazz on my phone, I began to relax. I finished smoking the joint and was in a state of heavenly bliss. *Awe, this is just what I needed.* I rested my head on my bath pillow and closed my eyes. That's when the voice emerged again.

You know it's time for you to take care of Philip, and then we're going back to Detroit to take care of Ricky. And don't worry; this time I won't let you ignore me. I'm not going away until we finish this once and for all.

As always, I ignored it. To respond or react to the voice would send me spiraling into a sphere of insanity. I couldn't let that happen. I knew that if I ever surrendered to the voice, it would take me down a destructive path of no return. Ignoring it was my only option.

After I finished bathing, I still felt anxious. The voice had me feeling unsettled as it continued whispering in the back of my head. It was then that I began using the pronoun "she" to refer to the voice. As the evening progressed, she wouldn't stop talking. At one point, I screamed, "Shut the fuck up!" but she ignored me. So, I decided to drink another double shot of tequila and drop a Percocet. I had to get some sleep. More importantly, I had to quiet the voice. I didn't like taking medically prescribed narcotics, but they were the only thing that would make her shut up, otherwise I would hear her chatter all night.

Later that night, when Sage came home, I was already in bed half asleep. I'm not sure if I was in bed early because I was high, drunk, or just overwhelmed by Philip's move to Atlanta I heard Sage call my name repeatedly, but I ignored her and pretended to be sound asleep.

The next morning, still feeling uneasy, I told Sage about my call with Junior. I explained how upset I became when he gave me the news about Philip's move to Atlanta. I also told her the entire torrid story of my marriage to Philip, including his physical abuse, his threats against Junior, and his bi-sexuality. As the hours passed, I continued sharing my life story with her, including the childhood rape that Ricky inflicted upon me. I explained that, as a result of my experiences with Ricky and Philip, I was still suffering. And because of those two individuals, I lost my Joey—the one true love of my life.

After many tear-filled hours, I finally finished spilling my guts. I had not told a soul, not even to Gigi, the entire gory details of the trauma I experienced at the hands of Philip and Ricky. For some reason, I felt relieved after sharing my story with Sage. However, I was surprised at how she reacted. Not only was she sympathetic to my story, she became angered by it, as if she was their victim instead of me.

"It's only a matter of time before they both get what's coming to them," she said. "And it's almost time."

Confused, I wondered where her anger came from.

"You must get past the misery of your experience with Philip and Ricky," Sage continued, sounding just like Gigi. "They're robbing you of the greatness that God wants for you. I didn't want to say anything before, but now I understand why you behave like you do. You're like the 'walking dead,' existing physically but dead on the inside."

I started crying. "I want to get better and leave my past behind," I said, "but I don't know how. Every time I think I've gotten over those two demons, something happens to remind me that I haven't."

Sage reached over and hugged me. "It's okay. I'll help you. I'm your friend. I promise I'll stay with you until those two tragedies are dead and buried. But first, I need you to do one thing for me."

I looked up at her "What's that?"

"I need you to get rid of all those drugs." She paused, waiting for me to reply, then continued. "You know what I'm talking about: those pills and that marijuana. You should probably stop drinking too. Before you can find your strength, you have to get rid of your crutches. You have to face the demons and pain in your life head on. That means with a clear, sober mind. Getting high only delays the inescapable; it doesn't make your problems go away. The longer you ignore a problem, the worse it gets. In your case, your issues with Philip and Ricky are like cancer cells that metastasize until you kill them."

I nodded. "You're right. I don't need anything to numb or deplete me. After all, I am the Kokuran, which means I already have everything I need to complete me. I guess it's time for me to blossom."

From that point forward, I began living a healthier lifestyle. I quit smoking weed and taking anti-depressants. I even reduced my alcohol consumption to only drinking wine occasionally while dining with Doc. I felt better immediately, as if a boulder had been lifted from my shoulders. The knot that had sought permanent residence in the pit of my stomach disappeared. More importantly, I felt happy, something I hadn't felt in a long time. The cloud of depression that seemed to loom in my peripheral view was gone.

And finally, once and for all, I was ready to put closure on my relationship with Joey. Even though I was ready to let him go, I didn't want to forget him, so I decided to get a tattoo in his memory. I told Sage about my plans, and she thought it was a good idea and agreed to accompany me for moral support.

The next day, Sage and I went to the tattoo parlor. She decided to get a tattoo as well. We both got tattoos on the inside of our wrists. I chose a black orchid with the letter J encased in the center of it, but Sage was very secretive about her tattoo. She kept it covered. When I inquired about it, she said, "It has a special meaning to me. I'll show you later and explain the significance of it."

I found it odd that she was so secretive about her tattoo, especially when she was so eager to go with me to the tattoo parlor. I thought that getting tattoos together would have been a shared experience, creating a sisterly bond similar to my outings with Zoe, but it wasn't. Then I remembered Sage's spiritual beliefs. Her tattoo probably had something to do with Buddhism.

Then we switched the conversation back to my tattoo. Sage grabbed my wrist and examined it. "Oh, Astrid, it's beautiful. Wait until you show it to your mother. She'll think you got it in her honor, since she loves orchids, and her initial is J as well.

"You're right; I hadn't thought about it that way. Gigi's real name is Josette, and everyone knows about her love of orchids. That's a good cover story. Some people might think I'm crazy for getting a tattoo with the first initial of my deceased ex-lover's name."

By then, Sage was ready to open her yoga studio in Atlantic Station. After she showed me her business plan, I decided to invest in it, becoming an equal partner. We agreed that she would handle the operations, and I would handle the finances. It was called the Lotus Blossom Yoga Studio. The décor was filled with Egyptian, Hindu, and Buddhist motifs, which symbolized rebirth, purification, eternal life, and some other spiritual stuff. Sage selected the white lotus flower for the business logo, which was in line with the rest of her spiritual revitalization decoration theme.

I spent a considerable amount of time at Sage's yoga studio helping her get it up and running. Truthfully, I was bored to death at the firm, especially since my workload had dwindled to nil. I was used to the hustle and bustle of a fast-paced work environment, which was a far cry from what my job had become. The only thing at work that held my interest were the resources at my disposal, which included Mr. Brown, the firm's top private investigator. So, I hired him to help me trace Di's whereabouts.

After three months, he discovered that Di had been living in California with a man prior to the incarceration she endured during her pregnancy with me. It was a long shot, but Mr. Brown said he would search for the mystery man. Hopefully, he could point us in the right direction, even if it led to a dead end.

Unfortunately, my search for Di was not enough of a distraction. I still found time to twiddle my thumbs at work. Perhaps Sage was right; I needed to stop procrastinating. I had wanted to leave my firm months earlier but delayed it, because I was afraid. It wasn't a fear of being unemployed that scared me; it was all the other unknowns: my identity and the overall life-change period. But seeing Sage in her studio and how happy she was made me want to find my own happy place.

Four

The Calm Before the Storm

After only a few weeks of negotiations, I completed my separation agreement with my employer. They were quite amenable to my terms, and I was more than satisfied with their generosity. I wish I could say the firm was sad to see me leave, but that was not the case. With lightning speed, they graciously accepted my proposal and cut me a huge check. They were obviously anticipating my departure, which didn't come as a total surprise to me.

Instead of starting a new job, I decided to take some time off to figure out what I really wanted to do with the next phase of my career. I was contemplating starting my own entertainment law firm or seeking a full-time professorship at a university. However, since I wasn't in a rush to do anything, I opted to continue working with Sage in her new yoga studio. Doing something totally different was exactly what I needed. Sage was equally happy for me to work with her, especially since we were business partners.

Although Sage and I had grown very close, there was something stealthy about her. She frequently disappeared for hours at a time. I knew she was dating, but she never mentioned anything about the men she dated. In fact, she never mentioned anything about her family or friends. Whenever I inquired about her personal life, she found a way to avoid answering me by deflecting the conversation. I didn't think anything of it; I figured she was private or hiding something, like the rest of us. I was the master at maintaining façades, so who was I to judge? Apart from that, I had no qualms about Sage. She was a great friend, which was exactly what I needed. She was developing into a good business partner too. In no time at all, the studio was operating at full capacity. We even hired two additional instructors.

To my amazement, I enjoyed working in the studio. It complemented my new healthy lifestyle. It had been three months since I had consumed alcohol or smoked weed. I also started exercising more and changed my diet. Unlike Sage, I wasn't a vegetarian, but I reduced my meat consumption and started eating more organic foods. I must say, my body was bangin' once again. Thanks to my workout regimen, I was almost as fit as I was in high school. I also started meditating, which helped to calm my anxiety.

The results of my healthy lifestyle were becoming noticeable to everyone. People at church, the studio, and in passing often complimented me on my fitness and vitality. My skin had naturally rejuvenated itself, such that my face appeared to be glowing, which made a few studio patrons ask if I was pregnant. That type of praise and feedback fueled me. It made me want to work harder on my health and overall wellness. I was slowly feeling better, inside and out.

While Gigi was happy about the changes I had made in my life, she was also skeptical. Sometimes, she would jokingly say, "You seem happy and upbeat. I hope you're not taking any of those happy pills." My response was always the same. I simply laughed and ignored her.

I never mentioned Sage when talking to Gigi. I didn't want her to drill me about Sage, and I certainly didn't want her to know that Sage was living with me. Gigi would request a full interrogation.

The only conversation that Gigi seemed to enjoy was talking about my relationship with Doc. Of course, she wanted to know about our sex life. She would often say, "Men in their fifties, sixties, and even seventies can still be great lovers. I've had a few older men myself, back when I was a young woman and recently too. And with very little disappointment."

I snickered. "Enough, Gigi. Must we always talk about your sex life? You're almost eighty years old, and you always seem to have sex on the brain."

"Well, how do you think I made it this far? You don't get to be my age living like a nun."

"Okay, Gigi, point noted. Enough about your sex life."

"Why are you so secretive about Doc's pushin' in the cushion?" she asked. "Is he knocking your back out, or is he the type who leaves the sheets neatly tucked in their corners?"

Gigi had me laughing so hard that I started choking. I was always evasive to Gigi's inquiries about my sex life with Doc. If I told her the truth, she would not have let me live it down. I usually said just enough to appease her curiosity.

Unfortunately, Gigi's comedic antics only served to temporarily shift my preoccupation with Philip's move to Atlanta. I was still struggling with the notion of it. Lately, no matter what was going on in my life, thoughts of Philip crept into my mind, accompanied by images of him harming me.

Although Philip lived in the suburbs, I was still concerned about running into him. I lived downtown, the core of Atlanta's social scene, so the probability of a chance encounter was high. I was still tormented by Philip, but I only realized it when he moved to Atlanta.

I told Sage about how threatened I felt by Philip's move to Atlanta. That's when she suggested I take a martial arts class. And so, I did. I was a quick study too. In addition to the sound defensive techniques, I found the training empowering. I began to feel stronger both physically and mentally.

By then my stamina had also improved, such that I could outpace Sage when we went jogging. I also noticed that my anxiety had subsided. I was rarely having sleepless nights, which was the last of my lingering ailments. But when they occurred occasionally, I used an over-the-counter sleep aid instead of the narcotics that Dr. Bina had prescribed. I felt like I was turning a corner in my life. My mind, body, and soul were getting stronger. I was slowly finding my essence, the core of my strength. I was rediscovering me.

One day after I finished meditating, I rested my head on the pillow and stared at the ceiling. I thought about Joey and smiled as I reflected on some of our happier times together. I missed him but in a different way, similar to the way I missed an old friend, not an ex-lover. Finally, I was no longer grieving over Joey. Perhaps Doc had something to do with that. We had been dating for about six months. I had grown very fond of him, even though we still had not consummated our relationship. Doc had shown me how to care and have intimacy without sex. However, I still hoped we would eventually have sex, because I wasn't sure how much longer I could endure our relationship without it.

Despite the absence of sex, Doc and I were becoming closer. His voice was the first I heard when I awoke in the morning and the last before I went to sleep. We also spent every weekend together, which culminated with me staying at his house. At Doc's insistence, I accepted the key he gave me to his house, and it became my second home.

One day I decided to surprise Doc and redecorate his master suite. I replaced his heavy brown drapes with light-blue sheers and a complementary bedding suite. I redid the master bath with a similar theme. When Doc came home, I told him to close his eyes as I led him to the bedroom. However, his reaction was different from what I expected. He seemed disappointed. "I like the new drapery and bedding, but why did you change them?

"I wanted a space in your home that was special for us. I didn't want to keep staring at the décor of your belated wife. When I'm here, I always feel like I'm in another woman's home.

You still have her belongings in this house. How do you expect me to feel?"

"I'm sorry. I didn't know you felt that way. That was insensitive of me. Truthfully, I didn't expect to ever fall in love again after my wife, Kathy passed away, so I had no thoughts about how another woman might feel about my home. Now that I'm in love with you, I'll do whatever it takes to keep you."

I listened patiently as his words, "in love," echoed in my head. I wondered how he could be in love with me. We had only been dating for six months, and we still had not had sex. Even though Doc and I had a close emotional connection, I wouldn't classify it as a great love. He certainly never made feel the way Joey did. The chemistry between Joey and me was undeniable. While I cared deeply for Doc, sparks were not flying between us, and I wasn't sure that the lack of sex was behind it. I was also starting to question why I was seeing him. Was I lonely? Was he a temporary fix? Was I using him has as a space filler? I wasn't sure about my feelings for Doc, but I knew we had not yet evolved to the place called love, at least not in my book.

"I was attracted to you when we first met," he said, "but I was uncomfortable with dating back then. Kathy had only been deceased two years, and I was just getting back out there. By the time I found the courage to look you up, you were already involved with Joey. So, I moved on, but I always said that if I ever got another chance with you, I would grab it. Now here we are today. I love you, and I don't want to lose you. We can redecorate the entire house if you want, or I can sell it and buy another one. It will be our home."

"Wow!" I said. "I wasn't expecting all that. Let's slow down a bit. We don't have to make any drastic decisions right away. I like your home, and since I've been spending a lot of time here, I wanted to add a little piece of me. That way, you'll think of me when I'm not here."

"Well, that's not a problem, because I think about you all the time anyway." He grabbed my hand. "Now, let's try out the shower in my new bathroom."

That surprised me, because Doc and I had not showered together since the embarrassing fiasco at Hilton Head a few months earlier.

"Are you sure?" I asked.

"Yes, tonight I want all of you, if that's okay."

I just smiled and nodded.

A few minutes later, I disrobed and then stepped into the shower. He came in behind me. He hugged me, and I turned around and kissed him.

"Can I wash your hair?" he asked.

I nodded. "Yes."

He began washing my hair and massaging my scalp. It felt good and relaxing. Then he began washing my entire body. His touch was soft and gentle; he washed me like I was a newborn baby. It aroused me; there was something sensual about it. Not to mention that a hot, steamy shower was always an aphrodisiac for me. It was the only time I really enjoyed giving a man head. But I decided I would follow Doc's lead, let him define the path of our ecstasy.

We stepped out of the shower, and Doc grabbed a large towel and quickly dried us off. Then he got some moisturizer and began applying it to my body. He started with my back and then worked his way around to the front. He dropped to his knees as he applied the moisturizer to my legs and thighs. Then he began kissing and licking the interior of my pussy. I felt my lava flow generously.

"OMG, you feel so good," I said. "What took you so long?"

He paused and looked up at me with a crooked smile. "Let's get in bed before I lay you out on this floor."

Seconds later, as I laid on my back, Doc grabbed my legs and pulled me down to center of the bed, away from the headboard. *Mmm . . . we're about to tear this bed up tonight,* I thought.

He continued using his fingers and his tongue to orally fuck me. After I climaxed, I wanted to reciprocate before he plunged inside of me and exploded. As I attempted to climb onto him, he stopped me. "Tonight, it's about making you feel good. Come and lay in my arms. We have plenty of time to explore the sexual depth of our relationship."

As I laid in Doc's arms, I tried to massage his penis and scrotum, but he moved my hands away. *Not this again,* I thought. I figured we had moved pass this celibacy shit. He needed to finish what he started; this wasn't a trial run. My pussy was revved up for round two, not for a shut down. I was confused, but I didn't react or say anything. I just laid in Docs arms, as I did on most nights, and went to sleep.

The next morning, Doc and I did our usual routine. He made breakfast, and then we went for a walk on a trail that surrounded the golf course that encased his home. I hoped he would bring up the previous night, because I really wanted to talk about it, but he didn't, so neither did I. He did bring up something equally important though.

"Now that we're getting serious, I feel there's something that I need to tell you." I thought he was going to share something pertaining to sex or his health, but it was a much bigger shocker. "It's about Dr. Bina."

I paused. "I think I need to sit down for this conversation."

"I don't think it's that serious, but we can sit down if you like."

Once we were seated on the bench, he continued. "Dr. Bina and I used to be involved romantically."

I looked at him in shock. "You were what?"

"Let me finish, and then I'll answer your questions."

I pursed my lips and nodded in agreement.

"I've known Elise, I mean Dr. Bina, for almost twenty years. She and I were on staff at the same hospital before she left to start her private practice. She and Kathy were close friends before she passed. I know what you're thinking, but it's not true. My relationship with Dr. Bina was strictly professional and platonic long before and after Kathy's death.

"Dr. Bina was a great comfort to my family and me during Kathy's last days. There were times after Kathy passed when I was such an emotional wreck that I didn't know if I was coming or going. Then one day, Dr. Bina suggested that I join her on a trip to Paris. She was kind, loving, and very attentive. She was right; I needed to get away. I was unaware of how the stress of Kathy's illness had weighed on me.

"After we returned, we continued seeing each other, but then I ended it. I told her that I liked her, but I wasn't ready to date seriously, let alone get into a new relationship. She said she understood, but then she became very persistent. She always found a way to let me know she was still interested in me. I often ignored her, but we remained friends.

"After you and I first met at the masquerade party and you never called me, I went out with a few other women, but nothing clicked. I found myself spending time with Dr. Bina once again, and the next thing I knew, we were in a relationship of sorts. While Dr. Bina is smart and beautiful, I didn't feel a romantic chemistry with her. After about six months, I knew the relationship wasn't going anywhere, so I ended it. Of course, she assumed that I needed more time because of Kathy, but that wasn't it. I just didn't like her that way, and I told her so emphatically.

However, she had difficulty accepting my lack of interest in her. Her behavior became bizarre. A few times, she showed up at my home without an invitation. She also frequently stopped by the hospital to say hello, which was usually followed by an invitation to dinner, the theater, or some other event. A few times, she showed up at a few events I was attending and acted as if I had invited her as my date. But eventually she backed off and resumed a normal discourse and interaction with me. I assumed her crush on me had dissolved, and we were simply platonic friends and colleagues. However, she did something recently that alarmed me. A few weeks ago, she confronted me at the hospital about my relationship with you. So, I told her the truth, that we were involved. I also told her that I was in love with you. That's when she started ranting and raving about you, behaving highly unprofessionally and unethically. But I stopped her. I would not let her divulge anything you might have shared with her."

"Wow," I said when he was finished. "That shit is really fucked up."

"Dr. Bina said something that I can't ignore," he added with a somber look. "She said that you're still in love with Joey and that you haven't gotten over him. So, I have to ask, are you?"

I was stunned and angered by Doc's words. "First of all, that bitch has no right to discuss my case with anyone. I'm going to sue her ass. But even worse, why didn't you tell me that you had an affair with her? Didn't you see the potential conflict of interest, my medical doctor referring me to his jilted ex-lover for psychotherapy?"

"No, I didn't see a conflict," he replied calmly. "You and I never dated, and my relationship with Dr. Bina ended well over a year before the incident with Joey. To my knowledge, she had moved on. She was quite cordial and respectful whenever I saw her in public, at church, and elsewhere. I had no reason to suspect she was harboring feelings for me.

"However, something else happened recently that has me seriously concerned. She came by the hospital a few days ago and told me that she was in love with me and has been since she and I went to Paris, which was almost five years ago. She seems to think I'm confused about my feelings, that I'm in love with her and not you and that I'm suffering from Superman syndrome, the need to rescue a damsel in distress.

"She became so irate and emotionally unhinged that security had to escort her out of the hospital. As she was leaving, she shouted, 'You belong to me, not her. I love you. I stood by you and your family while Kathy was dying. I'm the one who deserves to be with you, not Astrid. She's broken anyway, only she doesn't know it.' I was totally dumbfounded by her behavior."

"I can't believe this," I said. "This is déjà vu, another act of betrayal. All this time that I was seeking therapy from her, she was secretly in love with you. Well, it's a good thing I stopped seeing her long before you and I started dating." I paused for a moment. "You know, she's been calling me every week for the past few months trying to persuade me to resume therapy with her. How crazy is that?" I shook my head. "This is unbelievable. You should be worried less about my feelings for Joey and more about that stalker you have." I stood up. "I'm going home. This is way too much for me to handle."

Doc got up and followed me. "Don't leave like this. Please, Astrid, don't let this come between us."

I had heard those words before. Joey said the same thing when I found out about Pilar, his gold-digger baby mama. Maybe if I had left him then, my insecurity over Pilar, which triggered the events that followed, might not have happened, and Joey would still be alive. I refused to get caught up in another three-ring circus.

When we returned to Doc's home, I grabbed my things and said I was leaving. "Please, don't call me. I need some time to process this drama."

When I arrived home, Sage was not there. I felt stressed. It was too early for a drink, so I looked in my bathroom for my weed, but then I remembered I had thrown it away when I started my healthy living regimen. My breathing became labored, as if I was going to have an anxiety attack. Then I remembered the techniques that Sage said I should do when my stress level was elevated. I tried to meditate, but that shit wasn't working. So, I did the next best thing, looked for my weed. Ironically, I found a prescription that was written by Dr. Bina for my medical marijuana and quickly went down to the drugstore adjacent to my building for a quick refill. Unfortunately, they were out of marijuana cigarettes. That meant I had to drive to the drugstore across town. I did the forty-yard dash back to my condo, jumped in my car, and was on my way.

With all the midday traffic in Atlanta, it took me an hour to reach the drugstore. By the time I picked up my prescription, my anxiety had subsided. I decided not to use it but keep it on hand in case I needed it later.

When I entered my condo, Sage was there. "I can't stay long," she said. "I have to teach another class this afternoon."

Then she noticed the pharmacy bag sticking out of my purse. "What's in your bag?"

"It's my prescription marijuana," I said, not wanting to lie.

"Why, Astrid? You were doing so well."

As I tried to explain what happened with Doc and his affair with Dr. Bina, Sage interrupted. "Astrid, cut the bullshit. You've encountered another crisis, and your first reaction is to get high? This is a test. You can either deal with your issues head on with a sober mind, or you can deal with them in your usual cowardly way. So, what's it going to be? I know you're stronger than this."

"You're right," I said. "I don't need drugs or any other crutch to lean on when I have to face adversities."

Sage grabbed her things and headed toward the door. "You can tell me about your day when I get back from the studio."

After Sage left, I put my weed away and then took a shower and lounged around my condo. As I sat on the chaise lounge in the bedroom, I thought about Doc and Dr. Bina. I wasn't sure what to do about that situation. The easiest solution would have been just to end my relationship with Doc, but I wasn't sure I wanted to stop seeing him. And I sure as hell didn't want to see him with Dr. Bina.

Even though I hadn't been under Dr. Bina's care in months, I felt she had something on me that she would use, if necessary, to get Doc. The one time I should have trusted my instincts, I ignored them. I felt something was strange with Dr. Bina immediately following a few sessions with her. I could never pinpoint exactly what it was, but I knew something was wrong with her. Now my suspicions were confirmed. All this time, she was really crazy. What sane fifty-year-old woman held a crush for over five years on a man who had no interest in her? He had dumped her not once but twice, and yet she continued to believe he was in love with her. I always had a feeling that Dr. Bina's interests in me went beyond my mental health. I was confused and had no clue how to handle my dilemma with Doc. I would discuss the matter with Sage. Surely, she would help me figure it out.

When Sage came home, I shared the day's events with her. "What should I do?"

"Nothing right now. You should continue your relationship with Doc. He really cares for you. Let him handle the situation with Dr. Bina and see what happens. If she's crazy like you think she is, you need to watch your back. She could be a real threat to you. She may even try to hurt you. I think you should get a gun."

"What?" I exclaimed. "Do you think it's that serious? She's stalking Doc, not me."

"Well, you can't be too careful," Sage replied. "Doc's rejection of her may cause her to come after you. It's just a precaution. She may be harmless, but better safe than sorry."

"I don't know much about guns. Joey was an avid gun collector. I went to the range with him a few times, and he let me fire a few rounds, but that was it."

"Once you apply for a gun permit, you can take a class at the gun range," Sage said. "They will show you how to safely handle and shoot it. I'll go with you, if you want me there for support."

I nodded reluctantly. "I guess you're right. I'll apply for the license on Monday."

Later that evening, Doc called me several times, but I ignored his calls. He also sent me several text messages apologizing, but I didn't reply. I still felt a sense of betrayal. He should have told me about his relationship with Dr. Bina when we started dating, not six months later.

The next day, I agreed to go to brunch with Doc. During the meal, he apologized again. We agreed not to have any more secrets between us, no matter how small or immaterial we thought the subject matter was. We also talked at length about Dr. Bina. That's when I told him that I felt unsafe and was planning to purchase a gun.

"I've known Dr. Bina for years," he said. "I don't think she's a danger to either of us. I think she behaved like she did, because she was in shock. Now that she knows I'm unavailable and that we're together, she'll move on. She's an experienced psychiatrist; she'll get her emotions intact."

As Gigi would say, one thing for certain and two things for sure, "A woman is a woman, and her logic goes out the window when her heart is involved." I didn't need to be a psychologist to know that Dr. Bina was not going away that easily. No sirree.

"I hope you're right," I said. "I'm still going to buy a gun just to be on the safe side. Maybe you should too. While you think you know Dr. Bina, you really don't. She's a scorned woman, and that makes her dangerous. You need to be careful with her. Love can make people do terrible things, even kill."

"I think you're overreacting," Doc said. "Dr. Bina is not a threat to either of us. But I understand if you need a gun to feel safe. Besides, it's no big deal; most people here in Georgia own at least one firearm."

The next couple of weeks were uneventful. I did my usual routine, worked with Sage at the studio, and spent my evenings with Doc. Unfortunately, the sexual part of my relationship with Doc had become nonexistent, and I was growing tired of it. I began to question the relationship, feeling I might be better off single. What was the point of having a man when I still needed my vibrator?

When I started having thoughts about Damien, I knew I was at my wit's end with Doc. For a second, I thought about unblocking Damien's number and arranging a booty call. He didn't have much else to offer, but he was good at releasing my sexual tension.

My sexual frustration with Doc finally reached its peak when I exploded over breakfast. "I'm not happy, and I can't do this anymore, continue in a sexless relationship."

"I wanted our relationship to develop and grow outside of sex," he said. "I want a pure loving relationship with you. I was hoping we would be married before we engaged in sexual intercourse. Sex has a time and place in a relationship. If you do it too soon, it can be a distraction and cloud the purity of a relationship. I love you, and I want to marry you someday. I know it seems fast, but when you're my age, you can recognize the real thing when you find it. I know that you and I are the real deal. Besides, you can't put a time limit on love."

I'd heard those words before. That was the line that Joey had used to reel me in.

Doc took my hands and then dropped to his knees and pulled out a beautiful radiant-cut ten-carat diamond ring. "Will you marry me?" he asked as he slid the ring onto my finger.

Shocked, I paused before replying. "This seems too fast. I love you, but I'm not sure it's the depth of love that married people have for each other."

"Sustainable love develops over time," Doc said, "long after the infatuation has worn off. Besides, we have the main ingredients that will carry us through for a lifetime. But if you're not sure about marriage yet, I want you to wear the ring as a promise ring."

"Aren't we too old for that promise ring stuff?"

He laughed. "I don't care what label we use, as long as we're together."

"What about sex?" I asked. "How does that fit into our relationship? I'm sorry, but I don't want to wait until marriage before we have sex."

"Sweetheart, I want a wife, not just a sex partner, and I hope you want the same. Our relationship can be so much better if we exclude sex until marriage."

"Aren't you a bit of a hypocrite? Did you forget that we first met at a swingers' party? I've tried to respect your values and be patient with you, but I need sex. I don't have to do it every day, but I can't go months and years without it. So, if I can't have it with you, then you leave me no choice. I'll have to get it from someone else."

"I'm sorry you feel that way," Doc replied. "I was trying to help you experience a different kind of ecstasy that's beyond physical intimacy. But if you insist, we can start having sex immediately. As I said before, I don't want to lose you, so we'll do it your way."

I smiled. "Well, let's get this party started now."

Doc took me to his bedroom, and then we disrobed and got into bed. Doc performed oral sex on me, but when I attempted to return the favor, he stopped me and then relented. "Okay, I guess there's no turning back now."

I went down on him and noticed that he was having a little "flight" problem. However, once I stimulated him with my oral skills, his plane was in full throttle, and I took full advantage of it. I climbed on top of him and rode him until I had an orgasm. Then Doc gently rolled me onto my stomach and commenced to do his thing. When he climaxed, he let out a strange gasping sound, as if he was choking, followed by a loud sigh.

I looked at him. "Are you okay? I wanted to make sure you weren't having a heart attack or passing out on me."

He smiled but didn't respond as he readjusted his head on the pillow.

"Aren't you glad we finally did it?" I asked.

He smiled. "That's a loaded question. How can I object when I'm in a drunken orgasmic haze? I'll say yes to anything after you just fucked my brains out."

A few minutes later, I heard Doc snoring. *I guess my pussy was so good, I put his ass to sleep.*

While I watched Doc sleep, I wondered why I didn't feel the euphoria I was expecting after we had our first act of lovemaking. While Doc satisfied me sexually, something was missing. He didn't make me feel the way Joey did. I wondered if I was being unrealistic. Perhaps no man would ever measure up to Joey or even Damien, for that matter.

An hour later, Doc awoke, and we had a little pillow talk. "I was shy about having sex with you due to my condition," he said. "I promise that you can have as much sex as you want. I will never deny you again."

I smiled. "I'll hold you to that."

I was falling for Doc, and I didn't want to leave him just because he had an occasional erectile dysfunction. That wasn't a deal breaker for me. I felt safe with Doc, a void that I needed to fill, which had eluded me for years. Unlike Philip, Joey, and other men from my past, I believed Doc would never forsake or betray me. Perhaps he was the man that Gigi spoke of before I left Detroit.

Five

The Letter

Later that day, I went home feeling refreshed and stress-free. Doc had finally done his job and fed my starving libido. I smiled as I thought about him and looked at the enormous white diamond on my finger. He was not the type of man that I ever imagined being with, but he had far exceeded my expectations. He was definitely a keeper.

I went to the kitchen and decided to go through the mail that was piled on the table. However, I couldn't help but notice a large orange envelope that was handwritten to me with no address on it. I sat down and opened it. Inside was a white envelope and a flash drive. I took out the letter and read it.

Hello Astrid,

It's been a long time since we've communicated. If I must say, you are still beautiful. Don't bother trying to figure out my identity. It's impossible; I've made sure of that. So, let me get

> straight to the point. I want $1 million in cash, or I will send your sexy video to every major news network. I'm reasonable. I know you don't have a million dollars lying around, so I'll work with you. You can give me a quarter up front and the balance in installments. I'll provide details later.
>
> You can keep the flash drive. I have plenty of copies. In case you need some motivation, you should watch the video again. You and Marcus made one hot sexy video. I know you're exploring other career options. You might want to consider the adult film industry, because the camera loves your sexy body.
>
> I don't have to tell you to keep your mouth shut about this letter. I'm watching you, so don't do anything stupid or tell a soul about this business arrangement. I'll be in touch soon.

I was stunned. I didn't have a million dollars in liquidity; it would take me a few months to come up with that much cash. Furthermore, why was I being blackmailed for a sex video that contained doctored footage of me? I wasn't the person having sex with Marcus; it was some other woman.

Then I remembered Burke's response when I raised the same concern two years earlier: "It doesn't matter that you're not the actual person having sex in the video. The fact that you're in it at all is damaging enough. And in the court of public opinion, you will be labeled guilty as charged. When it comes to scandals, people run with ninety percent that's false and ignore the ten percent that's true."

Burke convinced me not to verify the video's authenticity. "Pursuing it could be more damaging than helpful to your reputation. Let it go, since the press has no knowledge of the video's existence."

So, I took his advice, which seemed to work until now.

For a moment, I thought the letter was sent as a cruel prank. I took the flash drive and watched the video on my computer, hoping it was not the sex video that Marcus made with him, me, and the mystery lady, but that was wishful thinking. I couldn't help but wonder why I was being blackmailed after all this time. I guess I would find out soon enough.

As I sat back in the chair, I felt an anxiety attack coming on. My breath became labored. Then the voice spoke to me. *Relax. Don't worry. We will get to the bottom of this. Once we find out this person's identity, we will dispose of him or her too, right along with Philip and Ricky.*

Ignoring the voice, I hid the envelope and its contents underneath some clothing in a dresser drawer. I needed to put the matter on pause and address it later.

Hours later, still feeling consumed by the letter, I felt that the motive wasn't simply money. It was something far more sinister, perhaps my destruction. Again, I wondered who was behind it. Because of Joey's death, I had a lot of enemies. The potential suspect list was endless, including Joey's family, friends, fans, baby mamas, and some of Marcus' following as well. However, I couldn't exclude Dr. Bina. She was well connected in Atlanta and could have uncovered the video. Given her obsession with Doc, she would stop at nothing to get me out of the way.

More importantly, I wondered how the letter got into my condo. It wasn't sent through the regular mail or by a courier service. Perhaps someone in my building was blackmailing me. Most of the residents knew my identity and about the scandal with Joey. Surely a few haters were among them.

Then Sage came to mind as a potential suspect, maybe the primary suspect. Looking back, I had let my guard down when it came to her. Perhaps Doc was right when he had raised concerns. Maybe I had overlooked something deceptive about Sage. She had been relentless in the manner in which she pursued our friendship and injected herself into my life. Perhaps she was pretending to be my friend to get close to me to discover my vulnerabilities and set me up for the kill.

Now that Sage was my primary suspect, I would have to be very careful with her. She was living in my house and had likely gone through all my personal information. How else would the blackmailer know my net worth? No one, including Gigi or Junior, knew the details of my finances. I felt scared and overwhelmed. Despite what the blackmailer said, I would have to tell someone. I could not deal with this by myself.

My initial thought was to contact Burke. His public relations firm had represented me after Joey died. Burke was also the person who mailed me copies of the sex video. He assured me that he sent me all the originals and duplicate copies. So, how could the sex video have surfaced? Furthermore, how many copies could be floating around out there among other would-be blackmailers? I wondered if Burke could be a suspect too.

The only person I could really trust to help me with the situation was Zoe. She used to be an assistant district attorney in the criminal division. Surely, she had experience in these matters. Besides, I knew she would have been upset with me for not coming to her for guidance. I was planning to visit with Zoe tomorrow, so I would tell her then.

When I arrived at Zoe's place, she was as big as a house. We exchanged pleasantries, hugged each other, and then moved to her sun porch, where we sipped sweet tea. She noticed I was on edge and wasted no time getting to the point. "Okay, Astrid, what's going on with you? You barely returned my calls, and when we do talk, the conversation is usually about you and your new best friend, Sage. I must admit, I'm a little jealous of Sage, but I know no one could ever take my place with you, right?"

"Girl, you're silly," I replied. "You know you're my one and only BFF. But enough about me, how are you and my little god baby doing?"

"Well, she's doing fine, but she's wreaking havoc on my body. I don't think I can make it another month. I had to take an early maternity leave, and I'm on a host of restrictions. I'm bored to death; I don't know what to do with myself. I've read about twenty books on parenting and raising children, and I'm more confused now than before I started. You're coming to the baby shower next Sunday, right? It will be scandalous if the godmother isn't here. My sister would never let me hear the end of it." She eyed me suspiciously. "And I guess I'll finally meet Sage, huh?"

I hesitated before responding, given my dilemma. "I'm sure she'll come if she's not working. The yoga studio is consuming all her time these days. I barely see her. Back to your shower. You know I wouldn't miss it for anything. Even though I'm still salty that your sister and cousins excluded me from planning the event."

"I had to keep the peace," Zoe replied. "My sister stopped speaking to me for a whole month when I told her that I wanted you to be the baby's godmother. She's still pissed at me. I told her to get over it. I love her, but I don't like her militant parenting style. She keeps her two daughters on lockdown. I told her that when they leave for college, they're going to go buck wild. She'll wish she hadn't been so strict." Suddenly, she shifted the conversation back to me. "Astrid, I know something's bothering you. What's wrong?"

By then, I had changed my mind. I didn't want to involve her if the blackmailer was indeed following me. Maybe I would tell her later. "I have some good news," I said. "I hired a PI to find my biological mother. He's already found some clues of her whereabouts. Apparently, she used to live in California."

"Astrid, are you sure you want to search for her?" Zoe asked with a worried look. "It's been a long time. What if she's deceased? She left you at birth. What if she doesn't want to be found? I think you should leave well enough alone."

"I thought you would be happy for me."

"I'm not trying to discourage you, but you've been through so much with Joey's death, and I don't want to see you disappointed or hurt again."

"I appreciate your concern, but I'll be okay. Searching for my biological mother is therapeutic. Joey's passing has given me added motivation to search for her. Besides, I have Sage around for moral support."

"Tell me more about Sage," Zoe said. "You two seem awfully close. I was surprised when you told me that she was your new roommate, and now you've gone into business with her, and you haven't even known her a year. I'm concerned about you and your dealings with her, particularly how she has infused herself into the crux of your life. Don't you find it a bit strange that this thirty-something-year-old woman has dropped into your life out of the blue? What's up with that?"

Prior to receiving the blackmail letter, I would have dismissed Zoe's concerns, but now I had my doubts. Not wanting to add to Zoe's suspicions, I pretended everything was copasetic between Sage and me. "Sage is cool. She's a bit of a health nut, but she's down to earth. Once you meet her, you can judge for yourself. Now, Madam Prosecutor, are you finished cross-examining me? Can you rest your case?"

We both laughed. "See?" she said. "This is what happens when you have too much time on your hands. You become paranoid about everything. My bad. Please, excuse my behavior. How's the yoga studio?"

"It's doing extremely well. We're thinking about expanding, maybe on the north side in Alpharetta."

Zoe became serious once again. "I'm not trying to tell you what to do, but I think you should wait awhile before you get too deep into this business with Sage. It's a private studio, which is much different than a franchise or a branded chain of fitness centers."

"First of all, let me correct you. It's a yoga wellness center, not a fitness center. Besides, you know when it comes to my money, I'm strictly business. I would never let friendship or family compromise my decisions. The yoga studio has turned out to be a great investment. It required very little upfront capital, and we're already turning a profit. Our classes are at full capacity, and we're turning people away. We get inquiries all the time about opening other locations. But now that you've mentioned franchises, I might look into franchising the studio; that's a good idea. You should come by after you have the baby. It will help you get that pre-baby body back faster too."

Zoe laughed. "At my age, it's going to take a miracle to get my hourglass figure back. "

"With a little exercise and a nip and tuck here and there, your body will be back in no time."

We both laughed, and then Zoe walked me to the door. "I really miss you," she said. Then she kissed me long and hard, as if she wanted to make love to me right then and there. She continued while tracing her fingers down the middle of my blouse to my crotch. "Maybe after I have the baby and get my body back, we can go away and spend some time together."

"Listen, Zoe, you know I love you, but only like a sister and nothing more. I need you to be okay with that."

"You're so beautiful," Zoe replied. "You can't blame a girl for trying. Don't be a stranger. Think about what I said about Sage. You need to keep an eye on her."

I hugged her. "I'll see you next Sunday."

As I drove home, I decided that for the moment, I'd wait and follow the blackmailer's instructions. There was certainly more to be revealed. However, in the meantime, I would do a background check on Sage. Zoe was right; it was strange how Sage seemed to wiggle her way into my life. And what a coincidence that she was the one who brought the blackmail letter into my home.

I remained conflicted about Sage. She seemed genuine and trustworthy. She was very caring, and she helped me get healthy and fit again. I was the one who invited her to live with me after she had already leased a place. The yoga studio was her idea and was thriving because of her, not me. Despite the circumstances, I didn't want to believe that she was out to hurt me. In my gut, I felt she was a true friend. I would reserve my judgment until I completed my investigation. For the moment, I would remain calm, as if nothing had changed between us.

As my mind shifted back to the blackmail, I decided to explore all my options on how to handle it. The possibility of not paying the blackmailer came to the top of my list. Sex videos were all over the place these days. Famous celebrities had sex videos leaked, either deliberately or criminally, and it didn't seem to ruin their lives. Times were different now; the shock value of sex was gone.

I had to step back and analyze the potential risks and consequences of the video getting out. Apart from embarrassment, what harm could it cause me? People had already formed opinions about me based on the press's spin on Joey's death. The damage to my reputation and my career had already been done; how much worse could it get? I know Gigi wouldn't have a problem with it. She would probably critique the video and give me some pointers on how to make the next one better.

Furthermore, what was to stop the blackmailer or some other person from blackmailing me again in the future? I would never know for certain how many of those videos were out there or who had them. It could become an endless waterfall if I wasn't careful. At some point, I would become unable to pay, and the sex video would be leaked anyway.

I had no choice but to hope the blackmailer left me alone long enough to figure out a solution before I had to pay up. I was surprised at how well I was handling the situation. A few months earlier, if I had received a blackmail letter, I would have fallen apart. I probably would have gotten drunk and doped up on everything I could find to numb the fear and anxiety brought on by the situation. I felt like I would come out of this crisis okay. Gigi was right; I was stronger than I realized. Maybe I had not lost my Kokuran strength. Perhaps it had been lying dormant, waiting for me to tap into it.

Six

Another Intermission with Chevalier

Once I made it home, I was feeling more in control. I decided to continue my life as normal, as if I had never seen the letter. I went into the kitchen and sorted through the piles of mail. After parsing out the junk mail, I went on my laptop.

As I checked my email, I noticed something in my inbox marked important and confidential. It was a note from one of the managing partners of a law firm in Chicago.

Ms. Johnson,

It has come to my attention that you have recently separated from Wyatt, Jones & Steinberg. Your reputation precedes you, and I would welcome the opportunity to discuss your continued interests in this specialized area. Please call me on the number provided on my attached business card at your convenience.

Signed,
Owen P. Witherspoon

That note came as a complete surprise and was highly unusual. My separation from Wyatt, Jones & Steinberg was supposed to be confidential. Technically, I was still on their roster for the next twelve months, the duration of the non-compete period. Rather than fret over the ethical concerns of the note, I would give Mr. Witherspoon a call. What was the harm in having a conversation with him? If nothing else, I might get a free trip to Chicago.

When Sage came home later that night, I asked if she had signed for the registered mail. "Yes. I also brought up a legal-sized orange envelope for you. The bellman at the front desk gave it to me. He said he thought it was from a courier service, but when he went to sign for it, the delivery person was gone. Once he realized it wasn't metered mail, he was going to throw it away, because they don't accept unofficial mail. But when I came to sign for the other letter, he mentioned it to me, and I told him that I would take it and make sure you got it. Did I do something wrong?"

"No, I was just wondering how the letter got here. It wasn't important. It was junk mail, so I threw it away.

Suddenly, my ring caught Sage's eye. "Wow, the sparkle and bling in that ring is blinding me. Why didn't you tell me about your engagement? Have you set a date?"

"This is a promise ring, and we're not engaged, so we haven't set a date. But if it was up to Doc, we would fly to Vegas and get married this weekend."

"Well, he's a great catch, a distinguished physician with no ex-wives or baby mama drama to contend with."

"That doesn't immunize him to drama. Any person over the age of forty has some type of baggage and drama in their life."

"Well, don't underestimate him," she said. "Women would line up for miles to marry a man like Doc."

I shrugged. "I think he's a keeper, but we'll see." My worries about the blackmail letter trumped my excitement about my pre-engagement to Doc. I wasn't in the mood to discuss the embellishments of being in love. I was more concerned about that damned letter.

After the day's event, I felt I deserved some wine. So, I poured a glass of merlot and reminded Sage of Zoe's baby shower.

"You know I can't make it," she said. "It's my turn to work at the studio this Sunday. Besides, I have plans later that evening."

"Why haven't you ever introduced me to any of your male friends?" I asked.

"Because you told me that you didn't want any of my male or female friends in your place. So, I've respected your house rules. Besides, I don't have anyone special like Doc in my life. The guys I date are strictly maintenance men, around for one purpose only."

We both laughed and continued talking about the rest of my day. I told her about the letter I received from the law firm in Chicago.

"Astrid, that's wonderful. You should explore all your options before you settle on your next career move."

"I don't know," I said. "I'm not sure I want to deal with the pressures and politics of working in a large law firm again. That's the part of the job I disliked most."

"You should at least check it out. This is a big change in your career. You've worked for large companies and commanded a high salary. The transition to private practice may not come with those big dollars though. You need to make sure you're making these decisions for the right reasons."

I nodded. "You're right. I'll call him on Monday."

I packed my overnight bag and headed to Doc's house. When I arrived, he greeted me in his bathrobe. "I waited for you. I know you like to shower together."

I grabbed his hand. "Then what are we waiting for?" I marched straight to the master suite and disrobed while Doc started the shower.

After I washed his back, he turned and faced me. I placed my towel on the tiled floor and then dropped to my knees and closed my eyes as I gave him head. I couldn't deep throat him though. That was something I shared with Joey, probably the only man to whom I could ever give that much of myself to. But Doc didn't mind; he was ecstatic over anything sexual that I did with him.

We continued our lovemaking in bed. Doc's confidence had certainly improved. Instead of me leading, he started directing me and became more vocal during our intimate exchanges. I liked the new-and-improved Doc. He was no disappointment. The shyness he once exhibited had disappeared.

The next morning, Doc and I prepared to leave for church. "Do you mind driving your own car?" he asked.

"No, but why?"

"Well, I'm meeting Elise after church today."

"You mean Dr. Bina? Oh, I forgot you two are on a first-name basis."

"It's not what you think. She's been distraught since she found out about our relationship. I want to try to help her."

"Tell that bitch to move on and get a life," I replied. "She needs to find a therapist and begin an intense treatment regimen."

Despite my words, I reluctantly agreed to Doc's request, and then we left for church. A few minutes after we were seated, Dr. Bina crossed over seven people just to sit next to Doc. Once she realized Doc was not paying any attention to her, she moved to another area of the church.

After the benediction, Doc was just about to walk me to my car when Dr. Bina approached. "Excuse me, Will," she said without acknowledging me. "Can I speak to you for a minute, please?"

Who the fuck is Will? I wondered. Then I remembered most of Doc's close friends and family called him that.

They stepped away and walked toward the front of the sanctuary. After fifteen minutes had passed, I decided to walk to my car and drive home. About thirty minutes later, Doc called my cell.

"Why didn't you wait for me?" he asked. It sounded like he was scolding me. "I wanted to walk you to your car."

"Because you were preoccupied trying to save your good friend, Elise. Get this straight, and don't ever forget it: I don't play second fiddle to anyone, and that's non-negotiable if want to be with me. I'll talk to you later. Goodbye."

Doc tried repeatedly to call me back, but I let his calls go straight to voicemail.

I was pissed at him for behaving like he had no clue why I was so upset. I felt disrespected by Dr. Bina's behavior and even angrier that Doc had allowed it. The situation reminded me of Joey and Pilar's co-parenting arrangement, which drove a wedge between us and ultimately led to the demise of our relationship.

Doc was much too old for me to train. I needed a man who was already assembled and willing to roll my way. Maybe it was time to pull back from the relationship before I got in too deep. Besides, I had a bigger problem than my love life to worry about: someone was blackmailing me, and that ordeal was far from over.

Later that night, I texted Doc and told him I needed to take some time away from our relationship, because I was having serious doubts about our future together. Instead of replying, Doc called me, but I sent his call to voicemail. He called back several more times, and each time I hit the "ignore" button. He finally sent me a text message: "I'm sorry for whatever I've done to make you feel this way about me. Please, take some time, but don't throw us away. I love you more than words can describe."

As I laid in bed that night, I kept thinking about the blackmail letter and who was behind it. More importantly, I was considering not complying with the blackmailer's demands. Maybe I could turn the tide and get the police involved. Extortion is a felony and could carry up to ten years. The blackmailer couldn't spend millions of dollars if he or she was locked up in prison; I wondered if this person had contemplated that risk. That's what I would do. I'd turn the tables on the blackmailer. I'd enlist my PI to help me uncover the person's identity, and then I'd get the police involved. I should have done that as soon as the letter first arrived. No more playing the victim. From this point forward, I would deal with my enemies head on.

I called my PI and asked him to come to Chicago for a meeting regarding a second job. I thought it would be better for us to meet in Chicago in case the blackmailer was also in Atlanta. We agreed to meet after I wrapped up my meeting with Mr. Witherspoon.

The next morning, I received a bouquet of flowers from Doc with a card that read, "I'm sorry, please forgive me. Love, Doc." However, I was unmoved by both and proceeded with my day.

Later that morning, Sage and I chatted briefly before she left for the studio. "You haven't been yourself lately," she said. "Is something wrong?"

"No, I've had a lot on my mind lately. I've decided to put my relationship with Doc on ice for a while. Our timing is just not in sync. He wants to move too fast for me. Besides, I need to focus on my next career move, which may or may not be in Atlanta. I'm leaving for Chicago in a few days. I'll deal with Doc when I return."

After a two-hour in-depth phone call with Mr. Witherspoon, we arranged for me to come to Chicago to meet with him. He wanted to send his private jet to pick me up, but I flew commercial instead, so I could make a mini-vacay out of the trip.

Before leaving Atlanta, I took off the promise ring that Doc had given me. The more I thought about Doc and Dr. Bina's so-called friendship, the more I became convinced that their past relationship was far more serious than he had led me to believe. I found it strange that he needed to tend to her while we were together instead of some other time when I was not around. Doc was clearly not ready for a serious commitment. I think we were both confused. He didn't measure up to Joey, and I didn't measure up to his beloved deceased wife, Kathy. I planned to return his ring when I got back from Chicago.

I met with Mr. Witherspoon and the other senior partners on Thursday, as scheduled. After six hours of an interrogation disguised as a business meeting, we concluded our day. Before I left, Mr. Witherspoon said, "I like you, and I think you would be an asset to our firm. We will be presenting you with an offer."

"Thank you," I replied. "I look forward to receiving it."

Later that evening, I met with my PI, Mr. Brown, at a restaurant not far from Mr. Witherspoon's offices. After discussing the particulars of my dilemma, Mr. Brown agreed to take the case. He gave me a disposable cell phone to use for our communications. We also agreed not to have any further direct contact in Atlanta, since my blackmailer and his or her associates were likely in Atlanta and in close proximity to me. He assured me that he would be able to find the blackmailer's identity. "Don't be surprised if the blackmailer turns out to be someone you're very close to," he cautioned, "someone that you least suspect."

"I just want this to go away, quickly and with finality!" I replied.

I spent the balance of the weekend visiting with my cousin Val. While we talked on the phone often, I had only seen her twice since Joey passed, due mainly to my avoidance. However, when we did connect, she was always barrels of fun. I knew spending time with her would be the perfect distraction. She would lift my spirits and have me laughing for days, which was just what I needed.

After spending most of the day shopping on Mag Mile, Val and I stopped in a restaurant to get a bite to eat. As the hostess walked us to our table, I looked over and saw an old familiar face. It was Chevalier (a.k.a. Chevy), seated with his family. I had not seen him in years, but he was still breathtaking, albeit a little older. He actually looked even better, if that was possible. I thought about walking over to his table to say hello but decided not to, as he was conversing with his daughter and had not noticed me.

About an hour later, while Val and I were engulfed in conversation, I turned and caught a glimpse of Chevy staring at me. I quickly turned away. Moments later, he approached our table and greeted us. After I introduced him to Val, he seemed excited to see me. He started talking casually to me, as if we were colleagues and no time had elapsed since our last encounter. He proceeded to invite me over to his house, which I found strange, since he was married.

"Please, call me," he said before leaving. "Let's meet for coffee, a drink, anything. I'd like to see you and catch up for old time's sake before you leave."

"Okay, I'll give you a call later," I said, startled by his boldness.

I watched him as he walked back to his table, settle his bill, and then leave with his family. I wondered if his wife scolded him when they got home. I certainly would not have approved of my husband asking another woman out for any occasion in my presence, business or otherwise. But Becky handled these situations very differently from Shaniqua.

"Mmm-umm, cuz. That's a tall glass of dark mocha delicious. Where did you find him? He's fine as hell, but did you see that wedding band he was wearing? It didn't seem to stop him though. Cuz, he was flirting with you. He had the audacity to ask you for a date with his wife seated only a few feet away. He's scandalous!"

"He's not like that," I replied, "and for the record, he wasn't asking me out on a date. I know he's married. We're old friends from my college days at Oxford, but we occasionally connect professionally."

"Mmm-hmm, well, he wasn't looking at you like you were just a friend. You know, I don't advocate messing with married men, but you might want to taste him once, just to shake off the dust, and ask for forgiveness later."

We both laughed.

"You and I know you haven't had any dick since Joey passed," she said, "and that's been two long years. Girl, you know that's not good for your mental well-being or the elasticity of your coochie. You really need to get some dick, and soon. If not with him then from someone else."

I smiled as I listened to Val's prescription for my sexual health and well-being. She had no idea that I was seriously dating Doc. Only Gigi and Sage knew.

"Astrid, you don't have to be in a relationship to have sex. Just find someone for a booty call. Men have been doing it for years."

I shook my head and laughed. "You know, you sound just like Gigi. On that note, let's get out of here before your husband files a missing persons report on us. We left your house at eight this morning; we've been gone over twelve hours."

Later that night, as I laid in bed, I thought about Chevy. The sight of him was refreshing. I wanted to see him, so I sent him a text message to let him know I would be in town for one day if he wanted to see me.

He responded immediately and asked me to meet him for breakfast.

When I walked in the restaurant promptly at 9 a.m., Chevy was already there. As I headed toward his table, he stood up and smiled. Then he greeted me with a hug and a long sensual kiss. I pulled back, because we were in a public place, not to mention he was a married man.

"I'm sorry," he said. "I'm just so happy to see you. I lost my head; you've always had that effect on me. I was hoping you wanted to get together last night. But anyway, here we are now.

And look at you. You continue to become more beautiful every time I see you."

I smiled. "Thanks. You always make me feel beautiful. So, tell me, how are you? And how's the family?"

"I'm fine. I wish I could say everything was fine at home too, but it's not. We decided to try to hang on for the sake of our daughter, but neither of us are happy. It's only a matter of time before we have to face the big D."

"Maybe not," I said. "Divorce doesn't have to be the end-all fix to your marital problems."

"I don't know. I'm not the kind of man who can fake happiness in my relationships."

"I guess that explains your behavior."

He smiled. "No, I've always been smitten over you. You'll always have a special place in my heart, whether or not we're single, married, or otherwise." He paused. "What else do you have planned for the rest of the day?"

"Not much."

"Let's spend the day together, okay?"

I eyed him suspiciously.

"I'm not suggesting we hook up or anything," he said. "I just want to spend a little more time with you, as much as your schedule permits."

"Okay," I said without any concern that he was married. Then we headed to the parking lot.

"Let's take my car," Chevy said. "We can get yours when you're ready to go back to your cousin's house."

Our first stop was the Triumph Towers, the high-rise building where Chevy's employer was located. He gave me a tour of his office, which resembled a small elegant banquet hall. It was filled with art-deco mahogany furniture including a matching desk and conference tables. Two prominent Picasso works were encased in the built-in wall space; however, it was the expansive view of the lake that was breathtaking. "Wow," I said, "this view alone is enough to make you want to come into the office and work every day."

"Unfortunately, most days I forget the lake is even there," he replied. "The demands of our clients don't allow for much downtime." Then he grabbed my hand. "I have one other place to show you."

We took the elevator to the penthouse. He said the apartment belonged to his company and was one of his perks. He gave me a quick tour, which consisted of the living room and kitchen, the library/office, and the powder room. To my surprise, he didn't show me the master suite or the second bedroom.

"This is very nice," I said as we walked toward the living room. "Do you spend much time here?"

Unfortunately, I spend a great deal of time here. Sometimes, it's easier to stay here than to drive over an hour to the suburbs to a home where I'm really not wanted. Not to mention dealing with the added stress of traffic."

"Okay, stop kidding," I said. "You know this was just a ruse to get me up here, so you can seduce me, right?"

He blushed, a slight smirk on his face. "No, that's not true. But I did want to spend time alone with you. I thought we could relax a bit and then go out a little later. But I'll confess to the ruse, if it works.

"If what works?"

"Astrid, I'm crazy about you. You know I've wanted you since I first laid eyes on you in England. We have a special chemistry that will bind us together forever."

"Maybe, but that's irrelevant now, because you're married. It seems that every time we meet up, one of us is either married or engaged. Maybe it's just not meant to be."

"I think it's the opposite. We are meant to be, and that's why we've never lost touch in over a decade. And we're obviously still very attracted to each other."

He paused, and neither of us spoke. As silence enveloped the room, Chevy took my hand. "I feel what you're trying to hide from me. Your feelings for me run deep, and you want me as much as I want you. But you're scared, and you're using the fact that I'm married to suppress your feelings."

I didn't bother to comment, because we obviously had two different perspectives on my feelings.

We made our way back to the living room, which was surrounded by wall-to-wall windows and panoramic views of Chicago's skyline. We sat on the curvy Euro-style leather sofa accompanied again by quiet awkwardness. Chevy broke the ice by offering me a cup of coffee from the mini barista station in the kitchen.

"Why didn't you show me the master suite?" I asked after a few sips.

He smiled and blushed slightly. "I didn't want to give you the wrong impression."

"What impression is that," I asked sarcastically, "the one where you want to sleep with me?"

"No, I mean yes. Okay, counselor, I'm guilty as charged."

"Well, are you going to show me the master? Don't be shy. Let me see it. You might get lucky."

With a huge smile on his face, Chevy stood up and then helped me to my feet. "If you insist."

About twenty steps later, we were standing in the master bedroom, nervous and apprehensive, like two inexperienced teenagers. I leaned against the dresser. "Are you going to just stand there, or are we going to christen this bed?"

Chevy let out a long sigh. "Okay, but I need to do something else first."

He gave me a long wet sensual kiss while putting his hands under my skirt, massaging my butt, and then fingering my vagina. After we came up for air, he put his finger in his mouth, the same finger that had been inside me. He sucked and licked his finger as if he was tasting a delectable sauce, just as he had done when we were at Oxford. "Let me undress you," he said.

"Whatever turns you on," I whispered.

Chevy slid my skirt down and pulled my shirt over my head. Then he released the hooks on my garter belt and rolled down my stockings, one leg at a time. He kissed my inner thighs and then worked his way up. He slid my panties to the side and used his tongue and lips to ingest me. The rhythmic tempo of his movements were sensual and exacting. He knew exactly where my G-spot was. I wasn't disturbed when I felt his finger gently enter my anus as he intensified his oral stimulation. I grabbed his head with both hands, joining in his passionate oral dance until I climaxed.

Afterwards, Chevy stood up and smiled. "Now that you've had the appetizer, we can get to the main course."

He picked me up and placed me gently on the bed. While lying beside him, I removed my bra and panties. As I started to get under the covers, Chevy stopped me. "I want to look at you, every inch of you." While staring at me, he repeatedly told me that I was beautiful and that my savory juices were the taste of perfection.

Then, without warning, Chevy rolled me onto my stomach, supported by all fours, and positioned himself between my legs behind me. After he penetrated me, I was surprised by his girth and the intensity of his strokes. After about three forceful thrusts, I fell flat on my stomach. He continued to deepen his strokes. He pushed one of my legs up to a ninety-degree angle and continued stroking me as if he was trying to insert his entire scrotum inside me. Then he let out a loud sigh and rested on my back.

Minutes later, we laid on our sides, still breathless. "Now that I've tasted you, I've gotta have you again," he said.

I didn't respond, my mind still floating around somewhere in orgasmic heaven.

Chevy got up and went to the bathroom. Moments later, he re-emerged with a warm soapy facecloth, which he used to wash my vagina and buttocks up, down, and inside out. While it was strange, at that moment, I thought briefly about Joey. Perhaps because he also used to wash my private parts during our sexual intermissions. Once Chevy finished, he tossed the facecloth on the floor and turned his attention back to me. He slid my body down to the center of the bed, pulled my legs over his shoulders, and forcefully penetrated me. There was something sexy about Chevy's brute roughness, perhaps because it was a contradiction to his normal demure disposition. That side of him turned me on and made me want to fuck him longer and harder. We continued making love in the missionary position until we both climaxed. Then we finally rested before falling asleep on the damp sheets, which were no longer tucked in their neat corner pockets.

Hours later, Chevy awoke and repeated what he had said earlier. "Now that I've tasted you, I've got to have you again. But not just for a night, I need to have you every night."

"What do you mean?" I asked. "You're married, and I'm not interested in turning this one-night stand into an affair. Don't get it twisted. I won't play the number two position for any man, and that includes you."

"I'm not asking you to play the role of a mistress," Chevy said calmly. "I told you that my marriage was in trouble, and we're on the verge of getting a divorce."

"No, Chevy," I said, my voice rising in pitch. "I don't want to have any part of you divorcing your wife. We're both just caught up in this lustful situation. This stolen intimacy may not mean anything to either of us tomorrow."

"Astrid, I'm in love with you and have been since we first met. But because of your circumstances, I never acted on my feelings. The only reason I got married was because I was getting to an age where people expected me to have a family. And it presented the right image for the firm. I was very fond of my wife, but I don't think I ever really loved her. I thought the physical aspects of our relationship would be enough, but it wasn't. And she, on the other hand, wanted the money and prestige of the lifestyle I could offer. It wasn't a real marriage for either of us; it was more of a business arrangement. The only good that came out of our marriage was our daughter. But we both know our marriage is doomed; it's just a matter of time. So, I hope you see that you're not the reason for the demise of my marriage; it was dying a slow death long before you showed up."

"Chevy, I've got a lot on my plate right now, and I don't want to complicate it further with a relationship. Even if you were single, I would feel the same. Please, don't put any expectations on me. Let's just enjoy the rest of our day and let tomorrow happen the way it's supposed to."

"Okay," he said, looking disappointed.

I sat up. "I'm hungry. Let's go out and get a bite to eat."

Chevy and I showered, dressed, and then off we went. At dinner, we laughed as we reminisced about our college days and our time at Oxford. In a strange way, having dinner with Chevy reminded me of Joey, of the happier times we shared together.

The night was quickly upon us, and it was getting late, so Chevy drove me to my car. As I was getting out, Chevy was about to say something, but I interrupted him with a kiss.

"Goodbye, Astrid," he said with sadness in his eyes. "Call me, please."

I didn't respond.

By the time I made it back to Val's house, she was asleep. But in true Val style, she left me a note on my pillow, which read: "I hope you had more than breakfast with Mr. Mocha delicious. I saw his big hands and big feet, need I say more . . .."

I smiled and went to sleep.

I flew back early Sunday morning, so I could attend Zoe's baby shower later that afternoon. While on the plane, I thought about my weekend in Chicago. The mini vacay was just what I needed. It provided a great distraction and an unexpected bonus of red-hot, blazing sex with Chevy. Despite his request, I had no intention of calling him. Playtime was over. It was time for me to get back to reality.

As soon as I arrived home, I opened the door to the scent of a dozen vases filled with red and white roses placed throughout every room in my home. I asked the housekeeper about the flowers, and she told me that she signed for them. I knew they were from Doc. He had called and texted me several times a day while I was in Chicago, but I had ignored his messages. I was still angry and had no interest in communicating with him.

I asked the housekeeper if she had seen Sage. She replied that she had not. It seemed lately that Sage and I were always missing each other, probably because she was spending all her time at the yoga studio. Once we hired the two part-time instructors, there was no need for me help out anymore, so I seldom went there.

It was time for me to head over to Zoe's house for the baby shower. I called Sage to see if she had changed her mind about attending, but she didn't answer.

By the time I arrived at Zoe's place, the festivities were underway. I managed to avoid playing the silly games. Once the activities started winding down, Zoe and I were finally able to talk.

"Where's Sage?" she asked, looking around.

"Oh, she couldn't make it. She had to work."

"Figures. I didn't expect her to come anyway. I don't think she likes me. Maybe she's jealous of our friendship." She eyed my tattoo. "So, now you're into body art? Let me guess: you and Sage have matching tattoos."

"We got tattoos on the same day," I admitted, "but I haven't seen Sage's tattoo. It's very personal to her, she keeps it covered."

"Astrid, I need to ask you something very personal," she said, changing the topic.

"Go ahead; you've never held your tongue before."

"Are you and Sage lovers?"

I laughed. "Absolutely not. Why would you think that?"

"You seem different since Sage has been in your life. I know how you felt about our shared intimacy and how private you were about it. It's cool; there's no judgment from me."

"For the last time, Sage and I are only friends. We're not swingers, lovers, or anything like that. I know it seems strange for me to have a roommate at my age, but it's cool. After Joey's death, I found myself stuck in a black hole, and Sage helped me get past that period and turn a corner in my life. Thanks to her, I've been able to start dating seriously again. I can never do enough to repay her for what she's done to help me. So, letting her live in my place for a short while is the least I can do."

Zoe shrugged. "Maybe I'm jealous."

"Girl, you are blessed. You have everything: a loving husband, a beautiful baby on the way, a great career, and this big-ass mansion that your husband bought you. You're living the American dream. I would trade places with you in a heartbeat. There's nothing fun or exciting about starting over at my age. Middle-aged people have too much baggage. You never know how wounded they are or if they have a hidden agenda. How do you find love in the middle of trying to figure all that shit out? At this stage of life, it feels like too much work." I shrugged. "But then, what's the alternative? Stay alone and grow old by myself?"

Zoe smiled. "Sometimes, I guess I overlook my blessings. Please, forgive me for being a bitch. You know this pregnancy has me emotionally unbalanced."

I reached over and hugged her. "I understand. You'll be okay." I glanced at my watch. "It's getting late. I need to head home. But call me as soon as you feel the first labor pain. I want to be at the hospital when my goddaughter enters the world."

As I drove off, Zoe waved goodbye. I continued looking at her standing on her porch until she was out of sight. Zoe and I had a strange connection. We seemed to know when something was bothering the other. We were worried about each other, uneasy about the changes occurring in our lives.

When I returned home, the first thing I did was begin my investigation of Sage. I went online and paid for a quick background check. To my surprise, there were several hundred Sage Brooks in the United States alone. I didn't have the energy to tackle that project with everything else that was going on in my life. Nonetheless, I remained suspicious of her.

I became upset as I pondered what to do about Sage. I no longer trusted her, but I had to be careful, because she was living in my home. The next step for me was getting her out of my house ASAP.

By then I was feeling foolish about my relationship with her. What was I thinking? I had befriended a complete stranger, moved her into my home, and started a business with her. And now she was possibly blackmailing me. How did I let that happen? For the first time since I met Sage, I was afraid of her. I wondered what her real purpose was for inserting herself into my life. Perhaps she was a con artist. Besides taking my money through extortion or otherwise, what else was she planning to do?

I had two choices: confront Sage directly or go to the police and let them remove her from my condo. However, my conscience wouldn't let me believe that Sage was evil and out to harm me. I needed to think about the situation a while longer before I made any decisions. Perhaps I'd consult with Doc. He always gave me good advice.

After avoiding his calls, I finally called Doc back. He apologized about the incident at church with Dr. Bina, so I agreed to see him again. However, my motives were somewhat selfish. I needed a place to stay while I figured out how to deal with Sage, and Doc's house was the perfect hideaway.

When I arrived, Doc was ecstatic to see me. He seemed kinder, sweeter, and more loving. Unfortunately, my sentiments for him were not quite the same, especially since I had reconnected with Chevy.

Spending time with Chevy reminded me of the fiery passion I desired in a man and in a relationship. It also reminded me that I was in control over whom I gave my heart to and shared my life with and, for that matter, whom I fucked. I didn't have to settle for what was considered safe, convenient, or the right thing to do where relationships were concerned. Hence, I didn't have to settle for Doc. For now, the wedding plans with Doc would have to be put on hold. I wasn't sure if I was ready for marriage with Doc, or with anyone for that matter. Besides, I had more important things to contend with than my future marital status.

Seven

Loving Two Ain't Easy To Do

While I had not planned to call Chevy, he had other intentions. He was texting and calling me the moment my plane landed in Atlanta. Initially, I ignored him, thinking he would see that I wasn't interested—but apparently not. After a while, his persistence paid off. I finally resumed talking to him, but only on the basis of a platonic friendship. The situation was made easier since Doc had recently been appointed to a new position at Emory Hospital and worked until midnight on most days. Even though I was staying at Doc's house, the only waking hours we spent together lately were at breakfast.

At first, my conversations with Chevy were friendly in nature, but gradually he revealed his true intent, which was to gain my affection. I must admit, I liked his attention and erotic chatter. Before I knew it, we were having phone sex and making plans to get together. While unintended, I found myself sliding into a love triangle.

I was all too aware of the deadly consequences of trying to love two and planned to end it as quickly as it had begun. While my feelings for Doc were not as strong as his, I didn't want to end our relationship just yet, nor hurt him by misleading or toying with his feelings. But I was excited by the fire that Chevy had ignited in me, which I needed like oxygen to breathe. I knew I would have to make a decision about my predicament soon; however, that would prove more difficult than expected. It seemed the more I tried to pull back from Chevy, the more he intensified his efforts.

I had been working at the yoga studio, doing paperwork, when Chevy called me. "Why don't you meet me for a drink after work today?"

I snickered. "You're so silly. You know I'm not in Chicago."

"Of course, but I'm here in Atlanta for one night. I'm staying at the JW downtown. I have a business meeting tomorrow, and then I'm leaving right after."

Reeling in shock, I didn't reply.

"I thought you would be happy about my surprise visit," he said after a long pause, "but I guess I was wrong."

"That's not true," I replied. "I'm happy you're here, but I already have plans for this evening that I can't change."

I waited for Chevy to respond, but he didn't say a word. I sensed he was disappointed. "Well, I guess I can meet you for a quick drink," I said finally.

"Okay, hurry," he replied. "I'll be waiting for you."

Truthfully, I wasn't pleased about Chevy's surprise visit. His timing couldn't have been worse. My plate was already overflowing with drama, and I didn't need to add him to it. I would have to stop Chevy in his tracks before things went any further. Besides, I had no interest in having a drawn-out affair with a married man.

At the hotel, I went straight to the restroom to do what I always had done when meeting a man: check out my swag and make sure my attire, hair, and face were on point. I looked pretty good wearing my royal-blue, A-line dress with a matching lace bra and thong panties. I was always up for a good tease, if for no other reason than to stroke my ego.

As I entered the dimly lit bar where Chevy was seated, I saw his wide smile and sparkling white teeth. He greeted me with a hug. "Hey beautiful, how are you?" he asked as he pulled out my chair.

I ordered a shot of tequila with lime and then gave him a serious look. "Chevy, we need to talk. You know I had a life well before we reconnected in Chicago." I proceeded to tell him about my relationship with Doc. His response was not what I expected.

"I knew you were seeing someone, because you don't like to be alone. That's probably why you married so young. And since you're not a 'loose, whorish' woman, I knew you'd be in a monogamous relationship. But that doesn't matter to me, because you're not in love with him. I felt your spirit the last time we were together. We connected in a way that few people ever do. I know you love me; you just don't want to acknowledge it, because it doesn't fit in that logical brain of yours. Love is illogical; you can't plan it or put all the pieces in a neat box. You fell in love with me in England, but because you were married, you didn't act on it. I'm not saying you didn't love that football player, but he's not here. Don't you see that God saved you for me and me for you? It's our time now. Let's not lose out on this second chance for real love and happiness."

Caught up in Chevy's words, I was speechless, unable to counter his perspective. "I need more time," I said finally. "I can't jump into another relationship now, and certainly not with some other woman's husband."

"As I said before when you were in Chicago, I'm going to take care of that situation. In fact, I've already started the divorce proceedings, and it has nothing to do with you. The unhappiness in my marriage was spilling over into every other aspect of my life. I just couldn't do it anymore. Not even for the sake of my daughter."

I tried to digest the words that emanated from Chevy's sensual lips, but I found it difficult to pay attention. As I looked at him, my pussy pulsated with desire. While my body wanted Chevy, my mind was conflicted. I repositioned myself and crossed my legs, hoping to suppress my lust.

I looked at my watch, not realizing that an hour had passed. I knew Doc would be waiting for me; he was leaving work early so that we could have a date night. "It's getting late," I said. "I need to get home."

"Please come up to my room before you leave," Chevy asked. "I know you can't stay, but can I at least hold you? The way you're acting, I'm not sure you want to see me again."

Before I could reply, Chevy interrupted. "I flew here today to spend time the with you, hoping to celebrate the start of a new life together, but now I'm uncertain about your feelings and our future. When I leave here, I may never see you again. I know how you are; you have a way of exiling people from your life. Please, babe, just give me five more minutes of your time."

"Okay, but I can't stay long. I told you I have another commitment."

As we rode up in the elevator, Chevy leaned over and kissed me, and then I knew I was in trouble. My lava began to flow. As soon as we were inside his room, we started kissing passionately. Then he pushed me down on the bed, lifted my dress, and practically tore off my panties. I didn't even try to resist him, especially since he immediately commenced to eating me out. Then he rolled me onto my stomach and penetrated me. All I could do was moan between his rough forceful strokes, hoping the feeling would last forever. Mere words could not describe the ecstasy I felt. It was as if I was hypnotized and would yield to his every command. Then, as his body stiffened, I heard him whisper, "Astrid, Astrid, Astrid," and then he let out a loud sigh before resting gently on my back.

We laid there quietly, both lost in thought for about five minutes before I broke the ice. "Chevy, I have to go now."

It was the first time that I'd ever made love with my clothes on. Chevy was still wearing his dress shirt and tie, which was soiled from my juices, and my dress was wrinkled and stained from Chevy's milky explosion.

I did a quick wash-up, grabbed my panties, and put them in my purse. I put on my sunglasses and opened the door, turning back to Chevy. "Goodbye."

Chevy stood in the doorway looking like a sad, lost puppy as I got on the elevator.

As I was driving to Doc's home, Chevy repeatedly called my cell phone, but I sent his calls to voicemail. That hadn't gone well. I went there to put the fire out, not add accelerant to it. Now, I was even more confused, not about Chevy but about my behavior. I had just made love to Chevy and was on my way to spend the night with Doc, and I had no guilty feelings about it.

When I arrived at Doc's home, he kissed me at the door, and then I went to the master suite and ran a bath. While bathing, I called Sage, and we chatted briefly about the things we usually talked about. I wanted her to think everything was copacetic between us. When I stepped out of the bathroom, Doc was standing at the door with a knowing look on his face. I think he had been eavesdropping.

"Are you okay?" I asked.

"Yes, I'm fine, but are you?"

"Yes, but I'm a little tired. I think I'll turn in early."

As I walked over to the bed, I noticed my purse had been moved and was neatly zipped. I couldn't remember if I had zipped it or not. I looked inside, and there were my moist panties, reeking of a strong odor of passion. I quickly put them in the net duffle bag that I used for my dirty clothes. Then I climbed into bed and went to sleep.

Later that night, Doc joined me in bed, where we held each other as we slept. I think he was surprised when I didn't initiate sex with him, which was unusual for me.

The next morning, Doc and I resumed our normal routine, as if we didn't have a care in the world. However, the intimacy I had shared with Chevy seemed to diminish my sexual appetite for Doc. Apart from that, everything else between us was the same. Together, Chevy and Doc summed up the perfect man for me, but separately, neither of them seemed to be enough. I needed Chevy's heated passion and Doc's nurturing qualities. But loving two was not an option. The end result of such a triangular relationship would surely be catastrophic. Nonetheless, ignoring my warnings to myself, I continued living my double life, talking to and texting Chevy daily while spending my nights and evenings with Doc.

While my two lovers distracted me from worries about my blackmail dilemma, I continued to be concerned about it. It was time to stop procrastinating and confront Sage about her involvement.

I had been staying at Doc's house for about a month when I told him that I was going back to my place. "Astrid, is everything okay? You seem preoccupied." He took my hand. "Do you still love me?" Before I could answer he interjected. "We've only had sex a few times since you returned from Chicago. If I hadn't initiated it, we probably wouldn't have had sex at all. This is not like you."

"I'm sorry. I've been under a lot of stress lately," I explained. "I'm worried about Gigi, and I'm at a crossroads with my career. I still owe Mr. Witherspoon an answer to their employment offer."

"Let me know if there's anything I can do to help."

"I will," I said as I hugged him.

I arrived home about thirty minutes before Sage. My timing was perfect. She came in, laid her gym bag on the floor, and sat on the sofa. Before she could say a word, I said, "Sage, we need to talk."

"Okay, no problem," she replied, giving me a concerned look. "What's wrong?"

"Who are you?" I asked, bypassing our usual small talk. "You don't have a driver's license, and you don't own a car or seem to want one. You catch the Marta bus everywhere, unless you're riding with me. And you seem to disappear all the time. Whenever I stop by the yoga studio, you're not there. Who is Sage Brooks? Because that person doesn't seem to exist. Are you in a witness protection program or something?"

"No," she said, a worried look on her face, "but I was in hiding, but not anymore."

I sat back in my chair. "Please explain."

"When I lived in New York, I dated a successful businessman, you know, a baller type. Then I found out from the Feds pursuing him that his wealth came from criminal activities. When I tried to leave him, he beat the shit out of me. That's when I disappeared. After moving around from state to state, I found my way to Atlanta."

Shocked by what I heard, I tried to process it. Sage's words sounded like something out of a movie. While her explanation was plausible, I still had doubts about her story and her identity.

"Let me assure you, you're not in any danger," Sage continued. "Apparently, the Feds convicted him. The last time I checked, he was doing life in upstate New York."

"Well, if I'm safe with you, then why am I being blackmailed? Are you blackmailing me?"

"What are you talking about?" she asked.

I paused and rested my hands in my lap, wondering how to handle the situation and whether or not to share the details with Sage. I gave her the orange envelope along with its contents: the blackmail letter and the USB drive that contained the sex video.

As she read the letter, her expression was just like mine when I first read it. "Astrid, I'm sorry about this. But I swear on everything I know and love that I'm not blackmailing you. Please, believe me. You're my friend. I would never hurt you, let alone try to extort money from you."

I didn't respond. Sage looked at the envelope. "I remember this envelope. I picked it up from the concierge a while back." She paused and eyed it closely. "It's been over a month since you got this letter. Has the blackmailer contacted you again?"

"No, not yet."

"Don't pay one cent," she said angrily. "Call his bluff, and let him release the video. Better yet, flip the script on his ass. This really pisses me off. You're a wonderful person. Why would someone want to do this to you?"

I was surprised by how upset Sage became. She reacted as if she was being blackmailed, not me. "Worst case, if the sex video is released, you can use it as an opportunity to tell your side of the story. Perhaps it will provide proof the footage was falsely edited. Even better, you can get the police involved and expose the blackmailer. I hope you see that you're the one in control; you're in the driver's seat."

"I thought about everything you said, including simply ignoring the letter," I replied, finally regaining my ability to speak. "But what about my job offer with the firm in Chicago? They won't hire me with a scandal hovering over me. It has taken two years to restore my reputation, and this sex video could ruin it again in five minutes."

"Astrid, do you really want to hitch your life to another corporate train? You're smart enough to do your own thing. You can chart your own course. You have no idea how talented you are. Your career is still in its prime. Firms will always want you on their team. I know you're worried about the financials, but the money will come in time, and lots of it."

As I listened to Sage, I hung onto her every word. She was right, I didn't want to join another corporate roster. I was ready to be my own boss and define my own destiny. It was then that I decided to reject Mr. Witherspoon's offer. I would formally communicate my decision later that week.

As we continued talking about my career, I forgot about my suspicions concerning Sage. Seeing how emotional she was over the letter, I knew she was not behind the blackmail, but that didn't erase my concerns about her identity.

"I do have one confession," Sage said. Then she took off the wrist band that she wore to cover her tattoo. It was identical to mine. She continued, "I know this seems weird but I feel a spiritual connection with you and that's why I got the same tattoo.

"You're right, that does seem a bit strange. I guess you can always change it later if you want to."

"No, I plan to keep it forever . . .."

Sage's tattoo was the least of my concerns. I interrupted and said, "Sage, I'm still uncomfortable with your circumstances."

"Astrid, my situation is what it is. I'll leave your home if that will make you feel better. But first let me help you get through this blackmail crisis. You need me now more than ever, okay?"

Despite my initial concerns about Sage, I believed her. "You don't have to leave," I said reluctantly, "and yes, I could use your help."

The truth was, I was scared about the blackmail situation. I felt safe knowing someone else was in the house with me. I didn't know what the blackmailer would do if I refused to pay him. Perhaps he might not release the sex video and resort to violence instead.

That's when I proceeded to tell her about the PI. For some reason, sharing the secret with Sage lessened the burden. We agreed that I would not do anything until I heard from either the blackmailer or Mr. Brown. In the meantime, I would continue my life as if I had never received the letter.

I continued to Skype with Chevy during the week while spending my weekends with Doc. However, Chevy conveniently came to Atlanta a few times a month on business. No matter the length of time, our visits always culminated in sex. Sometimes, I got wet in anticipation of seeing him. It always felt like we were making love for the first time and the last. While Chevy was aware of Doc, I went to great lengths to ensure that Doc had no knowledge of Chevy. It seemed that, for the moment, my deceptive double life was working.

One day while Chevy and I were talking, he informed me that his wife had agreed to fast-track their divorce and that it would be final within six months. "It's time for you to get rid of Doc," he said. "Once my divorce is final, I won't share you with another man. You'll have to make a choice: him or me. If it comes down to it, Astrid, I'll leave you for good this time. Forever!"

I was shocked by Chevy's ultimatum. I didn't want to lose him, but I wasn't sure I was ready to give up Doc either, so I did the next best thing. I lied. "I love you, and I want to be with you too. But I need time to let Doc down gently. He's a good person, and I don't want to hurt him any more than necessary. By the time your divorce is final, I'll be free to love you and only you. I promise."

The following Sunday morning, I woke up and went jogging before I went to church. Afterwards, Doc and I went to brunch, and then I headed home. On the way, I called Gigi. Although she sounded chipper, I sensed something was wrong.

"Gigi, did you go to church today?"

"Yes, but I came right home. I'm feeling a little tired today. I'm okay, so don't go worrying yourself."

"Where's Deana?"

"You know where she is, somewhere trying to save the world. All that education, and she doesn't have a cent to her name. She gives all her money to her church and those charities. And she works part-time and volunteers at the legal aid clinic. You know she has to use my credit card to put gas in that old, broken down hooptie she drives? It's a shame; she has a Harvard law degree, and she walks around here looking like she's homeless. But her heart is as good as gold. She is truly an angel. I know God has reserved a special place in heaven just for her."

Then, she switched the subject to my personal business—as always. "Well, how are you and Doc doing?"

"Fine."

"How's the sex? I know you did it with him by now."

I laughed. "Gigi, it's the same as before. It's very good."

"He seems like a very nice guy. I have a good feeling about him. I think he's good for you. When do you think I can meet him in person?"

"I guess when you come to Georgia. When are you coming, anyway?"

"I'm not sure," she replied. "Girl, you know I'm old and tired. I ain't had sex in a few years now."

"Gigi, what does your sex life have to do with you coming to Atlanta, or anything else, for that matter?"

She let out a soft laugh. "I'm just saying, I must be pretty old and tired if I'm not sexually active. You know, you can have sex for most of your life, as long as you can move around a little bit. The last man I had sex with was Alfred, a pharmacist at the hospital where I worked. Similar to you and Doc, he was much older than me, but we were together for years. Shortly after he retired, he had some health problems and moved into a senior living place. But we stayed in touch, and I visited him often. I usually brought him a plate of hot wings and a Viagra pill, and then I would climb in his bed, and we did our thing. The only reason we stopped was because the last time we did it, his oxygen tank stopped working, and the monitors went off, and the nurse rushed in and caught us."

We both burst into laughter.

"Gigi, quit it. You and your sex life are killing me."

Then Gigi's voice shifted to a serious tone. "I was planning to have a talk with you about your real mother, Di, but I think I've run out of time. So, I left some journals for you. I can see clearly now how my life was connected to you and Di in a special way that was different from my other children."

"Gigi, what are you talking about? You're not going anywhere. Besides, I thought you were going on vacation with me next month at my condo on the Cape. You know you can't go anywhere with me talking like that."

"I know, sweetie. I'm just talking. Anyway, Deana will handle everything if it ever becomes necessary."

"Well, that won't be for a long while. Didn't you say your nana lived past a hundred years old?"

"Yes, but she lived in the country, breathing fresh air, eating food off the plantation, and not inhaling all this pollution in the city. Baby girl, I'm feeling a little tired. I'm going to take a nap. You can call me later if you want."

"Okay, I love you. I'll talk to you later."

"Goodbye."

That was a first. I usually had to rush Gigi off the phone, but this time she did it to me. I didn't think too much about it though. After all, she was in her eighties and was slowing down, as all people did at her age.

When I arrived home, I pondered what to do about Doc and Chevy. I knew I couldn't keep juggling the two of them for long. I'm not sure if it was possible, but I felt like I was in love with them both. Neither of them were fulfilling alone, but together, they were adequate. But even as a package, something was still missing, the sense of utter fulfillment that Joey gave me. Perhaps I was looking for the impossible, Joey's likeness in someone else. I didn't need to waste time pondering that. I had more important things to contend with than my love life, mainly that damned blackmail letter.

Now that I had scratched Sage off the list, I was back at square one. I was even more concerned, because the blackmailer had not contacted me again since delivering the initial letter. I was worried and couldn't function with that hanging over my head.

I woke up the following morning and started my day as usual, which was to go straight to the bathroom and then to the kitchen for my first cup of coffee. While my coffee brewed, I turned on CNN and checked my cell phone to see if I had any messages.

The first thing I noticed was that I had several missed calls from Deana. That was strange, because she never called me late at night. Besides, everyone knew she went to sleep by nine unless she was doing something with her church. I checked my voicemail and saw that she had not left me a message. I didn't fret over it and decided I would call her later to make sure everything was okay.

I drank my coffee and then jumped in the shower, got dressed, and headed to work at the yoga studio. As I was driving, I noticed that Deana had texted me. It read, "Please call me ASAP." Since Deana rarely sent text messages, I decided to pull over and call her right away.

"Hey Deana, what's going on? I noticed you called me a few times last night."

She let out a long sigh. "It's not good. Gigi's back in the hospital. She had another stroke, and this one is much worse than the last. I think you need to come home."

"I'm on my way. Goodbye."

I made a U-turn and headed back to my condo to pack a suitcase. Two hours later, I was on a flight to Detroit.

Eight

Death's Knock At The Door

When I arrived at the hospital, most of my siblings were already there. The mood was just as I expected: cold, somber, and lamentable. The gloomy expression on everyone's face said it all: Gigi's condition was dire.

My sister, Nikki, took my hand and pulled me aside. "Let me talk to you before you go into Gigi's room," she said in her usual stone-cold demeanor. "Gigi is in a coma, and she's on oxygen, because she needs help breathing. I'm not going to lie; her condition is critical, and her prognosis doesn't look good. I told her years ago that she needed to change her diet and consider cardiac surgery, but she didn't listen. She was stubborn; she thought she could cure her heart disease with that Creole voodoo medicine stuff or with those orchids she grew. Of course, the stress she carried from you and your real mama, Dianne, didn't help matters."

As I listened to Nikki, tears rolled down my face. I was hurt, because Gigi was ill and the fact that there might be some merit to Nikki's cruel words. I knew my life's drama had brought added worry and stress to Gigi.

Nikki showed no reaction toward my emotional state. "There's no sense in getting upset, because there's nothing you can do. Deana's been praying all day. Perhaps you can join her."

Nikki had no emotions. She acted as if it was not her mother lying there. I wanted to curse her out and tell her to take that stick out of her ass and stop being such a bitch. But it wasn't the time or the place. I would deal with her later, because she was long overdue for an old-fashioned curse out and beat down.

Nikki and I had been engaged in a silent war for as long as I could remember. She had always had a passive-aggressive attitude toward me. When we were little kids, she often teased me and said I was not her little sister and would hit, kick, and pinch me when no one was watching. And when I shared a twin bed with her, she used to pretend to be asleep and deliberately push me out of the bed. Little did she know, I didn't mind, because it gave me an excuse to climb into bed with Gigi, which is where I wanted to be anyway. One would think that after all these years and the crisis at hand, she would show a little less resentment toward me. But silly me, I forgot who I was dealing with. There was no peace or love where Nikki and I were concerned.

I quickly dismissed Nikki as I headed toward Gigi's room, where I was met by Deana and Pastor Williams from Gigi's church. Even though Gigi had moved decades earlier from the infamous housing projects known as The Gardens, she continued to attend the same church. While the church had been renovated several times, it was still located around the corner from where The Gardens once stood—right in the middle of the hood, surrounded by nothing but urban blight and hopeful possibilities.

When I saw Pastor Williams, I knew things were not good for Gigi. "Ms. Astrid," he said after he greeted me, "I know you're busy, but please stop by the church when you have a moment."

"Okay," I said, puzzled by his request. "You know, Pastor, I can write you a check now."

As much as I liked Pastor Williams and his church, I hated its location. It reminded me of everything I wanted to forget: the harsh realities of poverty, my horrific childhood, and, of course Ricky, my molester.

He smiled. "That's not why I want you to stop by the church. Your mother left her journals with me for safekeeping. She wanted me to give them to you when the time came. And I think that time is now."

I stood there, scared to say anything but wondering what he was talking about. I felt tears forming in my eyes.

Deana must have sensed my apprehension. "Astrid, Pastor's request has nothing to do with planning Gigi's funeral. You know Gigi has probably already taken care of those details. In fact, I know she has. But that's irrelevant, 'cause if it's God's will, Gigi will pull through this and come home again."

I breathed a sigh of relief. "Pastor, I'll call your office tomorrow and schedule an appointment."

"That sounds good." He patted my shoulder before turning to leave.

Deana turned to me. "Brace yourself. I'll go with you."

I took a deep breath and then opened the door to Gigi's room. Despite her warning, I was not prepared for what awaited me. Gigi had lost a considerable amount of weight. She was frail, and her long, wavy, jet-black hair had become thin, silver strands. In addition to IV lines, she was hooked up to a ventilator, and it looked like it was doing most of the breathing for her.

Seeing her lying there like that, I could only sob. Deana hugged me as I cried uncontrollably. "Astrid, it's going to be okay. Just remember your faith."

After I calmed down, Deana released me. "I'll let you have some time alone with her. I'll be right outside the door if you need me."

As soon as Deana was gone, I leaned over and held Gigi's hand. I kissed it and then rubbed my face against hers before kissing her check. "Mommy," I whispered through the snot and tears running down my face, "I love you. Please don't leave me now. I'm begging you, please don't leave me." I don't know where those words came from. I had never called Gigi "Mommy" before. But as Gigi would say, one thing for certain and two things for sure, I did not want her to die. I wanted her to be healthy, just as she was a year earlier.

I couldn't bear to see Gigi like that or the thought of her not recovering. I grabbed some tissues and wiped the tears from my face and those that had spilled onto hers. Then I grabbed my purse and left her room.

As I was saying goodbye to everyone, Nikki offered me a ride to Gigi's house. I reluctantly accepted her offer, since I didn't have a car. As we drove, we had enough small talk about work and our kids to make it back to Gigi's house without getting into an argument. While it was a perfect time for me to cut into Nikki, I didn't bother. I was exhausted, and arguing with her hardly seemed worth it. We ordered pizza for dinner, and then I listened to her do what she loved best: talk about herself. As usual, she talked about her great accomplishments and how well her children were doing at their expensive boarding schools. After an hour of idle conversation, we retired to our respective bedrooms.

Once I was settled in bed, I began returning the many calls I had received, mainly from Doc, Chevy, and Sage. I was so consumed with worry about Gigi's stroke that I could barely remember the context of my conversations.

By the next morning, all my siblings had arrived. During breakfast, we had a meeting, led by Nikki, to discuss matters pertaining to Gigi's condition. We agreed not to notify the extended family for at least two weeks unless something changed. Since most of us lived outside of Detroit, we devised a schedule of who would stay with Deana and oversee Gigi's care as well as disseminate information to the siblings. Of course, that task fell to Deana and me. I didn't mind though. I had already planned to stay in Detroit while Gigi was in critical condition.

After the family meeting, I called Pastor Williams's office, and he told me to stop by at around three. I dreaded going to that appointment.

Once I arrived at his office, which was located in his church, we exchanged the normal clerical pleasantries. Then he proceeded with his disquisition. "I've known your mother for over forty years, and I've never met a stronger or braver woman. To have endured what she did from childhood and then rearing twelve kids alone with strong morals and conviction is no small feat. Not many people make it out of the Gardens and raise successful children like she did. Yes, she accomplished a lot, but not without scars and battle wounds. She cried many days in this church and in my office. And although she confessed her sins and accepted Christ as her Lord and Savior long ago, she still fell short, as all people do. However, she continued to fight for her glory and salvation."

Pastor Williams could no longer ignore the confusion on my face. "Listen, your mother was finally ready to talk to you and the rest of your siblings about her elusive past. She realized her acts of protection only led to lies and deception, which may have ultimately caused damage to some of her children, namely her oldest child, Dianne, your birth mother, and you. She knew her conscience and spirit would not be free until this conversation was had with you all.

"About a year ago, she came to me and told me about her illness and the talk she wanted to have with her children. Fearing a rapid decline in her health, she wanted her final days to be full of joy and happiness rather than scandal and hurt, which might come from that conversation. That's when I urged her to write a journal and leave it to her children upon her death. I assumed she would have left her journals for Deana, but she insisted that you receive them. She also left me with a letter that she wanted you to have after you read the journals."

"And what am I supposed to do with the knowledge of the journals after reading them?" I asked. "Am I supposed to make copies and give them to the siblings, or are they just for my eyes only?"

"I'm not sure. Perhaps the answer is at your discretion or in the letter. You don't have to make any decisions just yet. But for now, the journals are for your eyes only."

"Why don't you give me the letter now, and then I can sort all this out?"

"That's not how it works," he said in a scolding tone. "I promised your mother that I would handle this matter the way she wanted, and I intend to do that, down to the smallest detail. Understand?"

I nodded, and he continued. "Astrid, your mother said that you were the strongest of all her children and that you were most like her, even though she did not give birth to you. But even more so, she trusted you implicitly and knew that you would handle the contents of the journals as she would have expected. Your mother really admired the strength of your character. She often said that you were a Kokuran. Do you know what that means?"

"Yes, it's the black orchid flower which symbolizes beauty, strength, and power."

Nodding in agreement, Pastor Williams opened a drawer and pulled out two brown leather-bound journals. "Once again, I cannot stress upon you enough that these journals are to remain private and for your eyes only until you finish them and read the letter I'm holding for you. I trust I have your word?"

"Yes, Pastor Williams, you have my word.

"One more thing; time is of the essence, so you need to read the journals sooner rather than later," he added.

I plan to stay here at least a month, unless something changes in Gigi's condition. I should have both journals read by next week. Is that okay?"

"Sure, that's fine. I have no idea of the contents of those journals, so feel free to call me if you have any questions or encounter something that's troubling for you. And if for some reason I'm not available, my son, the associate pastor, is aware of your mother's request. He can assist you in my absence."

I stood up and put the journals in my oversized purse and thanked him. "I'll see you in a few weeks."

"Don't forget," he said, "you're always welcome to attend Sunday service with us."

I smiled. "Okay. Thanks, and goodbye."

By the time I made it to my car, I let out a loud sigh of relief. I was concerned about what Gigi might have shared with Pastor Williams, particularly as it pertained to me. For a minute, I thought he was going to bring up the trauma I experienced with Joey and the abuse I suffered at Philip's hands, but he didn't.

As I looked at the journals on the passenger seat, I was actually looking forward to reading them. I would finally learn why Gigi refused to talk about her past and why her parents disowned her. As far as I knew, she worked at a whorehouse and lived at home with her parents with her five illegitimate babies until she eloped and moved to Detroit. Her parents should have been glad that Pops even wanted to marry a woman in her predicament. I figured I would find out all the sordid details soon enough.

For some reason, I decided to take the scenic route back to Gigi's house, which took me by the mosque. I couldn't help but remember what happened to me the last time I was in the neighborhood: I saw Ricky. Unfortunately, no sooner had I thought about Ricky than I caught a glimpse of him. This time I didn't panic or have an anxiety attack. I pulled over and stared at him, hard and steadfast, the way an eagle stares at its prey. As I stared at him, the voice emerged. *You know what you have to do; you've waited long enough. It's time.*

Ignoring the voice, I continued watching him until he was out of sight. Then I began following him in my car. He walked briskly, as if he didn't have a care in the world, stopping to greet people along the way. Eventually, he made his way to a run-down apartment building. Something in me wanted sneak up on him and unleash a full-out attack, like a lion upon a gazelle, but that wasn't me. As much as I despised Ricky, I didn't have it in me to take his life, or anyone else's for that matter.

Without any more thought, I pulled out of the parking lot and sped away.

Once I made it to Gigi's house, I hid the journals in the bottom of my suitcase and then I headed to the hospital to see Gigi. When I arrived, Deana was already there reading Bible scriptures to Gigi. I greeted Gigi as if she could hear me and was not seriously ill.

"Hey Gigi. I can't stay long, but I wanted to stop by for a short visit before it got late. I saw Pastor Williams today. We had a long talk about you. I don't know what's in that letter, but I promise I will honor your wishes."

With a slight smile, Deana looked at me and nodded as if she was giving me her approval.

I bent over and hugged and kissed Gigi. Then I took her hand. "Please, come back to me," I whispered. "I need you. I'm not ready to let you go."

Deana put her arm around my shoulder. "Whatever happens to Gigi is God's will. You know how lively Gigi was; she would never want to live in a vegetative state."

I nodded. "I know you're right, but my feelings are what they are. I need her to stay with me a while longer."

Deana grabbed my hand and said, "let's go; we can devise a visiting schedule tomorrow after everyone leaves."

As I was driving home, I kept hearing a faint whisper, echoing, *Ricky, Ricky, Ricky.* I turned the radio up, but the whisper became louder. Feeling anxious, I pulled over to collect my thoughts. But the voice kept repeating the same words as if it were singing a verse in a song. *Ricky, Ricky, Ricky, It's time, It's time, It's time . . ..*

"Stop it, please be quiet!" I screamed. And just like that, it stopped.

By the time I made it to Gigi's house, most of my siblings were gone except for Nikki, and I wanted no part of her. I was in desperate need of some peace and quiet, so I went straight to my bedroom and closed the door.

Minutes later, I heard a knock. I opened my door and saw the last person I wanted to see or talk to: Nikki. There she was, stirring a cup of tea, standing tall and looking suspicious, as if she was up to no good. I knew she wasn't there to comfort me and that whatever words gushed from her mouth would be nasty and hurtful.

"I'm leaving in the morning, so Deana and you will have to hold things together. You know, Astrid, Gigi probably will not get better; you need to prepare yourself for the inevitable."

She paused as if waiting for me to reply, but I said nothing. "I hope you don't run off and do anything stupid when Gigi dies, like get yourself shot again or try to commit suicide, or better yet, find another man who beats you for a hobby. You'll probably end up in an insane asylum like your real mother. I'm not trying to be mean or cynical, but insanity runs in Gigi's family, and it's compounded when you add incest to it. You'll understand when you find out how Di was conceived."

I stood up. "Incest? What are you talking about?"

At first, she didn't respond. She just smiled and sipped her tea as she walked away. Then she turned back and smirked. "I guess you'll find out soon enough after you've read Gigi's journals."

I'm not sure when or if Gigi had knowledge of it, but Nikki had undoubtedly read her journals. Her painful words left me feeling perplexed. I never expected to read anything about incest in Gigi's life. Perhaps that explained why she never talked about her life in New Orleans.

Nikki seemed to enjoy taunting me with her advance scoop on the journals, especially knowing they were meant for my eyes only. One would think that with her long list of accomplishments, she would not have time to engage in this petty vendetta against me. Although I wasn't a psychologist, I knew Nikki's obsessive hatred toward me was not normal. Perhaps she was suffering from mental illness like her sister, Dianne. After all, they shared the same biological mother.

After showering and performing my usual bedtime rituals with Chevy and Doc, I found myself thinking about Ricky. I decided to do a quick background check on him. I grabbed my laptop and went straight to the state sex offenders list. Sure enough, there he was, photo and all, Richard Allen Jones (a.k.a. Ricky). I couldn't believe it; he was on the sex offenders list. Perhaps that explains why he was living in that run-down apartment. I was curious about what he had been doing the last thirty years. I needed to know more about him. Maybe it would give me closure and quiet the voice in my head. So, I sent an email to my PI and asked him to pull a report on Ricky and send it to me as soon as possible. I didn't bother to wait for his reply; I was exhausted and went to sleep.

The next morning, when I awoke, Nikki was already gone. She didn't say goodbye, leave a note, or anything. It didn't matter though; I was glad she was gone. I could not have spent another day in the same house with her.

As I opened the window shades, I noticed it was warm and cloudy, but I went for a quick jog anyway. Sure enough, I got caught in the rain and was soaked. However, when I returned, Chevy was standing on the porch waiting for me. I opened the door and invited him in.

While standing in the foyer, he said, "I thought I would surprise you and take you to breakfast. I flew in on a red eye, but I have to leave this afternoon. I know this is a very sad time for you. I can't cheer you up, but I can provide you with moral support and a little distraction."

Then he paused and said, "Oh, by the way, I brought this for you."

I opened the package. Inside was a dark grey jogging suit with a hooded sweatshirt. "What's this?" I asked.

"It's a promotional item from one of the clothing manufactures my firm represents." He pointed at the sweatshirt. "See? It has my company's name and logo on it."

"It's perfect," I replied. "In my rush to get here, I didn't pack any comfortable clothes to lounge in. I'm going to leave it here, so I'll always have it as a reminder of this day and your surprise visit in Detroit."

I was ecstatic to see Chevy. I hugged him and thanked him for the jogging suit. "I think I'll pass on the breakfast." I said, kissing him, "but I could really use a distraction." I rubbed the pelvic area at the front of his pants.

He was amazed as I led him to my bedroom, the only other bedroom in Gigi's house that had an en suite bathroom. I turned on the shower and began taking my clothes off. I looked at Chevy. "What are you waiting for?"

He smiled. "I didn't want to be presumptuous, but thanks for the invitation."

While we showered, Chevy washed my hair. It felt nice as he massaged my scalp. We finished and began drying off. I was momentarily confused when Chevy turned the shower back on. He must have put the dial on the hottest temperature, because the bathroom rapidly became hot and steamy. Then he sat me on the long counter and slid me to the edge, where he immersed his face deep inside me. As he orally fucked me, I held onto his head with one hand and the towel rack with the other. After minutes of me squirming and moaning, he resurfaced and grabbed me by my waist and penetrated me, thrusting as if he was riding a horse to the finish line. Both of us tried not to scream from ecstasy. After we climaxed, he rested his upper torso on top of me, due to exhaustion.

After a few minutes, he looked at me and smiled. "Do you want to go for round two?"

"I'm up for it if you are, but this time in the bed. This countertop is bruising my buttocks."

With no further talk, act two was on. Unlike before, Chevy made love to me slowly and gently as he held me tight. While the sex was nice, he must have sensed that I needed to be held more than I needed another orgasm.

I woke up an hour or so later to find Chevy sitting next to me. "Let's go out for lunch," he said, "and then I've got to get to the airport."

Hours later, we were saying goodbye. I had driven my car, so I could go straight to the hospital after we left the restaurant. Chevy made my day with his surprise visit. It was bold and perceptive of him, knowing I needed a little TLC.

While I liked Chevy, and my feelings for him were growing, there was still so much about him that I didn't know. Sex with him was superb, but the longevity of our relationship was questionable. I remained conflicted between him and Doc. I still wasn't ready to commit to Chevy or break things off with Doc. Besides, I knew Doc would come to Detroit on a moment's notice if I asked. But I was keeping him at bay to protect him while I went through this thing I had for Chevy.

When I arrived at the hospital, Gigi's condition was the same. This time, I didn't cry when I saw her. I kissed her and told her that I loved her and that I would sit with her in the hospital for years, if necessary.

I made myself comfortable in the recliner adjacent to Gigi's bed. I had brought a bag with all my mail, which Sage had forwarded to me, along with Gigi's journals. I decided to go through my mail first, starting with the pink envelope. It was Zoe's birth announcement, which included a picture of her new baby girl. To my surprise, she had named her daughter after me, Zora Astrid Patterson. I must say, she was the most beautiful baby I had seen in a long time. I smiled as I looked at her picture, which reminded me that there was light in all the darkness surrounding me. As much as I wanted to preoccupy myself with Zoe's baby, I knew I had to deal with the critical issues at hand, starting with Gigi's journals.

I pulled them out and stared at them. Part of me was curious about their content, while the other part of me was afraid. I was afraid of learning truths, lies, and alibis—afraid of knowing Gigi's deepest secrets, her pains and sufferings. And most of all, I was afraid of the effect that the knowledge of her legacy would have on my life.

I couldn't help but wonder why, after all these years, Gigi was finally ready to share her life story. I'm certain it had something to do with her illness. Perhaps the initial stroke had left her feeling unsure about her future, as if she was on the final leg of her life's journey. Not to worry though, I would find out soon enough.

Nine

A Seed of New Orleans

I started with the first journal entitled, *Gigi's Story: Part I.* It read as follows:

Just as I've always told my children, sometimes you need to examine your past to understand your present. You must look at the inception of everything to know how you ended up on the roads traveled and the various pit stops made along the way. Therefore, I guess the best place for me to start is with my grandfather, Henry Louis Thomassie II.

My grandfather, who was affectionately called Pop Henry, came to Louisiana from France just after slavery ended to complete his medical studies under the tutelage of Dr. Livingston, who owned one of the largest sugarcane plantations in Louisiana. As was common in those days, Pop

Henry lived in Dr. Livingston's home while under his apprenticeship. A small doctor's office was affixed to the main house, but most of their patient care was done at their patients' respective homes. Like most southern states at that time, former slaves continued to live on the plantations as farmhands or sharecroppers. Such was the case at the Livingston plantation. However, due to the legacy of French and Spanish rule in Louisiana, the relationship between master and slave was different from the other southern states, such as Mississippi and Alabama. From what I was told, the Louisiana slaves were treated better than the slaves who resided in the rest of the South. While that may be true, I don't think you can shed a positive light on slavery. So, I won't bother discussing that part of American history any further.

Getting back to Pop Henry, living in New Orleans was quite an impressionable experience for him. It was his first encounter with *gens de couleure libres* (free people of color), and the practice of *plaçage,* a form of common-law marriage between a white man and a colored woman. He enjoyed plantation life, especially being in the company of so many beautiful colored women. He was captivated by their unyielding strength, wisdom, sassy intellect, and curvaceous bodies, the result of the ethnic infusion of their French, Spanish, Native American, Caucasian, and African ancestry. While Pop Henry had eyes for the colored girls, he had no shortage of potential white female suitors as well. He was highly sought after by the daughters of several prominent plantation owners. By all accounts, Pop Henry was considered very handsome. He was just over six feet tall, with dark blond hair, blue eyes, and other model-like features. In addition to his sexy French accent, he had a boyish charm that attracted women to him like bees to honey, and he delighted in it. However, he knew his licentious behavior would have to come to an end, because his bride to be, Lisette, would soon be joining him.

Lisette and Pop Henry had a traditional long-distance courtship, which was common in those days. They wrote lengthy love letters that were filled with hidden, erotic desires and the excitement that would come from their intimate exchange, facilitated by marriage. Their letters often read more like short romance novels, which was normal in premarital courtships. It was not uncommon for couples to go months or years without feasting their eyes on each other until days prior to the marriage. But this did not bother Lisette, as she felt honored to be marrying a man like Pop Henry. She was proud and often boasted to friends that her fiancé was in America and would be sending for her when he completed his medical studies.

As planned, once Pop Henry finished his studies, he booked first-class passage for Lisette on the *St. Augustine*. As soon as she arrived in New Orleans, Pop Henry took her to a small parish church, where they were married, before he whisked her away to the plantation. Lisette was overjoyed by Pop Henry's affection and enthusiasm.

Dr. Livingston, who was elderly and widowed, had grown fond of Pop Henry and invited the newlyweds to live in the main house with him. The house was nothing short of grandiose. It was a sprawling white mansion that rested on a hilltop in the center of the plantation, surrounded by five hundred acres of sugar cane.

Lisette was happy to oblige Dr. Livingston's request, as his estate was exactly the type of home in which she envisioned raising a family with Pop Henry. And as far as Lisette was concerned, she wanted to start her family immediately, on their honeymoon night. However, the consummation of their marriage brought little jubilation to her. Her feelings had nothing to do with their sexual exchange but rather Pop Henry's indifference toward her afterwards. Once he completed his husbandly duties, he climbed out of bed and got dressed. "I'm going to one of the guest homes on the estate," he said politely. "I'll be staying there for the remainder of the night."

Confused and befuddled, Lisette didn't know what to think. She wondered frantically about what she might have done to cause her husband to leave her alone on their wedding night. She laid in bed, filled with anguish, tossing and turning until she fell asleep.

The next morning, when Pop Henry returned, Lisette asked, "Are you disappointed in me? Have I done something wrong?"

"No, my love," he replied without pause. "I am most pleased with you, but a man is permitted to have other pleasures, even from concubines, if he so desires."

"Concubine!!" Lisette cried in her native French tongue. "Are you telling me that you want to lie with another woman? If so, why did you bring me here, and why did you marry me?"

"Surely you know this is the way of a man. It is also the way of plantation life in America. But let me assure you that it will not interfere with my responsibility of being a good husband to you."

"What am I to do while you're enjoying the company of your concubines?" Lisette asked, still shocked and confused by what she was hearing.

"Am I to simply ignore this and pretend it's not happening? My father never engaged in such debauchery. My sisters and I always saw him emerge from mother's room when we awoke each morning."

"Lisette, we're in America now, and this is how things are, especially here in New Orleans. Soon you'll have plenty of babies to occupy your time. Besides, as a doctors' wife, you will be afforded a distinguished social life. We will attend extravagant galas with the most prominent people from parishes across the state. Give it time, and you will get used to things and be very happy as my wife. Besides, Dr. Livingston has promised to leave his plantation to me upon his death if I help him run it. While my family has a good name, we don't have this kind of fortune. I could never provide this type of life for you, not even as a doctor."

While Pop Henry had no intentions of leaving New Orleans, he did give Lisette that option. "You can either stay here and accept this way of life, or you can go back to France. Tell me what you want to do. But whatever you decide, you cannot change your mind or revisit this matter again. Understand?"

Lisette paused as she looked around the mansion, admiring its elegance and how the house staff treated her like royalty, seemingly at her beck and call. She smiled, knowing that no one from her small Parisian village went on to become wealthy and live in such opulence. She thought that Pop Henry would eventually lose interest in his concubines once they had children. She agreed that she would continue to live on the estate and adhere to Pop Henry's conditions.

Over the next few nights, Pop Henry repeated the same routine. At bedtime, he performed his husbandly duties and then disappeared until the next morning. Once Lisette became pregnant, he stopped sleeping in their marital bed altogether. Instead, he began spending all his nights away from home. That did not bode well with Lisette.

At times, she was conflicted by the promise she had made. Accepting her choice and being happy about it were two different things. She tried to understand Pop Henry's bed-hopping behavior, but she remained confused and saddened by it. When she complained and asked him to change his ways, he simply ignored her. Lisette assumed he was spending his time in town at one of the many seedy places in the French Quarter. However, she would soon know for certain where exactly Pop Henry was spending his time, and the knowledge of it devastated her.

One day Lisette decided to sneak down to one the guest homes on the other side of the estate, where Pop Henry was rumored to be staying. While not discussed, everyone knew they were the homes of the mistresses and *plaçage* relationships, and the wives knew to stay away. However, Lisette was defiant and wanted to go there anyway.

She hid behind a large oak tree and watched as white men went in and out of the cluster of homes. Just as she was about to leave, she saw Pop Henry emerge from one of the homes with a colored woman holding a baby. They sat on the swinging chair, drinking sweet tea and smiled affectionately as they talked to each other. Pop Henry also held and played with the baby with a joyful expression on his face. Stunned by the sight, Lisette slipped away and sobbed uncontrollably as she hurried back to the main house.

Now she knew the truth; Pop Henry had a fondness for the colored girls who resided on the estate and perhaps had fathered children with them. Even worse, he likely preferred being in their company instead of hers. Lisette never spoke of her trip to the guesthouse and never ventured there again. It was then that she resigned herself to accept the role of a wife living on a plantation.

Shortly after the birth of Pop Henry and Lisette's first child, Henry III, nicknamed Hank, Dr.

Livingston passed away and left the plantation to Pop Henry, as promised. It was then that Pop Henry changed his surname from Thomassie to Thomas. He felt that having a traditional American name gave him more entitlement to his inheritance. Thus, the plantation was renamed the Thomas Estate.

While Pop Henry focused on blending into the tapestry of the American culture, Lisette wanted to hold on to her Parisian roots. Instead of traditional Southern Cajun cooking, she insisted on French cuisine. She also spoke in her native French tongue and insisted everyone around her speak French as well. She went as far as to hold French lessons with the house staff; hence, most of the people on the plantation were bilingual.

Pop Henry and Lisette had two more children: a daughter, Mary, was born four years after Hank, and Buck was born almost ten years later. It was rumored that Pop Henry had ceased relations with Lisette after fathering Mary and that Buck was born during a drunken stupor. Unlike his older two children, Pop Henry showed little interest in Buck.

Over time, the family grew into a traditional southern family, attending church on Sunday, followed by family dinners and public galas mandated by their elite social standing. However,

Pop Henry's familial obligations had no effect on his appetite for colored girls. He continued to spend his evenings and nights in the guest homes.

In addition to the children Pop Henry had with Lisette, it was rumored that he had fathered children with several of the colored girls on the plantation. However, he was smitten by one girl in particular, Anna. She was a mulatto, born to a female slave who was part African and part Cherokee and her white slave owner. They said Pop Henry spent more time with Anna than with his wife. He even built Anna a small brick home on the estate, just a few feet away from the main house. As crazy as it sounds, that's how people behaved in those times.

Lisette had long gotten over her anguish about Pop Henry's behavior and accepted it. She was also keenly aware of Anna's presence in Pop Henry's life. Besides, she was well respected and knew she was queen of the plantation. She reveled in her role as "first lady."

Pop Henry and Anna had five children together, and he favored them as much as he favored his children with Lisette; however, he seemed proudest of his youngest daughter, Giselle, born only a few years after Buck. Her beauty was breathtaking. She had a rich, dark olive complexion with fine jet-black hair and the bluest of blue eyes.

She looked like an Egyptian queen. Pop Henry often paraded her around the main house and plantation, showing her off as if she was a prize of some sort. Everyone, including Lisette, showed high regard for Giselle's extraordinary beauty; everyone, that is, except her half-brother, Buck.

When Buck was about ten years old, he was playing with other white kids around the house when Giselle showed up. "May I play the game with you all?" she asked.

Buck walked over to her and slapped her so hard that she fell to the floor. While Giselle sat there holding her face and sobbing, Buck shouted, "You're nothing but a nigga! You don't belong here. You should be in the fields with the rest of them!"

Pop Henry must have heard Buck, because he walked in the room holding a leather strap and commenced to lashing him across his body until he was blue in the face. To add insult to his pain, Pop Henry made Buck apologize to Giselle.

"I'm sorry," Buck whispered while looking at the floor.

But Pop Henry wasn't finished yet. "Now get on your knees, and ask for her forgiveness."

Buck looked up at Pop Henry. "I said I was sorry. Isn't that enough? Why are you treating her like that? She's just another nigga girl."

In response, Pop Henry grabbed Buck by his collar and took him into the next room. Even though the door was closed, everyone heard Buck screaming in between the loud thumps and bumps.

Minutes later, Pop Henry emerged with his shirt covered in blood. He took Giselle back to Anna's house, told her what happened and to keep Giselle and the other little kids away from Buck. "That boy is not right in the head. I think he's got the head sickness, and there's no cure for it. He'll just turn into a raving mad dog over time.

"Lisette's family has been plagued by head sickness for generations, but her family kept it secret, fearing the knowledge of it would keep them from attaining proper marriages. She was right to keep her secret; I would not have married her otherwise. But it's too late now. I can only hope that none of my other children are afflicted by it."

After that incident, Pop Henry no longer brought Giselle to the main house. He also began keeping a close eye on Buck, knowing his illness would likely progress and become worse over time.

As Buck entered puberty, he started to become more rebellious and developed hatred toward the colored folks who lived on the plantation. His mischievous acts were often very dark and done in secret. People said he would steal dogs and hang them from trees, where they could be seen by the colored field hands.

Buck eventually found likeminded white boys, and they began harassing, beating, and even torturing colored boys at every opportunity. When Pop Henry learned of Buck's actions, he threatened to send him away, but Lisette begged him not to. Nonetheless, Pop Henry and Buck's relationship continued to be tense, and more physical altercations ensued. At least once a month, Pop Henry gave Buck a lashing. However, Pop Henry reached his limit when Buck brutally raped one of the colored girls who lived on the plantation. Buck was sent away to work for a farmer in Mississippi and told never to return.

Sadly, Buck's behavior continued to worsen, especially after he developed a fondness for corn liquor, which made his behavior more crazed and bizarre. It was said that his demonic behavior was not limited to the colored girls or the Negroes. It was also directed toward young pubescent white girls too, which resulted in him being forced to leave town after town.

Over the years, he moved around to various cities in the South to find work. His reputation eventually caught up to him, and it became difficult for him to get farm work. When he could no longer find employment, he reached out to Pop

Henry for help. To avoid bringing Buck back to New Orleans, Pop Henry bought him a small farm in Mississippi, so he could take care of himself. Nevertheless, Buck's farm was never prosperous, nor did he ever marry or have a family. He lived on his farm alone until he lost it many years later to his gambling debts.

By all accounts, Pop Henry was living the American dream. He was a wealthy businessman, and he had a wonderful family, excluding Buck, of course. Mary met and married a young pastor while finishing school up north. She and her husband started a family and returned to New Orleans for occasional visits. Following in his father's footsteps, Hank attended college and then medical school, with plans to work alongside Pop Henry in his medical practice.

Unfortunately, just as all her children became adults and left home, Lisette became seriously ill. She was afflicted by her family's head disease and unable to care for herself. She lost her mind, hearing voices, talking to herself, pretending to be other people, and, at times, not recognizing herself or anyone else. Based on the stories I heard about her, I believe she was suffering from schizophrenia. Ironically, it was Anna who cared for her. At Pop Henry's request, Anna moved into the main house and stayed there with Giselle until Lisette eventually died from a fever.

Pop Henry's life continued as normal, running the plantation and working in his medical practice, but he was becoming frail. Hank noticed his father's failing health and began coming home more often to visit.

It was during one of his visits that he noticed Giselle and gave special attention to her. She had blossomed into something spectacular, resembling a woman well beyond her age of fourteen. She looked even more exotic, standing at 5'7" with lean curves, rich olive skin, long black flowing hair, and blazing blue eyes. Although she was merely a teenager, and he was more than ten years her senior, Hank could not take his eyes off her. Her beauty mesmerized him. They began flirting with each other, even though he was engaged to be married to Ms. Katherine from a neighboring plantation.

The innocent flirting quickly became serious. Hank started coming home from the university almost every weekend, so he could spend time with Giselle. Even though they had to sneak around, they always found time to go skinny dipping in the swimming hole on the outskirts of the property. By then, they had engaged in far more than swimming. Hank had pierced Giselle's veil and felt the warmth of her loins and the depth of her silken vortex. He was spellbound and could not get enough of her.

One night, after they finished swimming, they laid on a blanket in each other's arms, staring at the moon. "I'm tired of sneaking around with you," Hank said. "I'm calling off my engagement to Katherine. I want you to be my wife. If Father won't let me marry you, then I'll never marry. You are the one I truly love."

"I love you too, and I want to marry you," Giselle responded, "but Pop Henry would never allow it. You know I can't pass for nothing white with this dark Cherokee blood running through my veins."'

"None of that matters to me. We'll go up north or leave the country if we have to."

"No, Hank. I can't leave New Orleans, and I can't leave my mama. I'll just be your *plaçage* wife, and we can live on the plantation with everyone else. By the time you finish your doctors' training, I'll be sixteen, and surely neither Mama nor Pop Henry will object."

"Alright, Giselle. As long as we're together."

Hank and Giselle continued sneaking around, hiding their love affair. It seemed everyone on the planation knew about it, except Pop Henry. But their secret would not last long.

One day, Pop Henry caught them in the kitchen of the main house kissing and became very angry with them. "This will not be permitted!" he yelled in his native French tongue. He pointed at the door. "Giselle, leave now! I'll speak to Anna about this later."

Once she was gone, Pop Henry turned to Hank. "I forbid you to lie with Giselle or any of Anna's girls. Their kinship is too close, and you might breed mongoloid babies or something worse. Besides, it's already been arranged for you to marry Ms. Katherine. She's a fine lady, and she'll make a good wife. This marriage will make a great union. Through her inheritance, the combined plantations will be the largest in Louisiana."

As Hank was about to speak, Pop Henry patted his shoulder. "Son, it's alright for you to have relations with the colored girls on the estate but not with Anna's daughters. Do you understand?"

Filled with sadness, Hank nodded. "Yes, Father, I understand."

He immediately packed up and went back to college, only returning for occasional visits.

While Hank and Giselle cooled off their amorous affair, their feelings for each other never diminished. That was evidenced two years later, when Pop Henry died suddenly from a heart attack. Hank and Giselle immediately resumed their love affair, even though he was already married. Similar to his father, Hank regularly visited the guest homes and started a *plaçage* relationship with Giselle. He and Giselle had two daughters within the next three years, and then, five years later, they had me. I was told that I was a spitting image of my mother, which is why my father wanted me to bear her name. I was born Giselle Josette Thomas and given the nickname Gigi.

The End.

By the time I finished reading the first journal, I had become intrigued with Gigi's story and was anxious to start on the second one. I knew it would be deep so I decided to take a short break. I went to the cafeteria, grabbed some coffee and a few snacks, and quickly returned to Gigi's room to resume reading.

Ten

A Spirit Lost & Found

The second journal was similarly titled, *Gigi's Story Part II.* It read as follows:

We were like so many other families in the south, living together in the same household with extended family members. That usually meant that generations of grandparents, aunts, uncles, and their children lived together, either in the same house or somewhere on the estate. In our case, it was slightly different because of the size and wealth that our sugar cane plantation afforded us. Our estate was huge, more like a self-contained town. We had several medicine ladies, carpenters, toolmakers, seamstresses, and, of course, the field hands. Everyone had nice homes, far better than the shacks the coloreds lived in on other plantations. Some of the other plantation owners were appalled by the way the coloreds lived on our estate, but it didn't bother Pop Henry or my father none. We were all happy living just as we were.

Life was good with my extended family too, which included lots of cousins, aunts and uncles, and my beloved Nana, who was also my maternal grandmother. As a priestess, Nana was admired like a celebrity and respected on our estate and nearby plantations.

There was never a shortage of fun times on the estate or limits to the imagination of my cousins and me. The only thing missing was my mother, Giselle. She died when I was a toddler, so Nana raised me until I was school age. Then I went to live in my Papa's house with his wife, Ms. Katherine, my two older sisters whom were born to my biological mother, and my baby brother, Louis, who was Papa and Ms. Katherine's only child. Unlike my sisters, I could not attend regular school or travel abroad. Papa said I didn't look white enough, so I had to be home schooled. I didn't mind though, because that meant I could spend more time playing with Louis.

Louis and I were nearly the same age and very close despite his illness, known today as hydrocephalus. Folks said the reason Louis was born sick was because Ms. Katherine and her family were cursed, but I didn't believe that, because Ms. Katherine was always kind to me. I couldn't imagine why anyone would want to put a curse on her. But maybe her parents did something that caused her to get hexed.

Papa wanted to send Louis away to a sanitarian, but Ms. Katherine wouldn't hear of it. She loved and hovered all over him. After years of trying to have a baby and several miscarriages, Louis was the only baby to live outside her womb. Thanks to Nana's medicines, he lived until he was nine years old.

By then, Nana was up in age. She spent most of her days working in her garden, and I worked alongside her every chance I could. I used to help her make medicines from all sorts of flowers. She was the one who introduced me to the orchid and its healing powers. She had the most beautiful garden. Sometimes, Ms. Katherine would bring her friends to see Nana's garden. There was never a shortage of compliments about the rare colors and exotic blooms. Nana grew plants and flowers that other folks couldn't grow in New Orleans. Since she was also a medicine woman, Nana grew some of the flowers to make medicines, but she grew most of the flowers simply for their beauty.

Nana taught me how to grow flowers in and outside their normal environments as well as the mystical healing powers of plants. But it was the orchids that she admired most. She said they were powerful and were connected to spirits, healing, and curses. She believed the energy and power of the orchid could be imparted into people. Her favorite orchid was the black orchid or, as she called it, the Kokuran.

"The Kokuran is symbolic of fertility, ecstasy, beauty, power, authority, and submission," she said. "These are traits of greatness that can be found in the lineage of royalty, renowned religious and political leaders, and other powerful people. These people have something extra special that sets them apart from others. You have those same qualities; you just haven't tapped into them yet, but you will one day when you're older, when you're in full blossom. And I'm not talking about your body. You will know when you have blossomed."

I didn't fully understand the meaning or the significance of the Kokuran back then, but I believed every word that came out of Nana's mouth. So, I decided to wait patiently until I blossomed. Papa didn't believe in voodoo and forbid us to talk about it, but most of my kinfolk believed in it and practiced it. They did it mostly in secret, so Papa wouldn't know.

My gardening time was limited, because Ms. Katherine insisted that I complete my studies, piano lessons, etiquette training, and other tasks befitting a wealthy plantation owner's daughter.

While it may seem strange, Ms. Katherine was very nice to my sisters and me despite the awkward circumstances. Back then, *plaçage* relationships were common in New Orleans, a part of everyday life, and the wives accepted it. But our plantation was different, because the wives and mistresses lived on the same property, and the children often mingled together. Sometimes, you couldn't tell whether or not a child belonged to a wife or a mistress. I heard that when Giselle passed away, my papa was devastated and no longer visited any women in the guest homes. He was grief-stricken and heartbroken for a long time.

As the years went by, following in the footsteps of my mother and sisters, I was tall with a build beyond my age, so Papa started keeping me close to home. I was not allowed to run freely around our estate as I had done before. Papa imposed the same restrictions on my older sisters when they were my age. He wanted to preserve us for marriage. Papa used to say, "Being virtuous will ensure a proper husband when the time comes." And that would have been my future if Uncle Buck had not shown up.

When I was about twelve years old, I met Uncle Buck for the first time. From the moment I saw him, I feared him. His appearance was ragged, and he smelled like he had been sleeping in the shed with the hunting dogs and bathed in whisky.

"You're the spitting image of your mother, perhaps even more beautiful," he said. "Your skin is much lighter than hers. So, you're Little Ms. Giselle?"

"Yes, but everyone calls me Gigi."

"Well, that's not a suitable name for a pretty girl like you. I'm going to call you Little Ms. Giselle. Is that alright?

I nodded shyly. "Yes."

"Well, get over here, and give your Uncle Buck a hug."

I didn't want to go near Uncle Buck, but Papa nudged me forward. "Go ahead now. Say hi to your uncle."

When I went to hug him, he started feeling my body all over while trying to stick his tongue in my mouth. As I struggled to pull away from him, I looked at my father and stepmother, hoping they would do something, but neither one of them said a word. When I finally pulled away from Uncle Buck with fear and trepidation embroidered across my face, I looked at Papa again, hoping he would say something to comfort me, but he didn't utter a word.

I ran out of the house and next door to the guest house where Nana lived. As she was seated in her rocking chair, I fell to my knees and cried while resting my head in her lap. I told her what uncle Buck had done to me.

Nana rubbed my head. "Oh, Lord, it was you in my dreams. Child, stay away from your Uncle Buck. He's got eyes for you."

"Nana, what are you talking about?"

"He wants to hurt you, to destroy you."

"Why?"

She paused and shook her head. "That man is evil. Some people are just born that way. Pop Henry thought Buck had a madness disease, a malfunction in his brain. But I knew different. He was born with an evil soul. That can't be fixed with any type of medicine. The only cure for that sickness is death, no different than putting a sick animal out of its misery.

"More importantly, the spirits told me that Buck came back to do one thing only: to harm and destroy. So, you'd better watch out for him. He has your father and Ms. Katherine fooled. Now that Pop Henry is gone, he'll try to take over the plantation."

"Nana, I'll just stay here with you."

"Your papa won't stand for that. He wants you to stay with his people."

"But I'm scared, Nana. I'm going to ask Papa to send Uncle Buck away."

"Child, that's not going to happen. But I'll put a protective shield around you."

"What's that?"

"You're too young to understand, but I'll take care of it tonight."

I felt relieved knowing that Nana would protect me, especially since she was a voodoo priestess.

Before I left, Nana gave me a red spice powder. She told me to sprinkle it by my door, and it would keep evil away from me, including Uncle Buck. And it worked. I would see Uncle Buck staring at me, but he never came near me or tried to touch me in any way.

One hot summer day, while playing in the fields with my cousins, we received some terrible news. My papa gathered everyone in front of the main house and told us that Nana had died in her sleep.

"What happened?" I asked.

"Nana was nearly a hundred years old," he said, "and that's what happens to old people."

Before I could say anything else, he looked at me and said, "I don't want to hear anything about spirits, conjuring, or anything of that sort. Do you hear me? We are a Christian family. Understand?"

I nodded, but I knew why Papa made that statement. Voodoo was widespread in New Orleans and quite popular on our estate. While Nana held the highest title of priestess, several other men and women on our estate practiced the craft, which included healing sick people, talking to the dead, casting spells, holding rituals, and so forth. These practices seemed normal to us, part of everyday life on the estate.

I was devastated by Nana's death. She had been more like my mother than my grandmother, showering me with an abundance of love and affection. While I had no memories of my mother, I was told that she was beautiful, like an Egyptian queen, and that papa was heartbroken when she died. Apart from that, not much was ever discussed about my mother.

Despite having three generations of doctors who owned and managed the estate, death refused to stay away. It visited our plantation quite often and sometimes unexpectedly.

A few weeks after Nana died, Papa had a heart attack and dropped dead. Everyone was nervous, because they knew Ms. Katherine could not run the plantation and that Uncle Buck would most likely take over. Unlike Papa, Uncle Buck did not hold any favor for colored people. He was pro-Jim Crow and believed in everything else that degraded and segregated Negroes and coloreds from white folks. Back then, I didn't know Negroes and coloreds were one and the same.

But that was not the worst of it. I learned that my papa and my mama were actually brother and sister, sharing the same father but having different mothers. So, my father was actually my uncle too.

Once Papa died, Uncle Buck quickly sobered up. He even bathed, shaved his face, and cut his hair. He looked distinguished, like an upstanding citizen. For the first time, I noticed that he had bright blue eyes and facial features like my papa.

Ms. Katherine wanted no part of Uncle Buck and quickly packed her belongings and moved back to her father's plantation. My two older sisters had left a few years earlier and eloped while studying abroad. So, the only people left in the main house were Uncle Buck, the live-in staff, and me. But that didn't last. He made the entire staff move out of the main house, and they only returned to work there during the day. He even fired the teacher who home-schooled me.

With each passing day, the field hands and most of my kinfolk fled the plantation. The flight had already started when Jim Crow came to Louisiana, but it was accelerated once Uncle Buck took over. I knew I needed to leave too, but I had nowhere to go. I was only twelve years old, and I had never left the plantation except to go to town occasionally to shop with Nana, Papa, or Ms. Katherine. When I asked some of my relatives to take me with them when they left the plantation, they refused. A few others flat out lied to me. When I showed up to their house with my suitcase, they were already gone.

As it turned out, I was not loved as much as I thought. I learned that most of my relatives were jealous of the way my mother and her children were treated, especially given that some of my cousins might have actually been my half-brothers and half-sisters. It was rumored that Papa had fathered other kids on the estate, but he only claimed my sisters and me. Nevertheless, I was left to fend for myself where Uncle Buck was concerned.

Everyone knew that Uncle Buck was crazy and had monstrous ways, but no one cared that I was alone in the house with him. I was trapped. I knew he would eventually do something bad to me or possibly even kill me, like he had done the hunting dogs. I had no one to protect me. I would just have to wait until the darkness came for me.

As the weeks went by, Uncle Buck paid me no mind. He was too preoccupied with his new status as a wealthy plantation owner. Thanks to his newfound wealth, his social life was very active, and he had plenty of women to frolic with. Sometimes, his lady friends would stay at the main house for days at a time.

To my surprise, Uncle Buck was kind to me. When he had gatherings in the main house, he made sure I was in my room. He often told me to continue with my studies and discussed sending me to a finishing school. And when he went into town, he would ask if I needed anything. I always said no, but he often brought back something anyway—silk scarves, scented oils, something more fitting for a woman than a teenage girl.

One day upon returning from town, he gave me some beautiful silk fabric, enough for at least three ball gowns. "Why did you buy me this fabric?" I asked.

"Ms. Giselle, you are growing up," he said. "Soon you will be old enough to attend balls or gain entrance to places in the French Quarter." He paused. "But with your kind, of course."

"Thank you for the fabric," I said, ignoring his last comment, and then retreated to my room.

Sometimes, Uncle Buck seemed genuinely concerned about me. Once I snuck down to the kitchen wearing only my nightgown to get a snack. While I was seated at the table, a man came into the kitchen, sat down, and began talking to me. Minutes later, Uncle Buck appeared and scolded the man. Then he turned to me. "Are you okay, Giselle?"

"Yes, I'm fine."

"It's late," he said in a mild voice. "You should go to your room and lock the door. You should never be in the company of man without a proper chaperone. Do you understand?"

"Yes, Uncle Buck. I'm sorry. Goodnight."

Uncle Buck continued with his life as plantation owner. He spent most of his time conducting business during the day and hanging out in the French Quarter at night. Since no one else lived in the main house, I would sneak out and go to one of the guest homes and spend the night there with one of my cousins. But in the early morning, I was often asked to leave, because everyone feared Uncle Buck.

Despite all the changes on the plantation, I still wanted to have a party for my thirteenth birthday, as was the tradition among the New Orleans elite social rank. The formal event was very important, as it marked the beginning of a girl's transition from childhood to that of a young woman. Some said the real purpose of the event was to provide a preview of females for future marriages, arranged or otherwise. It was usually a girl's last party before being presented at her debutante ball. But none of that mattered to me; I wanted to feel normal again, to have some fun and feel happy the way I did before my Papa died. So, I mustered the courage to ask Uncle Buck the big question, "May I have a birthday party?"

"Yes," he replied cheerfully. "I'll get the cook to organize it."

"Thank you, Uncle Buck," I said, feeling joyful and excited.

"Is that all? No hugs for your Uncle Buck?" he asked.

I reluctantly walked over and hugged him while making sure my face was turned away from his. He held me awkwardly tight before I slowly pulled away and returned to my room.

About two weeks later, I had my party. It was a joyous occasion and my last happy childhood memory. The few cousins who still resided on our estate and friends from nearby plantations were in all attendance. Although I received lots of nice gifts, Uncle Buck went over the top with his generosity. He bought me a thoroughbred horse, several silk ball gowns, and a beautiful diamond necklace that was certainly more appropriate for an adult woman than a girl my age. When I told him that I didn't ride, he said, "That's okay, I'll teach you. Your father and I used to enjoy riding together when we were kids."

I thought that was strange, because Papa never really talked about Uncle Buck, let alone horseback riding with him. It didn't matter though. Truth was, I was scared of horses. We had plenty of horses on our estate, but I had no interest in them, nor did I want to be anywhere near Uncle Buck's person.

That night, when I was asleep, I heard someone trying to open the door, but it was locked. I had heard those sounds on many nights before, but they were usually brief. I knew it was Uncle Buck and why he was trying to open my door.

That's when I devised a plan to run away. I planned to purchase a train ticket and leave Saturday morning, because Uncle Buck was usually drunk and stayed in the French Quarter over the weekend. Perhaps I would find Aunt Mary or go live with some other relatives who had already moved up North. Unfortunately, my plan never came to fruition.

When Friday came, Uncle Buck did not go out, as he usually did. Instead, he stayed home and drank whisky all day and night. That made me nervous, so I got some paprika and sprinkled it across my doorway, hoping it would be as effective as the red powder Nana had given me before she passed away. I locked my door and pushed my chest in front of it. Eventually, I fell asleep, hoping

I could still leave on Saturday or the next day, as soon as the opportunity presented itself.

In the quiet darkness of the early morning, someone rattled and turned the doorknob to my room, awakening me. I was afraid, because I knew who was behind the door. Minutes later, the door flew open, and Uncle Buck was standing there naked and holding a bottle of whisky.

"Don't make this difficult," he said drunkenly. "You know what I want. I'm going to do to you what I should have done to your mother years ago. The sins of a mother are always passed on to her daughter. It has to be done, so you'll know your place in life. Your kind will never be equal to white people. It doesn't matter how light or pale your skin is. And for those Niggas who are out there masquerading as white people, they should be hung from the tallest tree."

I was terrified as I listened to Uncle Buck's hateful rhetoric. I thought about jumping out the fourth-floor window to my death, but it was closed. As Uncle Buck approached, I tried to fight him off, but it only angered him. So, he beat me until I was unconscious. I awoke hours later with Uncle Buck whispering my name while gently wiping my face with a damp cloth as if he was sincerely caring for my wounds. Then I noticed my hands were tied over my head and my legs spread eagle and tied to the bedposts. He bound my mouth with a torn piece of bed sheet, and then he raped me. After he was finished, he punched my face repeatedly. I thought for sure that I would choke to death on my own blood.

I endured Uncle Buck's brutality for several days. He continued his acts of torture, using smelling salts to bring me back to consciousness, and then he raped me and beat me again until I passed out. The only thing I could remember was him calling my name. "Giselle, Giselle, wake up, my sweet Giselle." At some point, I realized Uncle Buck would probably kill me. It was then that I blacked out, and I believe my spirit left my body.

Days later, I awoke in a soaking tub at our cook's house surrounded by several ladies from the nearby plantations. I knew by their painted faces and formal white attire that I had been a part of some type of ritual. As I looked around the room, I felt a depth of pain that exceeded any words known to me. It was more than physical. My heart, soul, and spirit were traumatized. At that moment, I wished I was dead. I couldn't speak or move. All I could do was release the tears through the tightly wound bandages that covered my face. As I locked around to see where I was, I heard a faint voice in the background say, "She's back now. She'll be okay."

When I was lifted out of the tub on a gurney made from a bed sheet, a midwife came with her medicine bag and stitched my private areas for what seemed like hours. "You're all fixed now," she said when she was finished, "and in a few months, you'll be just like new again.

At some point, I heard another voice whisper, "Hallelujah! Hallelujah! I didn't think she was going to make it, but God had other plans for her. Hallelujah!"

A few months later, my recovery had progressed enough that I could eat solid foods again. Prior to that, my meal consumption was limited to drinking liquids from a straw due to fractured bones in my face. However, while my body was healing rapidly, my mind was not. It seemed to drift away often. But even worse, I felt alone, abandoned, sad, and angry.

I felt alone because I was alone. I couldn't understand why I had been treated so badly by my own kinfolk. None of them cared that I had no one to look after me once my papa died. Not even my older sisters thought enough of me to send for me, knowing my circumstances. They cared more about concealing their true ethnicity than helping me, their orphaned younger sister.

I had several other kinfolks who were still living on the estate. They knew that Uncle Buck hated colored people and had attacked a young girl on the estate once before, yet no one tried to rescue me. It was as if they left me to be eaten, like bait for the hunting dogs. Even the cook said everyone knew it was just a matter of time before Uncle Buck attacked me. It was as if I was chosen to be the sacrificial lamb. The knowledge of this left me feeling distraught and angry.

But I was also upset with Papa. I wondered why he overlooked Uncle Buck's inappropriate behavior toward me when he first arrived. He knew of Uncle Buck's predilection for violence toward girls and colored folks in general. Perhaps if he had sent him away, like Pop Henry did years earlier, he would have never been able to hurt me. I couldn't help but wonder if my darker skin color made me less worthy than my older sisters, who were light, bright, and damn near white. It didn't matter though, because Papa was gone and what was done was done. My thoughts of my Papa were never the same. Part of me hated him for not protecting me. I would be forever haunted by his indifference toward Uncle Buck's behavior toward me.

After much whispering about Uncle Buck, the cook finally told me what happened to him. Shortly after she found my nearly lifeless, bloody body lying in my bed, Uncle Buck disappeared.

However, a few days later, they found his dismembered body in a sack near the Mississippi River. No one ever spoke of him or his death after that, not even Aunt Mary. I was glad he was dead. I only wished I had been the one who killed him. I would have chopped him up in small pieces and then fed him to the alligators in the Bayou. I hated Uncle Buck, not only for what he had done to me, but also for all the other little girls he had hurt before me.

Aunt Mary and her family moved back to New Orleans to take over the plantation. She visited me at the cook's house and asked me to come back to the estate, so she could take care of me. "I know how much your papa loved his children, and he would want me to look after you. I promise you'll be safe and cared for, just as your father would have wanted."

I didn't respond, so she continued. "Just call when you're ready to come home. I'll send for you."

The cook said I could stay with her, but she thought things might be better for me back at the estate with Aunt Mary. Since I didn't want to overstay my welcome, I reluctantly decided to return home.

When I got there, I discovered Aunt Mary had redecorated the main house and given me a new bedroom with new furniture and bright yellow curtains. I resumed my home-schooling, and things seemed to go back to normal, my new normal. Despite Aunt Mary's kindness, I still felt sad and lonely. My home no longer felt like home, and I no longer visited the few relatives who still resided on the plantation. I hated them; they were no longer my kin. As far as I was concerned, they were just as responsible for what happened to me, knowing I was living in the house, alone, with a monster.

I rarely left the house. Most days I just sat on the porch swing and stared at the sky, daydreaming about the happy times I had as a child growing up on the plantation and also wondering if my mother or Nana could see me. Were they watching over me now?

One day, I happened to walk over to Nana's house when I noticed her garden. I was surprised that the flowers and plants were standing tall and robust. The orchids, her favorite flower, looked rich and vibrant. That was strange, because I was certain no one had bothered to maintain her garden. It was then that I felt Nana's spirit, and I knew she was tending her own garden. From that time forward, her garden became my garden, my place of solace and my salvation.

One day, while I was working in the garden, I passed out. I thought it was due to heat exhaustion, because it was about a hundred degrees outside. However, the doctor told me I was pregnant. I was shocked by the news. Without uttering a word, Aunt Mary and I were thinking the same thing. I was carrying a child sired by Uncle Buck.

"You don't have to keep it," Aunt Mary said, though she was deeply religious. "It might be born with the same madness disease that destroyed Buck. You know it wasn't completely his fault. His illness was hereditary, Mother's family was plagued by it. Just to be safe, when this child is born, we'll take it to an orphanage."

I wasn't going to wait that long. I was sure I was carrying evil inside me. Not only was Uncle Buck a madman and a rapist, he was also my father's brother and my mother's half-brother. Nothing good could come from such an incestuous union. I went to the midwife, so she could take care of it.

After examining me, she shook her head. "Although you're small, you're too far gone. I can't help you now, child."

I went home and cried myself to sleep. I was just beginning to feel normal again, and now I had been given a permanent reminder of Uncle Buck and his brutality. I figured I had no other choice but to kill myself. I could not bear any more pain. So, I went to Nana's house in search of the poisons and potions she kept. Surely she had something packed away that I could use for my purpose.

As I went through the boxes, I could not find anything but books and an old, worn Bible. I realized her medicine cabinet had probably been raided the day after she died. So, I laid down on the floor, sobbing, not realizing I was still holding the Bible.

As I laid the Bible on the floor, the pages flew open. Then I felt a warmth come over me, as if someone had placed a blanket over me. As I sobbed, I heard a faint voice say, "It will be alright."

I sat up and picked up the Bible. It was open to the book of Matthew. My eyes immediately seized on the following verse: "See that you do not despise one of these little ones. For I tell you that in heaven their angels always see the face of my Father who is in heaven" (Matthew 18:10). I wasn't sure how to interpret it, but I was certain it had something to do with my baby being an angel sent by God. It was then that I realized I wasn't carrying evil but something beautiful, a miracle of life. When I told Aunt Mary what happened, she said it was a message from God and that my baby and I would be okay.

About four months later, I gave birth to a baby girl. She was beautiful and perfect, with ten fingers and ten toes. I let Aunt Mary name her Dianne, but I called her by her nickname, Di.

One day, while nursing and looking into my baby's sweet little innocent face, I asked God not to take me away from her, as he had taken my mother and Nana from me. That was the first time I had ever prayed. "I promise you that I will never leave your side," I whispered to her. "And unlike my papa, I will always protect you. You will never know the pain that I've experienced."

I had transformed, by no choice of my own, from an innocent girl to a woman before my time. Giselle was gone. She died under Uncle Buck's hand. I wanted to forget everything associated with my childhood and start over. I wanted to forget the voice, Uncle Buck's voice, that last called me by my given name. Hence, I would no longer go by Giselle but by my second name instead. To the rest of the world, I would be known as Josette Thomas.

I continued to live at home with Aunt Mary and her husband. Her children were married with their own families and remained up north. They wanted no part of the south.

While working in my garden and taking care of my baby occupied most of my time, nothing could erase the nightmares of Uncle Buck that frequently paralyzed me in my sleep. I wanted to leave the plantation, but I was afraid to do so. It had become my prison and my refuge. I hated it and loved it at the same time. It had given me so much, but it had taken a lot from me as well.

By the time Di was a year old, I became restless. While my gardening and Di's cute, round face gave me joy, it was not enough to block out the pain and anger that still consumed me. It didn't help that people around me were always whispering and looking at me with pity, as if I were broken or damaged goods. I needed a distraction and a change of scenery. I was ready to spread my wings or at least venture off the estate and go into the city.

Since I was spoiled and considered unsuitable for a husband, I decided I didn't need one or want one, but that would not stop me from dating. I began spending time in the French Quarter. It was bursting at the seams with jazz, theaters, speakeasies, brothels, and plenty of other worldly activities to consume the time of wayward girls like me. It was just what I needed, one long endless party.

I attended parties in the mansions along Basin Street in Storyville, New Orleans' red-light district. The elegant mansions looked like any other ordinary family home situated in an opulent neighborhood. However, what was happening on the inside made them different from those other homes. Most were high-class brothels that resembled exclusive social clubs. In addition to the working girls, there were also single women, like me, who partied there. It was not unusual for wealthy businessmen, musicians, actors, and other famous people to patronize those establishments. While I never worked there, I did indulge in the festivities.

It was there where I thought I met my first true love, Dean. He was a tall, handsome musician, and he told me every lie a man could say to make a woman fall in love with him. "You are that special one who I've been searching for my entire life," he said. He even spoke of marriage and possibly taking Di and me with him back to his hometown of Philly.

I finally conceded to his persistent charm and began a courtship with him. After our first night of passion, he disappeared, leaving a pile of cash beneath the pillow where his head had rested next to mine. That's when I realized I was nothing more to him than a whore. Perhaps he even thought I worked at the brothel. Although disappointed, I had become hardened, so his degraded perception of me didn't bother me. In fact, I thought it was rather fitting. I didn't believe I was worthy of love from a man anyway. So, this was the next best thing: enjoy the company of a man while getting paid for it. However, a month later, my smile turned to worry. Dean had left more than cash behind. He left me pregnant with my second child, whom I named Deana.

When Deana was born, Di was thrilled. She acted as if I had given her a real baby doll. She would hug and kiss Deana all day if I let her. She was very protective of her and would often say, "This is my baby." Their closeness grew stronger as they got older.

Despite the circumstances, I had no regrets about having my babies. I loved them with every breath in me. Although not completely, they seemed to fill a void in my life. They were my reason for being.

Over the next few years, I continued to go deeper into the French Quarter's nightlife. It was during that time that I explored the depths of my sexuality, experimenting with men and women and occasionally, group love. I was looking for love from anyone, and I was willing to go pretty low to find it. Deep within, I was desperate for love like a hobo begging for spare change. Unfortunately, real love continued to evade me, but I carried on partying and trying to find it. Along the way, I had two more babies from gentlemen passersby who blew through New Orleans for one reason or another.

I loved my babies, but I didn't let them get in the way of my nefarious pleasures. My belly never swelled too large, so I usually partied until a few weeks before I gave birth. And then, about six months later, I'd stop nursing, put the baby on bottled milk, and place her in Aunt Mary's arms, so I could get back in the streets. Sometimes, I tried to stay home longer, but then the sadness would come and overwhelm me. The only time I felt happy was when I was drunk, smoking opium, or lying in the arms of a strange man. On a few occasions, I ran into some nice men, but I would quickly dismiss them. I was always drawn to the ones who came to play and not to stay. I was deeply conflicted, longing for love but scared and running away from it.

While Aunt Mary disapproved of my behavior, she never lectured me or threatened to kick me out of the house, perhaps because of my children. She loved and cared for my kids as if they were hers, so much so that my babies called her Mommy and me by my nickname, Gigi. However, she would occasionally look at me with pity in her eyes and say, "All you have to do is ask God for help, and he will help you. If you don't fix your hurt, you'll only end up hurting other people. You know what they say, 'Hurt people hurt people.'

Carrying around all that anger will only destroy you in the end."

She was right. I was still angry at some people and perhaps even angry at God. I was raised to believe that God would always protect me and provide for all my needs. But it seemed that he had forsaken me instead. My mother and Nana were taken from me when I was a young girl, and then my introduction to puberty came with forceful brutality. Where was God when my life was in such turmoil? Needless to say, my belief in God was doubtful back then. I looked for my spiritual fulfillment elsewhere, regardless of the consequences. But no matter how many men I laid with, nothing could replace the loneliness and emptiness I felt or remove the painful memory that Uncle Buck had burned inside me.

When I learned I was pregnant with baby number five, I decided to settle down and raise my girls. I was tired of running around in circles, looking for that imaginary love, or whatever else, to fill the piercing hole in my soul.

It was then that I became worried about Di. She had started clinging to me, became withdrawn, and barely spoke. She had also started wetting the bed. I was worried that she was becoming ill, possibly due to the incest or mental illness that plagued Papa's family. But I quickly dismissed that notion. I assumed she was spoiled and just needed lots of attention. She was always under my feet when she wasn't playing with her sisters. She refused to sleep in her room and slept in my bed instead, clinging to me for dear life. When I mentioned Di's behavior to Aunt Mary, she said Di was just spoiled and going through a phase; she would grow out of it.

One hot summer day, while I was walking with my girls down to the swimming hole, I met one of the men who worked in the fields. He was big, tall, dark, and muscular. He must have been about 6'6" and weighed at least 250 pounds. He greeted me shyly with a strong proper voice. "Hello, Ms. Thomas. You and your daughters look most enchanting today." As he walked away, he turned back and said, "My name is John Johnson, but they call me Big John."

I was stunned by how forward he was and how well he spoke. I had never heard a colored man or any of the field workers speak like he did. He didn't speak with the stereotypical southern drawl or with a Cajun dialect. He had a deep, baritone voice and spoke similar to proper educated white folks. In fact, he spoke better than my papa and some of the white businessmen I had met over the years. I must say, he left quite an impression on me.

The next time I went down to the swimming hole, I made a picnic for the girls and me. After we finished playing in the water, we ate, and I let the girls run around. Then, just as the sun was going down, Big John approached and asked if he could sit for a spell.

"When is your baby coming?" he asked as I rubbed my bulging stomach.

"In three months or so."

"Where's your husband?"

"I don't have a husband, and I don't need one. My girls and I are doing just fine by ourselves."

"I'm sorry; I didn't mean to offend you. I'm surprised that such a beautiful woman would be left alone with no husband or father for her children. That's not right. All children need a father just as their mama needs a man—I mean a husband."

I snickered. "I have four babies and another one on the way. Do I look like I'm suffering from the absence of a man? I've had more than my share of attention from men and, quite frankly, I'm tired of dealing with them. I just want to be a good mother and raise my girls to have a good life, and I don't need a man to help me do that, do I?"

I guess my sassy words left him speechless, because he didn't reply. Without asking my permission, he went into my picnic basket and grabbed a sandwich and began eating it. He proceeded to make small talk, and before I knew it, we were talking about anything and everything. He even had me laughing at his corny jokes. And when the girls got restless, he played with them until they were tired and ready to go home.

Big John helped me carry my belongings and the girls back to the main house. "May I call on you sometime, Ms. Thomas?"

"Do you see what shape I'm in?" I asked. "I'm pregnant, you know. I was spoiled when I was thirteen, and I've been a sinner ever since."

"You're not a sinner, and that spoiled stuff doesn't mean anything to me. You're still a good woman. I can tell by looking at you, beyond your exterior, inside here." He pointed to his heart. "And you're a good mother too. I see the affection you have for your girls. You've been hurt and you're acting out, that's all. It's not your fault you were mistreated and taken advantage of. There's no harm in looking for a man to love and cherish you. You are a queen. I hope you know that."

I smiled. "Well, folks call me a lot of names, but queen is not one of them. Why do you want to call on me anyway? I don't have anything. This plantation isn't mine, and it will never belong to me. When Aunt Mary passes, it will go to her heirs."

"Ms. Thomas, I don't care about any of that stuff. I'm really good at fixing cars, but no one will hire me around here. So, I'm going up north to get a factory job and then save enough money to open my own garage one day." He paused and looked at the ground. "And then maybe I'll marry a fine lady like you. We can be one big, happy family."

I looked at him cautiously. "Slow down, Mr. Big John. You don't even know me. But you can come up to the house tomorrow after supper and tell me more about your dreams and plans up north. And by the way, you can call me by my given name, Josette."

The next day, Big John rang the doorbell. Aunt Mary answered the door and frowned. "What do you want? You know the field hands are supposed to use the back door."

"Ma'am, I'm here to see Miss Josette," Big John said shyly.

"Wait here," Aunt Mary said as she closed the door. Then she called me into the kitchen. She was livid. "Gigi, I know you're not thinking about taking up with that man. I have accepted you, your wayward life, and your illegitimate babies, 'cause you all . . .." She paused and then lowered her voice to a whisper. "You look normal, like us, like regular white people. But now I have to put my foot down. If you take up with him, you must leave here. Do you know if you have children with that man, they might look like him? And then everyone will know for certain that you've laid with a Negro. There will be no turning back."

"Well, is that any worse than lying with my half-brother, like my mother did, or, for that matter, with my uncle who forced himself on me?"

Aunt Mary stood there, speechless. I turned away and went to the front porch, where Big John was waiting for me. I sat on the bench and kicked off my shoes, because my feet were swollen. Then, Big John began rubbing and massaging my feet, but not in an erotic way.

Minutes later, my baby girls came out, and everyone except Di played with Big John. He got on all fours and pretended he was a horse and rode them around on his back. When it got late, he read a story to them before it was time for me to bathe them and put them down for the night.

"If it's okay, I'd like to call on you again," he said. "Perhaps tomorrow. Would that be okay?"

I smiled. "Sure. I'm not going anywhere in my condition."

Big John and I saw each other the next day and all the days that followed. During his visits, he often talked about education and how important it was for me to educate my girls. Although Big John was a laborer, he was very smart. He said he wanted to go school and become a doctor, but his parents wouldn't let him. They needed him to work in the fields to help support the family. But he tried to keep up with his studies. He read books whenever he could. That's how he learned to read, write, do arithmetic, and speak so well.

I enjoyed listening to Big John talk for hours on end. He was a proud man and believed he could do or be anything. He didn't let his race or his economic circumstances limit his dreams. He hated the south, and when he left, he said he was never coming back.

Sometimes, he worked in the garden with me. I told him about Nana and her love for orchids, which I shared. He would often say, "There's snow up north, but you can have a garden in the summer and indoors too, all year round. I'm going to make sure you always have a garden to grow your orchids when we move up north."

I usually ignored him. I knew he was talking foolishly. Probably waiting around for me to have my baby, so he could taste my womanness and then disappear like the rest of them.

Other times, he would teasingly say, "You know you're going to be my wife one day. Just wait, you'll see."

I never responded to his comments. In the back of my mind, I wished his words were true, but I knew that was impossible.

Despite Aunt Mary's objections, I continued seeing Big John. I had grown very fond of him. He was the kindest, sweetest man I had ever known, and he made me feel special. He also made me feel safe and protected, a feeling I had not known since before Papa's death. Ironically, it was then that I noticed my nightmares about Uncle Buck had completely subsided. I couldn't help but think that meeting Big John had something to do with it.

When I came home from the hospital after having my fifth baby girl, my feelings for Big John were cemented. I knew I was falling in love with him. He visited me and took to my new baby as if she was his, admiring and doting on her, holding her, and rocking her when she cried. He was just as caring toward my other children except Di, who seemed to be afraid of him. But I knew, in time, she would grow to care for him as much as her sisters and I did.

I felt like I was experiencing real love from a man for the first time. Big John was outwardly affectionate. He would tell me he loved me throughout the day, and then, sometimes out of nowhere, he would say, "Woman, you know you're going to be my wife one day. And that day is coming real soon."

His words made me blush. I would smile and look away.

"That's okay," he would say. "I know you love me too, even though you never say it. I know you'll come around in time. I'm going to erase all those bad memories and show you how a queen is supposed to be treated."

As usual, I never responded to his remarks, I just smiled as I looked at his serious face. It felt good to be cared for in such a genuine way.

Big John was a special man. Not only did he love me, he loved my children as if he was their father. Our conversations always included my girls. He would often say, "One day we're going to do this with the girls" or "We're going to visit that place with the girls" or "I want the girls to go college and become doctors or lawyers."

Big John was very respectful of me. Even though I had been spoiled with five kids, he never attempted to have sex with me or brought up the subject. While he didn't have much money, he was very generous. He would often make things for me and my girls. He built a swing for my girls, he made me a jewelry box, and he even made me a cedar chest.

He was also very romantic. He always held my hand when we walked, and sometimes he would kiss my hands or the side of my face. He loved to brush my hair. Sometimes he would read to me from books by poets I had never heard of, such as Emily Dickinson, Henry David Thoreau, and Walt Whitman. To me, that was better than any foreplay or sex. But most of all, I loved Big John's adoration of me. Sometimes he called me Gigi, but most times he called me "Queen," "My Beautiful Queen," or some other name with "queen" in it. By then, I knew Big John truly loved me and that one day he would become my husband.

About a year from the day we first met, one Friday evening, Big John proposed. "I don't have a ring for you yet, but I want you to be my wife. Will you marry me?"

"Yes, I'll marry you," I replied, without hesitation. "I would be proud to be Mrs. Johnson. But when—"

Big John smiled with excitement and then cleared his throat. "Woman, you just made me the happiest man in New Orleans, but we're going to have a wait a little while before we get married—a few months at most. I'm leaving tomorrow morning for Detroit. My cousin has a job lined up for me in one of the automobile factories. Those jobs pay very well, four times the wages here."

My happiness about my engagement quickly faded as I listened to Big John explain why he was leaving me. He pulled out his handkerchief and wiped the tears that were slowly streaming down my face. "Listen, I have to do this for us," he said. "I'm not moving my wife into a shack, and you know we can't live on your family's estate. I have to be able to provide a home for you and our children. And the only way I can do that is to move to Detroit. It won't be for long, I promise."

"No, please, don't go," I replied. "We'll find a way to make it here. I don't need to live in a place like this estate. I'll be happy living anywhere as long as we're together."

Big John stepped back, as if he was becoming angry with me. "I don't have a cent to my name. I can't take care of me, let alone a family. Besides, I refuse to be relegated to living in these Jim Crow conditions. I don't feel like a man here. I'm nearly forty years old, and white folks around here still call me 'boy.' If I stay here, I'll end up with my head in a noose swinging from a tree. Do you want that to happen to me? I'm about to explode; I can't stay here any longer. You have been protected living on your family's plantation. You have no idea how cruel the world is beyond those gates. Your nearly white mulatto skin and kinship with the Thomas family has allowed you to live a privileged life, the complete opposite for most Negroes and coloreds living elsewhere. I don't want you to suffer any hardships being married to me."

Then he calmed himself down. "You're my queen. Let me be the best man I can be for you, for us. I'm going to work long enough to save money to find us a place to live, and then I'll be back for you and the girls. I promise. Once we're settled, I can start saving for my auto repair garage. In no time, we'll be on our way, and I can give you everything a queen deserves."

He took my hand while looking into my eyes. "I can't be a husband to you, or a father to those girls, if I don't feel like a man. Let me do this my way; please, try to understand."

I reluctantly agreed to Big John's plan. We hugged, and then he played with the children for a few minutes before we said our goodbyes. I cried as I watched him drive off. We loved each other, but I wasn't sure he would come back for me. I had five little girls and nothing to offer him but my burdens.

I told Aunt Mary that Big John had asked me to marry him.

"If you marry him, don't expect to come back here," she said. "You and your dark babies will not be welcomed. You will not embarrass my family by taking up with a man like him."

She meant every ugly word that flowed from her mouth. That was the first time I realized she was a racist. I think my papa was also a racist, even though he supposedly loved my mother. Perhaps the only reason he brought me and my sisters into his home was because we could more easily pass for white than the other children he fathered on the plantation.

Over the next few months, Aunt Mary continued to try to persuade me not to marry Big John. She even offered to keep my girls and raise them as hers and send me to Europe to be with my two older sisters in hopes that I might blend in and find a suitable white husband, as my sisters had done. But I was having no part of her nonsense. I had already found my true love. I would wait patiently for Big John to return for my babies and me.

Big John wrote a five-page letter to me every week detailing his life in Detroit and his undying love for me. I read each one repeatedly until the next one arrived as I counted down the days until his return.

It was exactly six months from the day of his departure that he returned, just like he promised. When he pulled up in his cousin's sedan, I wasted no time packing the car with our belongings and all my babies. However, before we drove off, I showed him the diamond necklace that Uncle Buck had given me when I was a girl. I never wore it, but I had held on to it, thinking that one day I could sell it if I ever needed money.

"Maybe you can sell this and use the money to help buy your garage," I said.

He smiled as he looked at the necklace. "I'll put it in the jar with the money I've already been saving. We'll have our garage in no time."

Before we hit the road for Detroit, we went to a church, where we were married. Big John gave me an antique gold wedding band. "I promise to buy you some diamonds later," he said as he slipped it onto my finger.

I was very proud of that ring. "I don't need anything else," I said. "Just promise you'll never stop loving me."

"I promise, Mrs. Johnson."

That's when we had our first French kiss.

I was happy to be Mrs. Johnson, and I was even happier to be leaving behind the estate and my painful past that came with it. The only thing I took with me were Nana's horticulture books, the synthetic black orchid flower that sat in a vase in her bedroom, and the gifts that Big John had given me. Nana's garden was the only memory I wanted to take with me. I was officially leaving Giselle behind and beginning my new life in Detroit as Mrs. Josette Johnson.

I never returned to New Orleans or had any contact with my two older sisters. Many years later, however, I did connect with a few relatives who had left the estate and moved up north. The rest is history.

The End.

Eleven

The Secret

After reading the last words in Gigi's journals, I let out a loud sigh. I didn't know if I should cry or get angry. I wondered how she had endured such a horrific childhood and became such an amazing woman. Even worse was realizing that she had lied to me, telling me that she was raised in a brothel, and one of the patrons raped her, leaving her pregnant with Di. Now I knew the truth, that she was born from a forbidden love between a brother and sister and then bore a child from rape by her uncle, the brother of her mother and father. Perhaps the incestuous nature of her rape was too much for her to fathom, so she made up a story about being raped by a stranger in a whorehouse.

Nonetheless, I was proud of Gigi's triumphant nature, persevering against all odds. I was impressed by the fact that she displayed no apparent scars from the tragedies of her childhood, while mine still haunted me. I was speechless as I looked at Gigi's frail body lying helpless in her hospital bed.

I understood why she chose to give me her journals. She knew I would understand her story, because it was also my story. Our lives mirrored each other. She was just like me, a girl raised without knowledge of her birth mother and who was sexually violated as a child. She knew the effects of my experience firsthand. She never wanted me to feel abandoned or alone, as she had felt growing up. She also knew the ramifications of carrying bitterness and hatred in her heart and the catastrophic effects it could have on one's life. This also explains why she was so persistent about me healing the wounds left by Ricky and Philip. More importantly, I knew why Gigi called me a Kokuran. It was because she was a Kokuran too, and she recognized those same qualities in me.

I wasn't sure what to do with my knowledge of the contents of Gigi's journals. Should I share them with my siblings, or keep them for myself? It was obvious that Nikki was aware of the journals and had probably read them, based on her comments about incest and mental illness. Still unsure, I decided to wait until I read the secret letter that Gigi's pastor was holding for me. Perhaps it contained instructions that would aid me in my decision.

I looked over at Gigi sleeping peacefully with the help of her breathing machine. At that moment, I realized the magnitude of her strength. She had lost her entire family at a young age, endured an abominable childhood, then found and lost the love of her life and was left to rear eleven children on her own. She persevered and never looked back. Gigi was a pillar of strength, and I knew I needed to follow in her footsteps. If she could overcome the obstacles in her life then I could do the same.

The next day, I went to see Pastor Williams.

"How do you feel?" he asked.

"I'm not sure. Never in a million years did I imagine Gigi's childhood to be the way it was, particularly the rape that left her pregnant with my real mother. I've always admired her strength, but I was clueless about how she developed it. Her hardships inadvertently gave her the wisdom and strength that she carried forward in her life. Knowing her story made me appreciate her even more. Our lives were very similar, and she wanted me to see that she had overcome the perils in her life to give me confidence to know that I could do the same."

"Well, I'm not sure what she expected you to learn from reading the journals, but I think after you read the letter, you'll have a better understanding."

He paused and took my hand. "Listen, time is of the essence. You need to read this letter and get back to me quickly."

"What's the hurry?" I asked.

"Perhaps you can call me within the next three days, alright?"

I nodded. "Yes, I will."

He handed me a letter-sized envelope with my name on it. It had a little weight to it, and I knew it contained some deep, serious stuff. *Gigi, what are you getting ready to reveal to me now*? I wondered. After reading her journals, there was nothing more she could say that would surprise me. Perhaps it was a list of rules on how to live out the rest of my life.

I was still reeling from Gigi's journals. I needed a break before I delved further into Gigi's past. I went back to her house, put the letter in my luggage, and continued with my double life, talking to Doc and Chevy. Even though I was sexting it up with Chevy, I still wasn't ready to cut my ties with Doc whom was very patient and understanding. He acted as if there was nothing wrong with our relationship nor suspected I was seeing another man.

The next day, Chevy flew to Detroit and gave me the distraction I needed, from sunset to sunrise. It wasn't just Chevy's sexual prowess that intrigued me, but it was something else that I could not label. Maybe it was the way he wooed me. Whenever he fucked me, he made me feel like I was on fire, wanting to go harder and deeper, right off the cliff's edge. During our climactic journey, I wanted to fuse with his body the way two pieces of metal are soldered together during their heated exchange. Not to mention he was fine as hell. He was a spectacular looking man with his piercing blue eyes and raven skin. And the cherry on top was the moans and poetic utterances he made with his sexy French accent in the midst of our passion. I couldn't get enough of him, but for some reason, I couldn't be anything more with him either.

After I returned from taking Chevy to the airport, it was time to get back to business. I needed to read Gigi's letter, so I could wrap up this business with her journals. I laid across my bed, staring at the envelope, knowing after reading it that my life would change yet again. The letter read as follows.

Dear Astrid,

If you're reading this letter, it means things are not going well for me. I'm either near death or already dead. By now, you've read my journals and understand my history and why I never wanted to talk about my past. Nothing good can come from facing bigotry and hatred. Some things you don't try to understand; you just move on and leave the ugliness behind. And if you're lucky enough to get a second chance at happiness, you grab it and never let go, which is what I experienced when I met and married Big John.

Joy and happiness had long left my vocabulary and only returned when Big John came into my life. He fulfilled the part of me that my babies could not. He gave me a family and made feel whole again. He showed me that I was a queen and helped me find my strength, which had been buried deep inside me. And yes, just like you, Astrid, I am a Kokuran. But it didn't start with me. It goes back to Nana and her mother. I hope you see that the depth of your strength runs deep. It's in your blood and the blood of your ancestors. So, as you read the rest of this letter, remember who you are and whose you are. Also, don't be quick to judge or condemn people for their mistakes. Most people would do better if they knew better.

Over the years, I learned to forgive the people who hurt me: my papa, my two sisters, even Uncle Buck. My forgiveness was not for them; it was for me. It gave me freedom and released the physical pain that was in the pit of my stomach and the hatred that caused me to place a death wish on everyone who had hurt me over the years. I didn't know it, but the hatred I was carrying put a chokehold on my life. It was robbing me of my joy, from appreciating the sun, the smell of spring, and all the wonderful blessings that God had bestowed upon me.

I need to reveal the secret I've been keeping from you. I hope you will understand my reasons and not harbor anger toward me for what I'm about to say. There's no easy way to say it other than to just say it. Your real mother, Di, has been living in Michigan for almost three years.

"What?" I shouted, shocked by what I had just read. Then I reread the sentence. I shook my head as I dropped the letter to the floor. I couldn't believe it. My mother was alive. All these years, she was alive, and Gigi never said a word to me. Gigi knew how I longed to know my real mother and the anguish I felt due to her absence from my life. How could Gigi have been so selfish?

I paused as I placed my hands on my temples. I cried out, "Why, Gigi? Why?"

My mind started wandering all over the place. Where had Di been all this time, and why didn't she reach out to me? Why did Gigi keep her presence a secret? My emotions were starting to boil. I felt anger, anxiety, excitement, and a bit of happiness. Tears streamed down my face, but I wasn't sure if they were tears of joy or sadness. But now was not the time for an emotional meltdown. I needed to finish reading the damned letter.

> I know the news of Di will come as a shock, but I didn't tell you about her because it was her wish for you not to see her when her health was in such decline. I only found out about Di three years ago, when Deana told me of her circumstances, that she was living in New York and was gravely ill. I went to visit her and eventually brought her back to Detroit, so I could care for her.
>
> I planned to tell you about Di after I got her settled. But no sooner had we returned to Detroit than I received the horrific news that Joey had shot you. I left immediately for Atlanta to see you, not knowing whether you would be dead or alive by the time I got to the hospital. Once I saw how critical your condition was, I knew your recovery, if any, would be long and intense. In the midst of your crisis, I was faced with one of the hardest decisions I ever had to make. I had two children who needed me at a crucial time in their lives. One daughter, who was terminally ill and preparing to

leave this world, and you, my other daughter, seriously injured with an uncertain prognosis. So, I decided to leave Deana in Detroit to look after Di while I stayed in Atlanta to take care of you. Besides, I knew Di would have wanted it that way. Her words to me were, "Please, take care of my baby." I've tried to honor my promise to her from the day you were born.

While you were recovering, your mental state remained fragile. I didn't think you could handle the shock of knowing Di was alive, so I decided not to tell you about her.

The situation continued to get worse. After I returned from taking care of you in Atlanta, I became aware that my health was failing too, and my time might be limited. So, I sought council and guidance from Pastor Williams. After many teary-eyed conversations, we decided I should write my journals and this letter.

I was never able to bring Di into my home to care for her due to the severity of her illness. Instead, I moved her into a nursing home. Since the nursing home was only a few miles away, I was able to spend time with her every day. Since I was retired, most days I spent the entire day with her, from breakfast to bedtime. It gave us a chance to have the relationship we never had. We talked as if we had never been separated. She told me her entire life story, including why she left and never came back. When she asked me to forgive her, I said, "There's no need. You've done nothing that warrants my forgiveness. But I, on the other hand, do need your forgiveness."

She smiled and said, "Hush, Gigi, I forgave you a long time ago."

She also told me that she and Deana stayed in touch over the years. Deana had even visited her a few times and gave her pictures of you while you were growing up. She was so proud of you and said she knew you were going to become something special. So, you're not a complete stranger to her.

Di had a smorgasbord of illnesses. The doctors said any one of them could cause her death at any time. She knew the severity of her illnesses and often said to me, "When the time comes, please don't let me linger, surviving on breathing machines and feeding tubes. The moment I can no longer sustain on my own, let me go. Let God's will be done. Gigi, I'm begging you, promise you'll carry out my wishes."

My response was always the same, "I promise." At least once a week, she repeated the same words about me carrying out her wishes. I loved her, and I didn't want to let her go, but it was hard watching her dwindle away right before my eyes. So, I knew when the time came, I would have no problem letting her go.

In addition to Di's physical ailments, she was also suffering from schizophrenia, which she most likely inherited from my paternal grandmother's lineage. After my initial stroke, I didn't see Di for over a month. When I finally made it back to see her, she had taken a turn for the worse. She was very weak and pretty much slept over the next few months before she lapsed into a coma.

After the doctors told me that Di's brain activity had declined to a persistent vegetative state, I made the difficult decision to break my promise to her. I did it for you. I moved her up north to Rosemont, a long-term care facility, knowing she would not likely awaken from her state.

My plan was to tell you about Di before she slipped into the coma, but things did not work out that way. I guess it was God's will.

I arranged for Rosemont to keep Di on life support until you were able to see her. I decided not to tell the other children about her. I wanted to leave that decision up to you, so you could decide how to memorialize her. Only three of us—Deana, Pastor Williams, and I know of Di's whereabouts. I gave specific instructions to Pastor Williams to oversee Di's final care. She will be taken off life support by the sixth month. I'm not sure how much time is left, but I hope you are able to see her before it's too late. Perhaps you can follow through on the promise I made to her. Maybe seeing her will give you peace and closure. Pastor Williams will help you get through this if I'm not around to assist you.

I'm sorry I couldn't tell you about Di sooner. I wanted to tell you about her when I first brought her back to Detroit, but she wouldn't let me. As her health deteriorated, I asked her many times, but her response was always the same. "I don't want her to see me like this. I don't want this to be her last memory of me. Just tell her I loved her, and I made a sacrifice to give her up, to give life to her and not take it away from her."

I hope you understand why I had to honor her wishes. It was the least that I could do for her. Unbeknownst to me, I failed your mother long ago and allowed things to happen to her that set her life on a path of destruction. But it was only when I started raising you that I realized what I had overlooked in Di. I was caught up in that vicious cycle of "hurt people hurting people." I didn't deliberately hurt Di, but when I failed to protect her, that's when I hurt her. I was so consumed by my own misery and hatred that I became selfish by trying to drown my sorrows through my reckless behavior: partying, whoring, drugging, and anything else that numbed my pain and distracted me from my reality. Worst of all, my anger blinded me from seeing that my own child was in trouble and reaching out for me to save her. Yes, while I was out partying, my baby girl was being molested right under my nose. I believe it was Aunt Mary's husband who did it. Di slept in Aunt Mary's bedroom until she was nearly five years old. But by the time I started putting the pieces together, decades later, it was too late. Di was grown and lost to the streets. When she left after you were born, it broke my heart. That's when I packed all her photos away and forbid anyone to speak of her.

Once I figured out that Ricky had molested you, I realized the signs I had missed when Di was in crisis. It was my failure to protect Di that made me intent on helping you. I saw the devastation that rape had on Di's life and mine, so I wanted to spare you that experience.

My sweet Astrid, I'm not sure if we will ever talk again. But I want you to own your strength and not let hatred and fear consume you. As Nana once told me, I had the traits of the Kokuran, and I just needed to tap into it to blossom. I tapped into mine long before I recognized it and subconsciously, throughout my life, as the need arose. To some extent, you've done the same. But now it's time for you to blossom. You're the only person holding you back from the glory and greatness that God has planned for you.

All my love,
Gigi

After getting over my shock of what I had read, I called Deana. She wasn't surprised to hear from me. "I knew you would be calling me. Pastor Williams told me he gave you the letter. Before you say anything, let's not start this conversation until I get home. I'll be there shortly."

I was angry and felt betrayed by Deana and Gigi. They had no right to keep me from my mother. Why was I not given a choice in the matter?

After an hour passed, I decided not to wait any longer for Deana. I was emotionally drained and physically exhausted. I felt like I had just completed a marathon and was down to my last few breaths. I didn't really care to talk to Deana or anyone else. I took a hot shower, ignored the calls and text messages I received from Doc and Chevy, and went to sleep.

The next morning, when I awoke, Deana was sitting in the kitchen waiting for me. By then, I had calmed down. Strangely, I wasn't angry anymore.

"Will you go with me to Rosemont to see D.?" I asked, without any preamble.

"Sure. Do you want Pastor Williams to meet us there?"

"No, I just want you to go with me." I paused. "What should I do?

"You don't have to figure it out now. You will know what to do when the time comes."

I headed to my room to get dressed before Deana started on her religious soapbox. The last thing I wanted to hear was her sermon on death.

The closer we got to the Rosemont, the faster my heart beat. I felt scared. It wasn't because Di was on life support but because my painted image of her was about to meet the reality of her.

As we walked through the hospital's cold, winding hallways, my anxiety grew. I grabbed Deana's hand and held it tight. As we were about to enter Di's room, fear made me stop at the door. I saw Di lying in her bed, as if she were sleeping.

Deana walked over to Di and began talking to her. She rubbed her hair and then kissed her cheek. "Astrid, don't be scared," she said, turning to me. "Come over here. It's okay; she's been waiting for you."

I walked over to Di's bed. She looked nothing like I imagined. She was still quite beautiful, despite the illness that had ravaged her body. My fear quietly subsided. I grabbed Di's hand and held it to my cheek. Then, I bent down and kissed her and rested my head on her chest. Suddenly, I was overtaken by a wave of emotion. I started bawling uncontrollably, similar to how I felt when I lost Joey. I couldn't explain it, but I felt a deep connection with Di, though we'd never met.

Moments later, Deana helped me compose myself.

"We need to let her complete her transition," I said, "so she can rest in peace. Can you call Pastor Williams and make the arrangements?"

"Sure, but what about the rest of the clan?"

"I would rather leave things as they are. Besides, my spirit is telling me that we need to move quickly. We don't have time to assemble everyone, and I don't want to deal with all the chaos and drama that would surround these circumstances." I paused and smiled at Deana. "God's waiting on her. She can't get her angel wings until we set her free."

Deana put her arm around me. "You're right, sweetie."

A few days later, we had a small memorial service for Di with only Pastor Williams, Deana, and me in attendance. I decided not to tell my siblings about Di, not then or ever. I cried a river of tears during her service. Although we were strangers, we were not; she had imprinted more than her DNA in me. My heart was entwined with hers and hers to mine. I felt as if I would miss her, despite having not been part of each other's lives.

After the service, Deana and I went home. I went to my room and climbed into bed. I couldn't sleep, as I was consumed with thoughts of Di and Gigi. I had lost my birth mother and feared I would soon lose my grandmother, the person who raised me. I couldn't help but wonder why this was happening now and why I was losing the two most important people in my life at the same time. Gigi had raised us not to question unexplainable life events; she always said they were God's will. But my faith was not like hers. I always struggled with understanding matters that defied life's natural order.

Deana knocked on my bedroom door and then opened it slightly. "Can I come in?"

"Sure. Is something wrong?"

"No, but I have something for you."

She sat on the edge of my bed and handed me a small black leather satchel.

"What's this?" I asked.

"It's for you. Di gave it to me to when we brought her back to Detroit. She knew her illness was terminal, and her days were short, and she wanted to leave something special for you to remember her by. She wanted me to hold on to them until . . .."

She didn't bother finishing her sentence. I unzipped the satchel and emptied the contents onto the bed. It contained several photos and a small digital audio recorder. One photo in particular stood out. It was a picture of Di holding me in the hospital when I was born. There were several other photos of her when she was young, in her twenties and thirties. There were also several pictures of me at different stages of life, including a picture of me holding Junior in the hospital the day he was born. I placed the pictures of us holding our babies next to each other. We looked like twins. I think Gigi saw the resemblance too. Perhaps, while she was rearing me, she felt like she was getting a second chance to raise Di.

After Deana and I looked through all the photos, I picked up the recorder and pushed play. When I heard Di's voice, it startled me, and I pressed stop right away. I couldn't take another grim walk down memory lane. I was still grappling with the horror of Gigi's life story; I wasn't ready for another one.

"What's wrong?" Deana asked.

"I can't do this right now. I know what's on this recorder. It's Di's life story and probably a message to me. It's too much."

"It's okay. Put it away. You can listen to it whenever you're ready, or never if that's what you decide."

I yawned and stretched. "I'm going to try to take a nap. It's been a long day."

"Okay, I'm going to the hospital to check on Gigi and then to church. Call me if you need anything or if you just want to talk."

"Okay. Goodbye."

I put the contents back into the satchel and placed it on my nightstand, turned off my phone, and closed my eyes.

When I awoke, my mind went straight to Di. I remained conflicted about her decision not to have any contact with me, especially when she returned to Detroit. She was definitely Gigi's daughter; they could both be very stubborn. There was no swaying them to the left or right when their minds were made up about a particular matter.

Seeing Di did not provide the closure I sought. In fact, it heightened my interest in her life, leaving me with even more questions. I wished I could ask her why she abandoned me and then reappeared later, only to conceal her existence from me. Deana probably knew the answer, but she would never divulge it. When it came to keeping secrets, her mouth was locked tighter than Fort Knox.

By then I figured the only way for me to understand Di's decision was to listen to her recording. I knew she was a former prostitute and had been incarcerated, so how much worse could her story be? There was no sense in delaying it. Perhaps I might finally get closure.

Twelve

Subjugation

I picked up the recorder, took a long, deep breath, and pressed play. Suddenly, Di's voice filled the room. It was eerie and much softer than I had imagined.

"I'm nervous, but I guess I'll start by saying, Astrid, my beautiful daughter, you're the best thing that ever happened to me. But the rest of my life after your birth seemed like a slow walk to hell. Like me, you're probably wondering how and when my life took a bad turn. There's no precise answer, just many contributing factors, some of which I only recently discovered. Since you're much smarter than me, perhaps you'll have a better chance of figuring out how I ended up on a one-way path to hell. My memory is not very good, so I'll start from the present day and work back to my childhood.

"I had been living like a gypsy, moving from state to state, city to city, wherever my drug-addicted lifestyle took me, but never Michigan. I eventually made it to New York and reconnected with my old friend, Kelly. Like me, she was still caught up in the life. We were both old, worn out, and still trying to get one more. I guess neither of us had the courage to commit suicide. We were already knocking on death's door; we knew that any day death would show up for us. But until then—"

"I always intended to get myself together, go home one day, and reunite with you. But for one reason or another, I could never stay clean or out of trouble long enough. My addiction led me to criminal behavior, which landed me in and out of jail for most of my adult life. I also spent time in several mental institutions. I wasted a lot of years, nearly my entire life, caught up in the throes of addiction. I never expected to live past age thirty, let alone fifty.

"By the time I was finally able to maintain my sobriety and ready to turn my life around, I received a devastating blow. After being hospitalized while suffering a serious bout of pneumonia, the doctor sat on my bed and said, 'Ms. Johnson, I'm sorry, but you are terminally ill. I don't know where to start. You are suffering from not one but from several illnesses. Your situation is unusual; most people would have already expired from any one of your illnesses having been left untreated.' He went on to list my diagnosis. By the time he read off the list of diseases, I was speechless.

"'How much time do I have?' I asked.

"He hesitated before responding. 'That's difficult to say,' he replied finally, 'especially in your case. It could be as short as six months or as long as two years. To be perfectly honest, the fact that you're still living and somewhat asymptomatic is a miracle. Perhaps somebody's prayers are working for you. But make no mistake, your condition will worsen over time.'

"The next day, I removed the IV lines, left the hospital, and went on a two-week drug binge. After winding up back in the hospital from a near-fatal overdose, I met Sister Nancy, who I credit for saving the bit of life I had left.

"Sister Nancy was a volunteer at the hospital and worked with distressed women. She was very kind, and I took an immediate liking to her. To my surprise, she had walked a similar path as a young girl before she found salvation with God and her convent.

"After spending a few weeks with me, Sister Nancy noticed some peculiarities in my behavior and persuaded me to see one of the staff psychiatrists. After a few sessions, I was diagnosed with schizophrenia. Unbeknownst to me, it was this disease that contributed to my cycle of drug use. Throughout my life, I had periodic migraines and blackouts, long periods without lucidity, and lived with the constant presence of voices directing my behavior. I thought my issues were side effects from the drugs. But every time I went into a drug rehab center, my symptoms got worse. I tried to ignore them, but they only seem to intensify as the drugs left my system. And after a month, I was back on the streets, looking for my next fix. Throughout my numerous hospital stays, none of the doctors ever evaluated me for a mental disease. My mental defects were always attributed to my drug abuse and not to mental illness. Perhaps my life would have been different if I had received the proper diagnosis and treatment.

"After I was discharged from the hospital, Sister Nancy arranged for me to move to a women's shelter run by her convent. Now that I was taking proper meds, my mind was stable, but it opened a floodgate for depression to rush back in. I felt a deep sadness as I looked over my life. I could see clearly as far back as my early childhood in New Orleans. Like an avalanche, the horrific memories I had blocked out for most of my life came barreling at me. They were the images of Aunt Mary's husband. While sleeping, he would awaken me and take me into the bathroom, where he repeatedly sexually abused me, from age three until I was about five years old. The act traumatized me to the point that I lost control of my bladder and my ability to speak for periods at a time. And because I was so young, I didn't have a vocabulary to articulate what was happening to me.

"The onset of these lost memories left me sobbing uncontrollably. Perhaps I was crying all the tears that I should have shed years earlier. Until then, I had not cried so profusely since the day I left you behind in the hospital.

"Sister Nancy noticed my melancholy state. 'Dianne, what can I do to help you?' she asked. 'You must make the most of each day, because tomorrow is not promised to anyone, not you or me. Every day that you wake up is a gift from God. He gives life, so that you can live life.'

"I understood Sister Nancy's comments, but I was dealing with a raging battle between my mind and body. Furthermore, I had not shared my recent setback with anyone at the convent. The problem was, now that my mind was healthy, my body was falling apart. Without the narcotics in my system, I was growing sicker and weaker by the day. On my last doctor visit, he said that I probably had, at most, two years left to live. That clock was real to me.

"I told Sister Nancy about you and how I hadn't seen my family in over thirty years. Now that I was sick, I probably would never see them again or have a relationship with you.

"'That's not true,' Sister Nancy said. 'We can help you reconnect with your family. We can arrange for them to come here, or we have a place near Detroit, if you would like to transfer there, so you can be close to your family.'

"'You don't understand,' I replied. 'I don't want to reunite with my family, only to become a burden to them later. Maybe I'll contact my sister Deana and decide later whether or not I should contact my mother and daughter.'

"I called Deana and told her about my medical condition. A week later, she came to visit me. To my surprise, Gigi was with her. I was happy to see them. Gigi hugged me so tight and held me a long time, as if she didn't want to let me go. It felt good. I needed that hug from her; it was long overdue. I felt her love flow right into my sickly body. In true Gigi style, without asking, she said, 'You're coming home with me as soon as we can make the arrangements.'

"I didn't argue with her; I just said 'Okay.'

"While I was okay with seeing Gigi and Deana, I was still conflicted about seeing you. My plan had always been to reconnect with you and become a part of your life again. But because of my drug addiction and now my illness, it doesn't seem like that's going to be possible. The last thing I want to do is bring more pain into your life. It doesn't seem fair to make my presence known to you while I'm uncertain how much time I have left. And between my illness and the effects of my lifelong drug abuse,

I am a pitiful sight, resembling a zombie from a horror movie. I don't want you to see me like this. I would rather your memories of me be from the photos taken earlier in my life than the image of me whittling away. I hope you can find it in your heart to understand my decision.

"After sharing my feelings about you with Sister Nancy, she suggested that I write a letter to you. However, it was difficult for me to write, since my illness left my hands trembling. So, Sister Nancy surprised me with the gift of the audio recorder that you're listening to now. I know it's not much, but my story and my heartfelt words are all I have left to give you. And I hope they answer all the questions you have for me.

"I think the best place for me to start is when I was teenager, the time when my life began spiraling out of control. I was like so many pubescent girls, headstrong and defiant. I thought I knew everything, ignoring Gigi's constant warnings, seeing them as unnecessary rants.

"It was fall, and the weather was unusually mild for that time of year in Detroit. Everyone was still wearing spring and summer attire. Of course, with my tall, thick, red-boned body, that meant my long legs and bulging DDs were amply displayed. I knew my body attracted a lot of attention from males of all ages, but I didn't care, and I did nothing to dissuade onlookers from gawking at me. I usually left the house wearing appropriate attire, but once I made it to school, I quickly removed the sweater that covered my low-cut blouse and took off the long skirt that covered my mini skirt, which was as short as my cheerleader skirt.

"Often, when I was at cheerleader practice, the coach would have to bar spectators from the gym, which included male teachers and students. They gathered around the gym as if I was a celebrity. Although my tall stature was unusual for a cheerleader, I was graceful and light on my feet, especially with my gymnastic skills. I guess the ballet classes Gigi made me take as a little girl were not a complete waste. Nonetheless, I liked the attention of boys and got plenty of it inside and outside of school.

"While I was quite flirtatious with boys and fooled around a bit with them, I had not yet had a real boyfriend. The boys in my school and neighborhood were cute, but they seemed immature, even though I was merely a teenager myself. For some reason, my eyes were always on the older boys around the neighborhood. However, that all changed when I met Malek, who later became my first love.

"I met Malek during my sophomore year of high school. At that time, we were still living in our home in the Boston Edison district, so I had to catch the Woodward bus to school each day. One day, while my girlfriends and I were waiting at the bus stop, Malek pulled up in his black, sapphire 500 S-Class Mercedes Benz. He rolled down his window and introduced himself and then offered us a ride to school. Sensing that he was trouble, we always said no. However, something about him caught my eye. It wasn't just because he was nice looking. I was also drawn to his 'bad boy' swag. He was about six feet tall with nightly complexion and wavy black hair with a beautiful smile that could light up any room. His garb was royal, and his disposition was like that of an Egyptian king. He wore sparkling diamonds in both ears, accompanied by his diamond bezel Rolex, which looked like something from a magazine. Even more striking was the large gold diamond-encrusted chains that dangled around his neck at various lengths over his silk muscle shirt. Of course, no wardrobe would be complete for a well-dressed man in Detroit without Crocs and Gators. Malek wore big blocks, little blocks, and every color they were made in, the entire crayon box. When it came to fashion, Malek was meticulous. The pleats in his pants were as perfect as the straight lines in his creases. Despite the intimidation of his celebrity-like appearance, he was very personable. He was quite charming, and he had a way with the ladies. He could woo any woman right out of her panties.

"After Malek's second visit with us at the bus stop, I noticed he had eyes for me. I couldn't help but blush as he braised us with his smooth seductive trash talk. He continued hanging out at the bus stop over the next few weeks, arriving every morning, as if he were clocking in for work. His pattern was always the same, a conversation full of playfulness while trying to convince my friends and I to take a ride with him in his fancy car. We always said no. We knew better. Street guys were bad news and off limits to us. However, I was smitten by Malek's attention and slowly started to yield to his flirtation. Then one day, I gave in and agreed to take a ride with him after school.

"I skipped cheerleader practice that day, so I could hang out with Malek and still make it home by curfew. Malek picked me up from school, and then we drove to Palmer Park. After driving around for a while, we found the perfect spot to have a little picnic. Malek popped the trunk of his car and pulled out a blanket and a basket with all the fixings. He spread the blanket on the ground and then pulled out a bottle of Cristal champagne. After he poured the champagne, he opened a bag from Sinbad's restaurant.

"'Sorry, baby,' he said. 'I don't cook, but I know where to get the best takeout.' I tried to help him make our plates, but he wouldn't let me. 'Today you're my princess,' he said. 'Let me serve you. Your wish is my command.'

"We both laughed, and then he proceeded to make the plates of food. After we finished eating, we engaged in small talk.

"'So, you're a spoiled rich girl?' he asked.

"'No, we're far from rich,' I replied. 'Unlike some of my neighbors, there are no fancy cars, maids, or butlers in our home. My mom makes me and my sisters clean the house like we're her maids. Pops works hard for our family, and that's why we have a nice home. He spends all his time working in his garage.'

"'Oh, wow,' he said. 'So, you're one of Big John's kids.'

"'Yes,' I replied, 'that's my Pops. There are eleven of us.'

"I was surprised when he told me that he knew Pops, but then Pops worked on cars for everyone from every walk of life; he didn't discriminate.

"'I know Big John,' he said. 'He worked on a couple of cars for me—not mine but the used cars I bought for the workers. Your father seems like a nice guy, and his business is booming. Everyone takes their cars to his shop. But I couldn't do it; I ain't never liked getting my hands dirty. Shit, I won't even change a flat tire. I'll just keep buying them and let people like your daddy fix them.'

"There was something cruel and condescending in the way Malek said, 'let other people, like your daddy, fix them,' but I didn't want to anger him, so I didn't say anything to him about it.

"Minutes later, I asked Malek to take me home, because I felt one of my migraines coming on. 'Relax,' he said as he pulled my head toward his lap. As I lay with my head in his lap, I told him about my migraines.

"'A few years ago, I started getting severe migraine headaches, and lately they've been occurring more often. Sometimes they're so strong, I feel like I'm going crazy. I hear noises that sound like whispers from one of those old portable transistor radios ringing constantly in my ears. On a few occasions, the migraines became so intense that I black out for hours at a time. Nothing seems to help. I used to take Aspirin, but after a while, that didn't help much. When they're really bad, I take some of Gigi's herbal medicines or sneak off somewhere and smoke a joint, which always seems to work.'

"Malek smiled. 'Okay, you're not as innocent as I thought you were.' He began to massage my scalp. 'I have something that will make those migraines go away forever,' he said. 'It's Cush.'

"'What's that?' I asked.

"'It's like weed,' he said, 'but it's better. It's a little stronger, and the high is better and faster. It will also help you relax.'

"'Is it dope?' I asked. 'I don't do drugs. Every now and then, my girls and I sneak a beer and share a joint, but that's all, nothing stronger than that.'

"'Well, I wouldn't classify Cush as anything heavy,' he replied. 'Like I said, it's just like weed, only better. Wait, I've got a joint in my car. Why don't you try it and judge for yourself?'

"I hesitated and then said, 'Okay, I'll smoke it with you.'

"Malek went to his car and got the Cush. It looked identical to a marijuana joint. He lit it and then gave it to me. I took two puffs and then gave it back to Malek, so he could take a hit, but he shook his head. 'No, this one's all for you. Take your time with it. I still have to work tonight, at least another ten hours. You only smoke Cush when you're winding your day down.'

"'Besides the obvious, do you have a real job?' I asked.

"He smiled. 'I'm not going to lie to you. Back in the day I did my thing, but that's over. Now I'm a legitimate businessman. I have a partner, and together we own a couple of nightclubs around the city.'

"'Oh, so that's how you afford all this stuff,' I said, pointing at his watch and clothes.

"He smiled. 'Yeah, something like that. Financially, we're doing okay, but we're really only scratching the surface. If I had it my way, I would turn Detroit into a smaller version of Las Vegas. I would put up hotels, high-end retail shops, and casinos downtown across the riverfront. But that's never going to happen. The big boys own the best properties downtown. They have the land locked up. So, people like us only get the leftover crumbs.'

"I shrugged. 'Well, you have to start somewhere,' I said.

"Suddenly, in the midst of our conversation, I nodded out, conscious but immobile. It was a feeling that I had never experienced before. Malek nudged my head softly. 'Wake up, sleeping beauty,' he said. 'I'd better get you home before your mother starts worrying about you.' To my surprise, when I awoke, it was already getting dark. I realized I had been asleep for a few hours and not a few minutes, as I thought initially.

"Malek dropped me off at the corner near my home. It was late, and with help from Deana, I was able to sneak in the house without Gigi noticing. Later that night, I told Deana about Malek, but she didn't share my excitement. She said, 'Don't you think he's too old for you? He's a street guy, and you know that Gigi and Pops would never approve of you dating a man like him.'

"'That's why I need you to help me keep him a secret,' I said. 'I really like him. I'm going to see him again tomorrow. Promise you won't tell anyone about me and Malek.'

"After a moment's hesitation, she nodded and said, 'Okay, I promise.'

"The next morning, Malek met me at the bus stop and took me straight downtown to his apartment on the riverfront. Once we entered his place, he pointed to the hallway and said, 'My bedroom is back there on the left. Make yourself comfortable. Give me a minute, and I'll join you. As I walked toward his bedroom, I felt uneasy. It wasn't because I was a virgin but because the scene was not playing out as I imagined it would. There was nothing loving or romantic about it. He didn't ask if I was hungry, thirsty, or anything. He seemed cold and detached. There would be no lovemaking with us, at least not that day. Losing my virginity would not be the way I fantasized about it. It would be nothing more than a meaningless sexual act.

"As I lay naked in Malek's bed, I looked around the room and wondered how many other girls had lost their virginity in that bed. Did Malek care about any of them, or were they all somewhere broken hearted? Would I end up like them? Although we had been flirting with each other for the past few weeks, we had only gone out one time. Surely, that wasn't enough time for him to develop serious feelings for me. There was no sense in fretting over my feelings now. Like it or not, I was about have sex with Malek. The moment I laid eyes on him, I knew he would be the man that I gave my virginity to. I felt lucky and honored that Malek was interested in me. All the girls in the neighborhood had a crush on him. I felt proud, as if I was dating a famous celebrity.

"Malek finally came into the bedroom. As he was taking his clothes off he said, 'Pull the covers back, and let me see that fine sexy ass.' After I pulled the covers back he said, 'Damn girl, all those tits and ass, I can't wait to play with all that.'

"I didn't respond. He climbed into bed and pulled me into his arms and said, 'Girl, why you look so serious? You need to relax? Hold up, I got something for you. He reached over into his drawer and pulled out a joint. He lit it and took a few hits and then he said, 'Here, smoke this, it will help you relax,' and it did.

"He looked me over and said, 'Mmm, mmm, mmm," and then he kissed me long and hard with his full succulent lips, as if he was trying to suck my breath away. After he finished kissing me, while running his fingers across my breast, he licked my face like an ice cream cone. 'Damn, girl. You're fine as hell, I'm going to take my time and enjoy all of this,' he said.

"That's when he attempted to penetrate me. While breathing hard, he said, 'Damn girl, why are you so tight?'

"I replied, ''Cause I've never had sex before.'

"Baffled, he rolled onto his side and looked at me. 'Are you telling me you're still a virgin?'

"I blushed slightly. 'Yeah,' I said. 'I've fooled around a bit, but I've never gone all the way."

"Shaking his head in confusion, he said, 'Get the fuck out of here. You're walking around here strapped like a video vixen, and ain't nobody hit that yet?'

"I nodded and said, 'That's right. I'm only fifteen. Why is that so hard for you to believe?'

"'Oh, that's right,' he said. 'I forget how young you are. Damn! You sure as hell don't look fifteen. You could easily pass for twenty-one. You may be young, but that body is ready.' He paused and in a low voice he said, 'I guess you're not taking any birth control pills or shots either?'

"I didn't respond, just turned slightly away from him. I felt embarrassed.

"'I know you're not trying to get a baby out of me, are you?' he asked.

"'No,' I said. 'Everything happened so fast. I thought we were going to date for a few months before we had sex, but here we are.'

"He laughed and said, 'Girl, you're crazy. Ain't nobody waitin' months to fuck, maybe at most a week or two.'

"He laid back on his pillow and smiled. 'Well, I'll be damned,' he said. 'I got a virgin in the bed with me. I ain't had one of those in years. Well, I'll just have to pull out, cause I'm not wearing a jimmy. I only wear those when I fuck with hoes, and that's not often.'

"For a few minutes, we were both quiet. Then he grabbed his phone and called his business partner. 'Man, something's come up,' he said, 'and I'm going to be tied up most of the day. I'll get back with you later.' Then he turned to me and said, 'Okay, pretty girl, this is your special day. It's all about you. Making you happy and keeping that pretty smile on your face.'

"It was then that I thought about how fortunate I was to be with Malek. Perhaps he would become my true love, the way Big John was for Gigi. I would be different from all the other girls that he had been with. We would become great lovers. I would join him in his bad boy world and become his ride-or-die chick. Everyone in the neighborhood would know I was Malek's girl, and they would respect and envy me.

"He rolled on top of me and said, 'Let's get this party started.' He said, 'I'll go slowly. It might hurt a little at first, but then it will feel better.

"Despite my outward maturity, I felt confused by the experience. Here I was, at age fifteen, losing my virginity to a man in his thirties. My parents would certainly disapprove, and Pops would have wanted to kill Malek if he knew about us. But I didn't see anything wrong with that picture. In fact, I felt proud to be lying with an older man instead of a boy my age."

"After completing the painful act of losing my virginity, he rolled over and went to sleep. No cuddling, pillow talk, or 'I love you' followed. So, I got up and went to the bathroom to clean myself up. As I looked in the mirror, I felt a pain in the pit of my stomach. *What have you done?* I wondered.

"I made my way to the kitchen looking for something to eat. As I rifled through his cabinets, I found a few boxes of cereal that were filled with bags of powdery white stuff. In fact, it seemed the cabinets and the refrigerator were packed with freezer bags and wrapped blocks of what I assumed were drugs. So, Malek had lied to me, he was a drug dealer. I started rationalizing his reasons for lying to me. But at the moment, Gigi's words crept through my mind, 'One thing for certain and two things for sure: When a man lies and deceives you, destruction awaits you.'

"As usual, I dismissed her words of wisdom and went on with my search for food. I found some orange juice instead. I poured a glassful, took a few sips, and then headed back to the bedroom. As I climbed into bed, Malek rolled over and reached for my glass. 'That's perfect,' he said. 'How you'd know I was thirsty?'

"He drank the entire glass with no regard for me and then lit another joint, but this time it was Cush. By then I could tell the difference. I also started to develop a fondness for it. It made me feel good, and it heightened my libido.

"Moments later, he pulled me over to him and said, 'I want everything. Now show me what you can do.'

"I didn't respond, but I knew what that meant. I was nervous. I knew I would have to do more than what I had done with the boys in my neighborhood.

After we finished round two, he said, 'I think you have a gift. You could make a lot of money with your body. You're fine as hell, and your stuff is off the chain. If you perform like you did for me, men will keep coming back for it and pay well for it too.'

"I was confused by his words. I knew the tranquility of the Cush had a lot to do with my sexual prowess. I was looking for love and enjoying making love to my man, not auditioning for a job. We continued to have sex on and off all day. By the end of the day, I had finally experienced that thing that had eluded me earlier, an orgasm, which paled in comparison to the four or five that Malek had.

"Malek dropped me off at the corner near my house at around seven that evening, the usual time I got in after cheerleading practice. As I was getting out the car, he gave me a Cush joint and said I should smoke it before I went to bed. Thanks to Deana, my day spent with Malek went unnoticed by Gigi.

"Over the next few days, Malek picked me up at the corner after school like clockwork. As soon as I got in his car, he gave me a Cush joint, and the party was on. Whenever I smoked Cush, I felt liberated with a heightened libido. Although I had no one else with whom to compare him, sex was great with Malek. I couldn't imagine that sex could be any better with any other man. I was blindly falling hard for Malek.

"By the end of the week, I had quit the cheerleading squad and was spending all my free time with Malek, telling numerous lies to Gigi to justify why I was getting home so late. Gigi saw straight through my lies. She would often yell at me and threaten to send me away to boarding school if I didn't change my behavior.

"By week three, I had started skipping classes and school altogether. Malek and I had grown very close and were totally in love. At least that's what I thought. Malek professed his love to me each and every day, especially during sex. He would often say, 'You belong to me now.' Then he would point at his heart and say, 'You're inside me now. You make my heart beat. I couldn't breathe if you were not in my life.'

"I was on cloud nine with my man, making love to him and smoking Cush all day. I was getting home later and later. I didn't care that Gigi was upset with me. I was numb to her screaming and yelling. I was waiting for her to throw me out, so I could move in with Malek, but she never did. She repeatedly warned me that if I kept acting up, I was going to pay dearly for the lesson she was trying to save me from.

"Weeks later, Gigi's warnings started to come to fruition. It was the day Malek revealed his true self, showing that he was none other than the son of Satan. He did the most sinister thing to me. He lured me into the devil's den, a place that would start my life spiraling out of control with such decay that it would last through the end of my days.

"By then, I had become reckless. I had practically quit school and had no regard for Gigi's household rules. I was under Malek's spell; at least that's what I thought until he disclosed to me the real contents of Cush. Unbeknownst to me, it was marijuana laced with heroin. So, I had already started developing an addiction to heroin but at a snail's pace.

"My life had slowly disintegrated into nothing but having sex with Malek, smoking Cush, and sleeping all day. Malek and I seemed happy with our mutual exchange. He kept me supplied with plenty of Cush joints, and I became his sex slave, allowing him to have complete control over my body. We even partied a few times with Carmen, one of his employees.

"One day, I was lying around and decided to smoke a Cush joint. But, when I looked in the place where Malek usually kept his stash, nothing was there. When Malek finally made it home, I expected him to have a few joints for me, but he didn't. He said his supply had dried up, but he should be back on deck in a few days.

"'I can't wait a few days,' I said. 'You need to go somewhere else to buy enough to hold me over.'

"He shouted, 'No, I don't fuck with everybody's shit. The entire city is dry now. If you can't wait, then you'll just have to snort a little blow. It's the same heroin we use to make Cush. Trust me, you'll like it. The high is the same but faster. It will relax you before you can count to five.'

"Stunned, I replied, 'Heroin? Why did you give me heroin? How could you do this to me? You of all people know how it destroys lives.'

"Ignoring my words, he pulled out a couple of packs of blow from his wallet, threw them on the table and said, 'Do you want this or not?'

"I was angry with Malek, but I was even more upset with myself for being so stupid and gullible. I thought I could sleep off my craving for Cush, but that was not the case. By nightfall, I became anxious and snorted one of the packs of blow. Later, I found out that Malek had told me another lie. Snorting blow was much worse than smoking Cush. My gradual slide into my addiction was over. I was deep into it, up to my neck.

"From that day forward, I increased my heroin intake daily. It wasn't a problem for me though, because my thirty-three-year-old lover was one of the biggest dope dealers in the city. I had no shortage of any drug I wanted. But, just when I was comfortable with my new addiction, Malek showed me another of his many dark faces.

"He began rationing my packs of blow. Some days he would leave me for hours without any drugs, to the point where I became ill. But when he returned, he usually had enough blow for me to feel better. However, on this particular day, he came home empty-handed. I walked into the living room, where Malek was counting money, and said, 'Malek, I'm feeling sick, I need a quick one.' He didn't respond, so I raised my voice. 'Malek, I'm sick.'

"In a nonchalant tone, he said, 'I told you to slow down on that stuff. You should have listened to me. I'm out of blow, so you'll have to wait a few hours. I'll get some for you when I go check on my spots. Anyway, I think it's time for you to start supporting your habit.'

"I looked at him in confusion and said, 'What are you talking about?'

"'Baby, you know I'm crazy about you, but all my women have to contribute to the cause.'

"Still confused, and becoming sicker by the minute, I said, 'Just give me a hit, and we can talk about it later. You know I'll help you in whatever way you need me.'

"He kept procrastinating, and then I started jonesing for the first time since I began snorting blow. I started having cold and hot sweats, my eyes were running, my arms were itching, and I felt nauseous. I even ran to the bathroom and vomited a few times. Before I knew it, I was on my knees begging him for a fix. His response? 'Well, I told you I'm out of packs. The only thing I have in the apartment is in a syringe in the refrigerator.'

"Without hesitation, I begged him to give it to me, and he had no reservations about it. So much for all the love he had for me. He knew the needle would take me over the edge, to a point of no return, and he didn't care one bit.

"Until that day, I had been delusional, denying my addiction, because I wasn't using a needle. I knew other heroin addicts who were using the needle and that they were willing to do anything and everything for a fix. While hanging out with Malek, I had seen such addicts behave desperately, willing to debase themselves, performing all sorts of sexual acts. I even saw a woman offer up her ten-year-old daughter for a fix. I looked down on them, thinking I would never lower myself to that level. I was just getting high, because the drugs were convenient for me. I always told myself that I was not an addict; I could quit at any time. However, there was no confusion when it came to the needle. I knew the needle was the final sign of a true addict.

"My delusional period was finally over. This was my first time using a syringe. Before then, I always smoked or snorted it. Once Malek injected the heroin in my arm, I fell deep into a false celestial abyss. The high was better than I ever imagined. Now I knew why heroin was so devastating. It felt better than an orgasm or any spiritual awakening. Until that time, the term, 'the devil is a liar' had no real significance to me, but thanks to heroin, I would find out very quickly.

"When I finally snapped out of my buzz coma, Malek told me he wanted me to work for him. I assumed he wanted me to work in one of his strip clubs, but that was not the case. He said, 'Since you're a minor, you can't work in the clubs. The police will shut us down if they catch you there. I have something better for you. I don't want you to burn out too quickly. With your looks, ballers will pay big money for you. I might also let you make a few movies—not the trashy kind but the more tasteful ones. I'm going to let you work private parties for now. In fact, you can start tonight. I want you to go with Carmen; she'll show you the ropes.'

"I knew what that meant. Carmen was a party girl, a straight-up call girl. She didn't walk the streets, but she was still a hoe, prostituting herself. 'Oh, I can't do that,' I said. 'Gigi would kill me. She would throw me out of the house for good. I'm only fifteen. Where would I live?'

"'Baby, I love you,' he said. 'I'll take care of you. You can always stay here, right beside your man.'

"'If you love me, why are trying to turn me into a whore?' I asked. 'You should help me get off the shit before it's too late.'

Without saying a word, Malek slapped me hard across the face, causing me to fall to the floor. My jaw was numb; I was sure he had dislocated or broken my jawbone. Then he was on top of me with a knife, holding the blade against my face. He said, 'Don't make me slice this beautiful face. Just do what I tell you, and you'll be okay. I don't like to beat my women, because I'm not that kind of man, but I will if I have to. So, don't get it twisted.'

"Then he got up, walked to his liquor cabinet, and lit a cigar as he poured himself a drink. *What a hypocrite,* I thought. There he was, drinking Balvenie premium scotch and smoking a cigar like a civilized businessman when he was nothing more than an arrogant, thugged-out, drug-dealing pimp.

"I was shocked as I wiped the tears from my face, still stinging from the slap. I wondered who this man was and how I got there. A few months earlier, I was a cheerleader standing at the bus stop, falling in love. Now I was addicted to drugs and being forced into prostitution. I was stronger than that; I could not let that happen to me. That's when I decided to leave Malek. I would disappear when Carmen and I went to the party at some professional ball player's home.

"A few minutes later, Malek pulled out a handkerchief and gently wiped the tears that were still flowing from my eyes. He started gently kissing my face, and then my lips. Then he said, 'Baby, I love you. Please, don't make me hurt you. This is an investment for your future too. Once we stack enough paper to invest in some other businesses, you'll be part owner. You can help run things or sit home and have a few babies if you want. You know that you and I will make beautiful babies together. I want to marry you one day, but we need to take care of business first. We need to get this money while we can.' He pulled out a few packs of blow and said, 'You can have as much of these as you like, and I'll even supply the needles, if that's your preference. All you have to do is your part. You know I love you, right? I won't let anyone hurt you, I promise. I won't let the rough guys have you either.'

"I didn't respond. I was young, but I wasn't that stupid. I realized at that moment that Malek was never my boyfriend. He had deliberately gotten me hooked on drugs to control me and lure me into prostitution. Gigi was right; it was a cruel world out there. She had warned me many times that something like this could happen, but I ignored her. Now, it was too late. I was caught up in something that I didn't know how to get out of. I was scared. Inside, I was crying for Gigi and Pops to save me, wishing Gigi had special powers that allowed her to see what was happening to me, so she could rescue me. But those were mere thoughts in my head.

"As we drove to Carmen's apartment, I felt one of my migraines come on. The pain was so intense that I started moaning and crying. I told Carman I was sick; I needed something. She knew exactly what I meant.

"'Hold on, we're almost at my place,' she said. 'Malek gave me a few packs of blow for you. I'll let you have them once we get to my place. I need to stop at this gas station and take care of something first, and then we'll go to my apartment. It's not far from here.'

"Before she left, she grabbed a gun from her purse and placed it in her jacket pocket. Then she showed me another gun in the console and said, 'Lock the door, and pay attention.' She pointed at the gun and said, 'Use it if you have to.'

"I wondered what else they were dragging me into. Without thinking, once Carmen was inside the gas station, I jumped in the driver's seat and sped off. Luckily, Pops had taught me how to drive a year earlier. I should have run away, left town, and went to a place where Malek would not be able to find me, but I didn't. I wanted to be in the safety and warmth of my parents' home, in my mother's arms.

"I knew Malek would be looking for me, so I parked near the Woodward bus line. I took the packs of blow out of Carmen's purse and then opened the trunk. That's when I saw the backpack. I grabbed it and placed Carmen's purse and keys in the trunk and then hopped on the bus to my home.

"I crept into the house at around one in the morning, climbed into bed with Deana, and held her hand tight. It was the first time I could ever remember feeling glad to be home, asleep in my room. I knew Gigi would be angry with me, so I prepared myself for it. But I also knew she loved me unconditionally and would give me another chance to get my act together. I would tell Gigi everything, about Malek and the drugs. She would make one of her concoctions and cure my addiction, or perhaps she and Pops would send me to a hospital or a rehab center, so I could get better. Once I was cured, I would go back to school and become a doctor like Pops wanted me to do. I had learned my lesson. No more lies, disrespecting, or disobeying Gigi's rules. I would be a good daughter from this point forward and make her proud of me.

"Sadly, the next day, things did not go as planned. That was the day that Pops was murdered while working in his garage. Now that Pops was gone, I couldn't burden Gigi with my problems. She had bigger things to worry about, like how she was going to support eleven kids with no husband or source of income. Besides, Gigi was also grieving. She had lost the one true love of her life. I knew she was in a different frame of mind, because she didn't yell at me when I sneaked back into the house after being away for three days. She seemed numb as she went about her day, making funeral arrangements.

"Needless to say, my grief for Pops was overshadowed by my fear of Malek. I was no longer delusional about Malek's feelings toward me. I knew my life was in danger and that Malek would not hesitate to kill me, not for running out on him but for stealing his drugs.

"I told Deana what happened, and she shared my concerns. We devised a plan for me to leave town later that night. But my departure became unnecessary. Later that evening, I learned that Malek and Carmen were found dead in Malek's car a few hours after Pops' body was found. They were supposedly killed for botching a big drug deal. I wasn't sure if I was in the clear, so I stayed in the house except to attend Pops' funeral.

"I had never been to a funeral before. It was the saddest day I could ever remember. Gigi must have cried all night, because her eyes were nearly swollen shut, as if she'd had an allergic reaction. Pops was beloved by so many people. The church was overflowing with mourners until there was standing room only. People greeted Gigi as they walked by the casket as if she was a celebrity. Deana and I sat on opposite sides of her. She held our hands so tight during the entire service, as if she would fall apart if she let them go. At times, I felt her trembling. I knew the depth of her pain was immeasurable.

"During the funeral repast service, Shelly, one of the neighborhood girls who attended Cass with me, asked if I had heard about Malek. I pretended to be indifferent and said, 'Yes, I heard he was shot.'

"She replied, 'Well, I hope you were not still seeing him. He was a real loser, nothing but a drug-dealing pimp. You know they found him in the car dead alongside his wife.'

"'His wife?' I asked. 'I didn't know he was married.'

"'Girl, everyone knew that skank, Carmen, was his wife. They were a real Bonnie and Clyde team. She did everything for him—tricked for him, pimped for him, sold drugs for him, and ultimately died for him. But they both got what they deserved after what they did to Mr. Big John. Torturing him like a dog before finally killing him.'

"'What are you talking about?' I shouted.

"'Oh, you didn't hear?'

"'No,' I said. 'Please tell me.'

"'It wasn't a robbery after all. They were looking for drugs at his garage. They said it was Malek who killed your father.'

"I couldn't believe what I was hearing. 'What do you mean, Malek killed Pops?' I said. 'He had no dealings with people like Malek or drug dealers of any sort.'

"'You know how kindhearted Mr. Big John was. There could have been drugs hidden in one of the cars in his shop. All I know is that something went down that had to do with drugs. They obviously didn't find what they were looking for, because Malek and his wife ended up dead too.'

"I was in total shock. I ran to the bathroom, went into a stall, and fell to my knees, crying. Pops was dead because of me. Malek probably wanted Pops to make me come to the garage, so he could retrieve his drugs, and then he would kill both of us, but Pops wouldn't do it. Pops, my beloved daddy, died to protect me.

"Deana came into the bathroom shortly after me and called my name, asking if I was alright. As I walked out of the stall, I cried out, 'This is all my fault! Gigi is going to hate me. How did I let this happen? I've destroyed everyone's life.' I hugged Deana as I continued sobbing and fell to the floor. 'Oh my God, Deana,' I said, 'what am I going to do? How can I ever fix this?' I was crying so hard, I threw up.

"'What are you talking about?' Deana said. 'This isn't your fault. Don't you remember your Bible? Regardless of what role you think you played in Pops' death, you didn't hasten his death. It was his time to go be with our real Father, our Lord and Savior, Jesus Christ.'

"Deana's words did not lift the burden that was weighing on my heart. She continued holding me as I cried with my head in her lap for what felt like hours. As she rubbed my back, she repeatedly sang a verse from 'Jesus Loves Me.' It's funny how some of the smallest things stay with you. I would go on to hear Deana's soft voice singing that verse at various times throughout my life.

"Later that night, as we were getting ready for bed, I told Deana the story that Shelly told me. She said, 'We must never talk about it again, ever. Nor should you ever speak of it to Gigi. Promise?' I promised that I would not.

"That night, I couldn't sleep. I went into the closet, where I hid the backpack full of drugs, and decided I had to get rid of it. Someone might link me to Malek and come looking for the drugs in our home and kill everyone. I took out enough to fill a small sandwich bag, enough to hold me over until I could go to a rehab center. Then I took Gigi's car, drove to Belle Isle, and threw the backpack over the bridge.

"When I returned home, Gigi was up waiting for me. She pushed me against the wall, collared me with both hands and shouted, 'For Christ's sake, your father just died. Can't you at least show him some respect in his death? His body is not even cold, and you're already running around with these no-good men. If you don't straighten up, you're going to have to leave here for good. I mean it!'

"'I'm sorry Gigi,' I responded. 'I promise I'll do better. I won't break curfew again.'

"She took her hands off me and walked back to the living room. I ran upstairs to my bedroom, where Deana was waiting up for me. 'Where have you been?' she whispered. I told her what I had done and that everything would be okay now.

"The next few weeks went by without incident. The only problem I had was my addiction. It seemed to worsen with my guilt over Pops' death. My drugs were almost gone, and I had yet to find a rehab center. Because I was a minor, I could not enter a drug treatment program without Gigi's consent. Gigi was going through enough with the financial difficulties we were having, and I didn't want to add to her worries with my addiction.

"Deana had a part-time job, but I was using all her money to support my habit. Over time, my addiction got worse, and it won out over my desire to be a good daughter. By the time we moved to the Gardens, I had obtained a fake ID and began working in a strip club to support my habit. It was around that time that Gigi finally kicked me out of the house.

"I realized later that my guilt over Pops' death and seeing the devastation that I had caused Gigi and my entire family made me hate myself. Gigi changed after Pops died. It was as if a part of her died too. So, I used the drugs to cover my pain. I wanted Gigi to hate me too because of what I had done to her. Because of me, she had lost her one true love, but I could never tell her the part I played in his death.

"By then, my addiction had gotten the best of me. When I could no longer work in the clubs, I was forced to work for a pimp, walking the streets of Detroit. He eventually sold me to another pimp, who made me work every truck stop along the interstate, from I-94 through I-15, until we finally stopped in California.

"By that point, I was a complete zombie, getting high to numb every fiber of my being. So many times, I wanted to overdose, but I couldn't do it. I guess all that time I spent in church with Gigi wasn't a total waste. I believed in God and I knew suicide was a sin that would leave my soul lingering in purgatory. Besides, I figured sooner or later the lifestyle I was living would lead to my inevitable death. And on several occasions, it almost did.

"Little did I know that one of those near-death experiences would lead to a miracle and one of the happiest moments of my life.

Thirteen

A Splendor Of Hope

"One evening, while working the strip near Hollywood Boulevard, I solicited an undercover policeman and was arrested. When my pimp bailed me out for two thousand dollars for the second time, he decided to teach me a lesson for my stupidity and gave me a ferocious beating, which included slicing my scalp from my neck to my forehead with a knife, right down to the white meat. However, he was nice enough to drive me to the hospital. Before he sped off, he said, 'You better be ready to go back to work tomorrow. I'll be looking for you.'

"Due to the severity of the beating and laceration, I was hospitalized for an entire week. During my stay, my heroin addiction was also treated, which allowed me to have a clear, sober mind. I hadn't felt sober, or felt anything for that matter, in over a year. It felt good, as if I had emerged from a deep sleep. I knew something was changing in me, because I was craving food instead of plotting how I was going to get my next fix.

"While I was there, a social worker also visited me several times. She said that since I was still young, I had time to turn my life around. She helped me get into a women's shelter that offered room, board, and drug treatment.

"After completing ninety days of the drug-treatment program, I was drug-free, healthy, and feeling good. A plastic surgeon affiliated with the shelter repaired the facial disfiguration that resulted from my beating. The only reminder of my old life was the thick scar across my head, but my hair covered most of it.

"I began taking GED classes in the morning and got a job cleaning luxury hotels and office buildings in the evening. My life was finally turning around. I even had thoughts about going to college and becoming a doctor like Pops wanted me to do. Once I got myself together, I would go back home, and Gigi would be proud of me. Maybe I could buy her a house to replace the one she lost when Pops died.

"One day, we were short staffed, so I was given the chore of cleaning one of the penthouse suites. It was beautiful. It looked like a luxury apartment, not at all like it was part of the hotel. It had two large bedrooms, three bathrooms, and a full gourmet kitchen with high-end stainless-steel appliances. The floors were made of black marble with an Oriental rug in what I assumed to be the living room. I decided to take a tour around the entire unit. The bedroom looked like a cloud with white bedding covering the oversized California king. I couldn't help myself; I jumped in the bed to feel how soft it was. While I was basking in the comforts of the goose-down comforter, I heard footsteps approaching the bedroom. I stood up just as a man entered.

"'You startled me,' I said. "I thought this suite was empty.'

"'I'm sorry,' he said. 'This is my home away from home. I have a lease on it.'

"'I'm almost finished,' I replied. 'I just have to change the linen and finish the bathroom in here, and then I can come back later to finish the rest.'

"'No, take your time,' he said. 'I prefer that you clean everything before you leave.'

"'Okay, but let me call the head maid, because three of us are supposed to clean your place. It could take me all night if I have to do it by myself.'

"'Well, I don't mind,' he said. 'I promise I won't get in your way.'

"I looked around at the size of his suite, realizing I would be dog tired after cleaning it by myself. But perhaps he would give me at least a twenty-dollar tip.

"I put on my headphones, and three hours later, I was done. As I was about to leave, he said, 'Wait I have something for you.' He gave me a tip, three hundred dollars, and thanked me for a job well done. Instead of catching the bus that night, I took a cab back to the women's shelter where I lived.

"The next day, my counselor asked me if I wanted a new job. She said that the gentleman whose suite I had cleaned the day before had requested me to be his private maid for the next six months. 'He's offering you a very high salary,' she said. 'When the six months are over, you can come back here, and we can help you find permanent housing. You'll still take your classes and attend counseling sessions here, but you'll live at the hotel.'

"'I don't know,' I said. 'Something seems fishy about it. Every man who's ever done anything nice for me has always ended up hurting me in the end, except my Pops. As Gigi would say, one thing for certain and two things for sure: men always have sex on the brain, and they will seize any opportunity to get it.'

"'Well, you're the one in control,' she replied. 'Make sure he knows that you're there to provide housecleaning services only. Do you know who he is? He's a Rackham. They're a very wealthy, powerful family, and they have a long political history in California. The Rackham Foundation is also a major benefactor to our organization. How often do people like us have access to such people? I hear that Paul's being groomed for a Senate seat and maybe even the presidency. If you play your cards right, he could probably help you get one of those high-paying government jobs. Before you know it, you'll have maids cleaning up for you."

"'Alright,' I replied. 'I'll give it a try. But I'm out of there the first sign of any inappropriate behavior.'

"The next day, I arrived at Mr. Rackham's suite. He left a note that said he would be gone for three days, along with a list of errands he wanted me to run, a set of car keys, and some cash. At first, I was going to drive his car, but then I decided not to. I was working an honest program, so I didn't dare touch his car, knowing I didn't have a driver's license. I took a taxi and ran all his errands, which used up all the money he left me.

"My second night there, I decided to order a pizza and then bathe in that enormous tub in his bathroom. I turned on the radio, closed my eyes, and rested my head on the soaking pillow. I felt like I was in heaven. When I opened my eyes, I was startled to see

Mr. Rackham standing in the doorway. 'Continue with your bath,' he said. 'Don't let me interrupt you. You look like an angel surrounded with clouds.'

"After he left, I grabbed a towel and locked the door. I proceeded to dry off and clean the bathroom. Then I went to the kitchen, where Mr. Rackham was reading his mail. He said, 'I'm sorry; my business concluded early, so I decided to come back.' I told him that I used the money he left for cab fare to run his errands.

"'Why didn't you take the car?' he asked. 'I left the keys for you.'

"'I don't have a driver's license,' I admitted.

"'Why not?' he asked. 'You're old enough to drive, aren't you?'

"'Yes, but I just moved here from New York, and I never got around to getting my license,' I explained.

"'This isn't New York, you know, so you can't depend on taxi or public transportation. You won't be able to get around here efficiently without a car. We'll have to get your license first thing tomorrow morning.'

"I snickered and said, 'I don't have a car, so I really don't need a license.'

"'Let's take care of the license first,' he said, 'and then we'll see about finding you a car.'

"I looked at him suspiciously and asked him why. He smiled and said, 'You're silly. You need a car, period. It's okay to accept a helping hand sometimes.'

"The next morning, he drove me to the DMV. We took care of all the requirements, and I emerged two hours later with my driver's license. Then Mr. Rackham suggested that I drive him around town to practice my driving skills.

"After driving around all day and then stopping for dinner, we went back to the hotel. We went to our respective rooms, and that was it. The next few weeks were very similar. Mr. Rackham usually traveled for three or four days and left me with a list of errands to run. It was business as usual.

"One weekend, I went on a retreat with the ladies from the shelter. When I returned, I found an envelope with my name on it and a small giftwrapped box. I opened it, and inside was a set of car keys. When I went to the parking garage, I found a cute red Volkswagen beetle. While I was happy for the car, it made me feel uneasy. I wondered what he was expecting in exchange. I was done with prostitution.

"When Mr. Rackham returned, I told him I could not accept the car. He said he knew of my circumstances and only wanted to help. He reassured me there were no strings attached. 'You can always leave it if you change your mind later and don't want it,' he said. I decided to keep it for the time being.

"The weekend was approaching, and Mr. Rackham invited me to attend a charity event with him. His only requirement was that I call him by his first name, Paul, instead of Mr. Rackham. He even bought me a formal dress and everything else I needed. As I got dressed, I felt like a princess in a fairytale.

"During the event, Paul held my hand as he proudly introduced me to his associates, where I heard several people say that Paul and I were a striking couple. Although there were at least two hundred people there, Paul and I were in a world by ourselves. We slow-danced on every song the band played. At times, it felt like Paul was not dancing but simply holding me tight, pressing his face and body against mine. That night, I experienced happiness beyond my imagination. I felt like I was someone else, and my tragic past didn't exist. I wanted to hold on to that feeling, at least for one night.

"When Paul and I returned to the suite, he opened a bottle of champagne, and we finished it. I guess we both forgot who we were, because he kissed me. The next thing I knew, we were making out. Then, he suddenly stopped and said, 'I'm sorry. I don't want you to feel pressured to be with me.'

"'It's okay,' I said. 'I want to.' I took his hand and walked him toward my room, but he stopped me.

"'No,' he said. 'I want you in my bed tonight.'

"Paul and I made love that night. Although I was not a virgin, I felt like I had made love for the very first time. After that, I slept in Paul's bed every night, and we made love at every opportunity.

"Paul's overnight travels became fewer and fewer, and soon we were spending all our days and nights together, during which Paul educated me and exposed me to a new world We visited historical landmarks and major tourist attractions in California, including Disneyland and the Napa wineries. We flew to Mexico often for romantic getaways, where we skinny dipped and made love on the white sandy beaches. I also accompanied Paul on several business trips and social engagements. Our dreamlike relationship went on for months without any hiccups. Paul's personality was surreal; he had great humility and was unmoved by his heritage as a member of a rich and powerful family. He was everything that defined a gentleman. Sometimes, when I was alone and reflecting on my newfound love, I thought about Gigi and how I was experiencing the same love and happiness she felt with Pops.

"One night, while I was lying in Paul's arms, he said, 'I love you and want you to stay with me. Will you? I'll pay for your college and even help you with medical school.' I agreed without hesitation.

"The next day, I woke up feeling tired and nauseous. I thought I was sick with the flu, but then the possibility of a pregnancy ran across my mind. I hadn't used birth control since I stopped tricking. I went to the free clinic and, sure enough, I was pregnant. The results shocked me. I didn't think I could get pregnant, given the abuse I had levied on my body. But more importantly, I felt scared and unsure whether or not I should tell Paul. I wondered if he would be angry or think I was trying to trap him into marrying me. Either way, the timing was bad. I was in no condition to be a mother.

"When Paul came home, I decided to tell him about the pregnancy. As soon as he sat down in the kitchen, I said, 'Paul, I'm sorry, but I'm pregnant.' At first, he didn't respond. Then he asked if I was sure. 'Yes,' I said. 'I know you're disappointed. Don't worry; I'm not going to keep it.'

"'Are you crazy?' he said. 'You're not getting rid of my baby. If you don't want her, give her to me when she's born, and let me and my family raise her.'

"'That's not it,' I said. 'What about your career and your political aspirations? And what about your family? This baby will surely have an impact on your plans, and with my past, it won't be good.'

"'None of that stuff matters to me,' he said. 'My career and political ambitions are my family's dreams, not mine. If it was up to me, I would be living abroad in some third-world country doing missionary work.' He paused and grabbed my hands. 'Don't worry about that stuff,' he continued. 'It will work itself out. I want you to have the baby. Our baby won't change any of my plans. Having you and now our baby will make my life complete.'

"I didn't respond as I stared at the floor, thinking how wonderful Paul was and that I could love him forever. He continued in a low whisper, 'Don't you want to have our baby girl? I'll take care of both of you.'

"'Yes, I do,' I said, 'but what makes you think this baby is a girl?'

"'I can't explain it,' he replied. 'I just have a feeling it's a girl, and she'll be beautiful, just like her mother.'

"At that moment, I felt happy and proud to be having Paul's baby. I knew Paul loved me. I thought that maybe God had forgiven me and was allowing me to have a second chance to turn my life around. I would go back to school and become a doctor and then marry Paul, a respectable man that Gigi would approve of. I would forget about Malek and all the mayhem he had created in my life. I would use my second chance to right all the wrongs of my past. Little did I know, my fairytale life would be short-lived.

"Paul left for a few days when I received a surprise visit from his mother. At first, she seemed concerned and quite pleasant as she explained that Paul called her and told her the good news, that I was expecting a child. 'You know, Paul has a big heart and would save the world if he could,' she said. 'When he was a kid, he used to bring home stray dogs and cats, and when he got older, he started bringing home stray people. So you see, you're no different, just another stray.' That's when she revealed the true intent of her visit. Without hesitation, she gave me a check for fifty thousand dollars and then told me she wanted me to get rid of the baby and get as far away from Paul as possible. 'If you come back, I won't be responsible for what happens to you,' she said. 'Paul has an important future ahead of him and I'm not going to let trash like you destroy it."

"'Paul and I love each other,' I replied. 'He's not going to let you run me off.'

"She smirked. 'He'll be upset at first,' she said, 'but he'll get over you. You're not the first piece of trash I've had to remove from Paul's life. Let me repeat myself: leave today on your own, or I'll have you removed permanently. It's that simple.' Then she walked to the door and opened it. 'Pack your belongings and leave now,' she said.

"Still reeling from the shock of her demands, I stood still in silence. Then two men, who looked like nightclub bouncers, walked through the door. Without saying a word, I knew they were there to throw me out of Paul's suite.

"I quickly gathered a few things. As I was approaching the door, Paul's mother handed me an envelope containing papers and the check she had offered me earlier. Then she said, 'Don't be foolish; take the money. By the way, I've made an appointment for you to see a doctor tomorrow to take care of your little problem. All the information you need is in this envelope. Everything has already been paid for. After it's done, I'll give you another check for an additional fifty thousand dollars. That should be enough to help you relocate far from here.

"'Listen,' she continued, 'I may seem like a bitch, but I'm doing what any mother would do to protect her children. You're still young and beautiful; you have plenty of time to find a husband and have a family with your own kind. Stay in your lane; you'll be happier that way. Don't expect to ever become a part of any blue-blooded family like the Rackhams. Did you really think I would let you sully my family's good name with your bastard child and your mutted race? The Rackham men have always played with women like you, but they knew where to draw the line. You see, sometimes Paul confuses fantasy with reality, which explains his temporary affection for you. But he can't continue to ignore his fate. Eventually, he'll come around and accept his place in this family, which doesn't include marrying or fathering children with the likes of you.'

"I didn't respond. I took the envelope, returned the check, and then I left. I went to my friend Kelly's apartment. Kelly and I met at rehab and became good friends. She and I were around the same age and had walked a similar dark path.

"When I arrived at Kelly's place, I asked if I could stay for a while, at least until I figure out a few things. She said I could stay as long as I needed to. 'Things are not going well for me in Cali,' I said, 'and I'm thinking about going back home after I take care of my situation.'

"'What situation?' she asked.

"'I had a one-night stand with a guy I met briefly about two months ago, and now I'm pregnant. But I'm going to take care of it this week.' Kelly said she understood. She had been there before.

"The next day, I went to see the doctor that Paul's mother had selected for me. To my surprise, it wasn't a free clinic; it was an actual doctors' office in a beautiful three-story glass building. After I checked in, the doctor asked me a few questions and then she examined me. 'Do you still want to proceed with the termination?' she asked. I told her I did. She gave me a few papers to sign and then stepped out of the room.

"As I looked at the papers, tears began rolling down my face. I kept thinking about how happy Paul was about the baby and how much he loved me. When the doctor returned, she saw my tears and said, 'We don't have to do this today or ever. I won't judge you either way. But you need to take care of it soon if want to terminate while you're still in the first trimester. Why don't we reschedule for next week? If I see you, it's fine, but if not, that's okay too.'

"I told Kelly I changed my mind and was keeping my baby. She said I was welcome to stay with her. She was planning to get a roommate anyway. She helped me get a job as a waitress in the restaurant where she worked. From there, things seemed to be going well for me. The next few weeks went by without incident. I didn't dare contact Paul, nor did he try to contact me. Deep inside, I was hoping Paul would find a way to contact me, but he never did. For some reason, I wasn't terribly bothered by it though. I was happy knowing that my baby, Paul's baby, was growing inside me.

"One night, while I was lying in bed, I heard someone hurriedly come into the apartment, but it wasn't Kelly. Before I could react, he was upon me and began attacking me. It felt like a nightmare, but it wasn't. Someone was beating, stomping, and kicking my entire body. Days later, I awoke in the hospital, black and blue and handcuffed to my bed. My court-appointed attorney said they found drugs in the apartment among my personal possessions. I explained that Kelly and I were both drug free and neither of us were associated with any persons using or selling drugs. Besides, it wasn't my apartment anyway. The police made a mistake. I told them Kelly could vouch for me.

"'Kelly seems to be MIA,' my attorney said. 'We can't find her anywhere. It looks like she boarded a plane to New York the same day that you were assaulted. The police say it looks like the assailants were searching for something, because the apartment was ransacked. Someone heard the noise and called the police, which probably saved your life. Someone has to account for the drugs that were found in the apartment. It wasn't a lot, but it was enough to get your probation revoked.'

"I didn't reply, still dazed and confused by what I was hearing. I just stared into space, trying to figure out what happened to me and how I was on my way to prison. My lawyer told me to take a plea, and I could be home in time to have my baby in a real hospital instead of a prison infirmary. So, I did. Before I left the hospital, my nurse told me to take it easy if I wanted to have a healthy baby. 'God must have covered you and your baby,' she said, 'because your injuries were not life threatening to you or your baby despite the beating you took.'

"The thought of going to prison terrified me. I had been to jail several times for short stays, but I was numb to it due to my drug addiction. Now that I was clean and sober, I worried about the environment. Would it be safe for my baby and me? Would the people who tried to kill me come after me while I was in prison? What happened to Kelly, who I thought was my friend? I wasn't sure if she set me up or was chased out of town. Either way, I could never have any contact with her.

"As it turned out, the conditions of my incarceration were not bad. I was placed in a special ward for pregnant women. With the exception of occasional periods of sadness brought on by the idle time that prison brings, I was okay. It was during that time that I realized that Paul's mother was responsible for my assault. If the neighbors had not called the police, I would have probably been killed. I realized I had to do whatever it took to save my baby. The answer was obvious. My baby's only chance for survival was with

Gigi. That's when I decided to go back home to Detroit after I was released.

"To ensure the baby's safety and that no one could trace her to Paul or me, I would let Gigi adopt her and not disclose the identity of the baby's father. That part would be easy. As an ex-prostitute and drug addict, it was highly conceivable that I got pregnant while tricking and didn't know who the father was. However, convincing Gigi to adopt my baby was another matter. She would either try to convince me to keep my baby, or she would want to know all the details behind my request, which would put her life and the baby's life at risk. I had selfishly brought harm to Gigi and my family before when I was dealing with Malek. I could never do that again, even if it meant I had to live in exile from my family. Sometimes a sacrifice is the only option.

"While riding the bus for three whole days, I came up with my plan. I would stay with Gigi until I had the baby, and then I would leave the hospital after the birth. Family meant everything to Gigi, and I knew she would never let my baby go into a foster home. She would have no choice but to keep her. I didn't want Gigi to be my baby's guardian; I wanted her to adopt her, so my name would not be associated with her. Even if Paul's mother found out about the baby later, knowing she was adopted might make her feel that neither my baby nor I were a threat to her family. But for my plan to work, I had to disappear. I had to abandon my child and my family. Maybe in five to ten years I could come back and reconnect with my baby and the rest of my family. I would explain my actions, and they would understand and forgive me once again.

"When I got to Detroit, I would make all the necessary arrangements for Gigi to adopt my baby. But I would have to do one more thing that would surely devastate her. I would leave her a letter stating that I was going back to my old life and that I was never returning. Paul's mother tried to kill her unborn grandchild and me to protect her family's name and honor. I was convinced she would stop at nothing and try to do it again. She would have no qualms about destroying my entire family in the process. I was responsible for Pops' death, and I swore I would never bring any more harm to my family.

"When I returned home, Gigi treated me as if nothing bad had happened between us. She was happy and excited about my pregnancy even after I explained the false circumstances that I made up surrounding my baby's conception. Gigi was a strong woman, but I could still see the pain in her eyes from losing Pops, the pain that I had caused.

"One day, while playing a board game with my siblings, I noticed Gigi staring at me. That's when I knew she knew I was responsible for Pops' death. But in true Gigi style, she never said anything about it, nor did she treat me unkindly. However, later that night, Deana confirmed my suspicion.

"Deana and I were very close; we shared a kindred spirit as if we were Siamese twins. Even though I was older than her, she was smarter and wiser than me. She was special; her heart was open, pure and not judgmental. She was also loyal and self-sacrificing. I knew that firsthand from all the things she had done for me. She kept my secrets when I was getting high. She even stole money to buy me drugs when I was sick. She always knew what I was thinking before the words came out of my mouth. She knew when I was in pain and the source of it before I told her. Gigi always said Deana had a gift of discernment, something that stemmed from our Creole roots. I never quite understood what she meant until then.

"Deana said that one day after I moved out, Gigi asked if she had heard the rumors, that some drug dealer named Malek had killed Pops. Before Deana could respond, Gigi asked, 'Was Malek Di's boyfriend?' Deana didn't answer, but Gigi said, 'I know the rumors are probably true.' Never again did Gigi inquire or have any further conversations on the topic.

"The day after I gave birth, Deana came to see me in the hospital. She said, 'I know you're planning to leave again, but why? You're going to break Gigi's heart.'

"'I don't have a choice,' I cried. 'It's the only way I can protect Astrid. Do you think I want to leave my baby?' I went on to explain how I met Paul and how his mother tried to have me killed. 'Our entire family will be at risk if I stay here. I can't bring any more harm to our family. Besides, I can't bear to look at the sadness in Gigi's eyes. She may not say it, but I know she blames me for Pops' death.'

"Deana reached over and hugged me and said, 'That's not true. Gigi loves you, and she has a forgiving heart. Where is your faith? The God I serve will not let that evil woman assassinate our family. There are twelve of us, now thirteen with Astrid. You need to stay here with your family where you belong. Together we can handle Paul and his bitch of a mother.'

"I was shocked by Deana's words. She rarely used profanity and had never spoken such harsh words before. I shook my head and said, 'Promise me that you'll help Gigi take care of Astrid. I'll come back in a few years. I promise I will.'

"With tears flowing down my face, I picked you up and said, 'You're so beautiful. Your little round face looks just like your father. Paul would have been elated if he had the opportunity to know you.' I turned to Deana and said, 'You know you can never speak of what I shared with you.'

"Deana told me that my secret was safe with her. She would take it to her grave if she had to. She also promised to watch over you as if you were her daughter. Then she leaned over and kissed me on my forehead. As she was leaving, she looked back at me and said, 'You're breaking my heart too.'

"As I wiped my tears away, I continued to think about Paul. I wondered why he had not tried to find me. With all his money, surely he could have hired private investigators. Maybe he came to his senses and took his place in the Rackham lineage and wanted nothing more to do with our child or me. I figured I'd never know, because I needed to disappear for good.

"Since the baby and I were doing well, my hospital stay was short, only three days. It saddened me, because I knew I would have to leave my baby once we were discharged. A few weeks prior to giving birth, I went to the Department of Children's Services to initiate the adoption process. It was then that the social worker inadvertently revealed that if I abandoned my baby, it would speed up the adoption process. So, that's what I decided to do.

"Day three arrived, and Gigi was coming to take us home at noon. That morning, I held you tight. I was hoping my scent would somehow stay in your memory. The hours passed quickly. I got dressed and then made sure the letter I had written for Gigi was placed with you in your crib. Then I took a taxi to the bus station and headed to Vegas.

"Unfortunately, like so many other addicts, I quickly fell back into my old patterns and began a vicious cycle of drug abuse. Needless to say, I never made it back to reconnect with you or anyone else in the family.

"A few years ago, I found myself in New York working at a seedy adult entertainment bar. I wasn't dancing, but I was engaging in other activities to support my drug habit. After trying to stave off a bad cold, I ended up in the hospital fighting off pneumonia where I met Sister Nancy.

"And here I am today, back in Detroit, taking one day at a time, facing my inevitable death. Well, that's it. That's my life and the reason why I had to let you go. Okay, this is the end. Goodbye."

And just like that, there was complete silence.

I must have been in shock. A few minutes elapsed before I noticed the recorder was still playing. Just as I was about to stop it, Di's voice came back.

"I have a few more things to say. Astrid, I loved you from the day I pushed you out of my womb and each and every day that followed throughout the haze of my addiction and brief moments of sobriety. I did the best I could, even though it was not good enough. I hope you understand why I had to leave you with Gigi and choose not to re-enter your life. Please find it in your heart to forgive me for the many hurts I've caused you. I too have suffered greatly for not having you in my life and for being forced to abandon you.

"Now that you know my story and that you do have a father, this should give you some closure. Leave the past in the past, and focus on the blessings you have on hand and that are forthcoming. You have a beautiful son, and before you know it, he'll be married, and our family tree will expand.

"Please heed my warning and do not attempt to contact Paul or his family; the consequences could be deadly. Nothing good can come from it but more heartache for you.

"In closing, please know that my heart has been filled with much joy and comfort knowing that you've had a good life. I knew you were going to be special and accomplish great things in your life. That's why I named you Astrid, divine and full of strength. May your heart hold all the joy and happiness that's possible."

I waited a few minutes more to make sure her audio was finished before I finally pressed stop. Then I took a deep breath and laid back on my bed and stared at the ceiling. I was too emotionally drained to feel anything. I couldn't cry, laugh, or feel anger.

I was sympathetic to Di's story, but I remained conflicted about her decision to abandon and later refuse to see me in her last days. But my spirit wouldn't let me be angry with her. I believed she thought she was doing the right thing. Perhaps in time I would be able to accept her choices.

I was surprised by Di's comments about my father. Part of me was happy to know he wasn't a random sperm donor and that I was actually conceived out of love. But Di should have known better. I was definitely going to search for Paul and his rotten mother. It was her fault that Di had been lost to the streets the second time. I wondered what kind of man Paul was, supposedly loving my mother in one breath and so easily accepting her disappearance in the next. For the moment, I'd put Mr. Paul Rackham on hold. I'd deal with him when I returned home to Atlanta.

I had been in Detroit for almost two months and decided to go home for a short stay. I was exhausted, and I needed a break. My hometown no longer felt like a safe haven, but more like a chamber of death. Besides, my leaving would allow me to avoid the conversation that Nikki and Deana felt we needed to have regarding Gigi's condition. That bitch Nikki wanted to pull the plug on Gigi the day after her stroke. As far as I was concerned, Nikki's opinion, medical or otherwise, didn't matter. My position was firm; as long as Gigi could breathe somewhat on her own, we would do everything possible to keep her alive. I was prepared to take legal action, if necessary.

Deana agreed to look after Gigi while I was in Atlanta. I had a lot to do when I got home: check on my home, my business with Sage and figure out what to do with my two lovers and the rest of the chaos in my life.

Fourteen

The Blackmail – Checkmate

On my return flight back to Atlanta, I reflected on the horrendous events of the past few weeks. In addition to Gigi's stroke, I had dealt with the shocking revelation of her life in New Orleans, meeting my mother for the first time, only to bury her a few days later, and learning the identity of my real father. I had experienced more drama in two months than most people have in a lifetime.

Strangely, while I had been haunted by Di's absence for most of my life, I hadn't given much thought to my father except as a lab specimen. But now that I knew the truth about my conception, I wanted to meet him, especially since Di was gone. My fantasies of reuniting with my mother were over, but perhaps I might have an opportunity to have a relationship with my father and my new extended family.

Then, I remembered the wicked witch on the throne—Paul's mother. I didn't think she'd be too happy to meet me. But perhaps her heart had softened. It had been decades since her initial encounter with Di. Multi-racial relationships were quite common now. They were no longer considered taboo, at least in America.

Doc picked me up from the airport and then took me to dinner. During the meal, he had a somber look on his face.

"Is it too late for us? Are we over?" he asked.

"I'm not sure how to answer you. My feelings haven't changed for you, but we've had some problems that are still unresolved. I'm open to trying to work things out if you are. Are you?"

"That depends on whether or not there's someone else in the picture," he said. "I sense a distance growing between us. Are you seeing someone else?"

"No one serious," I replied with thoughts of Chevy in mind. "If there was, I wouldn't be sitting here with you."

That seemed to lighten the mood. Doc's demeanor changed completely. Before I knew it, we were engulfed in laughter, and I had forgotten about Chevy, at least for the moment. By the time we finished our meal, I was tired and asked Doc to take me home. As Doc handed me my suitcase, he said, "I hope you'll find time for me this weekend." He pointed at his penis. "He misses you badly."

We both laughed, and I kissed him goodnight as I strolled into the lobby of my building.

When I entered my condo, Sage, as usual, had everything neatly organized. The place was spotless, and my mail lay on the kitchen table in neat piles labeled for each week I had been gone.

She also had a to-do list waiting for me. I looked at it and shook my head. "That girl needs to get a life."

Just as I settled in, relaxing on my sofa with a glass of wine, Sage came home. "Hey, Astrid. I wasn't expecting you tonight. I thought you were staying at Doc's house."

"No, I missed my home and sleeping in my own bed. Besides, I'm only here for a week before I return to Detroit, and I have a lot to catch up on before I leave."

Sage sat down beside me. "How's Gigi? I know there's a lot going on with your family. I'm here for you if need to talk or a shoulder to cry on."

"I don't know where to start," I replied. "The last few weeks have been surreal. I'm still in disbelief about what transpired. What I'm about to tell you is unbelievable."

Two hours later, after shedding a river of tears and going through a box of tissues, Sage was speechless. I told her everything, from the contents of Gigi's journals to meeting Di and learning the identity of my real father. "Astrid, I don't know what to say. This is a lot to take in. Are you alright? Can I help you?"

"I feel like I'm asleep and stuck in a nightmare that I can't wake up from," I said. "I want to go back to my life before all this happened, but I can't. Gigi's stroke and everything that followed kept replaying in my head, like an infinite loop. I know that only God can help Gigi, and as far as Di is concerned, maybe in time I will have peace about her decision regarding me. Of course, I wish I'd been able to spend time with her before she slipped into a coma, but it didn't work out that way. No sense in fretting over it now. But I do have something you can help me with; you can help me find Paul, my biological father."

Sage frowned with concern. "What about Di's warnings? Do you think searching for Paul is a good idea? Are you sure you want to open that can of worms? You know, the results might not be what you're expecting. What if Paul and his family don't want to have anything to do with you? Are you prepared for that?"

"Not really," I admitted, "but at least then I'll know for certain. It's the not knowing that I can't live with. Besides, my gut is telling me different, that Paul will embrace me when we finally meet. He doesn't know I exist, because his bitch-ass mother ran Di off and tried to kill her. I'll bet Paul has no idea about the role his mother played in Di's disappearance. Once I tell him the truth and let him listen to Di's audio recording, he'll have no choice but to believe me. If he wanted me when I was an embryo, he'll want me now. I just know it."

Sage shook her head. "I don't know, Astrid, this is a slippery slope. You need to be careful. But I'll help you in any way that I can."

"Thanks. I'm going to sleep on it awhile, and then I'll let you know what I decide to do next."

As I settled into bed, I looked at the text messages I had received from Chevy and Doc. Now that I was back in Atlanta, I wanted to spend time with Doc, but I had no intention of cutting off Chevy. I wanted to keep him too.

After talking to Doc and making plans for the following week, I hurriedly ended our call. I missed Chevy and looked forward to Skyping with him. Wearing a satin nightshirt, I dialed him on my computer. I caught him lying in bed, wearing nothing but his sexy chocolate skin. "Hey, Beautiful," he said. "You look sexy tonight wearing that white nightshirt. What else are you wearing?

I smiled. "Only my birthday suit.

"Oh, I wish I was there to see it. Why don't you unbutton it and move the screen back?"

"Okay, I see where this is going. You want a little porn action."

He grinned. "I'm not asking for any more than I'm willing to give. I'm not asking to see your pussy, not yet anyway. I just want to see a little more skin and those beautiful breasts. Don't act shy now; you know you like showing them off anyway, always wearing those cleavage-baring blouses."

Without hesitation, I smiled as I slowly unbuttoned all but the last button, to leave a little for his imagination. A little teasing never hurt. Then I began playing with myself under my nightshirt. That seemed to stir up a little heat in him. "Move the shirt, and let me see, baby," he said.

I smiled. "You first."

Chevy had no problem with nudity. He flipped his covers back, displaying his full-frontal nakedness and fully erect penis. "See what you've done to me? Every time I hear your voice, I get an erection." He continued talking to me as he stroked the shaft of penis. "Baby, let's quit wasting time. We've already done enough of that. I want us to live together. Give us a chance, and step out in faith with me."

Moments later, I saw the milky substance flow through Chevy's hands. "Baby, I've been on edge all day," he said. "I saved this for you."

"Well, now you can have a good night's sleep," I said. "Go clean yourself up, and I'll talk to you tomorrow."

"Astrid, I'm serious. Let's stop playing and do this, or I'm moving on—this time for good."

"Goodnight, Chevy," I replied. "Let's talk about this later."

Looking at Chevy's lean, naked torso and watching him masturbate aroused me. I got up and went into the bathroom and looked under the cabinet for one of my vibrators. I pulled out the box where I kept my sex toys, and all three of my vibrators were dead. I should have known that would be the case, since I hadn't used them in awhile. I decided to use the next best thing: my showerhead.

I climbed into the shower and turned it on high and closed my eyes as I recalled images of Chevy masturbating and making love to me as he had done when we were at Gigi's house. By then, the bathroom was full of steam, and my pussy was pulsating. I adjusted the intensity of the water flow, put one leg up on the bench, and held on the shower door as I positioned the showerhead just right, so the water would vigorously hit my G-spot. After about five minutes, I climaxed. It wasn't as good as my vibrator or Chevy, but it got the job done. I dried off and then went to bed.

By the time I awoke the next morning, Sage was already gone. I sat at the island, drinking my coffee and going through my mail, trying to decide which letter to open first. My decision was made when I came across a large, orange envelope. Just like before, it had not gone through the postal system. My stomach began to ache as I looked at the letter. I knew the subject of the contents before I opened it. Sure enough, it was another letter from the blackmailer.

Greetings Ms. Astrid,

It's been awhile since we've last spoke. You probably thought it was a prank or that I had developed a conscience and decided not to go through with our arrangement. I tried to spare you while you were visiting your sick mother, or shall I say "mothers."

Well, that would be incorrect, and since you didn't follow my instructions, you have forced my hand. I have to modify my request. Yes, I know you've hired Mr. Brown, your private investigator, to uncover my identity. I thought you were smarter than that, but you've been a naughty girl. So, now you'll have to pay. You have thirty days to come up with $1 million dollars in cash, or your sexy video will go viral. I will send instructions and account details later. Tell Mr. Brown to back off or face dire consequences. This isn't a game, I'm warning you for the last time. People can and will get hurt if you don't follow my instructions.

I was shocked, not by the blackmailer's request but by his knowledge of my activities. He clearly knew I was in Detroit and why I was there. More importantly, he knew of Di and my connection to her. I was still puzzled by the blackmailer's true motive. To go to this extent for a mere $1 million dollars just didn't make sense. The blackmailer had to want something more than money; I just didn't know what it was.

There was one more issue though. How was this blackmail letter and the prior letter delivered to me? Someone who was either living in or working in my building had to be involved. I still could not rule out Sage. While she appeared to be loyal, I didn't really know her, so I could not completely trust that she was not involved.

I had no choice except to be preemptive and to release the video myself. First, I would terminate Mr. Brown's services. I didn't want him or anyone else to get hurt. Then I would let Junior and the rest of my family know about the video. I would also have to inform Chevy and Doc. Maybe the news of my sex video would scare one of them off, and my dilemma would be over. I would choose the one who opted to stay with me.

That morning, I called Mr. Brown and explained that I was going in another direction with this matter. While my explanation was vague, Mr. Brown didn't question it. He agreed to send me a final report along with his invoice. "I'm sorry I couldn't find the source of the blackmail," he said, "but I think you'll be pleased with the other information I found. It's also included in my report." I thanked him and said goodbye, my curiosity piqued.

The next task on my list was to call Junior. I was nervous about telling him about the video, because that meant I would have to explain the details surrounding its origin. We had recently rebuilt our relationship, and I didn't want to do anything that would make him lose respect for me or want to pull away from me again. After procrastinating for about ten minutes, I finally dialed his number, and he answered in his usual cheerful voice.

"Hey son, I've got something serious to discuss with you," I said. After I explained the existence of the sex video and how it came to be, he was silent for a moment.

"Mom," he said finally, "why are you telling me this now? Did someone threaten to leak the video to the media?"

"No, someone informed me that they had seen a copy of the video, and it's only a matter of time before other people see it. I wanted to talk to you and the rest of the family about it before it goes viral." I went on to explain the circumstances of the video, how Marcus had falsely edited it to make it appear as if I was in it.

"Mom, that's unbelievable. Marcus and Joey were best friends; how could he betray Joey like that? Now I understand why Joey snapped and beat the hell out of Marcus. I probably would have done the same thing under the circumstances. Why didn't you tell me this when it first happened? Perhaps I could have helped or at least comforted you more."

"Son, that entire ordeal was very traumatic. It has taken me over a year to put it behind me, and now this sex video could make me re-live that nightmare all over again. Not to mention how it will scandalize Joey's name even further."

"Thanks for letting me know about the video, Mom. It's no big deal though; sex videos are all over the place these days. My only concern is you. I know how you value your privacy, not to mention how it could affect your career."

"As long as you're okay, that's all that matters. I can handle that other stuff."

"I'm proud of you, Mom, and that will never change. But promise me that you won't date any of my friends. If they see that sex video, they're going to want to date you. They already tease me about you and call you Mrs. Robinson from the classic movie, 'The Graduate.'"

We both laughed. "Okay son," I said, "I'll talk to you later."

I breathed a sigh of relief. That conversation was much easier than I expected. I only hoped the others would go just as smoothly.

Later that day, I held a video conference call with my siblings. I reiterated the story I had shared with Junior. Everyone but Nikki was supportive and understanding about my situation. Nikki was melodramatic. She acted as if we were a political family, and the sex video would scandalize our good name. "I can't believe you're going to drag our family through the mud with your antics. You've already done it once, and now you're going to do it again."

Before I could reply, my other sibling chimed in and shut her down. As we were about to conclude the call, Nikki said, "We need to discuss one more topic: Gigi's condition. How long are we going to let her stay on that breathing machine? We need to take her off it and let nature take its course."

"Listen, Nikki," I said, "I'm taking care of all Gigi's expenses, so there's no burden on you or anyone else in the family. She doesn't have any money that I'm aware of, so there's no big inheritance awaiting us. So, I have one question for you: why are you in such a hurry to kill our mother?"

She didn't respond. Moments later, she disconnected from the call. No one else commented so I concluded the call.

Now the only two people left to inform were Doc and Chevy.

When I arrived at Doc's house later that evening, he greeted me with a long kiss and a firm hug. "Maybe I should leave you for weeks at a time more often," I said when I came up for air, "if this is the type of welcome I can expect."

"No, please, don't leave me again," Doc replied. "You have no idea how much I've missed you. I was starting to worry that you met someone else in Detroit, especially since you're still not wearing the engagement ring."

Doc took my hand and walked toward the dining room, where he had the table beautifully set for a romantic candle-lit dinner. I smiled. "This is beautiful. But before we eat, I have something I need to tell you."

"Okay," he said as he sat down on the sofa.

"May I get a drink first?" Without waiting for an answer, I went to the butler pantry and poured a double shot of tequila and then sat next to Doc. "Listen, I'm not going to beat around the bush or attempt to whitewash things, so here it is. There's a sex video of me that will probably go viral in the next few weeks."

"With whom, may I ask?"

"With Joey's best friend, Marcus."

I waited for Doc to respond, but he didn't say a word, nor did his expression change. I explained how I wound up in a compromising position with Marcus and how he had edited the video and ultimately showed it to Joey, which resulted in their demise. To my surprise, Doc didn't question me about the details or attempt to engage in any further dialogue on the subject. His only words to me were, "Are you okay? What can I do to help you get through this?"

"Nothing. Just continue to give me your love and support. I care about you, and I hope that my dilemma doesn't cause you any embarrassment."

"I told you that I love you," he said, "and nothing is going to change that. Life is too short to let things like that get in the way of our happiness. Now let's eat before our dinner gets cold."

The evening continued to get better as night fell upon us. Doc and I showered together, made love, and then I fell asleep peacefully in his arms.

When I awoke the next morning, Doc was already gone. He called me just as I was pouring my coffee. "You must have really been tired. I tried to wake you, but you didn't budge. While I would have loved to sleep in with you this morning, I couldn't miss church today. Anyway, we have the rest of the day to spend together. Are you staying overnight again?"

"I'm sorry, but I have so much to do before I return to Detroit."

"I thought you would be home for at least two weeks."

"No, I'm leaving on Saturday. I told you that I couldn't leave Gigi alone in her condition. I'm the only one keeping her alive.

The rest of my siblings want to remove her life support. I can't let that happen, at least not yet."

"I understand," Doc replied. "Well, at least stay with me a few days before you leave."

"Okay, I'll try. I've got some business to prepare for Monday, so I'll come back tomorrow night. But we'll talk later. Love you."

Doc's reaction to my news of the sex video went over much better than I expected, especially given Doc's age and conservative values. Hopefully Chevy would be just as understanding.

Instead of using Skype, I called Chevy on his cell phone. "Hey sexy," he said. "Your roommate must be around, seeing as you're calling me on your cell phone."

As with my conversation with Doc, I decided not to skirt around the issue. "There's a sex video with me as the co-star that may go viral in the next few weeks."

"What did you just say?" Chevy asked. "What the hell are you talking about?"

"You heard me. I'm the co-star in a sex video that may hit the mass media in a few weeks. I can't say it any clearer than that."

Unlike Doc, Chevy wanted to know all the details. "You can't just blurt something out like this. I need to know more about your sex-capades. For starters, with whom, and when was it made, and why would you be so careless?"

"It's not that simple," I replied. "First of all, the video is fraudulent. The person who made the video cropped a picture of me and inserted it into the video. And because he's dead, I have no legal recourse."

"Wait a minute," Chevy said, "is this the same guy that Joey killed?"

"Yes, but that's irrelevant. What matters is the impact of the publicity on my loved ones."

"Astrid, how could you let something like this happen? In this day and age, you can't leave a sex video lying around. Your maid or anyone could have taken it."

"You're missing the fucking point!" I said. "This was not a keepsake that was stolen. The video is a fake! It's not me performing those sex acts; it's another woman. But that doesn't matter, because Marcus is dead, and it will be practically impossible to prove."

"I'm sorry," Chevy replied. "I wasn't trying to be insensitive. Forgive me, please."

"No problem. I just wanted to let you know before it's leaked to the media."

"I appreciate it, but I need to think about how best to handle the situation. I can't afford a scandal right now. I'm up for a new position with my company on top of dealing with this custody arrangement with my soon-to-be ex-wife. I can't be linked to any negative publicity right now."

"Okay, goodbye," I said and then hung up.

He called me back immediately, but I let his calls go straight to voicemail. So much for Chevy's compassion and empathy. It was a clear sign that he was not the kind of guy who would have my back and support me through life's storms. He was not the right man for me.

The next day, I finally accepted one of Chevy's calls. "Why don't we end this now before anything happens that might tarnish your image—"

"No, I'm sorry. I was being a jerk. I love you, and I'm not letting you get away from me again, not now or ever. Please forgive me for being so stupid." He paused. "I'll beg if I have to."

"Okay, I forgive you," I replied. "But listen, I've got a very busy week before I return to Detroit, so I won't have much time talk. But I miss you. Can you come for a visit while I'm there?"

"Absolutely. I'll make it happen. Take care of your business, babe, and get back to me when you can. I'm not going anywhere."

I could have used Chevy's initial response to my situation as a reason to end our relationship, which would have also allowed me to resolve my conflict between him and Doc. But I wasn't quite ready to let him go, even though his loyalty to me was now in question.

Now that my loved ones were informed about the sex video, the weight of the blackmail had lifted, but it was far from over. There were a lot of unanswered questions surrounding the blackmailer's true motive. I needed to do a little more work before I made any moves. Once it was behind me, I could focus on finding my biological father.

My first week at home was hectic. I planned to catch up with Zoe and Sage, but that proved difficult. I spent my days running around, taking care of business and most evenings with Doc while sneaking in a few Skype sessions with Chevy.

For some reason, Zoe had been calling me several times a day, but I was often too busy to take her calls. I did, however, manage to listen to her voicemails and reply to some of her text messages. I think she was struggling to adjust to motherhood. I warned her not take an extended maternity leave. With her Type-A workaholic personality, being a full-time mother would not be fulfilling. But she didn't take my advice, and she was probably going stir crazy.

It seemed that Sage and I were constantly missing each other as well. With the exception of her daily notes and the green health drink she made for me every morning, I could barely tell she was staying in the condo.

No matter how preoccupied I was during the day, the thought of my blackmail dilemma wouldn't go away. It often crept into the free space in my mind, reminding me that I had to decide how to deal with it soon.

Fifteen

Reconnecting with Burke

After disclosing the existence of the sex video to my family and the possibility of it going public, I thought I would feel relieved, but I didn't. The burden remained heavy on my mind. I couldn't fathom why someone wanted to blackmail me in the first place. As I pondered it, I was certain it wasn't about the money. What kind of blackmailer gave someone months to raise money? Such crimes usually occurred within days, not months. Even a two-bit street criminal knew to smash and dash when committing a crime to avoid being caught. Nope, this was not about my money; it never was. The reason was probably far worse than I could imagine.

After revisiting the obvious shortlist of suspects—Pilar, Marcus' family, or one of Joey's crazed fans—I quickly dismissed them. The blackmailer had to be someone who knew me and the circumstances surrounding the sex video, someone powerful enough to orchestrate this crime. I knew only one person who fit the bill: Burke. It was Burke who sent me copies of the sex video.

He assured me that he had sent me the original and the extra copies, but how could he have been certain no extra copies were circulating, and how could I be certain he was telling the truth? Nonetheless, given Burke's line of work and his highly unorthodox skills, anything was possible. One way or another, I would figure it out. If Burke wasn't the enemy, then maybe I could enlist his help.

I called Burke and asked for a meeting. Coincidently, he was in Atlanta, so he agreed to meet me for dinner. When I arrived at the restaurant, Burke was already seated and working on his second scotch. I ordered a shot of tequila and then quickly explained the issue at hand. "Someone is blackmailing me, and I think you know the source of it."

Startled by my abruptness, he choked on his drink before responding. "What are you talking about?"

"Don't act surprised, you know exactly what I'm talking about."

Red-faced and shocked, Burke was speechless as he stared at me.

"This ends now," I said. "Stop this immediately, or I'm going to the police and let the chips fall where they may."

"Astrid, let me assure that I don't know anything about you being blackmailed."

"Quit lying!" I replied. "I've done my homework. It's you; it can only be you.

"Astrid, I know your net worth, and a few extra million from you will have no effect on my bank account. Think about it: how would I benefit from blackmailing you?"

"Maybe not you directly, but perhaps one of your clients could."

"Astrid, you're paranoid. Think about your life and the circle of people in it. Who would hire me to blackmail you? I mean no disrespect, but I doubt very seriously that any one in my network knows you, let alone would have any interest in you. It's not like you're a celebrity or a political figure."

"Thanks a lot for letting me know that I'm a nobody," I said sarcastically.

"I'm sorry," he said. "That's not what I'm implying. I wanted to emphasize your importance to my constituents."

I paused as I thought about Burke's nameless clients. He was right. My life was simple, and none of his clients likely even knew me. I was back at square one.

"Okay, I need your help," I said finally. "I'm not paying the blackmailer, and I'm seriously considering getting the police involved." I explained the details surrounding the blackmail.

Burke shook his head in confusion. "Hold on; give me a week to look into this for you. If I don't get any answers, then I will notify the police with you."

For the first time since I'd known Burke, he wasn't his usual cocky self. He looked worried. I left him sitting at the bar nursing his third scotch. I knew he was not being completely forthcoming with me. He obviously had his suspicions about the source of the blackmail, but perhaps he was confused about the culprit and the reasons behind it.

I went back home, still stressed over the situation. However, I decided to take Burke's advice and wait for him to get back to me.

As I scanned my email, I saw Mr. Brown's name. As discussed, he had sent me the final invoice and two separate reports: one on Ricky and one on Di. I decided to ignore Ricky's report and read Di's instead. It essentially reflected the story she had told me on the recording. It said she had been working for Mr. Paul Rackham while living in the woman's shelter. She moved in with him as a full-time housekeeper, and later they became romantically involved. However, months later, they parted ways, and Di ended up pregnant and incarcerated. The timeline stopped there and then restarted with my birth and adoption in Detroit. Mr. Brown went on to note that Dianne had a long petty criminal record with time served in several correction facilities over a twenty-five-year stretch. In closing, he said, "My gut says Di was pregnant with you, and the father is most likely Paul Rackham. I don't have to tell you about the Rackhams' fortune; they own everything. Hope this helps."

Even though Mr. Brown was a day late on Paul's identity, it did validate what Di said about him being my father. However, while I should have been comforted by the news, my priority was unraveling my blackmailer's identity.

I replied to Mr. Brown's email, thanking him for his services and letting him know that his final check was in the mail.

A week later, Burke contacted me and arranged for us to meet again. He said that he found some information that may be of interest to me. I hoped that he had uncovered the source of the blackmail.

When I arrived at the hotel lounge where Burke was staying, he looked worried. "Astrid, when you resumed your search for your biological mother, it likely made some people nervous, because finding her would inevitably lead to the identity of your biological father, which I suspect is the real reason behind the blackmail. I believe the blackmail scheme was only meant to be a diversionary tactic. They were hoping it would distract you from your search, redirecting your attention elsewhere. I'm aware that you recently met and, unfortunately, buried your mother in Detroit. Perhaps she told you about her love affair with Paul Rackham." I nodded, so he continued. "Astrid, the Rackhams are very important people, and they are clients of mine."

"That doesn't surprise me," I said, "but I'm curious, when did you learn about my connection to the Rackham family?"

Burke told me that, years earlier when I was attending college and attempting to search for Di, I set off a chain of events. Ironically, while I was searching for Di, someone in the Rackham family was also looking into her whereabouts and stumbled upon me in the process. Since I had to disclose my relationship as Di's daughter during my investigation, my existence must have rattled a few cages with the Rackham family. Mrs. Rackham contacted Burke to track down Di and her baby to assess if damage control was needed.

Burke hired a private investigator and found that Di was lost in the spirals of her drug addiction and that she had given me up for adoption. He subsequently learned that I had been adopted by my grandmother and living a normal life under the impression that my father was an unknown patron of prostitution. Since I quickly abandoned my search for my mother and resumed my focus as wife and mother, no intervention was required. Hence, neither Di nor I were considered a threat to the Rackhams and were left alone, though we remained on their radar. However, for some reason Di seemed less of a concern to them than me. Burke was instructed to keep an eye on me to make sure I did not become a problem. So, he had been keeping tabs on me since I was in my early twenties.

Hence, my introductory meeting with Burke in the Carlton suites in Atlanta was not a coincidence. He arranged his stay there, so he could meet me. Helping me after the incident with Joey was not only for my benefit; it was for the Rackhams as well.

Burke often said, "A good journalist will create a story where there isn't one. They have a way of digging up dirt from the smallest crevices in one's life. They can easily and often do make something out of nothing." So, Burke had done what he did best: he manipulated the media to focus on the sensationalized three-ring circus of my relationship with Joey and Marcus. And it worked. The media remained focus on my present life and never looked into my past. Thus, my origin was never mentioned in the press.

Unbeknownst to me, Burke told me he had recently paid Mrs. Rackham a visit to provide an update on the matters he was managing for her family. As he ran down the list, he mentioned that Dianne was now deceased, hoping to get a reaction from her. But Mrs. Rackham maintained her usual stoic, ice-cold demeanor.

"Has something else happened that I should be concerned about?" she asked.

"No, I'm just doing the usual monitoring regarding these matters."

"Okay. You will let me know if something's wrong and then you'll take care of it, right?"

"No worries, Mrs. Rackham. I'll be in touch if there's a problem."

Knowing Mrs. Rackham's deceptive and deadly track record, Burke didn't believe a word she said. In fact, it was her calm demeanor that tipped her hand. Now Burke was certain that either she or someone from her clan was behind the blackmail. But why? They certainly didn't need the money.

Burke had an even greater concern. It seemed that Mrs. Rackham was no longer engaging him in matters of this nature. He wondered if she had doubts about his loyalty. He needed to get a handle on the situation. Mrs. Rackham was no one to trifle with. It was rumored that her family had a history of ties to the mob. There was no limit to what she would do under the auspices of protecting her family and their good name. He could potentially be in danger.

"Astrid, my only advice to you is to continue living your life as normal. I wouldn't worry about paying the blackmailer. I think the sex video will simply disappear. However, I cannot stress this enough: do not attempt to contact anyone in the Rackham family. They're very powerful. They've seated several presidents, you know. Their legacy goes back for generations. Mrs. Rackham is more dangerous than the men in her family; she'll stop at nothing to protect their dynasty. She will not welcome you into her family. Even if Paul does, she'll find a way to get rid of you. Let it go."

"Okay, I won't contact Paul or anyone else in his family," I replied.

As I was about to leave, I turned back. "Burke, there's still the matter of the sex video. Since someone or possibly some people have copies of it, what's to keep me from being blackmailed later? Maybe I should stick to my original plan and preemptively release the video myself. I don't want to profit from it; I just don't want it hanging over my head."

"Astrid, I made sure that Marcus' place was swept clean when we were looking for copies of the video. Only two people had possession of the videos: me and . . .." Burke paused without completing his sentence.

"Who?" I asked. "How do you know for certain that one of Marcus' houseguests didn't take a copy, or the police for that matter?"

"I have a hunch about the other person who might be involved," he said finally, "but I need to look into it further. Astrid, I need you to be patient awhile longer before you make any decisions about releasing the video. Just hold on. I promise I will get to the bottom of this, okay?"

"Okay, but if it's released, I expect you to clean up the fallout free of charge."

He smiled, but I could tell that he was still distressed about the situation. "This changes nothing. My advice to you is still the same. Do not contact the Rackhams, or be prepared to face your demise. I won't be able to do anything to help you if you do. Nor will anybody else."

Burke threw back his double shot of whisky and then patted my shoulder as he stood up. "Take care, I'll be in touch soon."

Burke's character was unrecognizable to me. He seemed petrified. I was more concerned about him than my blackmail dilemma.

Sixteen

Her Final Transition

After meeting with Burke, I decided to stay in Atlanta an additional week to tidy up a few more things before returning to Detroit.

I usually called Deana every day to get an update on Gigi. Unfortunately, her prognosis was always the same, which was not good news. I had been praying harder than I had ever prayed before, asking God to heal Gigi and let me have her awhile longer. I even promised to get married and stop fornicating if God gave me a little more time with her. So, every day that she was alive gave me hope. I honestly felt that she would recover from her stroke and be healthy once again. But it seemed I was the only one who believed that. Even Deana, with her devout religious beliefs, was not optimistic about Gigi's recovery.

I had spent the last two days with Doc and did not call Deana for my usual updates on Gigi. Since she had not called me, I assumed everything was okay. After Doc dropped me off at the airport on Saturday morning, I had a few minutes to spare, so I called Deana, but her phone went to voicemail. I texted her my arrival time and let her know that I planned to stop by the house and then go straight to the hospital to see Gigi. However, when I landed in Detroit, I still had not heard from her.

By the time, I arrived at Gigi's house, it was about three o'clock. I saw a few cars parked in the driveway, but when I entered the house, no one was there. That was odd. An eerie feeling came over me as looked around the quiet, empty house. I stopped dead in my tracks and dropped my suitcases where I stood. Then I jumped in my rental car and drove to the hospital.

I went straight to Gigi's room, but she wasn't there. I panicked and asked the nurse if she had been moved to another room.

"I'll check for you," the nurse replied. As she looked at her computer screen, I saw a concerned look come over her face. "Give me a minute," she said as she paged the doctor. That's when I knew that something was wrong.

Minutes later, Gigi's doctor approached me. "She's already been transferred."

"What are you talking about?" I asked. "Who transferred my mother, and where did they take her?"

He paused for a few seconds, but it felt like hours. "Your two sisters—Deana and your other sister, the physician from Boston, had her body moved to the funeral home."

The phrase "had her body moved to the funeral home" echoed in my head. Then I felt my legs give way. I gasped for air, as if I was choking. The pain of Gigi's death emanated from my toes and ran up through my entire body, culminating into a vocal explosion. I let out a scream that seemed to reverberate throughout the hospital. As the doctor held me, tears gushed from my eyes, blurring my vision. I struggled to catch my breath as the nurses gathered around me. I felt faint as they lifted me onto a stretcher and wheeled me into the emergency room. I vaguely saw the nurses and doctors scurrying around me, and then I heard someone say I was going into shock.

Hours later, I awoke with Deana standing over me and holding my hands. "Astrid, I'm sorry. I didn't want you to find out this way. Last night, Gigi was removed from the breathing machine, and she slipped away early this morning. Since you were already on your way here, I thought it was best to tell you after you had arrived."

Just then, the doctor entered. "I need to check your vitals one last time," he said. "If everything looks fine, you're free to go home." After looking at my chart and examining me he said, "Your vitals are good; you can go home now. I'll give you a prescription to help you get through this difficult time. Just stop by the pharmacy before you leave."

As Deana and I were leaving, a nurse handed Deana a large white envelope. "You must have forgotten these papers when you were here earlier today," the nurse said

Since Deana was pushing me in a wheelchair, I took the envelope. "Let me drive you home," Deana said, "and we'll come back tomorrow and get your car."

I could tell Deana was not herself She was unusually quiet, as if she was lost for words. Any other time, she would have been lecturing me and quoting Bible scriptures about death. Perhaps Gigi's loss was more than she could bear.

"What are these papers?" I asked as we drove home.

"Oh, just hospital stuff, the papers they make you sign when someone has passed away. Don't look at them; they will just make you more upset."

For some reason, I decided to look inside the envelope anyway. I poured the papers onto my lap. On top was a legal document that had recently been notarized. It said that Nikki had been given medical power of attorney over Gigi and that she had instructed the hospital to remove Gigi from the breathing machine. I continued looking through the papers and saw that Nikki had petitioned the court for medical power of attorney days after Gigi was hospitalized. Her secret legal actions had been in the works for weeks. No wonder she had stopped pressing us to make a decision about Gigi's breathing machine. She had this planned all along.

Deana looked over at me. "Listen, I didn't know anything about this medical power of attorney stuff. Nikki did this behind my back and everyone else's too. She tricked me into signing some papers awhile back, so I couldn't contest what she was trying to do. I'm an attorney; I should have known better than to sign anything without reading it. But that's my fault for trusting her. I never thought she would go that far. By the time I realized what she had done, it was too late. I was wondering why she kept showing up in town unexpectedly for no apparent reason. Luckily, one of the nurses called me and asked if I wanted to be there when they removed Gigi from the breathing machine; otherwise, I would not have known about it. Nikki didn't even bother to show up for Gigi's last hours. She only came to the hospital after she was notified that Gigi had passed away.

"Astrid, I know what you're thinking, but Gigi's gone now. We have to let her rest in peace. I think eventually we all would have made the same decision. Nikki just forced us to do it sooner."

I heard Deana talking, but I wasn't really listening to anything she said. My emotions were all over the place. I felt betrayed and hurt. More importantly, I felt angry. "That bitch," I whispered.

When we pulled up to Gigi's house, there were more cars parked nearby, so I knew people were in the house. Before we got out of the car, Deana grabbed my hand. "Astrid, let it go. Nikki will have to answer to God for her behavior, not to me or you."

I didn't respond. I just grabbed my purse and the envelope, got out of the car, and then slammed the door as hard as I could.

When I entered the house, several of my siblings and Gigi's close friends were seated throughout. I barely acknowledged them as my eyes bore into Nikki. She was standing in front of the fireplace, smiling and drinking tea, as if she was at a pleasurable social gathering. She smirked at me, as if to let me know she had got one over on me. At that moment she reminded me of the deceptive hurts that Philip had inflicted on me.

I dropped my purse and the envelope and went straight for Nikki. I grabbed her by her neck and pushed her to the floor. Then I punched her repeatedly as hard as I could With every blow, I saw a flashback of everyone who had ever hurt me, starting with Nikki when we were kids. I saw images of her pinching me and kicking me when no one was looking. Then I saw images of Ricky, Philip, Pilar, and finally, Marcus.

By the time the others pulled me off her, I was out of breath, and Nikki's face was covered in blood. "You're crazy!" she screamed. "I'm going to have you committed. Then you can be roommates in the same mental hospital with your real mother."

I tried to break loose from my brother's arm and let Nikki have it again. I felt like a raving animal. I didn't care if I hurt her. As far I was concerned, she deserved an ass kicking. It was long overdue.

Shaken from the altercation, Nikki went into the powder room. Deana grabbed my arm. "Astrid, have you lost your mind? You know Gigi would not approve of you behaving this way. Stop this right now!"

Shortly thereafter, Nikki emerged wearing sunglasses and carrying her jacket. Some of my siblings gathered around her, comforting her as she walked to the front door. I'm sure they had no idea why we were fighting or what she had done to Gigi.

By then I had calmed down and went into my bedroom. I sat on my bed, put my face in my hands, and began to cry. I felt like I was becoming unglued. While I had experienced the loss of Joey, it paled in comparison to losing Gigi. I was filled with anxiety and totally discombobulated. I started panicking, looking in my purse and in drawers, hoping to find a least one marijuana cigarette hidden somewhere, but to no avail.

Deana must have heard me crying. She came in my room and sat beside me and started humming lyrics from, "Jesus Loves Me."

I looked at Deana through my teary eyes. "Nikki had no right to take Gigi from me."

"You're giving Nikki too much power," Deana replied. "She didn't take Gigi away from us. It was her time to be with our Lord; otherwise, she would be here."

I turned to Deana and hugged her. "Thank you for everything. I'm tired. I'm going to take a shower and turn in early. This day has been too much for me."

While I was showering, I heard people whispering, but I couldn't make out what they were saying.

"Who's out there?" I shouted, but no one answered. At first, I thought it was the television, but then I remembered that I hadn't turned it on. Then the whispering suddenly stopped and I didn't think anything more about it.

I decided I would make the dreaded phone calls the next day. I took one of the pills the doctor gave me to help me sleep. As I laid in bed, I kept having thoughts of Gigi lying in her hospital bed. Even though she was in a coma, it had given me comfort knowing she was still alive. Now I felt afraid and alone. I wasn't sure how I was going to make it through the rest of my life without her. I guess I would find out soon enough.

The next morning, I called Junior and a few close friends and told them about Gigi's passing, and they all confirmed they would attend the funeral services. However, when I spoke to Sage, she said she would come to Detroit to support me, but she wasn't sure she would attend the funeral. I didn't try to persuade her otherwise.

Deana and I were at the funeral home as soon as it opened. Gigi had made her funeral arrangements in advance, so there was little for us to do except to see that her wishes were carried out.

By the time we arrived, she was already dressed and being prepared for viewing. She had the same peaceful look on her face that Di had when she passed away, but that gave me little comfort. However, to my surprise, I wasn't grief-stricken, perhaps because I was in denial or possibly, in shock.

Later that evening, I received text messages from Chevy and Doc that they had arrived in Detroit and wanted to see me, if I was up to it. I made up an excuse and decided not to see either of them.

The following day, we gathered at Gigi's church for a private family viewing. Clearly, the family was divided over the altercation Nikki and I had the previous day. Instead of sitting together as a family in the church pews, we were seated separately, on opposite sides of the church. Nikki and the other three youngest female siblings and their families sat on one side while the rest of us sat on the other. There we were, chocolate on one side and vanilla and caramel seated together on the other side. Gigi would have a fit if she knew we were behaving divisively. While she never allowed us to engage in discussions about the varied skin color of her children, it was always a subtle line of division among us. John Jr. seemed to be the only one indifferent about it.

After the viewing, I walked around the sanctuary, and I noticed neither Zoe nor Sage were there. Apparently, Zoe's baby was ill, so she could not make it. I never heard from Sage regarding her whereabouts.

Eventually, I made my way to the restroom, where I stumbled upon Sage. She was behaving strangely, as if she were hiding from someone. "I'm sorry I didn't come into the sanctuary," she whispered, "but I'm very uncomfortable at funerals. However, I wanted to let you know that I'm staying at the Westin if you need me."

"How long are you staying?" I asked.

"Maybe a week or two. Is that okay?"

"Let me introduce you to my family."

"No, I'm not feeling well. Maybe some other time."

That night, I was unable to sleep, so I packed a few things and went to the hotel where Sage was staying. I told her about my fight with Nikki and how it left me feeling.

"Close your eyes," she said. "I have something for you. I would never do this, but under the circumstances, it may be warranted."

When I opened my eyes, she had a few marijuana cigarettes for me. Sage knew exactly what I needed. I poured a glass of wine as I smoked my joint. My buzz kicked in, and I felt better and finally went to sleep.

The next morning, I arrived at Gigi's house just in time to get in one of the limousines. When I climbed in, my brother, John Jr., and his wife, Deana, and Junior, were already seated. The drive to the church was quiet and surreal. I felt like I was dreaming, but I knew I wasn't.

"Astrid, do you want a nurse or deacon to sit with you?" Deana asked.

"No, I'll be fine." I lied, I was feeling anxious. Deep inside, I was scared beyond my wits. I was terrified of not having Gigi around and scared about navigating the rest of my life without her. As old as I was, I was still a mama's girl, Gigi's baby girl. Nonetheless, the last thing I wanted was to have a meltdown in front of all those people. I kept telling myself not to fall apart at church.

I was numb throughout the service, except at the end, when they closed Gigi's casket. That's when my body started trembling. Then I heard a familiar voice say, "It's okay. I'm here now." Confused, I looked around, but no one was there. As I scanned the church, there wasn't a dry eye anywhere. Hours later, we laid Gigi to rest next to Di at the Woodlawn cemetery.

In keeping with tradition, we gathered at a restaurant for the repast. That's when I made my way over to Chevy. I was careful not to spend too much time with him, so as not to arouse any suspicions that we were dating. I did the same thing when I saw Doc, but Doc informed me that he had a crisis at home, and he was leaving early, returning to Atlanta. Things couldn't have worked out any better if I had planned it.

Junior wasn't able to stay long either, so I suggested he hitch a ride with Doc to the airport. That left me free to spend time with Chevy.

As I walked Doc and Junior to Doc's rental car, Doc seemed unusually quiet. Then he leaned in close. "Astrid, I'm not blind or stupid. When you get back to Atlanta, I want this extra-curricular shit with your boyfriend done, or it's over between us."

Shocked, I didn't respond. I just hugged him and Junior as I said my goodbyes.

I went back into the restaurant, where Chevy's piercing eyes were focused on me. I walked over to him and thanked him for coming.

"Well, you can thank me properly by coming to my hotel and staying the night with me," he said. "Besides, I have something very pleasing to share with you."

I smiled. "Okay, but I need to go to Gigi's house first and pack a few things."

By the time I made it back to Gigi's house, Nikki and her family were already there. She and I made eye contact but nothing more.

When I went into my room, I noticed some pamphlets lying on the nightstand. I glanced at them and saw they were about schizophrenia.

Minutes later, there was knock at door. It was Nikki. "Before you say anything, let me say I'm sorry about the way I handled the situation with Gigi's medical decision. I knew you and Deana would have left her on that machine for years. Gigi was my mother too, and I couldn't bear to see her body kept alive by a machine."

"She was breathing on her own," I said. "She just needed a little assistance."

"Astrid, you're in denial. I'm a doctor. Doesn't that count for something? If she were able to breathe independently, she would not have passed away."

"I don't believe you. You killed our mother, and I'll never forgive you for it."

"I didn't kill her; I simply let nature take its course. I hope you find it in your heart to forgive me one day." She paused. "I left those medical brochures for you. I know about Di's medical condition and that it deteriorated such that she was catatonic and placed in an institution somewhere up north. I also read Gigi's journals, so I know it's in her bloodline."

I didn't bother to correct her on the status of Di's condition. I just let her continue running her mouth.

"Astrid, I know you're angry with me, but you need to read that literature. If Di has schizophrenia, it's a strong possibility that you inherited it. Look, I'm not trying to hurt you. I only want to help you before it's too late. You need to at least consult with a psychiatrist. I'm concerned about you. Remember, we grew up together. I know things about you that the others don't. The way you used to play by yourself for hours with your imaginary friends and the way you fall apart every time you have a crisis. I'm concerned that since Gigi's gone, another big disaster is waiting for you."

"Listen, I'm an accomplished grown-ass woman, and I'll be okay," I replied. "In case you forgot, I'm a Kokuran."

"Don't give me that crazy Creole talk. You see what it did for Gigi? It landed her in an early grave."

I took a deep breath to keep from going ballistic on her. "Are you finished?"

She shook her head. "Astrid, that type of mental disorder will only get worse if left untreated."

I didn't feel like arguing with her, so to placate her, I said, I'd take a look at the brochures. Then she walked over and gave me a fake hug. "Goodbye," she said as she closed my door.

You stupid bitch, I thought. *You have no idea what you're talking about. Di is already dead, lying in an unmarked grave next to Gigi.*

I didn't believe anything that came out of Nikki's mouth. She was just like Philip, a complete narcissist. If anything, she needed psychotherapy. Walking around for years filled with hatred. She was the spitting image of her daddy, Big John, and she hated it. She had his skin color, his hair texture, and his gargantuan build. I always thought she was a tall exotic beauty. But like so many people, including myself, she struggled to see her own beauty.

After Nikki left, I found my mind drifting. Thoughts of Gigi crept in my head. I missed her, and an overwhelming wave of fear came over me. Then I heard the whispering again, but this time it sounded like chanting, similar to the background music in a horror film, creating a foreboding mood. I grabbed my head and shouted, "Be quiet!"

Just like that, it was silent. I thought it was strange, but I didn't dwell on it.

Seventeen

Unleashed

Earlier that day, I received several alerts on my phone that Mr. Brown had sent an email. I decided to check it before I left to meet Chevy. The email was essentially a formal notification that my case was being closed and asked if I had any final questions. That's when I decided to look at the report he had sent on Ricky a few weeks earlier.

It stated that Ricky had been incarcerated on and off for the last twenty years for varying degrees of sexual assault. Most recently, he had been linked to several unsolved rape cases in the Detroit area. However, he managed to avoid prosecution for those crimes. Apparently, he never left any DNA on his victims.

Reading the report angered me. It opened up an old wound, taking me back to when I was only eight years old, when he assaulted me. Something in me felt as if I could kill him if the opportunity ever presented itself. I closed my iPad and decided to switch my mindset to something more pleasant, like seeing Chevy, my tall, sexy chocolate deliciousness in the next hour.

As I packed my overnight bag, Deana called. "I hope you're still home. I need a favor from you. I left a package in my room, and I need you to bring it to me right away. Can you? I'm here at Gigi's church."

"Sure, I don't mind. I'll be there shortly."

Since nightfall was fast approaching, I decided to take Gigi's gun with me for safety. The last thing I needed was to get caught in that neighborhood without protection.

As I was about to pull off in my car, Sage startled me when she knocked on my window. I opened the door to let her in.

"Why are you dressed like that?" I asked. "All covered up, wearing a hoodie and sweat pants? You know you look like a teenage gangbanger, right?"

She looked at her attire and smiled. "Well, I went jogging and found myself in this area. When I realized it was about to rain, I detoured here, hoping you could give me a ride back to my hotel."

"Where have you been, and why are you carrying that backpack?" I asked. She didn't respond, so I continued. "When I didn't see you at Gigi's repast dinner, I assumed you left and went back to Atlanta."

"No, I went back to my hotel. You had enough people around. Besides, after what you told me about your sister, Nikki, I decided to stay away. I didn't need her interrogating me about you."

"Why don't you ride with me to the church, so we can catch up? Then I'll take you to your hotel."

"Sounds good to me."

As I drove, I told Sage about my conversation with Doc and his suspicions about Chevy.

"Astrid, leading on both of those men is not right. You need to stop fooling around before someone gets hurt. They both seem to genuinely care for you. You can't have it all. Just pick one, and then step out in faith like all other married people."

"You're right," I replied. "I'll make a decision this week, and I think I know who it's going to be."

By then, it was raining harder. I pulled up in front of the church and ran to the door, where Deana was waiting. I jumped out of the car and handed her the package.

"Where are you going in this nasty weather?" she asked.

I pointed to the car. "My friend Sage rode with me to the church. I'm taking her back to her hotel, and then I'm going to see my friend Chevy."

Deana leaned over slightly, straining to see inside the car. "It's raining so hard, I can't see anything. I don't see anybody. These reading glasses aren't worth two cents."

Confused by Deana's remarks, I thought, *She's getting old and turning into Gigi, but without the sex.*

As I pulled out the church parking lot, I saw a man walking briskly in the rain wearing a long black overcoat, holding an umbrella, and carrying a small grocery bag. Instinctively, my gut said it was Ricky. I drove closer to him and, sure enough, it was. Without uttering a word to Sage, I parked, grabbed Gigi's gun from my purse, and put it in my jacket pocket. Then I jumped out of the car and began following him.

"Astrid, what's wrong?" Sage shouted, getting out of the car. "Where are you going?" Ignoring her, I continued following him into the same apartment building I'd seen him enter before.

I stopped and shouted his name. He turned and looked at me. "Excuse me, Miss, but do I know you?"

"Perhaps you don't recognize me, since I'm not an eight-year-old child anymore. They should have thrown away the key when they locked you up the first time. I've seen your record; you graduated from raping little girls to raping grown women. You're an animal. They should have euthanized you."

He walked closer to me with a crooked grin on his face. "Oh, I know who you are. You're Gigi's little girl, Astrid." He shook his head as he stared at me the way a male lion looks at its prey. "Mmm, you're all grown up and still fine as all outdoors."

What happened next is a blur to me. "Stop," I said, my hand clutching Gigi's gun in my pocket. "Don't move any closer."

Ignoring my words, he continued toward me. "You followed me in here, so you must want some more of what I gave you before, but I'm going to finish it this time."

Before I could react, he grabbed me by my neck and dragged me into a janitorial closet. During the commotion, the gun fell out of my jacket, so I was defenseless. Somehow, he managed to pin me down and straddle his body on top of mine while holding a switchblade at my neck and unzipping his pants. Then, out of nowhere, a teenage boy appeared wearing a dark hoodie. He shot Ricky several times. All I heard was a loud pop, pop, pop! Blood splattered everywhere.

"Come on, Astrid," the boy said. "Let's get out of here."

Shocked by what had just unfolded right before my eyes, I just stood there, wondering who the boy was and how he knew my name.

The teenage boy stood up and fixed his hoodie. That's when I realized that it wasn't a boy at all; it was Sage.

"Sage, what have you done?

"Astrid, he was going to rape you again, but this time he was going to kill you. You know he's a serial rapist, and so do the police. They just don't have enough evidence to arrest him." She smirked. "Don't act so surprised. You knew this day would come. It lined up perfectly with our plans. Remember? We talked about it a few months ago."

I had no idea what Sage was talking about, but now was not the time to try to figure it out. We ran back to my car. Sage changed from her blood-soaked clothes and put them in her backpack, which she handed to me. "You need to burn this," she said. "You were never here. You have to behave as if nothing happened. You should go visit Chevy, as planned. I'll take a cab to my hotel, and then we can meet up tomorrow."

Still speechless, I said nothing.

"Astrid, shake it off. Pull yourself together. Drive normally, and don't say a word to anyone about what happened tonight, or both of us could end up in prison."

I drove to a nearby drugstore, where a cabstand was located, so Sage could get back to her hotel. Before she got out of the car, she gave me a slight slap on my face. "Astrid, promise you'll keep your mouth shut. You can't tell a soul."

"I promise."

I didn't bother to wait for Sage to get into a cab; I simply drove off. I was in such a frantic state that I couldn't remember how I made it to Chevy's hotel. I thought I was losing my mind, my grip on reality. Everything was a blur, as if the past few hours had not occurred. It seemed as if it was another bad dream, until I looked inside Sage's backpack and realized it was all too real.

I must have sat in the parking lot for at least an hour before I finally got out of my car. After much thought, I realized that Sage was right. I should stick with my original plans for the evening, and everything would be alright.

By the time I made it to Chevy's room, it was late. Not thinking clearly, I had grabbed the backpack along with my overnight bag.

"What took you so long?" Chevy asked as he opened the door. "I expected you hours ago. You seem frazzled, and you're soaking wet. Are you okay?" I didn't reply as he hugged me. "Take a warm shower and relax a bit," he said. "Then we can get our night started."

The last thing on my mind was sex, but Chevy was right about one thing: I needed to decompress. My anxiety level was through the roof, and my blood pressure probably was too. At any moment, my cork could pop.

I started the shower and turned the temperature to its hottest level. Once the steam was forming, I climbed in and sat down in the corner, trying to process how the night had unfolded. I had buried Gigi earlier in the day, and that night I had watched one of my best friends kill a person in cold blood. I had no idea what tomorrow would bring. I was worried sick. Should I go to the police and turn Sage in or wait for the police to find us? The longer I waited, the worse the consequences would be. For the moment, however, I decided to do nothing and see what the next day would bring.

Chevy knocked on the door. "Astrid, baby, are you alright? Do you need me to throw you a rescue line? You've been in there for forty-five minutes. There isn't that much dirt in China."

Minutes later, I emerged wearing the hotel's guest robe. I noticed Chevy had ordered room service, everything necessary to set the mood, including a food tray with oysters and a bottle Boërl & Kroff Brut champagne. While he was obviously in a romantic mood, he sensed that I was not. Chevy handed me a glass of champagne. "I know you're grieving about your mother, but I have some good news that might cheer you up a bit. I was going to wait until later to tell you this, but I think this is as good a time as any. My soon-to-be ex-wife has agreed to my settlement offer and visitation schedule with my daughter, so the only thing left is for the court to ratify the divorce."

"That's good," I said. "The sooner your divorce is final, the sooner you can move on with your life."

"There's more," he replied. "I was offered a new position with my firm; it's actually a promotion. I have a choice to either stay in Chicago or work out of our office in Atlanta. So, baby, you know what that means. We can start our new life together. I'm moving to Atlanta next month, and as soon as my divorce is final, I'm putting a ring on it and making you my wife. And I don't care what anyone might think or say about it. You are the love my life, and I want the world to know. Besides, we have a lot of lost time to make up. I love you, and you love me, and that's all that matters. I want to spend the rest of my life with you, and I want to start immediately."

Hearing Chevy's loving words made me realize how much he really loved me. At that moment, I knew he was the one for me. I would not make the same mistake I made with Joey and play games with the man I loved. Once I returned to Atlanta, I would end my relationship with Doc, and then I would be free to embark on the rest of my life with Chevy.

Chevy was right; it wasn't a mere coincidence that we had experienced a special connection for so many years. We belonged together; perhaps we were soulmates.

"Baby, you don't look happy about my news," Chevy said, studying my face.

"I'm very happy about your news," I replied, "but I'm still feeling despair from losing Gigi. The pain is deep and piercing; it's like nothing I've ever experienced. Please, understand. I'm excited about our future together, but I need a little time to close this gaping hole in my heart." Truthfully, I was more worried about what Sage had done to Ricky than Chevy's unexpurgated love for me.

Chevy sat down next to me and took my hand. "Baby, talk to me. You seem anxious and lost in your thoughts. Tell me what's on your mind. Don't hold back. We're about to be married soon and become one unit. What affects you also affects me and vice versa. Let me carry some of your burdens. You don't have to bear them alone."

As I thought about the promise I made to Sage, I pondered whether or not to tell Chevy what had happened. After all, Chevy wasn't just anyone; he was going to be my husband and life partner. Surely he would stand by my side and support me through anything. He had often professed his unconditional love for me.

I set my glass on the table and turned to Chevy. "Something really bad happened tonight, worse than anything you could imagine."

"What?" he asked while rubbing my shoulder and speaking in his sexy, comforting voice. "Maybe I can help."

"The problem is not with me but with my roommate, Sage."

"I've heard you talk about her, but you've never introduced us. Was she at the funeral service today?"

"Yes, briefly, but that's not the issue. She did something really bad, and I don't know what to do or whether I should tell you or anyone else what happened. Sage made me promise not to say anything about tonight. Besides, you may feel differently toward me after."

"Baby, nothing can be that bad. I love you, and nothing can tear us apart. I want to spend the rest of my life with you, which means through the ups and the downs."

I remained quiet, still unsure about sharing the night's dramatic events with him. Chevy waited patiently for me to continue. Finally, I blurted it out. "I witnessed Sage kill a man tonight."

"What?" Chevy shouted.

I explained how I had been molested by Ricky when I was a little girl and haunted by it my entire life. I also told him that I had shared my story with Sage and how upset she became by it. And when we saw Ricky earlier tonight as we were leaving the church, Sage followed him and killed him.

Chevy stared at me in disbelief, shaking his head slowly. "Astrid, none of this makes any sense. Why would Sage do such a thing?"

Before he could say another word, I unzipped Sage's backpack and showed him the bloody clothes and the gun. He stared inside the backpack for several minutes.

"Astrid, where did you get this gun?"

"It's Gigi's gun."

Then he pointed at the hoodie. "Is that the hoodie I gave you on my last visit to Detroit?"

I didn't respond. He took a clothing hanger and partially pulled out the hoodie, revealing his company's logo embroidered on the front. I was speechless. I hadn't noticed that Sage was wearing my hoodie.

"Well, Sage and I are roommates. She has access to everything in my place. We borrow each other's clothing from time to time. Perhaps she borrowed it without my knowledge."

"You told me you were leaving it in Detroit, so you would have something comfortable to lounge in. So, you must have given it to her. How else would she have gotten it?'

"I don't know. Why are you questioning me as if you don't believe me?"

"Baby, I believe you, but all this sounds so strange. This is very serious; a crime has been committed. We have to contact the police."

"But I didn't do anything. I had no idea that Sage was going to kill Ricky."

"But you were there when it happened. Do you know how that looks? You could be implicated in his murder. Even worse, how do you know you're not in danger? If Sage killed a man in cold blood right in front of you, what makes you think she won't come after you?" Worried and almost in tears, Chevy hugged me. "Oh my god, baby, how did you get into this mess?" He paused and stepped back. "Where is Sage? Do you have a photo of her?"

"No," I said, feeling confused. "Oh wait, we took a photo together at her yoga studio. I may still have it."

I scrolled through the photos on my phone until I found the picture taken during the grand opening. We were all wearing T-shirts with our names inscribed on them. I pulled up the image and enlarged it. "That's Sage, the woman standing in the middle of the group."

Chevy was perplexed by the photo. He stared at it for a long time. "Are you sure that's her?"

"Of course. Her name is written on her T-shirt."

Chevy looked at me as if he had seen a ghost. He shook his head slowly. "This can't be true. Astrid, you need to go back to your mother's house, and I'll figure something out. Don't say a word to anyone else about what you told me tonight. I'll call you in the morning, and then we'll take it from there."

"You want me to leave? But what about Sage? She knows where Gigi's house is. What if she comes after me?"

He didn't respond immediately. I saw tears in his eyes as he tried to rub them away. "I don't think you have to worry about Sage harming you. She has too much to lose."

Chevy helped me gather my things and then hugged me as we said goodbye. "Leave your backpack with me," he said. "I'll take care of it for you."

At first, I was confused by his request, but I trusted him, so I did as he asked.

"Baby, go home, and go straight to sleep. It's late, so I'll call you in the morning. Trust me; everything will be okay."

That was odd. It felt like Chevy had just thrown me out of his hotel room. But I felt relieved that I had shared my dilemma with him and that he was going to make sure everything was okay. Until then, I hadn't realized that Chevy was also a caretaker, my kind of man.

I did exactly what Chevy said. I went to Gig's house and popped a few of the pills the doctor gave me and then fell sound asleep.

The next morning, I called Chevy, but he didn't answer his phone, nor did the call go to his voicemail. That meant only one thing: he had blocked my calls. I called Sage, and the same thing happened.

When I turned on the morning news, Ricky's death was a breaking story. However, because he was a suspect in several unsolved rape cases, neither the media nor the police showed much empathy. In fact, they intimated that justice had been served and that his case would likely remain unsolved. After hearing that, I breathed a sigh of relief.

Over the next few days, I tried calling Chevy at work, but he was always unavailable for one reason or another. After several more attempts, he finally returned my call. His voice was almost unrecognizable. It wasn't the sweet, sexy voice that I had been conversing with over the past year. "Hello," he said sternly. "I know what happened to Ricky. I saw the report on the morning news before I left Detroit. I also threw your backpack and its contents into the hotel's incinerator. So I guess you're in the clear for now." He paused. "I'm sorry, Astrid, but I can't do this with you. It's over. Please leave me alone, and don't ever contact me again. You really need to get some help. Goodbye."

Just like that, he hung up. I burst into tears. I was deeply confused. I wondered how he could so easily flip the script on me and what I had done to cause him to behave that way. I was heartbroken yet again, but I had no choice but to respect his wishes.

Then the voice emerged again with an unfettered boldness. *That's good that he left on his own. That motherfucker was too weak for you anyway. Okay, enough wasting time discussing his punk ass. Men are and will forever be the least of your problems. Now that Gigi's gone, your business in Detroit is done. Let's get the fuck out of here and never look back.*

That time, I didn't ignore the voice. I did exactly what she said. I left Deana a note, packed my suitcase, and boarded a plane to Atlanta. However, unlike the prior flight, I felt different. Before I had been running away from something, which was very different from leaving something behind. Now I felt stronger, bolder, and even colder. Perhaps I had found what Gigi always said was within me, but which I could never really grasp—my inner strength.

I had forgotten I was a BAB (Bad Ass Bitch), someone far smarter and beautiful than most. I was a force to be reckoned with. The sweet, gentle, passive Astrid was gone. I was no longer turning the other cheek, excusing other people's bad behavior toward me. Whatever was dished out, I was serving back tenfold. I was no one to be taken lightly, no one to be fucked with, period.

I had been transformed. I had found my Kokuran strength and tapped into it.

While I pondered my courageous thoughts, the words that echoed through my head were foreign to me. They did not sound like me at all, but they were from me, the new me, or at least part of me.

Eighteen

Revealed

When I stepped off the plane in Atlanta, I knew I had a few important pieces of business to handle. First, deal with this blackmail shit once and for all. Second, find Sage. She was trouble, and I needed to get rid of her permanently. Third, deal with Doc. There was no sense in leading him on any further. I had no time for a relationship at the moment, but he was the least of my worries.

When I arrived at my condo, it was nice and tidy, just like Sage always left it. It was obvious she had been there recently when I saw the extra set of keys I had given her lying next to the mail on the kitchen island. I looked in Sage's room and saw that most of her belongings were gone. The only thing left was a box of short-haired wigs and a few items in the closet: her sexy evening gowns with tags still on them and her nightclub outfits, including that infamous cat suit. I remembered how she had the men and women dropping to their knees when she wore it. Not any woman could wear that cat suit, only a woman that was fierce enough to pull it off. And Sage wore it well with all the confidence and bravado to accompany it.

There were no other signs of her presence anywhere in my condo. It was as if she had never lived there. I assumed that, after what she did in Detroit, she took off. That was probably best under the circumstances. I had met some pretty wicked people over the years, but Sage took the prize. Zoe was right; I should not have cozied up with Sage so quickly. Now I understood why her behavior was so stealthy. She was a dark person: cunning, manipulative, deceptive, vindictive, and dangerous. And there was probably still more about her that I didn't know, but what I knew was enough for me. I was glad she was gone. There's no telling how much calamity and mayhem she could have stirred up in my life if she had stayed around.

For some reason, Zoe had been blowing up my cell phone over the past few days, leaving urgent messages for me to call. With everything else I was going through, I had ignored her calls. Her persistence was becoming annoying. I wondered what could be that important and what the hell she wanted with me. I wasn't up to her lesbian antics, and I wasn't in the mood for playing godmother to little Zora. My life was in a colossal state of turmoil, but I refused to let it destroy me or cause me to fall apart.

Back to my first order of business: I needed to call Burke. He had left me a message a few days earlier saying he had uncovered something I would find interesting. I gave him a call.

"I did some more digging, and just as I suspected, Paul's mother, Mrs. Rackham, is involved." He paused. "I'm sorry, but it gets worse. Do you remember when I told you that only one person besides me had access to the sex video?"

"Yes, and you were going to get back to me with the identity of the other person."

He let out a long sigh. "It was Zoe. Apparently, she has been in cahoots with Mrs. Rackham the entire time. I had no idea they were connected or had a reason for colluding against you."

Burke's words left me shocked and speechless.

He paused and asked, "Astrid, are you still there?"

"Yes, Burke, I'm still here."

"You're lucky. It's been rumored that back in the day Mrs. Rackham might have had you disposed of to keep you away from her son. I'm not sure what she's capable of doing today. That woman is dangerous and unpredictable. Unfortunately, I will be connected to the Rackham family as long as she's alive, through no choice of my own."

I wasn't really paying attention to what Burke was saying about Mrs. Rackham. Frankly, I didn't care to hear about her evil ways. I was too dismayed by Zoe's betrayal.

"Astrid, I know this hurts, but I'm not completely surprised. In my profession, I've seen these peculiar relationships many times over. Politics makes for strange bedfellows."

Burke's news about Zoe caught me off guard, but it was likely plausible, given Zoe's recent political aspirations and connection to me. I forgot that she had knowledge of my personal finances. I recalled discussing the subject with her when Joey and I were drafting our pre-nup. I had also given her a set of spare keys to my condo years earlier, when I made her my local emergency contact. She was in the perfect position to blackmail me, and I had completely missed it. The thought of Zoe blackmailing me or harming me in any way was unfathomable. I felt myself becoming unhinged and spiraling out of control yet again.

"Burke, this case is now closed."

"Wait, Astrid, I'm not finished yet."

"Well, I am. Goodbye."

He called me back a few times, but I sent his calls to voicemail. The old Astrid would have probably done something impulsive and reckless, but I decided not to do anything. I needed to marinate on this awhile longer before taking action.

I stared at the wall, consumed with thoughts of Zoe's betrayal. It was incomprehensible. In my heart, I knew Zoe loved me beyond limits. I wasn't ready to accept that she could betray me.

After talking to Burke, I tried calling Zoe, but this time my calls went straight to her voicemail. I suspected she might be avoiding me. No worries though. I would catch up with her in due time.

The next day, I called Doc, and we chatted as if there was no stress between us. He made no mention of the conversation we had back in Detroit regarding my extra-curricular activities with Chevy. In fact, he seemed anxious to resume our relationship and shift it up to a higher gear. His enthusiasm made me reconsider my plan to break up with him. Something about Doc always made me feel safe and secure and that he had unconditional love for me, unlike Chevy. It didn't matter that Doc didn't have a king cobra dick that took off like a rocket I finally understood what Doc was trying to convey: any relationship based solely on the physical was doomed from the start. I realized I had been captivated by Chevy's physical beauty and his sexual attributes. I wasn't the first or the last woman to be blindsided by a good piece of dick.

Doc and I arranged to get together later that week. "I want us to start over with a clean slate and leave the past behind," he said. "Can we do that?

"Yes, I think I would like that too."

"Before I proceed," Doc said, "I have something to tell you. I promised you no more secrets, especially where Dr. Bina is concerned, so I need to share this with you. While I was in Detroit attending your mother's funeral, she suffered a breakdown and attempted suicide. That's why I came back early."

Unmoved by Dr. Bina's mental health, I said, "I know she's your friend, but I don't care to talk about her."

As Doc attempted to say something, I cut him off. "Listen, I have to go. I'll call you later."

My mind was racing and getting ahead of me. Then I remembered I had a stash of marijuana hidden in my bathroom. I ran a warm lilac bath and brought a bottle of tequila in the bathroom with me. Two hours later, after soaking and indulging in my treats, I felt much better. I wrapped up the night by dropping a Percocet before going to bed.

The next morning I went to Zoe's office where she had resumed working. At first, her assistant tried to get rid of me, saying Zoe was unavailable and would be tied up in meetings all day.

"Well, I'll just wait," I said. "She has to come out of her office at some point today."

After waiting for thirty minutes, I sent Zoe a text message: "We need to talk now, or my next stop is to pay Mrs. Rackham a visit."

A few minutes later, her assistant approached me. "Mrs. Patterson will see you now."

Zoe and I did not greet each other in our usual affectionate manner. She was noticeably uncomfortable with my surprise visit. I stood in front of her desk and bent down to within an inch of her face. "Why the fuck are you blackmailing me?"

Zoe pushed her chair back, noticeably shaken. "Let me explain, Astrid. Things are not as they appear. Yes, I sent the blackmail letter and the sex video, but I did it to protect you."

"Oh, so this is how you protect me?"

Zoe held up her hands. "Wait, let me finish. About a year ago, I met Mrs. Rackham at a political fundraising event. Of course, the interest she showed in my political aspirations intrigued me. A few months later, she approached me at another event, but this time she wasn't as friendly. That's when she told me about you and your possible connection to her family. She had obviously done a background check on me. But what came next took me by surprise. She said if you ever attempted to contact her family, she would have you killed. I stood there, stunned and speechless, not sure how to respond. Then she said she knew of my close relationship with you and that perhaps I may have some influence over you.

"She said Paul was her only remaining son, the heir to her dynasty, and she couldn't have him maligned by the likes of you. She went on to say, 'It's a very narrow path to the white house, the most innocent mistakes are rarely forgiven, including having bastard children with ex-prostitutes.' It had taken her family many years to position themselves as part of this country's political landscape, and she was not going to allow anyone to destroy it. She said she would stop at nothing to protect her family's interests. That meant eliminating all obstacles and risks by any means necessary. 'Let me make it clearer for you,' she said. 'Get your friend Astrid under control, or I'll send her to a meat-processing factory, and not to work there. And believe me, I don't make idle threats.' As she started to walk away, she turned to me and said, 'By the way, now that we've talked, let me assure you that I wouldn't have a problem sending you there too, pregnant or not.'

Don't you see, Astrid? I had no choice. Our lives were in danger. So, that's when I came up with the blackmail scheme, hoping to distract you from looking for your biological mother. I knew that finding her would have inevitably led you straight to Paul, your biological father. Blackmailing you was only a ploy to buy more time, to keep Mrs. Rackham from harming you."

"That doesn't explain why you kept a copy of the sex video!" I yelled. "Why, Zoe? Why?"

"Astrid, I risked everything for you: my job, my reputation, and my license to practice law. While working on Marcus' case, I discovered that Burke and I missed some of the media devices that contained the video. That's when I retrieved it from the storage room and deleted it from the inventory log before I closed his case. I was planning to give you the flash drive, but I was waiting for the right time, when you were more stable and less frazzled over the loss of Joey. So, it's been in my safe all this time. To be frank, I forgot about it until I had that ominous conversation with Mrs. Rackham. She's a treacherous woman, Astrid. She threatened my entire family."

I didn't respond.

"Astrid, do you want something to happen to our children? Both Zora and Junior are at risk too. If you reveal yourself to Paul, there's no telling what Mrs. Rackham will do. It's not just your life at stake here."

"Relax," I said. "I'm not afraid of that bitch. She needs to be afraid of me. She's not the only one who will stop at nothing to protect her family."

Zoe shook her head in confusion. "This anger and bitterness doesn't sound like you. We both know you couldn't hurt a fly."

"Things are different now. That was the old Astrid. I have blossomed, and I handle things much differently these days. Trust me, the new me can do a lot more than hurt a fly."

"Astrid, this is serious. What are you going to do?

I could see that Zoe was terrified of Mrs. Rackham, so I tried to reassure her that I would not do anything to jeopardize her safety or mine. "Listen, the Rackhams are not that important to me. I've made it this far in my life without Paul. I can continue the rest of it without him. I promise I will never contact him or anyone in his family. Besides, nothing is more important to me than Junior, you, and my precious little goddaughter. Now that Gigi's gone, I don't want to lose any more of my loved ones. But what are you going to do? You're the one with the lofty political ambitions."

"Correction," Zoe replied. "Now that I have Zora and I've had a preview of how sinister politics are at the top of the pyramid, I'm no longer interested. I prefer playing politics in my own backyard, right here in Atlanta."

Breathing a sigh of relief, Zoe hugged me, and then we said goodbye. I saw Zoe standing in her office window watching me as I walked to my car. I knew Zoe all too well. She was still worried. Perhaps something else had her feeling unsettled about me.

As I drove home, I thought I should have gone to Hollywood. I had just given the performance of a lifetime. Yes, I had flat out lied to Zoe, but it was for her own good. Mrs. Rackham was not to be taken lightly. She obviously had Zoe and Burke terrified of her, but I wasn't afraid of her at all. *Huh, she'd better ask somebody!* I was the Kokuran, and she had no idea what I was capable of. I would deal with Mrs. Rackham and her son in due time.

Once I was settled at home, I called Burke and repeated the lie I had told Zoe. "I promised I would not have any contact with the Rackhams." He tried to reassure me that everything would be okay as long as I kept my promise. I heard him breathe a sigh of relief as we said goodbye. As with Zoe, I knew my business with him was not done as it related to the Rackham family. They would both be waiting in the wings, watching my every move.

Strangely, as I reflected on the pain and turmoil I had experienced over the past few months, I was numb. I felt a false sense of tranquility, as if everything was going to be okay. I didn't feel one iota of stress or anxiety, and I certainly had plenty of things to unravel me: the loss of Gigi and Di, Sage's horrendous crime, and my breakup with Chevy. But I was at peace. Then I thought about something Gigi said often, "Trials and tribulations were as much a part of life as the good times. And when storms come your way and knock you down, you have to get up, shake off the dust, and keep on steppin'". She was right, her words rang true to my ears.

Later that night, Doc and I made plans for a weekend getaway to Hilton Head. For some reason, my feelings toward Doc had changed. Ironically, they were much stronger than before my affair with Chevy. Perhaps because I knew Doc was crazy about me and would have my back always. Maybe I would keep him around a little longer, maybe indefinitely.

The next morning, I refocused on the business at hand. Now that this blackmail shit was done, I could scratch that off my list. My next item of business was to find Sage. That would be easier said than done. She was very private, and I didn't know much about her life in Atlanta outside of her work. When I called the yoga studio and inquired about her whereabouts, the manager said that Sage had not been there for weeks and had told them that she was taking a leave of absence to attend to family matters. She seemed to have fallen off the radar.

As I wondered about Sage, I wasn't sure whether I should forget about her or hire someone to help me find her. She clearly had something on me. She could say I was an accomplice in Ricky's murder or falsely accuse me of killing him. Furthermore, what would I do when I actually found her, ask her to pinky swear to keep the details of Ricky's murder our little secret?

The situation with Sage was complicated. As Gigi would say, one thing for certain and two things for sure: your past always has a way of catching up with you. She was right, I had to face my past head on now or it would come back later and destroy me. If I were ever linked to Ricky's murder, my life would be over. But in this case, I didn't have the luxury of being proactive. Sage had gone underground and knew how to find me whenever she wanted. I had no choice; I would have to deal with those consequences whenever they presented themselves.

Once again, I'd have to follow Gigi's words of wisdom: "Sometimes, when you're unsure how to solve a problem, if you wait patiently and do nothing, the solution will come to you." In this case, that's exactly what I would do.

Nineteen

Justice for Philip

As I was going through my mail, I noticed a letter from Deana. I wondered why she felt the need to communicate in such a formal manner. When I opened the envelope, it was a copy of Gigi's will. I thought it was rather quick to be dealing with Gigi's estate. But knowing Gigi, this was also part of her plan. She would not have wanted the disposition of her estate to be a laborious task for us.

Deana was named the executor of Gigi's estate. She didn't have much in terms of assets. She had left Deana her house and car and gave the rest of her children ten thousand dollars each with a request for us to donate the money to charity. Everything else she had, including a few stocks and bonds, she left to her church. However, she also gave me a second check, Di's money, to donate to a charity on her behalf. Gigi's generosity made me feel philanthropic. So, I decided to match her contribution and give a portion to Pastor Jay's church and a portion to a woman's shelter on behalf of Di.

The following day, I had several errands to run, and I drove my Range Rover instead of my sports car. Sage had convinced me to purchase the SUV after I went into business with her. She said I needed something less flashy to drive other than my Benz and Aston Martin cars, and I agreed. During that time, I also felt a need to tone down my image. I had spent years obsessed with my exterior packaging, and I was ready to shift my focus to my interior, my essence, the soul of me.

Later that afternoon, I delivered my financial gift to Pastor Jay. While there, we talked at length about Gigi's work in her church and how useful my donation would be for his community outreach programs. Before I left, Pastor Jay thanked me again. "I hope to you see you back in the church soon. Your church family can be a great comfort to you in your time of need."

"Yes, I know," I said. "I'll see you soon."

As I drove, I felt like I didn't have a care in the world. It was bright and sunny, so I decided to detour from my errands and swing by the mall to pick up a few things. A little shopping at Phipps was always in order.

As I was waiting in the valet parking lane, I noticed a man who resembled Philip walking past. I kept staring at him, and sure enough, it was Philip carrying a few packages to the self-parking area. So, I decided to follow him.

He drove down a long, winding two-lane country road for about an hour to a small rural town on the city's outskirts. It certainly was not his home. I recalled Junior mentioning that Philip and his wife had purchased a home in the suburb of Roswell, and this little town was at least two hours in the opposite direction. When Philip finally reached his destination, a small cottage-style home in a cul-de-sac, I figured he was up to no good, so I decided to wait and see what was up.

Minutes later, a strikingly buff young man driving a Porsche convertible pulled into the driveway behind Philip's car. He grabbed a gym bag and then rang the doorbell. Philip opened the door wearing a big smile. He cautiously looked around before greeting the man with a hug and a passionate kiss on the mouth.

I thought to myself: *Philip is unbelievable. He's living a double life; he's married with a new baby and living on the down low, an undercover gay lifestyle. Like they say, karma is a bitch; his wife gets no sympathy from me.*

I'm not sure what possessed me to stay there, but I sat outside of that house for two hours. As nightfall approached, I was about to leave, when Philip and the young man emerged from the front door. This time, there were no displays of affection on the front porch. The man in the Porsche took off first. Philip talked on his cell phone for about ten minutes before he took off. I followed him.

As I was following Philip, I felt an indescribable sense of rage toward him. Images of him beating me and verbally abusing me flickered before my eyes. It continued with images of his threats to harm Junior and take him away from me. The images got worse. I saw Philip repeatedly taunting me after I moved to Atlanta while I was dating Joey and the time after. The faster the images flickered in my head, the faster I drove. I blew my horn as I pulled alongside Philip on the wrong side of the road. Not knowing it was me, he lowered his window.

"Is something wrong?"

"Yes, motherfucker!" I shouted. "You're evil, a deadly parasite who needs to be exterminated. Now it's time for you to pay up for everything you did to me. Your ass is mine!"

Philip did a double-take as he finally recognized me. "Astrid, is that you?" Before I could respond, I saw fear and trepidation race across his face. "You're crazy," he said, and then he sped off.

I hit my accelerator and quickly caught up to him. The flickering images of him abusing me resumed, this time more graphic. All I could see was Phillip's arms going back as he threw punches toward some area on my body. With each blow that landed, I heard a thump that sounded like thunder.

I continued chasing him, trying to run him off the road. Because the roads were familiar to him, he was able to flank me a few times. But with the blink of an eye, I was back on his tail. Then he must have lost his way, because he turned down a side road surrounded by thick brush, which came to a dead end. That's when I knew it was over for him. I pushed down on the accelerator as hard as I could and T-boned his car. I hit him so hard that my airbag deployed, and sudden whiplash knocked me out momentarily.

When I regained consciousness, I saw Philip bent over in his car, his head face down in his airbag. I was sure he was dead. His car's windows were shattered I knew I had to leave quickly, before someone discovered Philip's car.

It was pitch black on the narrow, deserted road. Since there was no space to turn around, I had to drive in reverse. The whiplash left me in excruciating pain and unable to turn my neck, making it difficult to see behind me. When I got to the main road, I felt weak and tired, so I pulled over and rested on the shoulder. I breathed a sigh of relief knowing that from there it was a straight shot to the highway and then to my home. My eyes closed, I thought the aches and pains were worth it. I would do it all over again if that's what it took for me to get rid of Philip's ass. He was rotten, and he deserved to die.

I had no thoughts about the criminal aspects of what I had done. I felt invigorated as I told myself that the world was a better place without Philip in it. Although I had done a terrible thing, I didn't see it that way. I felt justified, as if I had performed an honorable act. Just as Philip had once basked in glory from the years of torture he unleashed on me, I could do the same to him. Sometimes, two wrongs could yield a righteous outcome.

As I was trying to adjust my rear-view mirror, I heard a loud horn that sounded like a train, with bright lights coming straight toward me at lightning speed.

Boom! Lights out!

There was nothing but darkness and silence for me once again. But this time, I was responsible for my injury. Instead of being grazed by a bullet, my SUV had been sideswiped by a semi-truck. The rescue team said I was lucky to be alive; the impact could have killed me. I guess it wasn't my time to die.

A lot of things were in place that day that I attribute to saving my life. For starters, my SUV was like a military vehicle, made to handle rough terrain and withstand off-road impact. And then there was the brush, the densely packed trees that cushioned my landing. All these elements contributed to saving my life;

however, it could have been divine intervention. Gigi was deeply religious, and she said that she prayed for God to keep a protective shield around me. Perhaps her prayers were answered.

Twenty

Chain Reaction

I awoke in the hospital a few days later with my hands strapped to the bed railings, which was protocol for the psychiatric ward. As I looked around, I saw Deana and Nikki sitting on a sofa having a conversation as if I wasn't there. At first, I thought Nikki had followed through on her threats to have me committed to a mental hospital; and to some extent, she had, maligning my character by exposing Di's schizophrenia and then claiming I had inherited the same disease. I had been placed in the mental ward for observation and treatment of my injuries. Since the driver of freightliner suffered no injuries, and due to my supposed mental state, the police did not conduct an extensive investigation on the accident. In fact, they never even questioned me.

Perhaps I needed to stay in the hospital for a little while, at least long enough to receive treatment for my neurological issues. While I could hear and understand everything around me, I was unable to convert my thoughts into words. The doctors said I didn't appear to have a traumatic brain injury, but my brain had most likely been jolted during the collision. Only time would reveal the extent of my injuries and my prognosis.

Deana noticed I was awake and walked over to my bed. She bent over and kissed me. "Astrid, I know you can hear me. You're like a cat; you have at least nine lives. I know you'll have a speedy recovery.

"Well at least she'll be safe here," Nikki said. "This is where she belongs. She can't take care of herself, always involved in some tragic event that causes her to end up in the ICU. You need to go ahead and petition the court for full power of attorney and have her permanently committed."

Deana walked and stood directly in front of Nikki, inches from her face. "Listen carefully, you bitch. If you do anything to harm Astrid, I promise you'll regret it. That beating Astrid gave you is nothing compared to what I'll do. I let you get away with manipulating Gigi's medical decisions, but I will not stand by and let you hurt Astrid."

She paused as if she was waiting for Nikki to reply, but Nikki didn't say a word, dumbfounded by Deana's abrasive stance. "No harm had better come to Astrid," Deana continued in a light voice as she turned away. "If it does, no matter how slight, I promise you'll regret it."

Nikki scoffed. "You're crazy too. I'm out of here. I'm done with you and the rest of the other illegitimate half-breeds my daddy adopted and tried to raise."

Nikki grabbed her purse and marched out of my room. "It will be a cold day in hell before you ever see me again!"

Ignoring Nikki's rants, Deana turned to me. "Don't worry, Astrid. You're not alone. I'm going to stay here in Atlanta until you're ready to come home. I'll be here as long as you need me." Then she kissed my forehead and left.

The next morning, Doc stopped by to visit. He looked sad and distraught. By then I presume he was keenly aware that I was being evaluated for various mental disorders. He might have actually seen my medical charts, since he was also on staff at Emory, where I was hospitalized. So much for doctor-patient privilege. I guess the men in white coats stood together like the men in blue.

Doc sat on my bed and held my hands. Then he bent down and kissed my hands and rubbed his face on them. When he sat up, he looked at me with teary eyes. "I love you and all those other people inside of you," he whispered. "I had my suspicions months ago that there might be something wrong with you, but I didn't want to face it. I thought that with my knowledge as a doctor and with our love, together, we could manage it. I used to hear you talking in the bathroom, as if you were holding an in-depth conversation with someone. When I inquired if you were talking to someone, you would either deny it or say you were on the phone with a friend. I knew that wasn't true, because your cell phone would be either on the charger plugged into the wall or in your purse. However, none of that matters to me. I'm in love with you, and I will help you get through your illness. And as soon as you're well enough, I want us to get married."

I was still heavily sedated and couldn't respond, but I understood everything Doc said. He kissed my cheek. "I'll see you soon," he said. I wanted to reach out to him, but all I could do was lie there with tears streaming slowly down my face as I watched him walk out the door.

Later that night, I awoke from a terrible nightmare. I was hysterical and cried out for Deana. A few hours later, she arrived. As soon as I saw her, I reached out to her, similar to the way an infant reaches for its mother. "What happened, and how did I get here?" I mumbled, still sobbing uncontrollably.

"Sweetie, what's wrong?" Deana asked, confused by my behavior. "I told you this before. You were in a terrible car accident. Don't you remember?"

"Where's Sage?" I cried. "She killed Philip and Ricky."

Deana frowned. "What are you talking about?"

"Philip is dead. Sage killed him. Junior will be so upset."

"Astrid, what are you talking about?"

I continued whimpering as I tried to explain, but my thoughts and speech were impaired, so Deana couldn't understand me. My doctor saw that I was becoming agitated and sedated me.

The next morning, Zoe and Deana were in my room. I was still groggy from the medicine I had been given the night before, but I was coherent enough to hear Deana's conversation with Zoe. "She had a rough night," Deana said. "She was delusional. She kept talking about folks being killed. Something about Philip being dead and her friend Sage killing someone."

"What about Philip and Sage?" Zoe asked.

Deana shrugged. "She wasn't making much sense. She was very unhappy when she learned that Philip had moved to Atlanta. Gigi and I told her that he was not a threat to her, and she should just go on with her life as if he wasn't living there. She paused. "I'm worried about her though. Maybe she's having a nervous breakdown. Perhaps Gigi's death and finding out about her real mother was too much for her to handle. You know, she's always been fragile, like a delicate flower."

Zoe was less concerned about my fragility than my comments about Sage. She became nervous as Deana told her about my outbursts regarding Sage killing Philip. She suspected my words were not merely delusional; perhaps there was some truth to them.

Then Zoe walked over and kissed me on my cheek. "I'll be back later," she said slowly as if I were deaf and reading her lips, "and I'll stay and visit with you awhile."

Zoe hurriedly left my room.

While I remained incoherent, I was able to make out what people were saying to me and about me. Since Deana was my temporary guardian, she was responsible for my medical decisions. I heard the doctor talk to Deana about me having a serious mental disorder, possibly schizophrenia. He suggested sending me to Lakeview for further psychological treatment. At first Deana resisted, saying all I needed was rest and a little prayer. But she changed her mind once the doctors showed her the observation they recorded of me. I never saw it, but it supposedly showed me having night terrors, intense crying spells, and several conversations with another person who wasn't there. When asked about it, I had no memory of those events.

Later that evening, Zoe returned to the hospital to visit me. By then I was heavily sedated again. She sat next to me on my bed. "Astrid, I know what you've done," she whispered.

"It wasn't me," I mumbled. "It was Sage."

"No, honey, there is no Sage; she's not real. It was you the whole time, pretending to be Sage." She pointed at my tattoo on the inside of my wrist. "I have proof from security footage taken from an apartment surveillance camera in Detroit. The person with this tattoo killed Ricky, and that person is you."

She took a deep breath before she continued. "I know it was also you who attempted to kill Philip. He survived the crash, and he's doing fine. I talked to him. You're lucky he refuses to identify you."

I figured the medicine had me confused, because I thought I heard Zoe say I was Sage.

"Listen, Astrid. You can never mention that Sage killed Ricky, not to anyone, not even to your doctors. They are bound by law to report any confessions that have to do with murder. Then it will only be a matter of time before the police put the pieces together. Once they start looking for Sage, it will lead them directly to you."

I didn't respond, so she grabbed me by the shoulders and shook me. "Astrid, I know you can hear me," she whispered. "You must never speak of Sage to anyone, not ever. Please blink or do something, so I'll know you understand me."

"Okay," I mumbled.

Zoe released me and relaxed somewhat. "Burke and I have everything under control. We're going to make all this stuff with Sage go away, and then you can start your life with a clean slate.

When you leave Lakeview, you can live a happy, healthy life. You know that I love you, and I'll always be here for you."

That's when I realized that Zoe was truly a friend, always risking everything to help me. I was truly blessed to have her in my life.

The next morning, I awoke to Zoe and Burke in my room. Like everyone else, they spoke about me and in my presence, as if I wasn't there or as if I couldn't understand. "I have tied up the loose ends on my part," Burke said, "but are you sure you've got the wreckage from this Sage person under control?"

Zoe nodded. "Yes. I've covered all the legal bases, and I've spoken to several doctors at Lakeview. They said, with medication, Astrid should be able to function at a hundred-percent capacity. With six months of treatment, she'll be as good as new, and no more Sage, period. But she'll probably be on medication for the rest of her life."

"I never saw anything in Astrid that suggested she might have a mental disorder," Burke said. "How did you find out?"

Zoe explained how she stumbled upon my illness in the course of her blackmail scheme. "After Mrs. Rackham coerced me to keep Astrid away from her family, I started tracking Astrid's activities. I put a surveillance trace on her communication devices and planted a listening device in her condo.

"The tricky part was delivering the blackmail letter. I knew Astrid would attempt to track down the source, so I used one of the street informants as a courier. And thanks to Astrid's PI, Mr. Brown, I knew when Astrid was getting close to finding her mother. However, the strange part was the silence in Astrid's condo. On several of her phone calls, Astrid mentioned that Sage was in Atlanta and referenced several conversations they had. But I could never trace a phone number to Sage, and I never picked up any audio on her in Astrid's condo. It was then that I shifted my focus to Sage and began to question her identity.

"Initially, I thought Sage might be a con, perhaps using someone else's identity. So, while Astrid was in Detroit, I entered her condo to obtain Sage's fingerprints to uncover her true identity. But the only fingerprints I found belonged to Astrid and her maid, which made me become even more curious about Sage.

"After the sweep of Astrid's condo failed to reveal anything, I pulled business documents from public records on the yoga studio that Sage and Astrid supposedly owned together. But again, there was no mention of Sage or any other business partner. So, I called the yoga studio and asked to speak to Sage and was told that she had taken an unspecified leave of absence to deal with family matters in Detroit. That was strange; I didn't recall Astrid mentioning that Sage was also from Detroit. That's when I asked the manager to fax over a document with Sage's full name on it.

"The next day, I was reviewing the document from the yoga studio when I noticed it only contained Astrid's information. I knew I would have to go directly to the yoga studio to sort this out. However, before leaving, I called the Detroit police department to inquire if they had a person by the name of Sage as a suspect in any crimes. The detective confirmed negative on my inquiry. Then I asked if they had any recent crimes that involved someone by the name of Ricky.

"The detective told me my timing was perfect. He was just closing the file and shipping it to the cold case department. There was a piece of security footage taken near an apartment building where a man by the name Richard, who was also suspected of being a serial rapist, was found murdered. The quality of the footage was very poor and didn't provide any leads. He said he could send it right over."

"When the file arrived, the footage was dark and grainy and further degraded by the heavy downpour. But I was able to see the profile of a person wearing a dark hoodie and jogging pants. When I zoomed in on the image, I saw a tattoo on the inside of the person's wrist. It was identical to the matching tattoo that Sage and Astrid had supposedly gotten a few months earlier. That's when I knew I had found Sage.

"The following day, I went back to the yoga studio and asked the manager about the two business owners, but the lady told me there was only one owner, Sage. I told her that couldn't be true, that my friend was part owner of the business, and her name was Astrid. The lady nodded and smiled. Then she dropped the bomb on me. She said sometimes she went by Miss Astrid, but she preferred to be called Sage.

"Confused, I took out my cell phone and pulled up a picture of Astrid and showed it to the lady. She smiled and said, 'Yes, that's Sage, your friend Miss Astrid. They're the same person.'

"The lady saw the confusion on my face. She grabbed a framed group photo taken during the grand opening with everyone wearing T-shirts with their names on them. Sure enough, there was Astrid wearing a T-shirt with the name 'Sage' inscribed on it. The lady also told me the mail is always addressed to Miss Astrid, but everyone, including the customers, called her Sage. They thought Sage was her nickname. That's when I began to put it all together.

"I returned to my office and looked at the security footage again, trying to see if the image I thought was Sage was indeed Astrid. As I stared at the image of the woman, grainy or not, it became crystal clear. It was Astrid."

"That's unbelievable," Burke exclaimed. "But what about the car accident with Philip? How does he fit into all of this?"

"Once Deana told me that Astrid kept repeating 'Sage killed Philip,' I decided to look into it. I found a police report that stated Philip was involved in a hit-and-run collision and taken to Grady Memorial Hospital. It also stated that they had no information on the identity of the other driver.

"I went to talk to Philip in my official capacity. I asked him a few standard questions, which he seemed reluctant to answer. Then I asked, 'Why were you on a deserted road in the middle of nowhere?' He said he was looking at investment properties and somehow got lost. The rest was a blur.

"I asked repeatedly, 'Are you sure you didn't see the driver who hit your vehicle?'

"His response was the same, 'I never saw the car or the person who hit me, and I can't remember much else before or after the collision.'

"My instincts told me that Philip was lying and that he probably had a good reason for it. If he named the other person in the accident, it might open a can of worms that he preferred to keep closed. I suspected he was hiding something, but I was less concerned about his secrets than Astrid's well-being. So, I gave him my card and told him to call me if he remembered anything. But I don't think he'll be calling. I'm certain he doesn't want to revisit the events surrounding the accident. Besides, when I was leaving, I saw a man who was buff with 'gay' written all over him go into his room. Something tells me there's a story behind that visit.

"I've spent a lot of time with Astrid over the years," Zoe continued, "and similar to you, I never saw any signs that she had a mental disorder. Sure, she was depressed over her divorce and following the incident with Joey, but that's to be expected. However, her doctors explained that people with mental disorders can go their entire lives without showing any symptoms. Usually, something catastrophic triggers the type of psychotic episode that Astrid experienced. It seems this Sage person had been around the past year, so something must have occurred then. But I have no idea what happened, since Astrid became a recluse after Joey died."

"Well, she'll get the help she needs at Lakeview and be back to normal in no time," Burke said.

Twenty-one

The Lakeview

When I arrived at Lakeview, which was secluded behind many winding tree-lined roads, it looked more like an opulent vacation resort than a mental hospital. In addition to the medical facility, there were tennis courts, a golf course, a swimming pool and fitness center, as well as a salon and spa services. The staff was exceptionally kind, not clinical or sterile in their approach. They behaved as if we were not in a hospital but a hotel. They referred to patients as guests, as if their stay was voluntary. To the contrary, only patients with serious illnesses were treated at Lakeview, and often it was a last resort before being committed to a long-term mental health facility.

Unlike other similar clinical institutions, I had a complete medical team assigned to me, which included a psychiatrist, two psychologists, and a nurse practitioner. Everyone knew that Lakeview was for the rich and famous, not for the poor and indigent. Not to mention that privacy and anonymity was assured.

After settling in, I spent the first week in the intake ward, which meant I was under twenty-four-hour observation. I was not allowed to interact with anyone or leave my room except when escorted and under the direct supervision of an aid. The quiet solitude did not bode well for my mental health; the silence was deafening.

It was also during that time that I reflected on the notion of me having schizophrenia and that I had created a character called Sage as my alter ego. It was rather ironic that I chose the name Sage, which means "to save" and the "wise one." Strangely, those were the qualities she exemplified in the role she played in my life.

It was hard for me to believe that Sage was not a real person, and that she was only a figment of my imagination. We had spent the past year hanging out together, going to places all over Atlanta, and no one ever approached me as if I was alone when we were out together. How could that be? Perhaps they thought I was crazy and left me alone with my lunacy.

After staring at white walls for a week, I was glad to finally move to my assigned room, which was more like a luxury studio apartment, except it didn't have a kitchenette. Of course, it had the usual safety features to keep the crazies from harming themselves, but otherwise it looked like any other apartment. However, this was an important week for me. It was the start of my intense therapy to understand the root cause of my illness.

I spent the next six weeks talking to my team about my emotional state and the possible triggers tied to my recent psychosis: my childhood rape, my abusive marriage, and the recent loss of loved ones. I wasn't sure how discussing my past was supposed to help me, but they were the doctors, not me.

There was one person I wanted to talk about, especially since it was her undoing that caused me to end up at Lakeview. But I remembered what Zoe told me, never to talk about Sage, not even with my doctors. So, I would have to help myself when it came to Sage's role in my life.

As I reflected on the duality of me, I struggled with seeing Sage and me as a single person instead of two separate individuals. She had been just as real as Zoe was to me; however, I remained deeply perplexed as to how she came into my life and the circumstances surrounding her presence in it. I recalled Gigi's advice: always start at the beginning to understand the ending. So, that's what I did; I examined the inception of Sage's entrance into my life.

I vaguely remembered when I began grade school while we were living in the Gardens that I started to feel alone. By then, Gigi was working full time and going to school in the evenings, so I was often left home with my siblings to watch over me. Gigi usually paired me with Nikki since we were the closest in age. However, Nikki resented being stuck with me. Perhaps that's why she eventually grew to hate me. Whenever Nikki and I visited her friends, they would exclude me from their activities and ignore me. Other times, when we were at the park, Nikki would stand by and do nothing as other kids teased and taunted me. When I cried to Gigi about it, Nikki would say, "Nobody's bothering her, she's just a whining, spoiled brat."

Gigi was busy and often tired; she didn't notice the depth of my pain. It seemed that my cries fell on deaf ears as the emotional state of my young life deteriorated further.

Nikki's behavior, coupled with the bullying at school, led me to feel lonely and isolated. It was around that time that I remember playing with an imaginary little girl who looked like a tomboy. She seemed to appear out of nowhere. We played board games and hopscotch in the play area just outside the back of my home. Although small in size, she was fearless. She carried a pocketknife, had a filthy mouth, and could fight better than most boys our age. Thanks to her, she even made the girls at school stop bullying me, but they still refused to befriend me.

However, it wasn't until Ricky assaulted me that I remember the little girl comforting me and telling me that her name was Sage. From that point forward, she maintained a daily presence in my life. After the incident with Ricky, I was terrified to walk back and forth to school. Even worse, Ricky made me feel terrified of men in general. In my mind, all men would rape at any opportunity. But Sage remained by my side, giving me the courage not to buckle under my fears. Sometimes, I would see Ricky in passing, which scared and angered me. But then Sage would say, "Don't worry. I promise we will take care of him when the time comes. Now that I'm here, he will never hurt you again."

Ricky had not only stolen my innocence, he had stolen the little bit of childhood happiness I had left in me, and I hated him for that. It was also at that time that I realized I did not have anyone to protect me, especially from men. That was the first time I longed for my father and became curious about his identity and whereabouts. Of course, that was well before all the lies I had been told about my father. Back then, all I knew was that I had a father, but he wasn't around. When I shared my thoughts of finding my real father with Sage, she said, "I'll help you find him when we get older, I promise."

However, the greatest gift that Sage gave me was the courage to leave home and attend Brookhaven. While I hated living in the Gardens, I was even more terrified of being away from Gigi. But Sage convinced me that it was the only way for me to truly be safe from Ricky and to have a better life. "You gotta leave the Gardens; it's not safe here for you. If you go to Brookhaven, you'll have a chance to live like the white people we see on television."

And she was right. Attending Brookhaven changed the trajectory of my life. In contrast to her youth and rough outward appearance, Sage was smart beyond her years. She was like Gigi when it came to her forethought and words of wisdom. But once I left for Brookhaven, Sage disappeared as suddenly as she had appeared.

However, after searching deep in my mind, I recalled a few occasions while I was married to Philip that Sage was there wiping my tears and helping me care for my wounds, reminding me that the wrath of Philip's brutality would pass. At first, her appearance in my life was sporadic. By the time I was going through my divorce, I was falling apart. There was a period when I was having suicidal thoughts. However, it was Sage who kept me from going overboard. "He's not worth it," she would whisper. "Hang on; this time shall pass. In the end, Philip will get what he's got coming. His day will come. I promise."

Back then, I was drinking excessively and dropping Vicodin like candy. I thought I was high, imagining Sage's existence, so I discounted her appearance. And once my divorce was final, she disappeared again.

By the time I met Joey, I was an emotional wreck from the aftermath of being married to Philip, which left me confused about love, sex, and relationships, period. Despite my desire not to love again, I found myself falling in love with Joey beyond my control. For many reasons though, my relationship with him was turbulent, unleashing anxiety and a host of other stressors in my life. To compound matters, unbeknownst to me, I was suffering full-blown PTSD after my divorce from Philip. That, coupled with the trauma from my childhood and feeling powerless in my relationship with Joey, triggered the re-appearance of Sage as a voice in my subconscious. However, I believe it was Gigi's initial stroke and near-death experience that ultimately pushed me over the edge, causing Sage to manifest once again as a physical being in my conscious life. Thus, Sage became my roommate, my confidante, my mentor, my business partner, and my warrior. She became everything I needed to overcome the perils in my life.

I closed my eyes and thought about Sage's re-emergence in my life. I remembered taking yoga classes and meeting her for the first time, jogging and going to the fitness center with her, and her accompanying me to the tattoo parlor. But as I reflected on those events and having numerous conversations with her throughout the year, I could see that no one was there.

I remembered that Joey had purchased the sexy cat suit and other evening gowns for me and that after he died, Zoe packed them up and stored them in the guest room closet. I remembered recently trying on the cat suit and feeling insecure, wishing I had the body and confidence to wear it.

I remembered hiring the maid and giving her keys to the condo and later giving her an envelope with cash to show my appreciation for the extra things she did, such as organizing my mail, reorganizing my furniture, and making healthy meals for me, including those green smoothies. Some of the conversations I thought I had with Sage were with my maid, including the blackmail scenario with the letters being brought into my condo, to outright accusing her of blackmailing me.

But then, there were some things I couldn't remember, such as buying those short-haired wigs, wearing the cat suit to the nightclub, and training to become a yoga instructor, let alone coming up with the idea to open the yoga studio. And I didn't remember when and why the maid suddenly quit.

Gigi had often credited me with having enormous strength that allowed me to overcome crises and still prosper. Little did she know that it was Sage who had stood by my side, giving me courage and confidence to persevere through my adversities. Sage was my rock, my strength, and my hero. She was a real person to me.

But how Sage's appearance had culminated in the death of someone puzzled me. I decided to shift my focus and work backwards, beginning with Ricky. I closed my eyes, so I could see what had really happened. It was as if I was watching a replay of a film, except the script was my life.

I saw the entire incident with Ricky unfold before my eyes. From the moment I followed him into the building through to the end, where I used my self-defense maneuvers to disable him. And then the rest that ensued . . ..

I remember vividly shooting Ricky. In a panic, I stepped outside through a rear door. I removed my hoodie and pulled my sleeves up, staring at my tattoo, specifically at the orchid. A few minutes elapsed before I used the gushing rain to wash my bloody face and hands. That was probably when I was captured on the security footage that Zoe referenced.

Realizing I needed to leave before someone saw me, I tied my hood tightly around my head and made a quick dash through the pouring rain to my car. Although it seemed surreal, that's exactly what happened. I had killed Ricky through no fault of my own. Nonetheless, I was still unsettled by it.

Trying to rationalize what I had done, I replayed the "what if" scenarios in my head. What if Deana had never asked me to come to Gigi's church that night? I would not have taken Gigi's gun and encountered Ricky. Alternatively, what if Ricky had just walked away from me and not attempted to attack me again? Perhaps I might not have shot him. But no matter the reason, I had killed Ricky and set off the chain of events that brought me to Lakeview.

Nonetheless, I could not begin to comprehend how I could stalk someone like an animal hunting its prey. But then I remembered it wasn't me, it was Sage. Although we shared the same body, she had a mind of her own.

Acknowledging Sage's existence was a pivotal moment for me. That's when I finally began to accept that I had a mental illness and needed help. It was something far more serious than my weed alone could handle.

Seeking psychological treatment while concealing Sage's existence would be a tremendous balancing act. As I pondered it, the answer came to me. I would just refer to Sage as "the person" and never mention her by name. I could never admit that Sage had manifested into a real person and became entwined into every aspect of my life. More importantly, I could never reveal that she had killed Ricky and attempted to kill Philip.

I paused and thought hard about it. Then I realized, once again, the depth of me. I was the Kokuran—my capabilities were endless. I would shrewdly keep my secret. After all, I had gone an entire year without exposing Sage to the people closest to me. Surely I could do the same with my doctors. My only concern was the antipsychotic drugs I was taking. Since the drugs took the edge off my sharpness, I was afraid I might unconsciously reveal something about Sage. But that was a chance I would have to take.

During therapy, I learned a lot about schizophrenia. "This disease is very difficult to diagnose," the doctor explained, "because it resembles several others, such as bi-polar and manic-depression disorders. It's frequently misdiagnosed, except when the most extreme symptoms are present. The disease is a psychosis, a type of mental illness in which a person cannot tell what is real from what is imagined. The exact cause of the disease is unknown; however, the major contributing factors are heredity, environmental, physiological, and chemical imbalances in the brain. While there is no cure for the disease, most of the symptoms can be managed with therapy and medication."

The doctor went on to explain that about one hundred thousand new cases were diagnosed every year, so the disease was more common than most people knew. "We're all ten minutes away from insanity," he said. "There are probably thousands more who have the disease and don't even know it."

After an hour, I had enough education on schizophrenia. Quite frankly, I learned more than I cared to know about it. But I had no choice but to follow their treatment program, which included education about my supposed condition.

During the second phase of my treatment, I began intensive therapy to understand the depth of my delusional state. "The loss of your mother may have triggered your psychosis," the doctor said, "but we need to determine if your psychosis is temporary, episodic, or permanent."

"How are you going to determine that?" I asked.

"Through hypnosis, of course," he replied.

"No, you can't do that!" I shouted, worried I might divulge something about Sage or Ricky's death.

He laughed. "I'm just kidding. Right now, your prognosis is good. Your condition appears to be stable, but we don't know if it will remain that way or if you'll have another psychotic episode later. And contrary to the myths, we don't like to over medicate our patients. When you were in the hospital, you were having nightmares and then acting as if someone was comforting you. Do you remember those incidents, and do you know who the person was that was comforting you?"

"Yes and yes. I'm embarrassed to say that I was sobbing over the loss of my mother, Gigi, who was actually the grandmother who raised me. Throughout my life, whenever I was in pain, I would reach out to Gigi for comfort. But apparently, what I thought was occurring in my dreams was my actual behavior."

He pursed his lips. "I can't help you if you're not honest with me."

"I'm telling the truth," I protested. "I have no reason to lie."

We continued to have similar discussions over the next six weeks. The truth was, as I reflected over the past year that I spent with Sage, I wasn't sure when Sage took over my mind or actions. Through my therapy sessions, I realized that there were periods of time for which I could not account, too many to attempt to recall.

During my last session, I asked if my illness could cause me to harm anyone, commit murder, or snap. His response surprised me. "We're all capable of harming or even killing someone, accidentally or intentionally. All you need are the right conditions: a weapon, motivation arising from a threat or something more heinous, and the opportunity. If any of these three elements are present, then the possibility of harm can occur. However, the converse is true as well. So, to answer your question, you are no more prone to hurt someone than anyone else."

I was relieved to hear his words, but it didn't help me understand what happened with Ricky at the hands of Sage, the hands we shared.

Sometimes when I was alone, I thought about Ricky and how conflicted I felt about his death. My emotions varied, ranging from guilt to relief, despair, and indifference. While I concluded that my actions were justified, because killing Ricky was self-defense under those circumstances, I still felt uncomfortable with it.

I had carried hatred toward Ricky for many years and wanted revenge. I always hoped that a horrendous death would befall him at someone's hands, including mine. However, Gigi raised me to believe that vengeance did not belong to me and that I had to learn to forgive people, even those who hurt me. I was supposed to forgive Ricky just as she forgave her Uncle Buck. Perhaps it was easier for Gigi to forgive her assailant, knowing he had been punished immediately for his act. I, on the other hand, could not forgive Ricky so easily, and I paid dearly for it. My hatred for him kept me stuck in time, forever stealing a piece of my happiness and eventually landing me in a bed at Lakeview.

After three months of intensive therapy, I was finally starting to gain acceptance and understanding about my illness. My doctor said people with my condition often create imaginary alter egos to cope with crises or traumatic life events. They become overwhelmed, retreating in their subconscious. But once the crisis has been averted, the alter ego usually goes away. However, an alter ego could recur depending on the depth of illness and the success of the treatment protocol. The key was having the right skills to manage the trigger symptoms. In my case, this meant my condition could be managed and that my long-term prognosis was good.

By month four, I breathed a sigh of relief. I had made it through the most difficult part of my treatment without revealing Sage. The next phase was modified to include group therapy. My sessions were focused on grieving and coping with high levels of stress. It was also when I was finally permitted to have visitors. All other forms of communication were still off limits. While Zoe and Deana visited often, Doc never came to see me. When I asked Zoe and Deana if they had seen or heard from Doc, their answer was always the same: no, without much dialogue. It was obvious they were avoiding talking about Doc with me.

I was allowed to write one letter to Doc, but he never wrote back. I figured my illness was too much for him to handle and, like Chevy, he didn't want to have anything to do with me. However, I thought Doc would have at least been honest and told me to my face that he wanted to cut ties. Perhaps he was waiting for me to get out of Lakeview before he broke the news, fearing my medical condition was too fragile to handle a breakup. No sense in fretting over the unknown; I would face Doc when I was discharged from Lakeview in two months.

One day, while sitting poolside, I noticed that I was feeling good. For the first time in a long time, my mind, body, and soul were in harmony. Prior to my arrival at Lakeview, I was skeptical about the effectiveness of psychotherapy. I thought it was only for crazy or weak people; however, I obviously fell somewhere in the middle of that spectrum. I had to admit that, apart from the side effects of the meds, the treatment protocol seemed to be working. My team of doctors were very encouraging, often telling me that I could resume a normal life outside of Lakeview in no time at all.

While I had been successful in concealing Sage from my doctors, I was left with many unanswered questions about her. Sage had infused herself into my life, only I didn't know when and how much of my life had become hers. Those lines remained blurred. I realized I would probably never be able to completely sort out those details, so I didn't bother to pursue it. Besides, despite recent events, I knew Sage came into my life to help, not harm me. And that was good enough for me. It was then that I concluded she would never be a threat to me. As far as I was concerned, the issue with Sage was closed.

I had been at Lakeview about five months when Nikki paid me a surprise visit. Initially, I thought it was odd, but she had convinced Deana that she was deeply sorry for her past behavior toward me. She wanted to apologize and start over, forge a real sisterly bond with me. She was very kind, almost unrecognizable, as she expressed genuine concern about my health and well-being.

"Astrid, I'm sorry about everything," Nikki said. "You have every right to dislike me. I haven't always been very nice to you, let alone much of a sister to you. But I want a second chance. I want us to be close the way Gigi wanted us to be. I also have a confession to make. The reason I've been unkind to you over the years was because I was jealous of you. I was the youngest girl, and Gigi acted as if I didn't exist once she brought you home from the hospital. It wasn't just Gigi that spoiled you, it seemed everyone else in the family did as well. Your presence made me feel invisible. But it wasn't until I read Gigi's journals and learned that she too was raised by her grandmother that I fully understood why she was overly attentive to you. Please forgive me, and let's start over. Gigi always wanted us to be close. This would certainly make her happy while she's watching us from heaven."

"Okay," I replied cautiously. "But one day at time."

We hugged. "I hear you're quite the painter," she said. "Can I see some of your work?"

I led her into the gallery, where my artwork was displayed, and showed her my two paintings: a picture of Gigi bending over, tending her garden and my favorite, a spectacular image of a black orchid.

"Astrid, these are beautiful," Nikki said. "I had no idea you were such a talented artist."

We walked next door to the art studio, and I showed her a painting that I had started with Doc and me standing side by side on his yacht. "I'm almost finished," I said proudly. "I plan to give it to Doc as a gift the next time I see him. I can't wait to go sailing with him again."

"You need to get that thought out of your head," Nikki replied. Then she covered her mouth with her hand. "Oh, that's right. No one told you about Doc?

"What happened to Doc?" I asked, concerned.

Ignoring my question, Nikki became preoccupied with her purse. Then she pulled out a compact mirror and retouched her lipstick. "I'm sorry, but I forgot. Deana said she spoke to your doctors, and they agreed it was best that you were not told about Doc." She grinned slightly. "I'm very sorry, me and my big mouth."

Nikki showed no empathy and seemed to be glowing as she taunted me while withholding the news about Doc. That's when I realized she was up to no good. Her visit was merely a ploy to hurt me in some way.

"You've already spilled the beans," I said impatiently, "so you might as well tell me what happened."

In response, she pulled out a slip of paper. "Well, your friend Doc is dead. It was a tragic set of circumstances. I think they said his lover or maybe his ex-lover killed him." She looked at the paper. "The woman's name was Dr. Elise Bina. Apparently, it was a murder-suicide. It happened last month; it was all over the medical community. I'm surprised you didn't hear about it, since the incident occurred right here in Atlanta. I'm sure it was in the local news."

Hearing that Doc had been killed at Dr. Bina's hands didn't come as a complete surprise. I knew she was unstable and could snap at any time. I tried to tell Doc about Dr. Bina many times, but he ignored my warnings. Nonetheless, I was shattered by the news of his death, knowing I would never see him again. But mourning Doc would have to come much later. First, I had to listen to more of Nikki's agonizing commentary.

"Oh, I forgot, your access to media is controlled here. You can't get the news in the crazy hospital."

I stood there in deep shock and silence as my mind wandered. Then I snapped and I tried to choke the life out of

Nikki. If the orderlies had not pulled me off, I believe I would have succeeded. I forgot that Nikki was the devil, a wolf in sheep's clothing. She came to visit me, pretending to make amends when all along she wanted to destroy me, put a dagger in my heart. But then I remembered, months earlier, her referencing that I should be committed permanently. She knew I was leaving Lakeview the next month, and this was her last-ditch effort to have me permanently confined there or to some other mental institution. That's when I realized the extent of Nikki's unending hatred for me.

Unfortunately, the confrontation with Nikki set my treatment progress back, causing my doctors to extend my stay. My depression worsened, and I fell into a semi-catatonic state. Once again, I was given heavy doses of antipsychotic drugs with debilitating side effects. I slowly slipped into a place where I could retreat to the bowels of my mind permanently. But then I thought about Gigi's journals and all the pain and suffering she had endured and overcame. If she could rise from the ashes of her life, surely I could do the same. That's when I tapped into my inner strength and found my way back to reality and to the road of recovery.

A few months later, my condition improved to the point where I was before Nikki's infamous visit. I was also painting again and allowed to have a short list of visitors Deana, Zoe, and Burke.

Needless to say, by then I was growing tired of Lakeview and looking forward to finally being discharged at the end of the month. I was leaving Lakeview soon, one way or another.

Twenty-two

The Kokuran – In Full Blossom

It was my birthday when Zoe, Deana, and Burke paid me a surprise visit. They brought a cake, and we had a small celebration. Deana wanted to invite Junior, but I didn't want him to see me, mainly because I was keeping my illness a secret from him and everyone else. Most people thought I was distraught after Gigi's passing and was relaxing somewhere out of the country on an extended vacation. Truth was, I was embarrassed about having a mental disorder and being a guest at Lakeview.

A few hours later, my party was over. I felt sad as I watched everyone leave, wishing I could go with them. I was anxious to get back to having a normal life, whatever that was. I missed my old life and living in the moment. I missed watching the sunset through the panoramic views of the windows in my condo. I missed my career, brokering business deals with rich and famous clients. I missed intimacy with a man. There was no better feeling than lying in a man's arms after a night of hot, steamy, passionate sex.

Sometimes I thought about the yoga studio, but I wasn't sure how I felt about it. Deana seemed to like it though, especially since she was managing it, along with my other business affairs.

However, what I missed most was Gigi. If she were alive, she would be right by my side giving me love and encouragement to get well. She would help me see past my pain and mistakes. She would also help me understand Sage and her presence in my life. But that would never be. I would have to learn how to live without Gigi even though when she died, she took a part of me. Hopefully, all the good she instilled in me was stored within my brain and heart, so I could use them to guide me through the rest of my days.

As I thought about Gigi, I closed my eyes and saw pages full of her Creole idioms, colloquialisms and admonitions. One in particular popped into my head: "One thing for certain and two things for sure: if you look hard enough, you can always find a silver lining or a glimmer of light in darkness." Those were not mere words; they were prophetic. I had already experienced situations that required me to see the light in the darkness, and I would certainly have to embrace more in the days to come.

In terms of Di, the one who brought me into this craziness, my feelings were conflicted. Some days I longed to have had a relationship with her, while other days I was angry with her for abandoning me and then subsequently reappearing, only to conceal her presence from me. Perhaps, in time, I would figure out my feelings for her. For the moment, my heart won't let me mourn for a stranger.

Whenever I found myself feeling melancholy about my life, I would shift my mind to my future. Such mind drifts usually ended with me counting down the days for my next restart before my meds kicked in.

It was time for my evening meds, which relaxed me to the point that I felt like a zombie. I had no energy to move but was not tired enough to sleep. I usually just stared out the window until I became sleepy. My mind would drift into a subconscious state, such that I was often unaware of my surroundings. I hated taking so many meds, but I followed the treatment plan to ensure I was discharged as planned with no restrictions.

Unbeknownst to me, I had a surprise visitor that day, but I would not learn about it or the identity of the person until much later. Apparently, after Burke, Deana, and Zoe left, Burke made a phone call to the mystery person. "Everyone is gone, and she's been sedated, so you can see her now," he said.

The mystery person was none other than Paul, my biological father. He didn't come inside my room; he just looked at me through the window on the door. Then, he pulled Burke aside. "I trust you will handle this," he said. "I want her to have the best care and everything she needs, but she can never be linked to me. No one can ever know of her relation to my family."

"Of course, Paul. But what about your mother? She's the one who's out of control."

"I'm afraid that Mother's sudden health crisis has taken a turn for the worse," Paul replied. "I'm sure she won't be a problem where Astrid's concerned anymore."

And then, like an apparition, Paul was gone. But it didn't matter to me, because I never knew he was there. However, I was far from done with Paul. I would deal with him and his wicked mother in the next episode of my life.

As my stay at Lakeview came to an end, I learned I would need to take meds for the rest of my life. Otherwise, I could risk another psychotic breakdown or worse. But I wasn't bothered by it. I was willing to do whatever was necessary to function normally in the outside world.

During my last two weeks at Lakeview, I convinced one of my doctors to give me medicinal marijuana to counter the side effects of my meds. I was given a marijuana pill instead of a cigarette, since smoking of any kind was not allowed on the premises. But any form of marijuana was fine with me. It seemed to make me feel better, but it could have been a placebo effect.

One day, while I was in the gallery painting, a nurse stopped by. "What a beautiful flower," she said. "It looks like a lotus."

"Yes, it's a lotus blossom," I said. "It has many different meanings. In the Egyptian culture, it symbolizes rebirth. In the Hindu culture, it symbolizes beauty, fertility, prosperity, spirituality, and eternity. And in Buddhism, it symbolizes purity.

"I used to paint black orchids, the Kokuran, in memory of my mother and in memory of me, the person I used to be. But now the orchid has matured; it's in full blossom. In time, one by one, all the petals will fall off until no buds are left, and the stem can be cut back for hopeful rebirth or tossed away forever. Of course, you can always buy a new one and start over, repeating the process, knowing it will end the same. So, why bother teasing yourself, gleaning your eyes on a mysterious beauty that will eventually fade into permanent darkness? But now I fancy the lotus blossom. It's more relevant to me since the orchid has fully blossomed. It's time for rebirth, to evolve and transform into something even greater."

The nurse seemed confused by what I said about the orchid and the lotus flowers, but she continued to indulge me, as if nothing was wrong. She was probably used to patients giving verbal dissertations on one topic or another. But my rant probably had more to do with the fact that I had stopped taking all but one of my meds and my marijuana pills. I knew I would not be able to function in society taking a catalog of drugs that included anti-psychotics, anti-depressants, and a host of other mood stabilizers. Taking those combined meds was enough to make any person appear insane. People would think I was crazy or using heroin or something worse, because my meds zapped my energy and slowed me down to a drooling nod. I didn't believe I needed to take all that medication anyway. My doctor said my illness was probably triggered by a childhood trauma, and Ricky's death had cured that problem.

While at Lakeview, I read tons of literature on mental illness and found that many cases shared common and overlapping symptoms with schizophrenia, such as a nervous breakdown, which was a temporary condition. So, I concluded that's what had happened to me; I had a nervous breakdown. Who wouldn't fall apart with so much death surrounding them in the last few years? But now I was feeling better and had emerged from the symptoms of my illness.

My departure day finally arrived, and I was so elated about leaving that I hardly slept the night before. My suitcases were packed three hours before Deana arrived to take me home. After she signed the papers for my release, we took my suitcases to my Aston Martin. Seeing my car made me light up like a Christmas tree. It was the first sign that I was on my way back to a normal life.

"May I drive?" I asked. "I promise to be careful."

"Sure, it's your car anyway," Deana replied.

I climbed into the driver's side and waited for the seat to automatically adjust perfectly to my body. Then, I paused and took a deep breath, inhaling the smell of the leather seats, which reminded me of my old life. The part of me that was once happy, self-assured, and proud of the person I set out to be. The part of me that had blossomed, affirming my essence as the Kokuran—strong, bold, and powerful.

Deana held out my cell phone. "Here you go. I know you're anxious to get your hands on this thing."

I smiled with excitement. "Thanks. You must have read my mind." I turned on my cell phone and scrolled through my contacts, looking for Damien's name. Once I found it, I unblocked his number. Now that Chevy and Doc were no longer in my life, I might need a little something from Damien to sustain me while I searched for the next Mr. Right.

Then, I adjusted the rear-view mirror, where I saw an unexpected person seated in the backseat. It was Sage, wearing an assured grin on her face, letting me know she was still nearby if I ever needed her. However, I didn't stumble or shutter at the sight, because I already knew she was still present within me. I smiled and gave her a quick wink to acknowledge her. Then, I pulled off, heading toward my condo and looking forward to beginning the next chapter of my life.

As I drove, I thought about the question Gigi often asked me: "When are you going to blossom?"

Gigi, I hope you can see me, I said in my mind. *No more playing the victim. Those days are over. I have finally blossomed!*

Gigi was right. My strength was always within me, lying dormant and waiting patiently to be released. While I had known the attributes of the Kokuran, I had only recently uncovered my darker side. Those qualities had nothing to do with the Kokuran, but were nonetheless still part of me: vindictive, venomous, and deadly. However, the entirety of me was not revealed until my fears and pain imploded like a volcano and pushed me to the razor's edge of the dark side, the point where people snap and often never return.

The revelation of these characteristics was frightening and empowering. While they could help me, they could also hurt me if I didn't control them. Put simply, that meant I had to control Sage. After all, it was Sage who had unleashed the darkness in me. But Sage and I were one and the same, so all I had to do was control me.

It was then that I had an epiphany. I had dealt with and resolved my struggles with power and control when I lost Joey. I recalled the awakening that enabled me to reflect on my life's journey, realizing I was neither weak nor a victim but rather a triumphant survivor, affirming that my inner and outer being were one and the same.

I had overcome the knowledge of being abandoned at birth by my mother, being molested as a child, cancer, and an abusive marriage, all of which left me feeling broken, bitter, and profoundly confused. And in the midst of my perplexity, I was blessed to have a second chance at love. However, due to my PTSD, I wasn't ready for love again, and I had single-handedly destroyed it. Then, after climbing out of the pits of sorrow and self-loathing, I found my way back. And, just when I was finally moving on with my life, pain and misery revisited me with an unending ferocity, dismantling all the progress I had made and taking more loved ones away from me.

Reflecting on the whirlpool of my recent drama, I knew I had to shake it off. Otherwise, I would spiral back down into a psychotic pit. My mind became consumed with negative thoughts, overtaking my serenity. I felt an anxiety attack approaching and knew I needed to collect myself.

Scanning the roadside, I noticed a sign with directions for a nearby pet park. I made up a story about wanting to get a dog and suggested to Deana that we stop there. Deana, sweet and gullible, was clueless as to what was really going on. She loved dogs and was eager to stop. She jumped out of the car and ran ahead of me.

I stayed behind for a moment, trying to pull myself together. I took a marijuana pill, drank some water, and relaxed against the headrest. I closed my eyes, and in the midst of my thinking, Gigi's two favorite scriptures came to mind: "No weapons that form against me shall prosper" and "In your mercy put an end to my haters, and send destruction on all those who are against my soul; for I am your servant."

In my interpretation, those scriptures validated and reaffirmed what I was duty bound to complete. I could not give power to anything that was trying to steal, kill, and destroy my spirit, the lifeblood of me. I had to destroy my enemies before they destroyed me. I would start with Paul and the rest of the Rackham family. I would make them pay for what they had done to Di and to me.

As for my other enemies, Nikki and Philip, I had something for them too, if necessary. But I wasn't worried; they were no threat to me as long as I was vigilant in my suit of armor. Besides, I had something extra: my Kokuran strength. I didn't need Gigi to lean on or a flower to remind me of my strength. Just like my DNA, the attributes of the Kokuran were forever embedded within me—beautiful, mysterious, strong, and powerful.

With one difference though: I had evolved.

My strength had expanded, transcended, darkened, and amended.

I was the Kokuran, and I was in full blossom.

THE END

About Jordin Mack

I am a native Detroiter who was raised amidst the harsh conditions of inner-city urban life where I saw the darkest of bad times and the brightest of good times. I went on to attend college, earning a Master's degree in Business and embarked on a long career in Corporate America. Then, one day, I was reflecting on how I used to enjoy the art of writing, so I decided to stop thinking about it and just did it – I started writing again. After all, dreams have no expiration date.

It is the trilogy of my experiences in urban, academia, and corporate life that provide the unique style in my literary expression.

An Excerpt From my Blog:

"Dreams have no expiration date." I've heard those words several times throughout my life and simply ignored them. Then, a few years ago, someone said them to me again; but that time, they resonated with me. So, here I am today, pursuing my creative and entrepreneurial endeavors while also pushing the limits to become my bigger, better, and badder self. This is not a static journey, but one that will be defined over time. It's never too late to start living your dreams…